I0708514

Also by Terez Mertes Rose

Off Balance
Outside the Limelight
A Dancer's Guide to Africa
Ballet Orphans

Other Stages

Ballet Theatre Chronicles
Book 4

Terez Mertes Rose

Published in the United States
Classical Girl Press - www.classicalgirlpress.org
Cover design by James T. Egan, Bookfly Design, LLC
Formatting by Polgarus Studio

ISBN (print): 979-8-9885212-1-1
ISBN (ebook): 979-8-9885212-0-4

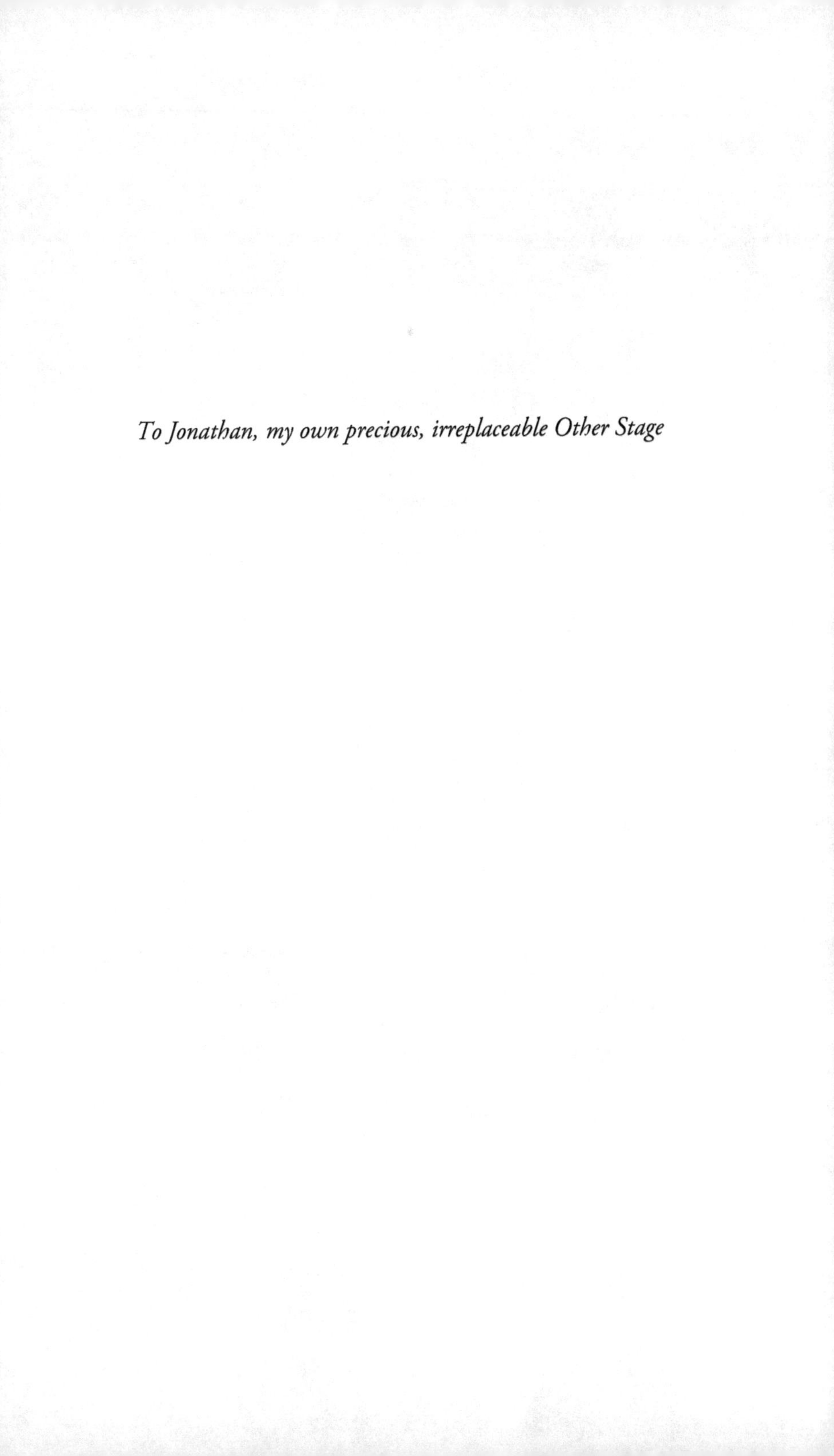

To Jonathan, my own precious, irreplaceable Other Stage

"We come altogether fresh and raw into the several stages of life, and often find ourselves without experience, despite our years."
~ Francois de La Rochefoucauld

"There's nothing called a perfect parent, so just be a real one."
~ Sue Atkins

Prologue

December 2007

Once Katrina Devries and Javier Torres, principal dancers with San Francisco's West Coast Ballet Theatre, made the decision to create a family together—not just talk about it but proceed with the actual deed—things happened fast.

They were in Los Angeles, having just guest-performed the leads in a regional company's *Nutcracker* production, something they did annually. The taxi had dropped them off at their hotel, and as they made their way through the opulent lobby, silent except for the sound of a burbling fountain, their last words in the taxi echoed in Katrina's head. Javier had brought it up first.

We said last year that we'd do it if we felt the same, one year later. I feel the same.

I do, too.

Which means …

Yes.

Now?

Yes. Right now. Before we lose our nerve.

Neither of them spoke as they waited for the elevator. Only once the doors swung open did Javier speak. "Your room or mine?" His voice sounding strained.

She tried to speak but all that came out was a squeak. She cleared her throat. "Mine."

"All right." He punched the button for her floor and then reached over and took her hand. His was cold. So was hers.

This same event, last year, had spawned the initial conversation between them. Javier, having just broken up with a needy girlfriend, had declared himself off women for life, and told Katrina the lone thing he regretted was the diminished chance he'd have a son, something that would have made his traditional-minded family back in Cuba so happy. Katrina had jokingly offered to be a part of the solution, and the idea, joke or not, quickly found root. The two of them, never romantically involved, still loved each other deeply. They'd been close friends since arriving together at the WCBT, as teens, seventeen years earlier. A baby, they mused. A little one they could raise together and nurture and love, all of it independent of romance and marriage, which went bad most of the time anyway, they agreed. A child they'd keep close through the tender years, something neither of them had truly experienced, having been pulled so young from their respective households to train.

She thought about April, one of the ballet masters and Katrina's longtime friend in the company. April was married and had two children. The more she thought about it, the more she realized she wanted what April had. Those two little girls, precious and wide-eyed, clinging to their mother's thighs during visits to studio rehearsals, were now growing into young ladies.

She wanted a child. She wanted a family.

But of course no one acted impulsively on such a big decision. One year, she and Javier had agreed. If they felt the same way, one year later, if neither of them had gotten involved in a relationship, then they'd talk. Actually, do more than talk.

That time had come.

The elevator pinged open to Katrina's floor and they walked in silence to her room, awkward as strangers.

The irony of this was that they were longtime partners, paired up constantly because they had such good chemistry and knew each other's bodies so well. His hands had clasped, grabbed and stroked almost every inch of her leotard-clad body. He'd clutched her inner thighs, had his face wedged between her legs in lifts and twists. Their sweat mingled indiscriminately as he encircled her waist, or she hung on to his shoulders, his torso, immersed in all the choreography's demands. Offstage they held hands, something they'd done since the day of their arrival. And yet, here they were now, inside her room, warily circling one another.

He excused himself to use the bathroom, and she could hear the distinct male sound of his stream hitting the water. She sat on the bed's edge and told herself firmly to view this as simply another pas de deux they were about to rehearse. One of those private sessions, just the two of them, trying to figure out why the partnered lift and its descent didn't quite work.

He came out of the bathroom and she rose nervously. "That one?" She pointed to the second, unused bed.

"Sure." He went to the mini-bar and assessed its contents. "I need a tequila. You?"

"If there's a Courvoisier brandy, I'll take it."

He poured the contents of the little bottle into a water glass and handed it to her.

She took nervous sips, watching him gulp down his tequila and return to peruse the other contents of the mini-bar cabinet.

"Chips?" He fished out a bag and held it up.

She shook her head. "No thank you."

He ripped open the bag and munched the chips, one after another, focused on the act as if each chip were providing him with sustenance. She took another sip of her brandy and then recklessly tossed the rest down. The liquid burned her throat, her chest, but steadied her.

He glanced her way. "Another?"

"Is there more Courvoisier?"

He sifted around. "There's a Grand Marnier. Will that work?"

She nodded, holding out her glass. He opened the little bottle and poured in its contents.

He stuffed the last of the chips into his mouth, crumpled the bag and tossed it into the trash can. He grabbed another mini bottle for himself, and gulped it down, right from the bottle. He stared at the bottle in his hand afterward, as if searching for a tutorial on how to impregnate your best friend with whom your entire relationship had been platonic. "Please don't take offense if I don't look you in the eye," he said, gaze still locked on the bottle.

"I won't. You know, we should look at this like a trip to the dentist. The way your mind goes elsewhere, and if you relax into your thoughts, the business gets done fast. No eye contact involved at all."

He looked over at her, his relief evident. "It's no wonder you're my closest female friend. You're so perfect for me."

"I'd say the same about you."

"We should get married."

This made them both laugh and wrinkle their noses. They didn't want a marriage. They wanted a child.

He drew a deep breath, and exhaled loudly. "Let's do this thing."

"I'll just get in the bed now," she said. "Maybe we keep our shirts on?"

"Yes. I think that would be a good idea."

She slid under the sheets and, within its safe confines, pulled off her leggings and underwear, dropping them to the floor.

Javier gestured to the overhead lights. "Can we turn these off?"

"Yes, of course. Whatever makes you more comfortable."

He clicked off the room lights but left the bathroom light on, before making his way over to the other side of the bed. She heard rather than saw him remove his own clothes, and felt the bed shift as he joined her. They remained far apart. The gulf between them now seemed impossible to traverse.

"I'm sorry, Katja," he said in a low, pained voice. "I'm going to have to … stroke myself first."

She could feel her face go hot and was grateful for the darkness. "Of course. Go ahead. I understand." He'd once confessed to her that it was while dating the needy girlfriend that he'd ceased feeling physically attracted to females. It was only men he desired now. He'd been happier since then, she knew. But right now? She didn't even want to know what, or whom, he was thinking of. Instead, she tried to relax, think about flowers and meadows as, beside her, he worked his hands busily.

A moment later he spoke in a voice strained with uncertain excitement. "All right. I think I can try now."

She jumped cat- like when she felt his hand on her thigh, and they both laughed nervously. "I'm going to need to touch you down there," he explained. "To guide myself in."

"Of course. Okay."

This was going to be a disaster, she thought with a sinking heart. She knew her body; down below it was tense and dry and tight. Nothing was going to be guided in there. "I'm sorry," she said, "but I'm going to need something, um, slippery first."

"Oh. All right. That makes sense."

"Excuse me." She slipped out of bed and went into the bathroom, assessing her options. Shampoo, conditioner, shower gel, lotion— none of it was right. She peered into her own toiletries kit, sifting around, until she found eye makeup remover. The first ingredient was mineral oil. If it was safe enough to use so close to the eyes, it would surely work for lubrication as well.

Before stepping back out, she modestly wrapped one of the towels around her waist and caught a glimpse of her pale face in the mirror. She looked terrified.

He was staring at the ceiling, his hands once again below the sheets, as she slipped back into the bed with him. "Okay, my turn to, um, take care of things," she said. "Before you try."

"Sure."

She poured some of the liquid onto the tips of her fingers and stroked, the way an operating-room nurse might wipe down an incision area with alcohol and iodine just before the surgeon made his slice. With oily fingers, she carefully put the lid back on the makeup remover and set it on her nightstand. "Ready," she said, trying to sound casual.

"Great," he replied, and it oddly comforted her that his voice sounded strained.

Neither of them moved. Javier reached over and took her hand. "I hope you don't think less of me if I admit that I am petrified right now."

Which made her laugh, because he was the one always so calm before a performance. Meanwhile she wrestled with anxiety and nerves, particularly before opening nights of big, important ballets, where sometimes she'd throw up from the stress of her lead role.

"You're laughing at me," he exclaimed, and rolled over to face her. He was laughing now too, and when she wriggled a little so that her left leg hooked one of his, from there it was no big deal for him to roll on top of her. They smiled at each other with a playfulness that faded as the gravity of what they were about to attempt came over them both.

"We're doing this," he said, wonder in his voice.

"We are," she marveled.

"Here goes," he said, and before she could reply, he thrust himself in.

It hurt, much more than she'd expected. Not that she'd ever found sex to be an easy, comfortable experience. But if professional ballet had taught her anything about life, it was that to obtain the big prizes, you had to expect the big hurt. You had to seek it out and embrace it.

So she embraced the pain, the shock, and just beyond it, the triumph.

A baby. This creation of a family no one could take from her. A tiny human she and Javier could chuckle over, the baby's amazement after touching a kitten for the first time (like April's Jen), or their shocked recoil at their first taste of frosting (like April's Kylie). Javier and her, sharing challenges, triumphs, and every wonderful thing in between.

So pleasurable was the image, she let slip a happy little groan as Javier worked above her, his own groans of pleasure growing audible too.

So much to feel optimistic about.

October 2011

Chapter 1

Katrina

The audience went wild over Dario. He'd been allowed to run onstage to join his parents after their performance, a miniature Javier with lighter skin and hazel eyes, only now registering the 2000 people watching him. Katrina, sticky and spent, still catching her breath, felt her maternal instincts kick into high gear. She stroked Dario's warm mop of silky brown hair as he looked around, bewildered. He looked so vulnerable, so small, even though today was his third birthday. It was the outsized nature of the stage, the overhead lights, the sea of faces from the audience, mostly obscured by the darkened auditorium, that overwhelmed unless it was your world. Dario registered the applause and cries of approval with wide eyes before turning to Javier and raising his arms imploringly. Javier's regal stage expression relaxed into an indulgent smile as he lifted Dario and settled him on one hip.

The applause continued. Javier took a courtly step to the side and gestured with his free arm to Katrina. She curtseyed, leg behind her in a deep lunge, hand to her heart, full of gratitude not just to the audience but for all life had given her. Their son's birthday! Raising him with Javier, all together, like a true family. It was everything she could have asked for. She rose from her curtsey and beamed at the audience. Dario, as if sensing what came next, wiggled out of Javier's grip, down to the ground, so that he could perfectly mirror his father, in a bow from the waist, complete with sweeping arm flourish. Katrina didn't know whether to laugh at Dario's adorableness or cry that her baby was growing up too fast.

From the auditorium came a collective coo of delight, which Dario rewarded with a second bow, just as courtly and refined. The crowd ate it up, roaring their approval, which made Dario nervously clutch at Javier's hand.

After a final bow with the ensemble cast behind them, the applause finally slowed, and the heavy gold curtains separating audience from stage came down. The overhead backstage lights blazed on and everyone from the cast burst into their own applause and cheers. Their final stop on tour, the final performance. Ninety minutes from San Francisco, they were already geared up for their back-home celebrations. Which, for Katrina and Javier, meant Dario's birthday party.

April, herself a former company dancer, had been with Dario in the green room watching the performance on the closed-circuit television where he could see his parents dance, and shout whenever he liked. Now she stepped out of the downstage-right wing and held out her slender arms to Dario. "Aren't you the clever boy?" she exclaimed, as Dario ran to her. "Bowing just like your daddy!" She picked him up and gave him a hug, grinning at Katrina over his wriggling body.

Katrina felt a warm hand envelop hers. It was Javier, watching April and Dario as well. "Our little boy is getting older," he said.

"So quickly, it seems." Katrina reached with her free hand to pluck at her costume's shoulder straps, uncomfortably digging into her shoulder. "Unzip my bodice?" she asked, presenting her back to him.

He unzipped it halfway and immediately the pressure eased. His fingers kneaded the sore, indented spots where the straps had been, eliciting from her a groan of relief.

"That feels wonderful. Thank you."

"You're welcome."

"I love having Dario with us today. It was darling, seeing him bow, trying to imitate you."

"Overnight he's changed," Javier mused. "Suddenly he's like a little man." His hands grew still, and when Katrina twisted around in query, she saw that a rapt expression had come over his face.

"What is it?" she asked.

"I've just made a very important decision. One I've been brooding over for weeks. Suddenly the answer is effortless."

She studied his handsome, familiar face. Even though their relationship was once again purely platonic, she'd felt a tiny bit of romantic love toward him since their days of trying to get her pregnant. Now, as he gazed intently into her eyes, a thrill spread through her and settled in her belly.

He was going to say, "Let's get married!"

And she was going to tell him, "Yes, yes, *yes!*"

It was the next step for them. Never mind that he was more into men these days and she preferred celibacy. They loved each other deeply. They were already living together. It would make his family in Cuba so happy.

"Tell me more," she urged, but before he could respond, others approached, including the production manager, who wanted a word with Javier.

"Mama! Mama!" Dario cried, running back toward her, "April is coming to our party too! She has a present for me!"

Katrina grabbed at Javier's hand before they separated. "Tell me later."

"Tonight at home. After the party," he promised.

Home was a beautifully restored Edwardian three-bedroom duplex in Hayes Valley, not far from where April and her family lived. With the inheritance her grandmother had left her, Katrina had bought the property years back, a hot real-estate tip from April's husband that had quickly paid off. It had two floors, a large living room, a sunny kitchen and a tiny enclosed backyard. Javier had moved in before Dario's birth, staying for the first year, as planned, and simply never leaving, a win for them all.

The birthday-party invitations had been extended to two dozen people, but within the hour over forty people crowded the rooms, including Javier's broad circle of friends, company colleagues and administrators, and her own beloved friends—Alice, Montserrat and April—fellow moms working in the performing arts, all of them her lifeline since Dario's birth.

The lone stranger among the guests was a handsome, genial man named Brent. Katrina struggled to place him and realized that he'd spoken with her and Javier after last year's gala. He was a dermatologist, at the gala with his wife, who'd looked amused as he'd stammered words of praise for Javier's power and cat-like grace.

This time, Brent was alone. He caught sight of her and came over.

"I absolutely love your house and its décor." He smiled at her warmly. "The elegance of it suits you and Javier perfectly."

"Thank you," she replied. "How nice to see you here. Your wife didn't join you?"

"No, I came alone." He hesitated, as if it were an awkward subject. "I didn't imagine a young boy's birthday party would interest her," he added. "Our two boys are in their early twenties."

"Well, it's so nice of you to join us here today." She wasn't sure what else to add. How well did he know Javier? Was he just attracted to the glamour of the setup? What did one say to a dermatologist, anyway? Her own skin was pale and unblemished; it was a ballet-dancer thing, like long hair.

To her relief, Alice approached and joined the conversation. Alice had once danced with the company, but now worked in Symphony administration. When Brent heard this, he admitted he was more familiar with the classical-music world than ballet, but that Javier had really wanted him here today. Katrina listened as the two of them chatted about the fall lineup at the Symphony, but Brent's last sentence played over and over in her head.

Javier really wanted me to be here.

Why would Javier invite a casual acquaintance to a little boy's birthday party?

By nine o'clock, the last of the revelers had left. Katrina tucked a fussy, overstimulated Dario into his bed where, miraculously, he fell asleep the instant his head hit the pillow.

The party room was a mess. Blue streamers sagged from the ceiling and balloons rustled, bumping into one another on the confetti-strewn floor. The table held a dozen plates, some encrusted with frosting or pooled with melted ice cream. Javier took the plates and set to work in the kitchen, as she cleaned the living room. When she joined him in the kitchen afterward, they worked in a relaxed silence. She studied his face, marveling at the way his adult features were so similar to their son's. Both had a high, smooth forehead and a strong chin that jutted out when they were being stubborn.

"The party went well," he said.

"It did." She gave a happy little sigh.

Javier glanced at her. "Tired?"

"A little. Still wired, though, too. What an eventful day." She thought of his news, the "important decision" still to come, and it sent a shiver of excitement through her.

"Our son turning three. It still feels like a small miracle."

"It does," she agreed.

They wiped down counters, put away unused beverages, stowed

the leftover cake. Javier made them coffee and they returned to the living room with their cups, settling on either end of the couch. She decided she couldn't wait any longer. Ignoring her coffee, she drew a deep breath and plunged in. "You said you had news to share. A big decision made."

He smiled. "I'll have to tell him you remembered. He said I shouldn't bring it up, otherwise."

Him.

Something froze in her. The proprietary tone in his voice, the softening in his eyes, spoke volumes. Only not the volumes she'd been expecting.

She remembered the lone unattached male at the party. Her insides clenched.

"The dermatologist. Brent." She had to force the name out. "You've gotten involved with him." She wanted more than anything for him to look perplexed and ask what she was talking about.

"You're good." He chuckled and shook his head. "Yes, and yes."

She felt dizzy, as though she'd just taken a hit of a powerful intoxicant, only one that made her feel bad instead of good, delivering far too much clarity. "It started last year, didn't it?" she asked through numb lips. "You met him, right after the gala performance."

"That was it. He was with his wife," Javier said. "Soon to be ex-wife. Ironically, she's the ballet lover, not him. He'd gone to the performance as a favor to her."

"I remember him stumbling all over his words, praising you."

"He did. It was charming. We encountered each other a second time a month later, and laughed about it. At a party thrown by a mutual friend. I think it shocked us both, how quickly we connected after that. How intensely."

This was a nightmare. She wanted to slow down the momentum,

at the least, but it was like a boulder rolling down a hill. "Is it love?" she asked.

Please say no. Please say no.

He didn't respond immediately. Instead, he gazed down at the cup of coffee in his hand.

"Katja, he's asked me to move in with him."

She couldn't speak. She couldn't move.

"Yes, it's love," he added. "I'm head over heels. We both are."

His golden-brown eyes had grown brighter. "A change makes sense, on so many levels. We're too tight in these rooms anyway. Three of us and two bedrooms."

"But wait." She found her wits again. "There's the study downstairs. That's three bedrooms. We have plenty of room."

"The downstairs room is for your parents."

"They're rarely here. Two times a year, at most."

"No. It's for them. You gifted it to them."

True. She'd felt bad that Grandmother had willed her the bulk of her estate. In return, she'd bought the house, with the proceeds from selling the Paris apartment, so that her parents, moving constantly, could have a stateside home base. "Then we'll put Dario back in my room, I don't mind. I like having him close. He still doesn't sleep well through the night."

"He needs a room of his own. He cries because he knows one of us is right there."

"I can't bear to hear him cry."

"He's three. He *needs* to cry and solve it himself. That's what Brent told me."

"Brent, the dermatologist, who's now a child expert too?"

"He's raised two boys of his own."

"All right, fine." She thought fast. "But what about your family in Cuba?"

He looked bewildered. "What do they have to do with this?"

How to explain what she'd been expecting to hear without making a fool of herself? "I'd thought, I mean, the two of us, together in this way …" She cut off her attempts when she saw his confusion deepen. "Your family thinks you're straight and in a relationship with the mother of your child. If you move out, will you tell them why?"

She watched as sorrow shadowed his face. "Yes, I'll tell them. They might not approve, but it's not their choice. It's mine, and I've made it. It's time I come out. It's long overdue."

Her panicking mind seized on a more debatable issue. "Where does Brent live?"

"He's found a place in the Upper Fillmore. Just off Pine, near the shops. It's charming."

"That's too far!" she protested. "It's the other side of San Francisco!"

"It's an Uber ride, that's all."

"It's too far. This is what we said we'd avoid. It will traumatize Dario."

Javier shook his head. "This is not what we said we'd avoid. We agreed we'd never ship our child off at an early age to train for something like ballet. You and I were both only eight. That was the scenario we said we'd avoid at all costs. This situation couldn't be more different. I'm stretching his world, that's all. He knows you're here, and home base is here. He knows that if I bring him over to my new home for a night or two, it can be his 'home away from home.' Brent's home is big; Dario will have his own permanent room.

"And this is a good time, actually," he continued with renewed energy. "He's not a baby anymore. You saw him this afternoon, onstage—he took that bow like a pro. He wants to be a little man. I couldn't be happier. It shows he's a normal, curious, three-year-old boy who's eager to address the world around him. Do you remember how he was so slow to talk, when Alice's son was chattering away? Or how he wasn't interested in walking, even at twelve months? This is all good. It's the right timing, and the right direction."

She realized there would be no talking him out of anything.

There went her dream. Her stupid, romantic, little-girl's dream of a happily ever after. Further, now everyone at the company would know. She'd loved their cover. Her implied domestic partnership with Javier kept her from getting hit on. She didn't want to be "a single mom." She didn't want anything to change.

"Just … give me one more week before you tell anyone at the studios. Can we do that?" She hated the way her voice trembled.

His determined expression softened. "*Mi amor,* of course," he soothed.

They sipped their coffees in silence. All too soon he finished his and glanced at his watch. "I'm sorry to do this, but Brent's expecting me. I'll be spending the night there."

This was how it would be now. "Sure," she managed. "Okay."

He left to collect his things, and in a matter of minutes he was out the door with a "see you in company class, give Dario a kiss for me in the morning" tossed over his shoulder. She sank back into the sofa and listened to the sound of his car starting up from their narrow strip of a driveway. Then he drove away. She stayed there for another five minutes, unmoving, wondering how the day could have started so fabulously and ended so poorly.

She took a sip of the now-tepid coffee and set it down. She considered heading upstairs to bed, but knew that any attempt to sleep, with her mind churning, would be futile.

April. She could call April. She was a night owl, and had told Katrina she could always call for help, no matter the hour.

Feeling almost panicky with anxiety, she punched in the numbers, and as soon as she heard April's voice, she began to cry.

April was a soothing, sympathetic listener and Katrina explained, through tears, what had happened.

"Sweetie," April said. "Three deep breaths. Tomorrow we start rehearsing full steam for the gala and the season. Focus on your work; none of that has changed for either you or Javier. Agreed?"

"Agreed." Katrina gave a little sniff.

"Tomorrow I'll ring Alice and Montserrat and see if they're free for the evening. I hereby propose an emergency meeting of the mom squad."

The anxiety eased its grip on her. "That would be great."

"In the meantime, make yourself a chamomile tea and read a really boring book."

"Okay. Good night. Thank you, April. Thank you so much."

Chapter 2

April

"Can I have bacon with my eggs?" Jen, April Manning's fifteen-year-old daughter, asked.

"No bacon today. Just scrambled eggs." April set down the spatula beside the stovetop and regarded her wearily. She hadn't slept well last night after Katrina's call, aching for her and her news. Katrina alone hadn't seen Javier's departure coming, which went to show you how people remained in denial for as long as possible, rather than face an uncomfortable reality.

"Phooey." Jen made a face. "Can you at least grate some cheddar cheese on mine? They're not so plain that way."

"Fine. Give me your plate and pull the shredded cheese out of the fridge."

April took Jen's plate, scooped some eggs and tossed a handful of cheddar from the bag Jen offered her. She gave the plate fifteen seconds in the microwave to melt the cheese and handed it back to her daughter.

"Thanks, Mom." Jen smiled. "This looks better."

"You're welcome."

April caught sight of herself in the mirror on the side wall, the one that reflected the backyard garden and seemed to fill the kitchen itself with green by day. She'd maintained her ballet dancer's slimness, but a 46-year-old mother's slimness was different from the svelte 26-year-old she'd been when she'd met and fallen in love with Russell. Her hair was shorter now, too. She'd cut it off when Kylie was a baby and toddler Jen would yank on the long braid like it was a dinner-bell rope. Back then, there were enough challenges in her life without her hair being one of them.

"Why does the coffee taste funny?" Russell, already lost in his bubble of work-day concentration, looked up from his place at the far end of the table.

April took a first sip of her own coffee and recoiled. "Did you run some vinegar through the coffee maker yesterday, by any chance?"

"Oh." Russell paused, brow furrowed. "I did. But I ran clean water through it after that."

"Did you run water through twice?"

"I guess not."

"That explains it."

"I'm sorry." He looked sheepish. "Here I thought I was being nice, giving you a good cup of coffee after your days on the road."

"Well, thanks for the thought." She sighed as she dumped the contents of her cup into the sink, followed by the mostly full pot of coffee. "I'll have better coffee for us in five minutes."

"Thanks, love," he said, already distracted by something of greater interest on the laptop open before him.

As Jen ate her eggs, April paused to study her daughter more closely. She was so lovely, with her long golden hair and fine-boned features, that April wanted to reach out, grab her, and hold on. Like herself, Jen had decided early on that she wanted to be a ballet dancer. Her moods and needs were uncomplicated: she loved her circle of friends at school, and she loved ballet.

This morning, Jen wanted to talk about the *Nutcracker* rehearsals, now in full swing. She was a student at the company's ballet school, cast as a toy soldier in the Act 1 battle scene, and as a dragonfly in the Act II opening scene. Her greatest coup was having just been chosen to understudy the lead role of Clara. "I know there's two of us as understudies and four official Claras," she told April, "so I might not ever be able to actually dance it, but I'm so proud to be there, learning the role."

"As you should be!" April gave Jen an approving nod, before glancing at her watch. "It's getting late. Where's your sister?"

"Dunno." Jen shrugged. "I heard her, though. She's awake."

"Coming," April heard from the hallway, and a moment later, her youngest emerged. April smiled at Kylie. Her little pixie, her beloved fairy-sprite, who couldn't have been more different from Jen. Short brown hair that she insisted on cutting herself, intense hazel eyes that changed from greenish to brownish according to what she wore. Skinny as a grasshopper. Thirteen months younger than Jen, Kylie marched to her own drummer. As a high school freshman, life was about to get more challenging for April's quirky, stubborn, independent-minded daughter.

"Good morning, Kylie-button." April gestured to the egg pan. "Come bring me a plate."

Kylie peered over at the stove and grimaced. "I really don't feel like eggs today."

"Why? They're here and they're ready."

"I'm not hungry. They're so heavy, they might make me retch. And I think it would be rude to retch when the rest of you are trying to eat."

"Gee. Thanks for your consideration."

"No problem. So, if I promise to eat eggs the next time, can I just have Cheerios today?"

April sighed. "All right, but have a big bowl."

"Okay. Hi Dad," she offered, as she went to retrieve the cereal from the cabinet.

"Hey, sweetie. How goes?"

"Meh."

"Why just 'meh'?"

"It's Monday."

"Monday is great! It means you can dive in." His eyes gleamed. The challenges of being a high-level director at the tech corporation he'd helped start up, years earlier, appealed to him. He worked long hours and had his share of struggles, but he loved the work.

The coffee gave one last asthmatic wheeze and a final burp. "Russell, new coffee is ready," April called over her shoulder as she took a serving of the unloved scrambled eggs.

"Mom?" Kylie called out. "Would you drive me to school today?"

April groaned as she set down the spoon and turned to face her daughter. "Kylie, I told you, it's just not convenient in the way your middle school was. You can't get into the habit of this. It was twice the week before I went on tour, and twice the week before that."

"It's the first time this week," Kylie argued.

"That's because it's Monday."

"What's the problem?" Russell asked Kylie as he rose and poured himself a fresh coffee.

"In the mornings I just don't want to talk to anyone."

"So you put in your earbuds and tune out the world. Problem solved."

"It's not an auditory issue, Dad. I need my psychic space. A full bus stresses me out."

"That's ridiculous," Russell said. "You need to just grin and bear it."

She offered no reply. Instead her face grew stony and she plunged her spoon into her Cheerios and milk so forcefully that a spray of milk shot up and splashed the tablecloth.

Another challenging week, then, April decided. How silly to have thought that high school meant she could back off on parenting. Or maybe not silly. Jen, this time last year, had shooed her away merrily, strode onto the high school campus with a glad smile, and never looked back.

She studied her unhappy child, which made her think of her unhappy friend. "I have a deal to propose," she told Kylie. "The moms are meeting tonight."

"And you need a babysitter," she cut in swiftly. "Deal. In exchange for a ride to school today I'll watch them tonight. But I still get to pocket the money if the other moms insist on paying me, okay?"

April smiled. "Fair trade."

"Good." Kylie smiled back.

"Jen?" April glanced her way.

"No thanks, the bus works for me." She rose from the table, empty plate in hand. "Gotta go get ready for school!"

Monday mornings, April joined the other ballet masters in the office of Anders, their boss and the company's artistic director, for an informal meeting. As ballet masters, she, Ben and Curtis taught company class, supervised rehearsals, coached individual dancers, offered input on casting, and support to visiting choreographers. The West Coast Ballet Theatre, with its 55 dancers, 100 performances annually and a $30 million budget, could afford, and needed, three of them. All former company principals, Anders had chosen them because they knew the company repertoire inside and out, and they knew how to get along with him, how to run things with efficiency and no drama.

Today, the four of them rehashed the tour, its bumps, its triumphs, and today's return to studio rehearsals. The November gala had risen to the forefront in importance, followed by the *Nutcracker* run, through December. Then there was spring repertory season, with its six programs, part of which they'd already started rehearsing.

Javier knocked on the half-opened door and joined the group. He murmured to Anders as the others laughingly argued over which of them had had the noisier hotel rooms while on tour.

Anders gestured for quiet and pointed to Javier.

They all regarded Javier, who wore a mysterious smile. "I've proposed to Anders that he make some changes to the gala," he said. "A new commissioned piece."

"It would have to be a pretty remarkable commission to change things around," said Ben.

"I'd say it's remarkable." Javier's smile broadened. "From Edwin Hess."

The ballet masters all froze, speechless. April found her voice first. "Are we talking *the* Edwin Hess?"

Javier nodded.

Edwin Hess: charismatic, British, rising-star choreographer, just turned thirty. Anders had expressed interest in hiring him three years earlier, but the recent blockbuster success of the film that had featured his choreography now meant that trying for a Hess commission was like reaching for the moon.

Javier explained how a friend of a friend, connected to the London ballet scene, had learned Hess had an unexpected opening in his current schedule. Further back-and-forthing had revealed that he'd consider creating a piece for Anders and the company's gala, if the price were right.

"If we could make it happen, that would be extraordinary," Anders said. "We can easily shift things in the program to accommodate it."

"Who would dance it?" April glanced at Javier. "I assume you'll want it for yourself and Katrina?"

"Not exactly," he replied. "Katrina, yes. But with a new partner.

As for myself, I'll keep the *Don Quixote* pas de deux and choose another dancer. Mind you, both new partners will be of the highest caliber. Young ones who are starting to make a mark here." He turned to Anders. "Let's talk later, you and I. What do you think of a Cuban couple?" Javier's eyes gleamed.

A smile spread across Anders' face. "I think that could prove to be very exciting."

April, meanwhile, could only think of Katrina. This would be one shock announcement right on the heels of last night's. "How is Katrina going to like this idea?" she asked Javier.

"She'll be thrilled. Having a celebrity choreographer set a new commission on you is a dream scenario for any dancer. And I haven't mentioned the best part. If it goes well, Hess will consider expanding the piece into a full ballet for next year's repertory season."

This was huge. A gift falling from the sky.

"Ben, get his people on the phone today," Anders said. "Confirm that Hess is serious, and how much he's asking."

A phone call came in for Anders, ending the meeting. As the others left the office, April gestured for Javier to walk separately with her. Only when they were out of earshot did she speak.

"Katrina called me last night and gave me the news."

"I thought she might."

"I was anticipating this situation sooner or later. I'm on your side as much as hers. But, well, are you sure that you want to dump this second thing on Katrina right now?"

"It's time. Time for both changes." His shoulders rose and fell abruptly. "She doesn't seem to need men in that other way. Being a mother wholly fulfills her." He stopped and turned to look at April, his expression sorrowful. "It brings me no satisfaction to say this. I know she's hurting. I know it will be an adjustment. But to not act now would be a mistake."

"I understand."

They began walking again. "I'll do everything I can to help her through the transition," he said. "But she'll need your support, too."

"She has mine, and more. Our mom group is meeting up tonight."

"I'm glad to hear it. I want her to be happy."

First day back from the West Coast tour meant diving right in, prioritizing different programs, each with its own sense of urgency. April arrived early for the first rehearsal, giving her the chance to chat with Dena, one of her favorite dancers. Anders had only recently given Dena the green light to rehearse and perform again, after she'd been sidelined for a brain tumor and its removal, eighteen months ago. Although residual facial paralysis still dogged her, her motivation was high, her eyes bright. She was a newlywed, too, married to a wonderful guy who'd been by her side through her recuperation.

April saw Katrina step into the studio and look around. When she spied April, she walked over. "The Don Q rehearsal with Javier was canceled," she said. She looked tired and mournful. "What do you suppose that was about?"

"Couldn't tell you," April said, which wasn't actually a lie. Anders never wanted the ballet masters to speak publicly of decisions made in his office. "But lucky you, it frees you to have some relaxing you-time."

"I'd rather be working. Rehearsing with Javier."

"Go grab a nap in a quiet place. You'll feel much better. And that will pep you up for tonight's party."

Dena glanced at them quizzically. "A party, huh? I thought Dario's party was yesterday."

"It was. Tonight is just our mom group," April explained. "At Montserrat's house."

Dena knew the members of their mom group; she'd even joined them once or twice while sidelined, to keep up her spirits. "I love your group," she said. "Tell Alice and Montserrat I say hi."

"I will." April said. "In fact, if you're free, you're more than welcome to join us." She looked in query at Katrina, who nodded.

"Actually, I'd like that. The hubby has a class to teach tonight. But would I be barging in?" Dena's glance flickered over Katrina.

"No, you wouldn't." Katrina sounded firm. "The more the merrier. And that's our goal—to be merry. Can we get Kylie to watch over the kids?" she asked April.

"I already booked her," April assured her.

"Good," Katrina said. "Let's all plan to have fun tonight."

After she left, Dena shot April a bemused look. "What's up with her?"

"Oh, you know." April kept her tone vague. "Stuff. She just needs a little boost from friends."

Dena grew thoughtful. "This is a fun coincidence, because just last week my brother-in-law brought up Montserrat. He's a classical musician too, a pianist, and when he heard that I knew her, he said he'd love to meet her. He's trying to network in the classical music community here. He knows her reputation and that she sometimes works with young artists to help them further their careers. Any chance I could bring him along? He's very charming. I'm sure he'd be happy to entertain us with some piano playing. He's very good, by the way."

"Well, my goal for tonight is to make Katrina relax, enjoy herself," April said.

"He'll help with that, all right," Dena said, and began to chuckle.

"Why? What's so funny?"

"All right, you should be aware that he's really good looking. And a flirt. But not in an icky way. There's something refreshing and real about him."

April thought of Katrina, the sadness on her face. She was too young and pretty to play the grieving-widow card. "Bring him along. You're right, Montserrat likes meeting young artists."

"Cool," Dena said. "I'll text him right now."

"Seven o'clock, Montserrat's house."

"We'll be there."

Chapter 3

Kylie

Montserrat and her family lived in a pretty house on Potrero Hill, with an amazing view of the San Francisco skyline. At her house that night, the moms settled into the living room while Kylie herded her three charges into the playroom. Kylie liked the little kids well enough. She'd known Granger and Dario since the day they were each born. Granger, Alice's son, had just turned three, like Dario. Years ago, Katrina and Alice had been dancers in the company together, competing for the same promotion, but Katrina had won out. Everyone thought it was hilarious when, years later, they were pregnant at the same time, due one week apart, like it was a competition again. This time, Alice won. Granger was born five days earlier than Dario, even though Katrina had been due first.

Granger picked up a red foam-rubber block and studied it warily. "Throw it," Kylie encouraged. But he only squinted at her in confusion as if she'd told him to fly. "Like this," Kylie said, and tossed its twin, a blue foam-rubber block, to Dario, who caught it, more out of coincidence than skill. He looked shocked to see it in his hands and promptly threw it at Granger.

"Do you go to school?" Emma, Montserrat's daughter asked her, coming to sit next to her on the floor. Emma was five and already very lady-like.

"I do. And do you?"

Emma nodded solemnly. "In the mornings."

"Did you have a good day at school today?"

"I guess so." Emma wiggled around to get more comfortable. "We drank apple juice, but a little bit got on my dress."

"Oh, dear. Was that messy?"

"It was only a small amount." Emma looked at her earnestly. "My mommy wasn't mad."

"I'm glad to hear that, Emma."

Emma rose, went over to the toy shelf and pulled out a children's card game. "Will you play this with me?" she asked.

"Sure. As long as the boys don't need me to play referee."

She let Emma explain the card game's directions, even though it was pretty obvious to anyone but a kid. But she liked Emma's calm, and the way she kept glancing at Kylie to make sure she approved.

She was glad this job had come up. It was a distraction from the reality that high school wasn't working out like she'd thought. The memory of the day's poetry presentation, the blank looks and the laughter that had followed, still made her ears burn in shame.

Why did none of her classmates like classical music? Why was it seen as so weird of her, that she chose a piece of classical music instead of rock or R&B for the project? The assignment had been to write something while listening to music that inspired you. You brought in the music and played it as you stood in front of the others and read your poem. She'd chosen Schumann and his Violin Concerto, after a conversation with Montserrat about his life and his amazing music. Montserrat was the violinist featured in the CD recording too, which had made it even more cool.

The concerto's slow movement was so pretty, with this sense of warmth and underlying security, even though the music was in a minor key. It had an unbearable sweetness that made her heart ache.

Because just a few months later, Schumann went mad, threw himself into the Rhine, and was committed to an insane asylum.

It was like you could hear it in the music. Not the madness, but the way Schumann had maybe caught a glimpse of the great beyond. Listening to his music as she wrote, the poem had all but written itself.

> *An awareness crystallizes inside of me*
> *Rays of illumination cast into every dark corner of the psyche*
> *Here, the understanding*
> *Here the devotion. To the pursuit of the sacred, the ineffable*
> *A normal life, gone.*
> *To slave, instead, and arrive at the place where mortal meets divine*
> *The pinnacle. A sweetness, a golden light*
> *A place of such perfection, one dissolves upon witnessing it*
> *To capture both realms, a hero's journey, a price must be paid*
> *The price of one's life.*

It went on like that for three more stanzas. Afterward, she called Montserrat and read it over the phone, and both of them agreed that Kylie had hit the ball out of the park.

Except that, in the classroom that day, her classmates had hated it.

Once she'd finished reading it out loud, she stood there in front of them, shaking from nerves and the poem's intensity, clutching the sides of the podium. All the students were supposed to clap when the presenter had finished, but only a few did. Most had blank looks on their faces. Then the snorts of laughter started, muffled at first, but growing louder until the teacher had to wave her arms and tell everyone to settle down, that this was not an appropriate response.

What a terrible mistake it had been to share her thoughts, her special music. She'd wanted to curl up and disappear, undo the entire presentation. Better to have just begged off, even taking an F for the assignment.

"I want, I want!" Granger cried, waking Kylie from her reverie. He rose and snatched the Huberman sphere from Dario, which expanded from a cantaloupe-sized sphere into one as big as a three-dimensional hula hoop. Kylie had to find Dario a new toy, then she showed Granger how to expand and contract the Huberman sphere. Then it was Emma's turn. The calming influence of being around little kids who didn't overthink anything began to soothe her.

Montserrat hadn't asked about the poem and Kylie hadn't offered any comments. She hoped it stayed that way. She could hear Montserrat now, from the other room, telling the other moms about a recent guest performance in a quartet. "The pages of the score were fluttering from the air flow onstage," she was saying. "I must have been right under the source. Every time I'd turn my page, it would start fluttering again. Sometimes the page would lift up and start to turn on its own. I'd slap it down if I wasn't playing, but otherwise I had to wait and just wing it. The others in the quartet were mortified afterward, but I told them, no biggie, that was live performing for you. Speaking of which, don't forget my young-artist event in two and a half weeks with the quintet. Down the Peninsula in Menlo Park. You'll all be there?"

"It's on my calendar," Kylie's mom said, and Kylie made a mental note to tell her mom she wanted to go, too.

"Wouldn't miss it," Alice said, and Katrina murmured something Kylie couldn't hear.

The doorbell sounded and a few seconds later, Kylie heard the sound of Dena's cheery voice. Then, strangely, an unfamiliar guy's voice, which had never happened in one of the mom-group gatherings before. Kylie cocked her head in the voice's direction. She could tell he was an adult, but a younger one. His voice had a richness, a hint of laughter, something that drew you in.

Intrigued, she went and took a peek.

Bingo. An adult, but younger than the moms. "Hi, Kylie," Dena called out, and the stranger turned her way as well.

"Hey, there," he said. "Hi!"

He was gorgeous. She froze, struck dumb. "Hi," she managed finally.

"Hey! Littles!" he exclaimed as the three kids swarmed out, equal parts curiosity and trepidation over the new arrivals.

"That's my youngest daughter, Kylie," her mom was saying. "She's our indispensable child watcher when we moms gather."

"Nice to meet you, Kylie," he said. "I'm David."

His smile was warm and friendly. He was suntanned and wore a loose aquamarine shirt with the sleeves rolled up, like he'd just gotten off a yacht or a Caribbean beach. The tan and the shirt's color made his blue eyes stand out. His hair was sun-bleached blond and untamed, curls and waves that seemed like a gold halo.

"I forgot to ask you, Kylie," Montserrat said. "How did your music poem go?"

Could there have been a worse time for the question? Her face grew warm. She studied her fingernails. "Meh," she mumbled.

"What do you mean?" Montserrat prodded.

"The other kids couldn't relate to it."

Montserrat turned to the others. "Kylie wrote this poem set to Schumann's music, and it was so amazing."

"What was it about?" David asked.

Great. Now she had to bumble around with words in front of this god. Face hot, she tried to explain in the shortest, easiest way possible. "It was about life and art and how Schumann was teetering on the edge of madness when he wrote his violin concerto, and maybe that's why the slow movement was so amazing."

David, to her relief, didn't give her a blank look. "Schumann's great," he said. "Did you know he was an excellent writer himself? A music critic, a really good one, very perceptive and forward-thinking about the music of his time. He was the founder and editor of this popular music journal and would use two pseudonyms in his reviews, except the names are eluding me."

"Florestan and Eusebius." The words came out before Kylie could censor them—this would have been the world's worst time to screw up, but to her relief, David and Montserrat nodded. "I wouldn't know the difference between them," Kylie admitted. "I just remember their names."

"Florestan was the wilder one," David said. "Outspoken, passionate and rather impetuous. Eusebius was mild-mannered, more kind and contemplative in his writing. Or did I get the two switched around wrong?" he asked Montserrat.

"No, you got it right."

"Well done, Kylie," David said. "I'm impressed." He smiled at her. She felt something in her stomach leap up and resettle somewhere below her belly, which made her feel like she needed to sit down.

The group's focus shifted—thank God for that—to the fact that David wanted to play the piano for all of them. As the others debated over what they wanted to hear, Kylie glanced over at the kids, who were all seated by their respective moms, legs in crisscross-applesauce, behaving angelically. She decided it meant she could stay and listen as well, so she perched herself on the padded edge of her mom's armchair.

Music decisions made, David set himself up at Montserrat's piano. From the first notes he played, Kylie felt this glowing thing descend and warm her from the inside. It made all the bad feelings, the pessimism about school, fade from her mind. After a lyrical Chopin waltz, he played something Beethoven-ish, a sonata that was dense and passionate. To Kylie's ears, it all sounded incredible. Alice was nodding thoughtfully. She worked at the Symphony, and Kylie could tell she, too, was impressed. Everyone was.

"Those were lovely," Montserrat said after he finished. "Now tell me what you want from me."

"I could use a job."

"I have an accompanist already. With a conservatory pedigree."

"I was conservatory-trained through my teens. In San Francisco. Accepted to Julliard."

"And this is where you tell us you tossed the opportunity aside and went elsewhere with your life," Montserrat said.

David looked surprised. "It's that obvious?"

"By your playing, your talent and training are clear. And by the glitz, the embellishment, I can tell you decided to strike out on your own and go for a more crowd-pleasing style."

He laughed out loud. "Montserrat, you could be a fortune teller. You nailed it. I've made my living over the past several years by performing what people want to hear, in the way they want to hear it. The reality is, being a crowd-pleaser pays really well."

"Why do you want my opinion, then?" Montserrat asked.

David grew serious. "Because being around Dena, my sister-in-law here, is making me want to … I don't know. Be a more pure artist. Try harder. Reconnect with the art."

"Here's a thought, David." Kylie's mom spoke up. "At the studios, we're minus a rehearsal accompanist. They're looking for a seasoned, classically trained pianist. At the least, you could audition to be on the roster as a substitute accompanist. It pays well."

"Working there in the room with the dancers?"

Kylie saw his gaze zero in on Katrina.

Of course. Always Katrina, the company star. Kylie watched David watch Katrina. Probably check her left hand to see if she wore a ring. Katrina's expression remained neutral but her cheeks pinkened.

"Give me your contact information," her mom said. "I'll get you in to audition with Elsa, our lead accompanist. You'll need to pass scrutiny with both her and Anders, our artistic director. Anders, by the way, is a classically trained pianist. They're both set in what they want in an accompanist. A clean, classical, unobtrusive sound. For what it's worth, I'd check the ego at the door."

"I can do that. Easy-peasy."

Montserrat had left the room and returned now with her violin and bow in one hand, sheet music in the other. She waved the sheets at him. "Dvorak's Piano Quintet in A major. Are you familiar with it?"

"I am."

"Can you play the third movement?"

"As in, right now?"

"Yes."

His eyes lit up and Kylie could tell he was someone who liked a challenge. "I think I could give it a good shot."

Montserrat handed the score to him. "Look it over while I tune up. I'll cover for the other instruments where it makes sense." She looked at everyone else. "You ladies don't mind, do you?"

"Absolutely not," Alice declared, and all the others agreed.

David pored over the music score, expression bright with interest. He played little passages here and there as Montserrat tuned her violin. When she finished, he looked up.

"Ready?" Montserrat asked him.

He nodded.

"Go for it."

They both launched into the music. It was spirited and exciting, full of catchy phrases and beautiful melodies that got passed from one instrument to the next. Kylie had never heard the music before and made a mental note to check out more Dvorak. It was amazing how, with just their two instruments, Montserrat and David made such a rich sound, told such a full musical story. Kylie knew Montserrat had been performing as a concert soloist for over fifteen years. That David could keep up with her made him seem even more god-like.

They played the movement all the way through. When they finished, Montserrat lowered her violin and smiled at David. "I have to admit, I wouldn't have expected you to keep up so beautifully with the classical repertoire."

David gave a modest nod. "The classics were my first love. It's how I spend my 'me' time at the piano. Chopin and Beethoven are the teachers I worship and try to emulate."

"Let's keep in touch," Montserrat said, and Kylie knew that was a huge win for him.

"Yes," her mom told David, with the same interest in her voice. "The West Coast Ballet Theatre will be in touch too."

Best. News. Ever.

Chapter 4

Katrina

She and Kylie were in Cairo, confusingly, and they were sharing a plate of *koshari* that Nabila had made. Sharing was the wrong word. Kylie had turned so that she could eat it all, even as Katrina tried to tell her, over Kylie's shoulder, "I need some too. I need it more than you." But no words came out, so she could only hum her disapproval and wait behind Kylie for her turn. A hot breeze stirred the palm trees above them, shading the two of them from too much sun, a good thing, because a ballet dancer treasured her smooth, pale skin. Kylie wasn't a ballet dancer but they were the same age, which was to say mere girls. Growing girls, absorbing everything. And Katrina was hungry, so hungry. Longing for that koshari.

A little boy in the other room stirred restlessly, making noisy whimpers because he must have wanted some too. Or wanted his mother. Where was his mother? Why was she being neglectful?

Katrina's eyes flew open in alarm to reveal the darkness of her bedroom. What could she have been thinking? *She* was the mother. Although Javier hadn't officially moved yet, she was the only adult in the house tonight—the new normal—and she had to maintain vigilance. She lay there in the dark, heart thumping, but no further sound came from the monitor in Dario's bedroom. Her heart rate gradually slowed. Dario, clearly, had fallen back to sleep on his own, just like Javier was always saying he would, and should.

She glanced at the clock and saw it was approaching 2:00AM. She settled back into her pillows and let the energy of the curious dream reverberate in her. She and Kylie, the same age—what a bizarre concept. And the feeling of being in Cairo had seemed so real, even though it had been such a long time ago. When was the last time she'd thought of Cairo? Years and years. Decades, even.

She'd just turned eight when she and her parents moved there, following a year in London. Before that, it had been a year in Barcelona. Her father was a Distinguished Fellow of Literature, which meant that a lot of universities around the world wanted him as a guest lecturer. Home was Amsterdam, although, of her parents, only her father was Dutch. Her mother was French, but she, too, called Amsterdam home, because when she married the great poet, Sandor De Vries, his home became hers. It all sounded very romantic to Katja, whose full name was Katrina, but no one used it because it was stuffy and formal.

They arrived in Cairo in early summer. Her mother, spent from the move and the blistering heat, turned down proposals to go exploring. Katja was eager for adventure, but was warned that girls here stayed mostly inside, never running or being boisterous in public, which sounded completely unfair. She loved to climb trees and race boys. She was happiest when she was in motion. So she proposed to her father that she dress like a boy, tucking her blond braid down her shirt, so that, out in public, no one would know she was a girl. To prove it, she donned her disguise and strutted through the living room just like a boy would. Her father laughed and laughed, declaring her a born actress, and agreeing to the plan.

Cairo was heat, blazing sun and busy, crowded streets. Everything seemed to be hues of brown, tan and gold except for the Nile River, which had its own different hues of blue. The city was noisy like nothing Katja had ever known, full of traffic at all hours, with cars honking to warn off other drivers or simply to greet someone familiar. There were as many reasons to honk as there were hours of the day. Then there were the tinny broadcast calls to prayer, echoing throughout the city, five times a day, starting well before sunrise.

She and her father explored all sorts of neighborhoods, as well as the Egyptian Museum and the Khan el-Khalili bazaar. From a street vendor they bought chilled *karkadeh*, tea red as rubies from the hibiscus flower petals they were made from. They ate *koshari*, a dish layered with rice, macaroni and lentils, topped with chickpeas, crispy onions, and tangy, spicy tomato sauce. It was so good, Katja could have eaten it every day for the rest of her life. When she told her father this, he smiled broadly and announced he would tell Zahra, their housekeeper and cook, to put it on their menu regularly.

Her boy disguise worked. If anything, it was her father who drew attention because, like most Dutchmen, he was tall. She, too, was tall, particularly for a girl just turned eight, and lanky like her father as well. She wasn't pretty—she'd noticed this in London last year, when trying to adapt to the new, uncomfortable ritual of school. Her ears stuck out and so did her jaw, and only her long blonde hair, too pale and straight to be pretty, marked her as a girl. She sensed her parents might have wanted a son, but she was their only child. But her father always told people she was the apple of his eye, that he wouldn't exchange her for a dozen boys, and that always made her feel good.

She loved their new life. She'd go to sleep each night, tired and contented. Her parents had made new friends who'd sometimes visit late in the evening. From her bed, Katja listened to their voices, her father's rich laughter, her mother's gentler voice, with the scent of the visitors' cigarette smoke wafting her way. She loved this feeling, an utter assurance that her parents would always be there—no matter where "there" was that year. It changed. It didn't matter to her. What mattered was being together, ever ready for the next adventure.

Once her father assumed his duties at the university, Katja had to seek out a new best friend. Her mother still preferred to stay indoors, leaving shopping errands for Nabila, the hired girl who helped Zahra with the cleaning and cooking. In Nabila, Katja instantly sensed an ally. Nabila was younger and more playful than the other adults in the household. Like Zahra, she was Egyptian, with warm brown eyes, lustrous black hair held back with a jeweled clip, and a dusting of tiny freckles across the bridge of her nose that made her especially pretty in Katja's mind. She spoke good English and taught Katja songs and phrases in Arabic, and soon Katja could pick up bits of conversation between Nabila and Zahra.

Nabila wasn't afraid to appear un-ladylike from time to time, which Katja loved. She told her father one night how they'd raced down the block, and she'd been so much faster than Nabila that she'd looped back around and still won the race.

Nabila, listening in, nodded and chuckled.

"Always in movement, my Katja." Her father reached over and fondly tussled Katja's hair. "She just can't keep still."

"I have two sisters like that," Nabila said. "They're born dancers. The younger one, Katja's age, is only in training, but the other is a professional."

"*Raqs Sharqi?*" her father asked Nabila.

The words meant nothing to Katja, but they made Nabila's face light up. "Indeed, yes!"

Her father's expression softened. "A beautiful tradition. Such artful dancing. I saw a performance, many years back, that I'll never forget."

Nabila looked even more pleased. "I'm so happy to hear this. I'll have to tell my mother. She was a *Raqs Sharqi* dancer of considerable renown thirty years ago."

"Well my goodness," he said. "That's something!"

Katja was sold, even without knowing anything more. She tugged at her father's arm. "I want to see this dancing! I want to be a dancer, too. May I visit them, Papa? Please?"

"You're supposed to wait for an invitation," he scolded, but Nabila only smiled.

"I would love to introduce Katja to my family. I'll arrange a visit on a day when both sisters are there."

Her father's eyes twinkled. "Excellent. A fine addition to my daughter's education here."

Three days later, she and Nabila took a bus, then a long walk, past throngs of people and shops squeezed closely together, to arrive at Nabila's home, in a tall apartment building. Once inside, Nabila gestured to a living room where a handful of people were gathered. Egyptian pop music blared as an older woman with pulled-back hair and a still-beautiful face gave instructions to a skinny, long-legged girl who looked about Katja's age. Female voices in an adjacent kitchen called out to each other amid the clanging of pots and pans. It all felt like a party was about to erupt.

In the living room, the skinny girl began to dance, moving her hips in an alluring circle. She wore a low-cut filmy skirt and skimpy top, her hair held back by a long, glittery, blue and silver scarf that flowed down her shoulders. Katja, by Nabila's side, watched in awed silence.

"That's my mother and my younger sister," Nabila murmured. Katja barely took in her words, mesmerized as she was by the girl's grace in motion. Nabila's mother called out something in Arabic over the music and demonstrated with her hands. The girl nodded and shifted to a different set of moves, leaning back, even as her hips kept swiveling. Now her shoulders shimmied, making them seem disconnected from the rest of her. And her expression while she was doing all this—she looked almost bored, like she'd been doing this amazing dancing every day of her life and it was no big deal.

Katja had never envied another girl as much as she did Nabila's little sister. She was like a princess. The girl rolled her wrists, her hands, making them look like flowers unfurling. It was like art that moved. If her father had been there, he'd have instantly composed a poem. "The dancing," she said to Nabila in a daze. "What did you say it was called?"

"*Raqs Sharqi*," Nabila replied. "In English, it's 'belly dancing.'"

The music stopped and attention turned to Nabila and Katja's arrival. Katja felt shy and gawky as Nabila introduced her. Another sister named Yasmine joined them. She was stunningly beautiful, about Nabila's age and height with the same creamy honey-colored skin and eyes, only no freckles, and there was something about her that gave off an electric energy. This, surely, was the professional dancer. Katja shook with excitement.

"Show Yasmine the newest movement," Nabila told her younger sister. Their mother turned the music back on, and Katja and the others watched the girl dance again.

"No," Yasmine said afterwards. "Not enough. Do it like this." She demonstrated, and if Katja had thought the younger sister could dance and move, it was nothing like a professional. Yasmine's body moved like a wave, first the head, then chest, then belly, then hips. Katja hadn't before realized movement could be liquid, but there was no other way to describe it. She felt an ache deep inside her, and she became limp with longing.

I want to dance like this.
I want it so much.

The scene seared itself onto Katja's mind. She played it over and over in her head, and dreamt about it that night. The next morning she rose early, intent on teaching herself the steps, which made Nabila laugh when Katja informed her of the decision. Nabila stopped laughing as soon as she saw Katja's hurt expression. "It's in the blood," she tried to explain to Katja. "My sisters take after our mother. They were born to dance."

"I was too," Katja argued stubbornly. "I just know it."

"Perhaps. But you must learn somehow."

"Could your mother or sisters teach me?"

"They're too busy. But—" Nabila paused thoughtfully. "We have a videotape collection. Yasmine's performances, as well as those of other famous dancers."

"Could I borrow them? I'd be extra careful."

Nabila looked over at the family television, rarely on because there were only a few channels available, all with boring programs. "It wouldn't work without a VCR."

"I'll ask my father to buy one."

"They're very expensive here."

"I'm going to ask him."

Nabila laughed. "Look at that stubborn chin. You're a girl who gets what she wants, aren't you?"

"Only when I really, really want it."

Katja went to work on her father, who soon threw up his hands in surrender and said he'd check with the university's audio-visual department to see if they had loaners for faculty.

They did. It all came together. Nabila brought over two videocassettes, and thereafter a new one every week. Katja watched the videos closely in the heat of the afternoon while the others napped. She took in the hypnotic movement of the dancers' hips and arms, the arched back, the contracting belly, and worked all afternoon to replicate them in front of her bedroom mirror. It was her practice. Her religion. Her art. It was everything. Trying to move like Yasmine was hard and frustrating, but she never let that stop her.

I want, I want, I want.

School, her mother reminded her, was about to start, which made Katja feel sick with anxiety. Last year, in London, she'd hated it. From a year of homeschooling when they lived in Barcelona, she'd been two grade levels ahead of her British classmates, and had felt bored and lonely, made worse by the fact that she had a stammer that made the other kids laugh at her. There was a British school in Cairo her parents were planning to send her to, and she wanted none of it. It would cut into her dance practice time. To show her parents how serious she was about her dance education, she gave a performance, complete with a costume (four of her mother's scarves tucked out of her shorts, like a dress) and music. Her father's eyes shone with pride and afterwards, he, Nabila and her mother all clapped and cheered. But her mother looked worried, too. Katja overheard her parents talking in the kitchen later that evening and crept closer to listen.

"She's extraordinary when she moves," her father was saying. "She's a budding artist. Last year in London, when she only had school, she wilted! Here she blooms. I say we homeschool her again. She's self-motivated, and we have all the books she needs, right here. And have you heard her in the kitchen with Zahra and Nabila? She speaks Arabic with them. Her fifth language! Don't tell me she's not getting an extraordinary education."

"Sandor, I agree," her mother replied. "It's just that …"

"What?"

"My mother wouldn't approve."

"Your mother is not Katrina's parent. We are."

But then, Grandmother announced a visit, and overnight, the household changed. Her father seemed less jovial; Zahra and Nabila were assigned double the amount of tasks to get the house spotless, and her mother got her hair styled and bought a new dress. Not an Egyptian one. A Parisian one. She didn't look happy about wearing it.

Grandmother arrived late one afternoon, a tall, elegant woman, dressed in a snug-fitting skirt and jacket, apparently "a Chanel," as Katja heard Zahra tell Nabila.

"Come say hello to your grandmother," her mother told her in French, her voice as strained as her smile.

Katja had been instructed to wear what felt like her most uncomfortable clothes. She also had to wind her blond hair into a bun. It wasn't pretty at all; without her shiny curtain of long hair she felt plain and dull. But she knew her manners.

At dinner, she kept stealing glances at this stern woman, who was both familiar and not. The Chanel suit she still wore puzzled Katja. Why should Grandmother opt for such constraining clothing in such a hot environment? Didn't she understand that flowing, light garments were much better here?

Over the next few days, Katja couldn't decide if her mother was glad or uncomfortable that her mother was there. A little of both, she decided. Grandmother didn't talk much to her father, which surprised Katja. He was the most interesting man she knew. He always made a lot of friends, university types, educated and intelligent, and everyone liked him. Why didn't Grandmother? She didn't like the evening his university friends came over, either.

The following night was quieter, and Grandmother seemed to

enjoy it more. She sat on the couch with Katja and inquired about her hobbies, which Katja told her were reading and dancing.

Grandmother's eyes lit with interest. She asked to see the books, nodding in satisfaction at their titles, their thickness, and the fact that they were in an assortment of languages—German, English, French, and a children's book in Spanish. "She reads well for such a young girl," Grandmother told her parents, who nodded proudly.

"You enjoy dance, too?" Grandmother asked.

"Oh, yes! I want to become a professional dancer. I've been teaching myself."

This got Grandmother's full attention. She seemed excited, even. "Tell me how you teach yourself," she said.

"I watch videos of dancers, because I'm not allowed to attend an actual performance, but a video is good and from it I've learned a lot. Then I practice the movements in my bedroom for an hour every day, where there's a mirror. I think I've gotten good. Would you like to see me perform?"

"No," Katja's mother cut in swiftly, and Katja eyed her in confusion.

"I would love to see my granddaughter dance, Marine," Grandmother said, and by the way she spoke, Katja could tell Grandmother was still The Boss, even though her father was The Boss as well.

"Sandor?" Her mother's voice sounded strained.

"Marine," he said gently. "Of course Katja must show your mother her dance. She's proud of it. So are we. She's a beautiful dancer."

Her mother looked trapped. Katja couldn't understand why. "All right," her mother said.

Katja raced to put on her costume and grab her music. Her father adjusted the living room lights to spotlight her. She began her dance, slow movements at first, growing into bigger ones. Soon, that dreamy feeling came over her, where her body seemed to respond to the music on its own, like she herself were only a bystander. It began to feel like a dream, her back arching, dipping into a backbend, arms coiling and uncoiling like serpents, as her hips undulated through it all. As the last notes sounded, she struck a final pose, knowing it had been her best dancing yet.

Her father applauded enthusiastically but her mother was more subdued, not even meeting Katja's gaze. Grandmother didn't clap. Katja paused in confusion. Had she danced poorly, after all?

"Excuse me." Grandmother rose swiftly from the couch and retreated into the guest room as Katja's parents exchanged looks.

"I think I should go in there," her mother said.

"Did Grandmother not like my dancing?" Katja asked her father, once her mother had left the room. "Was I bad?"

"You were beautiful. Amazing. I'm thinking perhaps your grandmother was expecting something more like the dancing she prefers."

"What kind would that be?"

"Ballet." His lip curled. Clearly he didn't share the feeling.

She went to bed that evening overhearing their voices, sometimes raised in protest (her mother) and responded to with firmness (Grandmother) and then her father's reasonable voice. She knew that soon he'd make them laugh, even Grandmother, and all would be well. But Grandmother's sharp, raised voice roused her as she was drifting off.

"I will not see her turned into a wild bohemian, Sandor, simply because it pleases you to be one yourself."

"You have no choice, Hélène."

"Oh, I do. Ask my daughter. And just who do you think subsidizes your opulent—and decidedly unbohemian—residence?"

Except they didn't live in Bohemia, Katja thought sleepily. They lived in Cairo, so Grandmother must have been talking about something else. Reassured, she slipped off, into a dream world, until an agitated voice alerted her.

"Take her, then, you old witch!" she heard her father exclaim, except he'd said *bruha vieja,* which was Spanish and Grandmother only spoke French, so that proved it was a dream.

"There'll be less drama if we simply pack and leave," Grandmother replied. "Less time for her to think about it. I checked, and there are seats on tomorrow's afternoon flight to Paris. I'll book them."

"*Maman*, this is so cruel of you," her mother protested in a broken voice.

"I will never forgive you for this," her father said in a low, menacing voice, which, even for a dream, didn't sound anything like him.

"I don't need your drama, Sandor. I am doing this for her. We are not so different, in the end, the three of us. We all want what's best for her."

The next morning, Katja entered the kitchen to find Grandmother seated, in her Chanel suit again, calmly drinking coffee. Her parents, there at the table with their coffees as well, didn't look up to greet her. But Grandmother was all smiles as she wished Katja a good morning. "Your parents tell me you love an adventure."

"Oh, I do!"

"You and I are going to embark on an adventure. We are going to return to Paris, where you will study and prepare for the chance to study dance at one of the finest institutions in the dance world."

Katja hesitated. An adventure! Studying dance at an important school! But her parents weren't happy about what Grandmother was proposing. Her mother looked up and Katja now saw her eyes were puffy and red, like she'd been crying.

A bad feeling took hold. "My parents are going too, yes? Because that's how our adventures work."

Her mother gave a great sob and rose from her seat, knocking over the chair. Ignoring it, she hurried out of the kitchen and into the bathroom, where Katja could hear her crying. Now Katja was scared. "Papa?" She turned to her father. "What's happening? Why is Mama upset?"

He tried to smile. "We are thinking that we will miss you very much. Because we won't be going with you, Katja. I need to stay here and teach, so you will live with Grandmother."

"When? Do I leave next year?"

He looked down at his cup of coffee. "You leave today."

The dream last night. It hadn't been a dream. Her thoughts scrambled.

"I can't go without my parents!" she told Grandmother.

In place of a response, Grandmother gave an elegant shrug.

Katja turned wildly to her father. "Papa?"

Her father shook his head. "This isn't what I want. But your grandmother has persuaded us that it's in your best interest."

"No! Being here in Cairo with you and Mama is what's best for me!" Horror came over her. "Where's Nabila? I need to be with Nabila! She's my best friend!"

"We've asked her to stay home today," her father said.

"I want her! She's going to help me become a better belly dancer."

"You are a spoiled little girl too used to getting your way," Grandmother cut in sharply. "There will be no more belly dancing. You are to pack two bags and be ready to leave with me in three hours."

She rose and sailed out of the room. Katja stared at her father in shock, who was blinking fast like he was about to cry. He hadn't fought back. Her parents were going to let *la bruha vieja* take her from them.

A blur, the next few hours. Her mother, packing Katja's bags and crying, while Katja sat on her bed, stunned and incapable of thought. A bath. Dressing in uncomfortable clothes. A taxi arriving. Hugs from her parents. And now a cold numbness consumed her and she couldn't even speak.

The airport. A flight. She said nothing to *la bruha vieja*, vowing to give Grandmother the silent treatment, which always made her parents break down and give her what she wanted.

Grandmother didn't break down. Not on the flight, or at Charles De Gaulle airport, or on the drive through a dark, rainy Paris, to Grandmother's flat. Periodic glances at Grandmother's calm, determined face told Katja all she needed to know.

The witch had won. She'd prevailed. Katja had just lost everything that mattered to her, and Grandmother didn't care.

Paris was terrible. Grandmother's flat in the 1st *arondissement* was dark, cold and formal, like a museum, with nowhere comfortable to sit. The windows had double panes and even though she could see cars, there weren't enough honking noises outside. The silence inside, which she now knew Grandmother preferred, felt utterly lonely. Day after day, it always seemed to be twilight and drizzling. Even London hadn't been like this.

She wept into her pillow nightly, missing her parents with a ferocity that made her hyperventilate. The grey feeling never went away. The weather, Grandmother's strictness, the absence of her father's voice and his cheerful energy, made her want to crawl into bed and never come out.

There was traditional schooling again, and like in London the previous year, the other students jeered at her when she tried to talk and instead stuttered. She made no friends. Worse, there were no dance classes like she'd been promised. Instead, there was only talk of it. Talk, talk, talk, among Grandmother and her friends. They all agreed that, for the Paris Opera Ballet School, it was better for her to have no ballet lessons prior, than to have bad ballet lessons. And no *danse du ventre*—belly dancing—Grandmother had warned. No hips moving, ever again. Gyrating hips were bad, apparently, and she'd been bad for doing them so well.

One day an older woman, a friend of Grandmother's, came over, bringing with her a Russian couple. To Katrina's shocked surprise, she was instructed to strip to her underpants, and refrain from trying to cover her chest with her arms. And Grandmother had thought belly dancing was indecent? It was a terrible, mortifying experience, made more so by the fact that they treated her like an animal on sale at the market. As the women watched, the man roped her around the waist with one arm, and with his free hand, took her back leg and lifted it behind her. He nudged her standing leg's foot so that the toes pointed to the side. "Relax your muscles," he commanded in heavily accented French, and she tried to do as she was told. Next, she stood on both feet and he gripped her behind the waist and pressed against her shoulder so she arched all the way back, easily reaching the floor behind her. This she could do, thanks to her dance practice in Cairo. Only now it wasn't such a bad thing, apparently.

Back up she came. The Russian woman approached and she and the man bent to study her feet, flexing and arching each one, murmuring to each other in Russian. They asked her to take three steps and curtsey, to the right, and to the left. Finally they released her and she ran to cover herself. Ten minutes later, they left. "They know ballet bodies," was all Grandmother would say to Katja. "We needed to know." And that was it. Eventually she gleaned the visit's significance from eavesdropping on Grandmother and her friend, even though she knew a proper young lady didn't eavesdrop. It turned out the Russian couple was affiliated with an important ballet school in Russia, the Vaganova Academy, and the meeting had been a favor to see if Katja were a good fit for the equally important Paris Opera Ballet School. Katja leaned closer to the open door to catch Grandmother's next words.

"He told us that, if it were a Vaganova audition, they would take her. That she had it all—lines, extensions, feet, flexibility."

"Tiens! C'est la bonne nouvelle, ça! Felicitations, ma chère Hélène."

Grandmother and her friend thought it was good news. Katja's gut wrenched in fear that Grandmother planned to send her to Russia, but the feeling faded when they went on to talk about how the Paris Opera Ballet School now had a new facility, an entire campus in Nanterre, just outside Paris, complete with weekday boarding, and how splendidly it might all work out.

But that would be January, at the earliest, Grandmother told her, and otherwise, next fall. And in the meantime, Katja was to learn how to swallow her unhappiness and cope.

A dreary eternity later—six whole weeks—Grandmother greeted her after school with good news. "I've just received word from my contact at the Paris Opera Ballet School. A young student has dropped out. There will be one opening in your level at the School, following Christmas break. You've been invited to audition."

Katja hesitated. "And that ballet school will include *school* school, too?"

"Yes. You will study academics in the morning and dance in the afternoon."

"And all the other students will be dancers, too?"

"Correct."

This news cheered her up. No more of the classroom she hated.

A chance to dance every single day. Her spirits began to lift until the following Sunday, when her parents told her, on their weekly phone call, that they couldn't be with her on Christmas or New Year's this year. Her mother sounded carefully vague about the reason, but her father was more blunt. "Apparently it's not our choice," he told her over the protests of her mother in the background. "It's your grandmother's mandate."

"What?" she gasped. "Papa, why?"

"Ask your grandmother."

After the call, she stormed to Grandmother, angry as she'd ever been about anything. "They say you aren't allowing them to come here for the holidays," she burst out, aware that she was being very impolite and unladylike.

Grandmother nodded.

"But why?" she cried.

Grandmother regarded her impassively. "Your audition for the Paris Opera Ballet School is the first week of January. I won't have anything distracting you from that. It's too important."

"I want my parents!"

"They're not the proper influence for you at this time."

"It's Christmas!"

"This audition is more important."

"No it's not! You're mean and I hate you," cried Katja. "I wish you were dead so I could be back with my parents."

Grandmother slapped her so hard the sound seemed to echo through the room. Katja's face burst into pain. She recoiled, stunned. She'd never been slapped before; her parents had never hit her, ever. She and Grandmother stared at each other.

"You do not speak to your grandmother in such a way." Grandmother's voice shook, her eyes full of fire.

Katja burst into tears and ran to her bedroom. She slammed the door, unspeakably bad manners and all, and threw herself on her bed, sobbing for all that she'd lost.

She must have fallen asleep, because the room was darker when she opened her eyes, and she was no longer alone. Grandmother stood looking down at her, not fiery-eyed anymore. More pensive. Almost sad.

"Your audition is ten days after Christmas, which means three days after the New Year," she told Katja. "It will determine your life. I do not exaggerate. My instincts tell me that with your grace, musicality and body type, you have the capacity to be an extraordinary ballet dancer. The best of the best. But perhaps it was wrong of me to try so hard. It has to come from you. All of it. If you don't have the drive for the ballet world—and it is cruel, exacting and unforgiving—so be it. Next school year, you can return to live with your parents. I'll intervene no more."

Katja didn't know what to say. They regarded each other warily in the dimming light. Outside, rain began to fall, a soft patter on the roof.

Finally Grandmother spoke again. "What do you want most, granddaughter? Aside from being with your parents again?"

It was an unusual question. Grandmother had never asked her opinion, her thoughts, on anything. "I want to be the best dancer in the world," she replied.

Grandmother studied her. "There is pain and disappointment in training to be the best, which you can't imagine. Only discipline and hard work and the ability to accept harsh conditions, harsh criticism will bring you that prize."

She sat on the edge of Katja's bed. "If you think I am harsh, it's nothing compared to what they will be. They will work you beyond fatigue, criticize your slightest faults, push you beyond your endurance. Above all will hang the terror of being rejected, expelled.

You will be ranked, you will be weighed, and if you are found lacking, you will not be invited to return the following year. Complaining is unacceptable. Obedience is everything. You have to have exceptional resistance to pain to succeed as a dancer of the Paris Opera Ballet. As a professional ballet dancer everywhere."

"If no one is allowed to complain, how do you know so much?" Katja challenged.

Grandmother's expression didn't change. "I was a student at the Paris Opera Ballet School, a *petit rat,* as students there are referred to, when I was ten. I trained for a year at the School and at the end, I re-auditioned for a place in one of its six divisions, as every student must do, every year. I was not reselected. It felt like the end of the world. Even though it had been a painful, too-challenging world. The teachers, all former dancers and students themselves, were cruel, unforgiving, because this was how they, too, were taught. Only the best students, the ones who could handle the pressure, survived it all. I can't know what the conditions are now, in this new facility. But you will be there, alone and fending for yourself, Sunday evening to Friday evening, when you'll return home for two nights. I ask myself now if you're ready for it. I ask myself why I would subject my lovely young granddaughter to such a challenge."

Grandmother thought she was lovely. This startled Katja as much as the announcement that Grandmother had once been a student there. She was seeing Grandmother in an entirely new light. "Why didn't you tell me you wanted to be a dancer as much as I do?" she asked.

"Because I don't find rehashing the past to be of any help. I was young, it ended poorly, I survived the disappointment and moved on with my life. I was never meant to be a professional ballet dancer. My involvement in ballet is as a longtime patron. As for the past, my advice to you, granddaughter, is to leave it in the past. To hold onto it is foolish and exhausting."

She cocked her head and regarded Katrina. "You're younger than I was—far too young for a life decision—but the opportunity is about to present itself to you. The Paris Opera Ballet School produces the best of the best dancers, but now you know what price it will come at. Do you still want to proceed with the audition?"

Katja began to shake, in excitement and a little bit of fear, too. She felt as though she were standing on the high-dive board of an enormous pool, preparing to dive in, even though she didn't yet know how to swim.

"I do."

"Because we can turn down the invitation and you can enjoy Christmas and New Year's with your parents, without the pressures of training for ballet. I'll let it be your choice."

She hardly dared breathe. She considered the delight of seeing her parents, spending day after day alongside her father.

She couldn't. Grandmother was right. The audition was everything.

"No. They should stay in Cairo."

Grandmother gave a little sigh. Katja couldn't tell if it meant she was relieved or worried.

"So be it."

Chapter 5

Katrina

Javier moved out officially on Saturday afternoon. Brent had rented a pickup and together they carted out Javier's belongings and loaded them into the truck bed. For Katrina, it all felt profoundly destabilizing. He left items behind, anything that might have created a gap in the décor or destroyed the illusion that both parents still lived under the same roof. "Whatever's needed to keep Dario feeling secure and loved," he said. "And you, too, *mi amor*." His eyes brimmed with solicitude. "I am still wholly committed to being Dario's father and your partner in parenting him. Just from a different place."

He was being extra kind this morning. It had shaken her, his phone call last night from Brent's, the "great, thrilling" news about the Edwin Hess commission. A done deal on Friday afternoon, he announced, that Anders would make official on Monday. A daring new piece, set on her by a celebrity choreographer. Yes, exciting news. But the price: losing Don Q for the gala and thus losing Javier, on the heels of his moving out. His enthusiasm for her "amazing good fortune" only served to highlight his own pleasure with the setup, this chance to establish a second partnership with a young, new, supremely talented dancer.

Dario, sleepy from his nap, looked as uneasy as she felt. Her heart gave a sorrowful lurch, watching him stand there, his blankie in one hand, his favorite dinosaur clutched in the other. He was wearing his battered Hot Wheels slippers, which had to be forcefully removed each night, only on the condition, he made them promise, that his slippers remain right there, by his bed, so he could slip them on again the instant he arose the next day. He came over to her and she sat and pulled him onto her lap. His light brown hair was sweetly tousled, his cheeks pink. His cheeks had lost none of their baby fullness, and it was pure intoxication, pressing her cheek against his, nuzzling the warm smoothness, the sweet smell of his skin.

As Javier and Brent worked, Javier glanced at Dario periodically, assessing his reaction to the moving boxes and Brent. At one point Javier squatted down next to him.

"Remember how I explained this, little man? It's time for you to have your own room, so I'm moving these things to Brent's, where I'll sleep now."

"Okay, Papi," Dario said obediently.

"And remember, you'll have your own room there, too."

"Yes, Papi."

Brent seemed to intuit Dario's little boy's urge to "hang out with the men." "Dario," he suggested, "why don't you help your dad carry this last box?"

Dario slid off Katrina's lap and hurried over to Javier, who shifted his grip on the box to accommodate Dario's tiny hands. Dario, for his part, emitted little groans, and took on a labored expression as he slowly moved with Javier through the front door, which Brent held open for them.

When they returned, Dario was flushed and excited. "Papi says I can go with them to move the boxes into his room!" he said, the words all rushed and garbled in that darling three-year-old's way, even though everyone agreed that, for his age, he spoke quite well.

"He needs my help, Mama! I have to go!"

Oh, the sweetness of his puffed-out chest, his little shoulders pulled back. Her little boy, growing up so fast.

Please not so fast, she wanted to cry. *I'm not ready for this.*

Daily ballet class was the core around which she'd built her world since her days at the Paris Opera Ballet School. The routine and cadence of company class was unchanging, even as each year brought departures and new arrivals. This year the new dancer everyone was watching was the ultra-talented Palmira, just eighteen, bypassed over apprentice status to join as a full corps de ballet member. Her parents had been Cuban ballet stars and she'd trained in their elite Miami school before Anders snagged her to finish her training with the WCBT's ballet school. New, as well, was David the pianist, who, in spite of his low status among the four accompanists, had been selected to play for the day's company class. Which meant Anders approved of him. Katrina flashed David a polite smile, which he returned, but she didn't approach him to chat. This was her quiet, centering time. Today the news would come out, not just about the Edwin Hess commission and new partnering, but Javier's changes in his personal life. She shook the worrisome thoughts from her mind and focused on warming her protesting muscles, slowly rotating ankles, hips, and performing gentle extensions. It grounded her like nothing else, making her world feel safe and manageable. She had her strength, her health, she reminded herself, and in this line of work that was everything.

Javier arrived. To her relief, he took the same place in front of her at the barre, as he'd done for twenty-one years now. He smiled lovingly and kissed her forehead like he always did. It gave her the sense that all would work out fine. The feeling continued as Curtis, the senior ballet master, arrived to teach the class. Pliés, tendus, dégagés, rondes de jambe, one exercise into the next, followed by center work of adagio, small jumps, pirouettes. She and Javier both worked hard, focusing only on their bodies, their craft. A big, sweeping grand allegro across the diagonal, in groups, completed the morning's work. As class ended, Ben appeared at the doorway. He gestured for her, Javier, Palmira and a young, talented, freckle-faced soloist named Jimmy, to join him. "Anders has some changes to discuss with the four of you," he told them.

It was time.

When Anders greeted them, turning first to Palmira and Jimmy, Katrina watched Palmira's pretty brown eyes fill with uncertainty. This sort of big, big news had career-changing implications. She remembered what it had felt like to be that new, unseasoned dancer, handed a role that, quite possibly, was too big of a challenge. She'd danced the lead role in opening night of *The Sleeping Beauty* at age sixteen, mere months after her arrival. That performance had catapulted her to fame, paving the way for promotion after promotion.

"Congratulations." Anders addressed Jimmy first. "You are the recipient of a big opportunity. Edwin Hess has accepted our request for a commission. He will create a piece this month, setting it on Katrina and you. You've proven to be a fast study. We'll present it in the gala."

Jimmy looked stunned. "That's fantastic," he stammered. "I can't believe this."

Anders gave him a curt nod. "It's my feeling that you're ready for this kind of challenge."

"Oh, I am! Yes sir, I very much am!"

"Excellent. Please don't disappoint me." He turned next to Palmira. "You will, in turn, dance the *Don Quixote* pas de deux with Javier." Palmira's expression passed from shock to elation to trepidation. No surprise. Javier was as prestigious a partner as she could ever hope for.

"Do you believe you're up to the task?" Anders asked her.

"I do. I am," Palmira managed, looking both thrilled and terrified.

"You have six and a half weeks to prove you can do it. You danced Kitri's solo beautifully for the student recital last spring, so I'm confident. I'll have April oversee the Don Q rehearsals—learn all you can from her."

"I will."

He gave the two younger dancers a nod of dismissal. Jimmy and Palmira bolted, as if afraid Anders might call out that he'd changed his mind.

Anders rose from behind his desk and came around to perch himself on the front side. "Right, you two. Let's talk about the new change in your lives." His eyes settled on Katrina. Through the years, his looks seemed unchanging: a handsome, boyish face, a soulful gaze in his grey eyes whenever the matter at hand grew personal. "Javier told me this morning. I wondered what had been dragging your spirits down last week. Now I know." He chuckled. "In all candor, I was afraid you were going to tell me you were pregnant again."

This made her laugh too. "No. One child is plenty for me. And I'm fine with everything now. I just needed a few days to adjust."

Javier reached for her hand. "We promise you, Anders, this won't affect our professional partnership in the least." He gave her hand a squeeze. "Agreed?" he asked her.

"Absolutely."

"Good," Anders said. "And Katja. Know that I care." His expression, so caring and solicitous, warmed the part of her that had felt so chilled of late.

"Thank you."

"Lucinda will want to talk to you about this new development," he added. "Plan to stop by her office before you leave for the day."

"I can do that."

She didn't have a rehearsal in the day's final spot. Principals had less frequent rehearsals and more press-related obligations, so visits to Lucinda in Public Relations were familiar. At four o'clock, she knocked on Lucinda's office door on the executive level and was invited in.

Lucinda had grown more physically substantial in the years Katrina had known her, but so had her authority. She had an abundance of honey-colored hair to make up for the weight that accumulated—Lucinda joked that every time a dancer was told to drop a few pounds, they dropped them off in her office for her to take on. She smiled infrequently, and reserved most of her smiles for dancers like Katrina and Javier, because they never resisted her will, her suggestions, and they were WCBT moneymakers. "You make my job easy," she'd told Katrina with an approving nod, and the little girl still inside Katrina melted. In many ways, Lucinda was the still-living embodiment of Grandmother.

"Right, then. Let's speak frankly," Lucinda said. "You and Javier, going your separate ways. How are we going to spin this? Do we allude to the sexual—or not—nature of your relationship?"

She felt heat flood her face. "Really, I don't know if this is appropriate."

Lucinda leaned across her desk. "Honey. Don't be stupid. You and I have to figure this out, here in private. Word is going to get out and interviewers will ask about that. The two of you have a child together. The assumption has been that it was a romantic setup. All well presented. We can pat ourselves on the back for that. And I know you— you've been enjoying the shield it's put around you. We've gotten a lot of mileage out of your purity, your 'above it all' demeanor. You're very Marie Taglioni. Women ate up that prima-ballerina Madonna type, back in the day. What was it, eighteenth century?"

"Nineteenth."

"Fine, nineteenth century. She danced like an angel, but she was a woman, a mother, a family type. Very relatable. It's worked for you, too, and it's been brilliant."

It *had* been brilliant. She hadn't wanted it to end.

For a moment, Lucinda looked as sad as Katrina felt. But Lucinda's sad expression lasted mere seconds. "Anyway, we're moving on, because life moves on. Javier and I will have a talk. He's clearly ready to come out. Not in a noisy way. And of course we'll ignore the social media chatter, the rumors and speculation. But he can't deny that he hasn't aligned himself in a different partnership. So. You can't either."

Katrina nodded, resigned, as a feeling of despondency washed over her.

Lucinda fell silent, but Katrina sensed her scrutiny. "Never you mind," she said finally. "We'll come up with something. How about that posh English guy who's had a crush on you since forever."

"Martin?"

"Yes. Him. Invite him to join you out more often. He'll be flattered."

"We already go out every other month or so. I wouldn't want him to get the wrong idea."

"Yes, but if you want the cover, that's the way to go. If it looks like you have a boyfriend you won't get hit on, and I know you prefer that."

"I'm also a mother. That's a perfectly good reason not to date."

"Single mothers date, honey. Especially hot single mothers, which would include you."

Katrina wrinkled her nose. "It's just not my thing."

Lucinda's intercom buzzed. "Fritzie from *The Chronicle* is here," announced her assistant over the speaker.

"Thanks," Lucinda replied. "We're wrapping things up."

She and Lucinda both rose. "Keep me in the loop," Lucinda told her. "And call your guy."

She swallowed her reluctance. "All right. I will."

Chapter 6

April

Edwin Hess burst upon the scene like a king, amid trumpeting praise and flourishes. The WCBT's executive director had brought three bottles of Veuve Cliquot to Anders' office, and despite the early hour, the staff celebrated, raising full glasses to toast Edwin. April kept her sips tiny; their workday had just begun. Edwin, who wouldn't start rehearsing until the next day, was still on London time, where it was 5PM. Even if it hadn't been London time, she got the sense their guest of honor would have been in a party mood. He had that manic, restless gleam in his eyes.

He'd dressed stylishly, in tight jeans and an orange blazer, a fine wool scarf draped around his neck. A three-day stubble beard made his good looks edgier, a look April sensed he was cultivating to make up for his slim build and short stature. The suede chukka boots he wore easily added two inches to his height.

"We are so very, very glad you're here." Gil, the company's winsome director of development, shot Edwin a dazzling smile. Gil was married to Lana, a principal dancer, a relationship April secretly felt served him better than Lana. "What a gift you are, to our development team. I think it took less than an hour, following the press release, for the phones to start ringing. Donors asking me, one after another, 'How can I be a part of this? How can I financially support this treasure?'"

They smiled broadly at each other. Gil continued in a lower, more personal voice that didn't allow April to eavesdrop anymore. Whatever praise Gil was heaping on Edwin's plate, it worked. They looked like best friends.

Edwin didn't seem interested in talking with her, the lone female present. It was clear he bonded better with males. He confirmed this when he announced to Anders that, in working alongside a ballet master in rehearsals, he wanted either Ben or Curtis.

"No problem," Anders said.

"Agreed!" April pasted a bright smile on her face, reminding herself that she didn't need Edwin Hess to like her, or even notice her. He just needed to produce a winner for Anders and the company. "Cheers. To a winning endeavor." She raised her glass high and the others followed suit.

Edwin, laughing, seized the open Veuve Cliquot bottle and poured the rest into his glass, catching the fizzy overflow with a noisy slurp.

"Looks like I should open that third bottle," the executive director said, a little bemused.

"I'll do the honors," Gil cut in swiftly, and within seconds he'd popped open the bottle and poured more champagne into both Edwin's glass and his own.

"Now *this* is what I call a party." Edwin's voice was rich with satisfaction, and April saw Anders, Ben and Curtis direct approving nods to Gil.

They were happy. Edwin was happy. She saw the alarm in Ben's eyes as Edwin refilled first Curtis's and then Ben's glass to the brim. Hiding her grin, she mentally toasted Ben.

Here's to working with someone who's a real piece of work. Good luck!

Just before April's first rehearsal of the day, Ben appeared with Rebecca, a former company dancer and Dena's older sister. She'd always been a beauty, and now her glossy brown hair hung shorter, free and unencumbered. There was new spirit in her eyes as well. "Here's your new rehearsal assistant," Ben told April.

Surprised and pleased, she smiled at Rebecca. "I'm so glad to see you back here."

"Glad to be here," she replied, which sounded as ambivalent as her situation.

Rebecca had shocked all by turning down her contract renewal last spring. But then, confusingly, she'd renewed it after all, and promptly left for Brussels, ostensibly to help Anders' ex-wife and former work partner, Sabine, with her smaller ballet company. April sensed there'd been more beneath it all, high drama involving Rebecca, Ben and Anders, but knew better than to pry.

Ben was Anders' second in command, a job neither she nor Curtis had wanted, but escorting Rebecca seemed like a task he was happy to do. He waited to speak until Rebecca left to greet her former peers. "Anders says your job is to keep her out of his hair and keep her in line." He grinned, which made him look adorably boyish. "We all know her skill in getting under his skin. She's on contract through the season, so she is to help out and assist you in rehearsals."

"Wonderful. It's great to have her back."

Ben eyes softened. "It is."

Once Ben departed for his own rehearsal studio, April called out for the dancers' attention. "Today let's run through the ballroom waltz, all of it, without stopping. It'll be rough, I realize, but just keep going." She turned to Rebecca. "Are you ready to give your new job a try?"

Rebecca held up a clipboard with paper and a pen. "You tell me your comments and I write them down?"

"Yup."

"Then I'm good to go."

The sixteen dancers took their places as Elsa, the rehearsal's accompanist, began to play. April studied the dancers, their steps, and murmured to Rebecca. Her new assistant was well acquainted with the ballet, the ensemble look required, and offered a few insights of her own. Afterward, April gave the dancers their notes, and scrutinized a tricky passage where the dancers ran and leapt, crisscrossing lines without bumping into each other.

The three hours flew. Rehearsal culminated with one last run-through and a few final observations from April. Afterward, as the dancers milled around, grabbing their bags, chatting, she and Rebecca smiled at each other. "Is this thoroughly weird?" April asked.

"If not thoroughly, then still pretty much."

"How was Brussels? How's Sabine? How are *you* doing, really? I have so many questions. Are you free for lunch?"

"Ben and I are meeting up, but why don't you join us?"

April hesitated.

"Alice will be there." Rebecca smiled at April's surprise. "I know, friendships change. So does life." She shrugged philosophically but offered no further comment.

April wanted to see Alice, and she wanted to drink in the energy of this newly emancipated Rebecca. "Sure. I'm game."

Ben had booked a table at a nearby French brasserie, a lunchtime splurge known for its classic décor and Parisian touch, including tables crowded too closely together. But the charm of the place was undeniable, with its rich oak paneling, wall hangings depicting Parisian scenes, and the restaurant's always excellent bowl of French onion soup. Ben and Rebecca both ordered the *moules frites* and Alice, like April, ordered the French onion soup and a house salad. Alice was all smiles, wearing the dazed expression of an overworked parent who rarely took actual lunches but instead used the time to squeeze in more work or errands.

"When's the last time you had a sit-down lunch in a restaurant?" April asked her.

"I'm certain it hasn't been that long. Didn't we meet up, right after that one holiday?"

"We did. That was Easter."

"Oh. That long, huh?"

April chuckled. "Glad you're here. It's good to see you relax, if only for an hour."

"The same goes for you, I'm sure."

"I eat out with Anders once a week," April said. "That's always a sit-down event."

"That's not relaxing. Not in the least. You should be paid double for those times."

"He foots the bill. Does that count?"

A snort was Alice's only response, but her lips had curled into a grin. Alice loved to hate Anders. He'd been her boss when she was a dancer, and he'd held all the power, which irked her now. "I don't know how Ben tolerates him the way he does."

"Because Anders pays him very, very well?"

"Anders is lucky to have him on board," Alice said.

"Agreed."

Over their meals, Rebecca gave the group a recap of her six months in Brussels. She'd become close friends with a choreographer, a friend of Sabine's as well. Leila Bertrand was her name. "She's building an impressive roster of commissions within the European circuit. Her work is amazing," Rebecca said. "She's classically trained, but uses that as a base for including more contemporary movement. It's all so fresh and inventive. Anders should find out more about her through Sabine."

"Actually, he knows about Leila," Ben said. "I think he'd agree with your assessment."

Rebecca's eyes lit up. "So, why not the company here for her first big North American commission? That would be so perfect."

Ben shook his head. "My hunch is that it's not the right timing just yet. Granted, Anders would be open to meeting Leila if she were in the area, ask to see some of her work, maybe even allow her to stage an in-studio demonstration. He already takes two or three of these meetings each month. Talented choreographers. But it's more complicated than just picking something appealing. Untried here in North America means a certain risk. Marketing has some input, and Anders has to be prepared to defend his choice to the board of trustees. Ultimately, our goal is to sell the maximum number of tickets, which the tried and true regularly produces."

"It's the artistic director's responsibility to be introducing big new ideas," Rebecca argued. "Anders has the clout, the reputation for excellence. His endorsement could help launch a promising choreographer's career. But it's always been male choreographers."

"He's used females in the past," Ben said, a bit defensively.

"All three of them," Alice quipped, which made Rebecca and April grin. Alice might not have been working for the WCBT anymore, but clearly she'd stayed on top of things. "Three in fifteen years. And close to a dozen male choreographers each year, on average, means we're looking at …" She turned to Rebecca. "You're the recent college graduate. Do the math."

"Some are duplicates, you know," Ben interrupted. "Our in-house choreographer has given the company nine new ballets in that time period."

"Fine," Rebecca said. "We'll subtract those. It still means there are well over 150 opportunities going to males versus three opportunities for females."

April winced. That was a lot. Even Ben looked less confident.

"Of course I recognize the gender inequality," he said, "but the ballet world has plenty of females in charge. They essentially run the ballet schools everywhere you go. They occupy very high positions."

"But they all still defer to the artistic directors, who are nearly all males. Except for pioneers like Sabine, and she says she's had to work ten times as hard merely to be considered 'one of them.'"

"And she's been highly successful," Ben said. "There you have it. So, as they say, become the change you want to see in the world."

Rebecca eyed Ben speculatively. "Oh, I plan to do my best," she said in a low, confident voice. "I'll make you boys wonder what hit you."

"Uh oh. Look out, world." He sounded half-joking, half-concerned, as the server came to clear their table.

Rebecca's mood had mellowed, and now she affectionally roped an arm around Ben, reaching over with the other hand to pat his thigh. He grew limp with infatuation, which she pretended not to notice. "Ladies, what am I going to do with this guy?" she asked.

Alice chuckled. "I've a hunch you'll figure out something." She glanced at her watch. "I hate to eat and run, but I've got a meeting I need to prep for. This was wonderful, though. Thanks for including me."

April rose with her. "I'll join you. I need to catch Anders before the end of lunch hour."

"Put your money away," Rebecca said as she and Alice took out their wallets. "Ben's got this."

"Fine, but we've got the next one." Alice shrugged back into her suit jacket. "Thank you. Great to see you both."

The wind was brisk outside, but the sun delivered its signature October warmth. The two of them walked the three blocks, through pedestrian traffic, past restaurants and shops.

"I knew you were friends with Ben, back from your dancing days with the company," April said, "but how did you grow close with Rebecca?"

"Last spring, she was in need of some support and encouragement when trying to make a decision about her future. Ben brought her over and she and I had a good heart-to-heart."

"I remember your own days, just before your decision," April mused. "I ached for you."

"Yeah, it can feel like a journey in the dark, down a bumpy road, without a road map. I'm glad she made the choices she did. She looks so happy and confident."

"She does. Care to speculate on what's up with her and Ben?"

"That was hard to miss, wasn't it? Definitely something there, but they seem to be playing their cards carefully."

"Boy, is he smitten."

"Cute to see, isn't it?" She grinned at April. "Remember the days of feeling that way?"

"Not really," April admitted.

"Yeah, me neither."

"Parenting."

"Yup."

They stopped for a red light.

"So how's the Granger beast these days?" April asked.

"Well, here's a conundrum for you. Granger's discovered his little man-tool. I got the report from his daycare. Apparently he slides his hand down there and strokes it during story time. I was told how that, in and of itself, wasn't abnormal, but it got problematic the other day when he invited the other boys to come look at his new toy, and did they have one too, and could he see it?"

April began to laugh. "How embarrassing was *that* conversation?"

The light turned green and they crossed the street. "I'm sure my face was bright red. They were very PC about, not wanting to shame a three-year-old for being curious about his body, but yeah, the invitation he extended to the other boys didn't go over well with the teachers."

"What was Niles' response?"

"My dear husband wasn't concerned in the least. He says it's an absentminded comfort thing for Granger. So, great. Some kids suck their thumb, and our kid … well, everything's just a stage, right?"

"Absolutely," April assured her. "He's learning about his body, that's all. It's age and developmentally appropriate. Now if he gets to high school and tries that, that's a problem."

They both snorted with laughter.

"What's it like, having high-school kids?" Alice asked.

"So much easier than the early years." April sighed happily. "They're maturing nicely and are learning how to handle their own challenges. Kylie still has a way to go, but I'm confident she'll follow Jen's lead and be enjoying high school in no time." April hesitated over the last words; they were Russell's and not hers. But his conviction that Kylie was just fine had persuaded her as well. And Kylie was proving responsible about coming home each afternoon to an empty house and settling into homework. With Jen at the ballet school every afternoon, it meant both her girls were set and on their way to maturity.

The hard work was done.

What a relief.

Chapter 7

Kylie

The high school's cafeteria was cavernous, with overhead fluorescent lights casting a pale glare throughout. At lunchtime, the room echoed noisily with the sound of clashing conversations, rustling lunch sacks and the clatter of plastic cafeteria trays against Formica tables. Kylie, alone, scanned the room.

The anxiety of not being sure where to sit had built to such a high level, she felt sick. Every day it was the same risk. If Marisa and Lacey, who had the class before lunch together, found an open table, they'd grab it and save a space for Kylie. But if there were no empty tables, they'd just find seats where they could. Sometimes it meant the last two seats at the table. Which meant no room for Kylie, and she'd have to find her own spot alone, like a loser. This had only happened four times since school started, a month earlier. But three of the times had been last week. Today the same familiar knots formed in her stomach until she spied Marisa and Lacey in the far corner, seated at a table that still held room for her.

She bought a carton of milk to go with her sack lunch and hurried over to join them. After a quick greeting to her, they returned to their own discussion. They were rehashing something they'd done the afternoon before, eliciting a stab of disappointment in Kylie that they hadn't thought to invite her, too.

Lacey had been Kylie's best friend since first grade, and they'd invited Marisa into their group three years ago, to be nice to the new student. But now, you'd have thought that it was the other way around, with Kylie being the new one, the third wheel.

"And what about afterwards, at the pizza place?" Marisa said to Lacey. "That guy with the sexy brown eyes? He was flirting with you in such a big way."

"Do you think so?" Lacey's expression brightened. "He never talked to me, though. Just to his friends."

Lacey, like Jen, was pretty, always catching the boys' attention with her honey-blonde hair and clear blue eyes. Marisa wasn't as pretty; in truth, she wasn't pretty at all, with her bulging eyes and Miss Piggy nose, but she was flirtatious and confident. "But he was talking *about* you," Marisa replied. "Remember that? The design on the back of your tee shirt."

"I guess he was. And he was cute."

They went on and on. Kylie could think of nothing to add. If she told them about David, they'd ask where he went to school and she'd have to admit he was a college graduate already. That would go over like a lead balloon.

"Excuse me." A cool voice interrupted their conversation. "Those seats taken?"

Startled, they looked up to see Freeda Ogden-Hernandez and her two friends. Freeda was gesturing to the just-vacated spot at the table's other end.

Freeda Ogden-Hernandez was a little scary, and not just to Kylie. She was beautiful in a mature, edgy sort of way, with porcelain skin, jet black hair and big eyes that tilted at the corners, like a cat's. Her mother was a district judge, her father a big name in finance. She was rebellious and got into trouble a lot, and wasn't afraid to act scornful about people or issues, whether they were popular or not.

Marisa's eyes widened. "No! I mean, sure, go ahead, and no, they aren't taken."

Freeda gave Lacey a nod—pretty looks like Lacey's merited an acknowledgement of her built-in status—and sat down with her friends. Kylie didn't mind that she herself had been ignored. Better ignored than mocked.

Marisa and Lucy returned to their own conversation, analyzing, piece by piece, every little detail of their afternoon out. From the other end of the table came more interesting conversation. "Eww! He's not hot," one of the girls exclaimed. "He's much too old!"

"Older men can be hot," Freeda said with a sly grin. "Pierce Brosnan in *The Thomas Crown Affair?* I'd totally go after an older man like that."

"But the rule was supposed to be someone in real life," one of the other girls said. "Someone here in San Francisco. Like Gavin Newsom."

"Mayor McHottie, oh yeah," Freeda agreed. "Except he's lieutenant governor now, so technically he's in Sacramento, not San Francisco."

"Close enough. Anyway, that was mine. You have to come up with your own."

"I've totally got one," Freeda said. "Anders Gunst."

"Who's he?"

"Director of the West Coast Ballet Theatre, you idiot."

Kylie had perked up instantly at the familiar name. She felt proud, as if she'd played some part in Anders' refined good looks and his charisma.

"It's that German mystique," Freeda mused. "It's so sexy. And the way he speaks perfect English without a trace of a German accent— it makes him so cosmopolitan."

"Except he's not German," Kylie blurted out, and the three girls turned to look at her in surprise, making her feel as if she'd been eavesdropping. But how could she *not* have heard them? "He's Danish."

"No, he's German," Freeda said. "I know because he and my mom spoke German together at last year's gala."

"Well, Anders speaks Danish, English, French and German."

"How would *you* know, anyway?" Freeda challenged.

"He's my mom's boss and I've heard him speak Danish. Danes are really good at foreign languages. Most of them speak several. Like the Dutch. Like Katrina. Devries, I mean," she added.

"You don't have to add the 'Devries' part," Freeda said. "I knew who you were talking about. Everyone knows Katrina Devries. Right?" She turned to her friends who bobbed their heads.

"I'm friends with Katrina." Kylie tried to not sound like she was bragging. "She and my mom have always been really close. Like, for decades."

Freeda looked unimpressed. "My mom is friends with Nancy Pelosi from way back. It doesn't mean I go around telling people I'm friends with Nancy Pelosi."

"It's more than that," Kylie protested, and out of the corner of her eye, she saw Lacey and Marisa shrink in their seats. No one was supposed to contradict or challenge the queen bee. "I spent the evening with Katrina last week, in fact. Well, I was mostly watching her son and a few other kids. And you know Javier Torres?"

"Of course I do." Freeda retorted.

"So, he and Katrina live together and have a little boy."

"This isn't news."

"—And they've just separated."

Freeda perked up. "You're kidding. They're breaking up?"

"Yeah. Javier wanted to move on to someone else." She knew better than to elaborate on the fact that "someone else" was a guy. Let Javier come out publicly, first. "But it wasn't hostile or anything. They're still good friends, and partners onstage. They have to be, don't they? My mom's helping Katrina through the transition."

"Who's your mom?" Freeda asked.

"April Manning."

Freeda scrunched her nose. "Never heard of her."

"She's a ballet master with the West Coast Ballet Theatre. Before that, she was a principal dancer. She was really good. Almost as good as Katrina."

"When?"

"Back in the '90s."

"Ancient history." Freeda turned back to her friends. Kylie caught Marisa and Lacey exchanging private, loaded glances.

What had she done wrong? She was going to scream if they told her this was like the poetry reading, and that she needed to just keep her mouth shut. She wasn't going to do that.

She hated high school. Hated all the mysterious rules and codes of conduct that the others seemed to know about and she didn't. It was like one big, giant minefield.

At school's end, Freeda stopped Kylie in the hall as her two friends stood behind her, grinning. "So I texted my mom," Freeda began. "She says she knew April Manning. That she was an amazing dancer. Like Katrina, just like you said. Only your mom didn't stop at one kid. She could have kept on dancing if she'd just had the one child. My mom thinks her having the second child was a mistake."

She loved hearing her mom praised. And there was no higher compliment than "she was amazing" and "like Katrina." But the second part. And the malicious gleam in Freeda's eyes as she asked, "You're the first child, right?"

Freeda had to have known about Jen, golden Jen Garvey, a queen bee in her own right.

"No." Kylie clutched the strap of her backpack like she was a sky jumper and that was the thing you yanked to activate your parachute so that you wouldn't continue your free-fall down to the hard, unforgiving ground. "I'm the second child."

"Oh. Whoops." Laughter filled Freeda's voice, and her two friends snorted like horses.

She did her best to brush off their laughter, pretend like it didn't hurt. Face burning, she made her way to the bus. She would go straight to the WCBT studios, she decided. Visit the kind people there who liked her for who she was.

After getting off the bus, she walked the two blocks to the studios. There, Kylie greeted the security guys and made her way to Wardrobe. The department was located in the theater, which itself was connected to the main building via a subterranean walkway that used to spook Kylie as a kid. The department was a surprisingly large area, a warren of connected rooms. Kylie loved the way it was a world in and of itself. It felt homier than home. Like going to your grandma's and your aunts were there, and everyone was enjoying a cup of tea and cookies. Although the Wardrobe ladies weren't sipping tea and eating cookies, and the one time Kylie had tried to drink her chocolate milk in the room, they'd all freaked out. No food or drink near the costumes. They were too valuable, too hard to clean if there was a stain.

She entered the room with its pleasing smell of laundry soap, spray starch and clean clothes, where what looked like *The Sleeping Beauty* costumes dominated the central working space. There were lots of tutus, each one having been stored detached from its jeweled, sparkling bodice and hung on its side, grouped together spoon style. To the left, she saw several workers cutting, stitching, ironing, pinning fabrics to a dressmakers' mannequin. To the right, the ironing tables. Further back, more clusters of working people. You could hear the hum of activity, not just the voices but the soft hiss of the industrial steamers, the rumble of enormous dryers, and the *tack-*

tack-tack-tack of the sewing machines.

She spied Betty, the Wardrobe mistress, always pink-cheeked and smiling, and went over to say hi. She waved to everyone she knew as she went, which was a lot of people. Wardrobe staffing didn't turn over the way the dancer roster did, and there'd only been a few changes in the department for as long as she could remember. Her mom had always been fond of Betty, telling Kylie and Jen how much Betty reminded her of her deceased mom. Same age and shape, same boundless warmth and comfort.

"Hi Kylie-button." Betty tucked an errant grey curl behind her ear and smiled at Kylie. "I'm so glad you came by. I miss seeing you here weekly, like in your middle-school years. But you're all independent now. A high school student! My, how time flies."

"Look at all these pretty costumes," Kylie exclaimed before Betty could ask her anything about school. "Are they from *The Sleeping Beauty*?"

Her ploy worked. Betty smiled. "Correct. They're being loaned out to Seattle this season. In turn, they'll loan us their *Alice in Wonderland* costumes next season. So that's our work this week, making sure these are all in pristine shape and ready to be shipped."

There were over 300 costumes for *The Sleeping Beauty*. They were all amazing. Kylie observed one of Betty's assistants nearby working on the Silver Fairy's costume for Act III. Betty herself was working on a different tutu that featured a peach-colored bodice with matching lace, dotted with Swarovski crystals and pearls. The tutu attached to the bodice was plush and fluffed out like the Silver Fairy costume, with a peach and gold lace embellishment layer, decorated with gold beads and crystals on appliqued gold trim.

"That's so fancy," Kylie murmured, reaching out to caress a bead. "It's like something royalty would wear."

"Precisely the point," Betty said. "Do you know your price tags for tutus?"

"I think my mom said 2500 dollars on average?"

"Correct again."

"But these ones are fancier." Kylie fingered one of the tiny crystal nuggets.

Betty nodded. "They're closer to 5000 dollars. And the most ornate costumes here can hit the 10,000 dollar mark. That, plus the scenery, is what makes *The Sleeping Beauty* an expensive production."

"Good thing the costumes last a long time."

"True. Especially if you take really good care of them, which we do. Speaking of which, I've got something to show you." Betty reached over and picked up a Princess Aurora costume. Aurora was the lead character, and this glittery white tutu and bodice was worn in the Act III Wedding Day scene. "This was your mama's costume, Kylie. The first year we premiered these costumes, back in 1992, she was opening-night Aurora. It was a sight to see. She was like a fairy princess, so pretty and light on her feet."

Kylie reached over. How strange to see the tutu, run her hand over the bodice's sweat-darkened interior. She couldn't imagine her mom as a principal dancer like Katrina. Kylie figured, even then, her mom must have been helping the younger dancers, offering them support whenever she could. That was one of the skills she was well known for. Sometimes it made Kylie feel jealous when her mom focused more on "her girls" at the studios than on her own flesh-and-blood girls. Like Katrina. Did Katrina appreciate all that her mom did for her, Kylie wondered?

Sometimes she thought not.

She ran into David in the hallway on her way out, which rendered her speechless with delight. All the hours she'd spent dreaming about him since meeting him, and here he was, gazing at her with the same unaffected pleasure.

"Kylie! How's it going?"

"Great! How are you?"

"Oh, I'm liking it here." He gestured back toward the studios. "This is so much fun. It's interesting, it's challenging, my job changes every day. But you know what the best thing is? Playing so much classical music. I was thinking about you this morning, in fact. How you'd love that I now get to do this."

He'd been thinking about her. Maybe at the precise moment she'd been thinking about him. Her day, her world, exploded into sunshine and happiness.

"You're right," she said. "It's so cool!"

"How's school, by the way?"

"Truthfully, it sucks. The other girls in my class make fun of me, even my so-called best friends. Am I that awful? Don't answer that."

"Of course you're not awful. You're amazing."

"Tell them that."

"I will. I'll go tell them how wrong they've got it."

"Sure!" she joked back. "Come pick me up from school. We get out at 2:50pm."

"Oh, darn." A mock slap to his forehead. "I have *work*. That thing I keep forgetting."

They both broke up with laughter over that.

He looked at his watch. "Whoops, speaking of which, gotta get back to it. Nice to run into you, though!"

"You too!"

He took off in the direction of the studios, walking briskly. She watched him until he turned a corner. She stayed beyond that, drawing in deep breaths this air he'd just breathed, as if that would allow her to hold onto him.

Happiness, for a moment longer.

Chapter 8

Katrina

When Katrina made her way to the smaller studio for their first rehearsal with Edwin Hess, she was surprised to see a crowd had shown up, along with a television film crew. His assistant was there to capture some footage, which he planned to post on social media. Lucinda was there as the official company mouthpiece. Beside her stood Anders and Curtis, the ballet master chosen to support Edwin at his rehearsals.

Edwin was being interviewed. A reporter from a local news station held up a mic as her associate filmed from three feet away. "I'm very much looking forward to taking on this commission," Edwin was saying in his posh British accent. "The West Coast Ballet Theatre just gets better and better, drawing top dancers, utilizing top choreography. They reside mostly on the traditional side of contemporary ballet, so I might be asking the dancers to step outside their comfort zones. But in a company with this caliber of dancers, I'm certain they'll meet my expectations. Possibly even exceed them!"

His eyes lit up when he saw Katrina. "My newest muse!" He beckoned her forward with one arm out.

It felt strange, being a prop in his speech, his presentation, without having yet been introduced to him. She wasn't sure whether to shake his hand and say "nice to meet you" or act like they were already friends, as his gesture seemed to imply. But the cameraman was filming and both the reporter and Lucinda were beaming, so she went with it, stepping in and accepting his one-armed hug.

He took a step back, mugging a theatrical assessment of her. "I've been looking forward to working with you. Your grace, your strength, this sense, when you dance, that you can take on every challenge thrown at you. This is what a choreographer loves to work with. I can't wait to get started!"

"Edwin," the reporter asked, "can you tell us what the ballet will be about?"

"I'm seeing a contemporary ballet about contemporary love. The romantic, crazy kind, that sweeps you up and rearranges your emotions."

The reporter's next question, directed to Hess alone, allowed Katrina to edge away and claim a spot in the corner to put on her pointe shoes. She saw Jimmy arrive and waved him over. He gave her a smile that seemed both happy and nervous.

She, too, felt nervous about this unorthodox new partnership. Jimmy, a soloist and seventeen years her junior was, to her, that most exotic of Americans, a farm boy from East Texas. He spoke with a folksy, southern accent and wore boots and a cowboy hat when he went out at night with the other dancers. He was sweet-faced, completely without guile, and danced like a young god. It was a lot to take in.

He came and sat beside her. "I'm nervous as anything," he admitted. "He's a celebrity. A genius. I know he specifically chose you, but what if he doesn't like me?"

She patted his knee with an ease that surprised even her. "We're a pair. We tell him that's not negotiable."

"Really?" His eyes, wide and innocent, searched her face. "You're the greatest for saying that. I just hope I can be a good partner and make you proud."

"Let's start!" Edwin called out, and she and Jimmy both joined him in the center, still in front of the camera and the visitors. "The first sixty-four counts. Here's what I have in mind. I'm feeling melodic, romantic vibes."

He called out movements, sometimes demonstrating, other times merely using his fingers. Chaîné turns, interwoven movements, step-steps into overhead grand-jeté lifts. Everything felt lyrical and reassuringly classical.

So far, so good.

In the second hour, however, once the news crew and visitors had left, Edwin revealed his more unconventional side.

He gave her and Jimmy a contorted pose to hold, arms and legs pretzeled, backs arched, with Jimmy supporting most of her weight with one arm. "Here, you are seeking the truth about love," he said in a singsongy cadence. "It is, in fact, as if the truth were a shard, like glass, which the other person—the lover—has hidden deep within, beneath layers and layers of herself. You must force her to surrender it, opening her arms, her legs, to pry it free, because you need it too. Do you see? The truth she swallowed, the answers she holds, belong to you."

He hadn't told them to release the pose, even though their muscles were shaking with exertion. "Until then, your sense of love, its definition, cannot belong entirely to you. Which makes you fallible, unreal, a mere whiff of this element of change, of *transformation*." He fell silent and raised his hands high, like a priest celebrating Mass.

"I'm sorry," Jimmy burst out in a strained voice, "I can't hold this pose any longer."

Edwin pivoted and regarded Jimmy ecstatically. "That's it! That's it exactly! Keep it! Hold it close!"

She and Jimmy finally toppled, laughing helplessly. Edwin

pointed at them and nodded decisively, as if that had been his end result all along.

That evening, over one of their bi-monthly dinner dates, she told Martin about the rehearsal. "Goodness," Martin said, "even I've heard of Edwin Hess. From that movie. Not that I liked the movie, but that's beside the point. He's world-renowned. And a fellow Brit—how positively *splendid.*"

Martin was every inch the English gentleman, like something out of a Masterpiece Theatre Edwardian drama. A private-equity analyst, he was tall and fleshy, with thick brown hair that flopped over into his eyes when he grew animated by a story he was telling. His hands would demonstrate with ever-broadening circles, before he'd finally push the hair back into place. He not only knew that her father was a renowned poet, he had actually bought a book of his poetry, and could recite lines from memory. He rarely mentioned Dario by name. Although he politely inquired about him at every meet-up, she sensed he wished Dario didn't exist.

An amiable river of unstoppable (and frequently dull) conversation flowed from Martin. She visualized herself in a boat, bobbing along, no fear that it might capsize, no concerns for where it might carry her, because, in the end, she felt safe inside the vessel that was Martin's company. He'd never made any demands on her, and had always allowed her to call the shots in the relationship. Which meant keeping it platonic.

The restaurant on Gough Street was full, a rich aroma of garlic and roasting meat perfuming the air. Servers bustled amid the clink of silver against china and the hum of animated conversation. Their waiter brought over two cocktails, compliments of the house. The owners loved it when Katrina showed up at their restaurant, because she was a recognizable figure in San Francisco and it looked good for their business. A familiar dance critic a few tables away gave her a respectful nod and smile, which she returned. She was aware that others, too, were regarding her, murmuring among themselves.

That's Katrina Devries! She eats! Or at least she drinks.

"Anyway, congratulations on the Hess commission." Martin raised his glass to hers. "It sounds like an excellent opportunity for you and your company."

She clinked his glass and smiled, aiming to project confidence. "I hope it works out well. Right now, it's too soon to know."

"So you won't be dancing the *Don Quixote* pas de deux with Javier?"

"I won't. We have a young, new dancer, Cuban-trained. Javier's keen to work with her."

"He seemed to be in an excellent mood tonight."

"Yes, well, there've been changes in our lives of late."

"Really? Do tell."

"He's … well, he's in a relationship. A serious one. In fact, he's moved out."

How bitter the words still felt in her mouth.

Martin looked puzzled. "I don't understand. He was there at the house. Everything seemed so much like it's always been. In fact, what I did notice was that Javier greeted me more warmly than usual."

"He's there with Dario tonight. And he was glad to see you, I suppose, because he wants me to have a social life. He trusts you; he likes you."

"He does?" Martin beamed. "That's wonderful to hear. I was afraid he found me a bit dull."

In truth, Javier did. But dull also meant safe. Just as Martin's awkwardness around Dario meant he'd never represent a threat in the Daddy-replacement department.

"This new relationship," Martin began. "Is it a he or a she?"

She could be candid; he was long familiar with their situation. "A he. Named Brent."

"Poor dear." Martin seemed genuinely sympathetic. "This is a big change for you, too."

"It is." A walnut-sized lump filled her throat. "But we'll be fine, Dario and I. We're adapting." She thought about Lucinda's directive, to be seen with Martin even more. "You'll be pleased to know that our PR director approves of you, too. She says you should be my cover now. So other single men won't bother me."

"*Really?*" he breathed.

His eyes gleamed and she wanted to kick herself for voicing the thought out loud. Before she could add any sort of caveat, the waiter approached with their meals. As he ground fresh black pepper onto each plate, she glanced around the restaurant. She was shocked to see David Lavigne across the room entertaining four young women and realized that they were company dancers, all smiles, their hair long down their backs, leaning in to better hear the story David was telling. Or perhaps leaning in to be closer to him. They were all clearly entranced by him.

No surprise. People—especially females—liked him and were drawn to his flirtatious nature. Even older, married women like Elsa, the lead accompanist, or Betty in Wardrobe. But in direct contrast to his chatty, extroverted manner, he'd arrive in the studio with a book tucked under one arm, which he'd read when he wasn't playing the piano. And he wouldn't just glance through the book, either, but wholly immerse himself in it. When the ballet master called out for him to recommence playing, he'd snap back into action quickly, but she'd catch the enraptured expression still on his face. And then there was the meditation. She'd chanced upon him, over the lunch hour one day, cross-legged and silent in one of the quiet nooks she herself favored. His eyes had remained closed, his body perfectly still, undistracted by her presence, which had seemed so advanced and elevated that it unnerved her more than the easy-going jokester had.

"How's your little son doing?" Martin inquired once the waiter had departed.

"He's doing relatively well, given the circumstances. He's now in a regular twin bed. Javier thought he'd transition better if we replaced his double bed and Dario's toddler bed with two twins. One is still 'Daddy's bed,' which seems to comfort him. But it's still a big change."

"Aha." Martin paused for a respectful beat. "Did I tell you about the most curious incident I had, a few months back, involving a very old bookstore and a ferret?"

Inwardly, she sighed. "No, you didn't! Do tell."

He commenced a long-winded story that only required her to appear interested. She injected the occasional "oh, really?" and "how do you like *that*?" from time to time, relaxing into his chatter, when she noted, out of the corner of her eye, that David and his harem were leaving.

Martin noticed too. He could be very observant, even as he droned on with one of his stories. "Who was that?" he asked.

"What do you mean?" she asked, flustered.

"Did you know him? The young man with the pretty girls?"

"They're company dancers and he's a new accompanist. The girls were all eyes, weren't they? They're sweet, but so impressionable."

"He's a bit young for you, I think."

She shot him a frosty look. "What are you saying? He's an accompanist. That's the only role he plays in my world."

"Of course. Forgive me."

The waiter came to clear away their plates. They declined dessert but ordered espressos, which they sipped in a reflective silence. When the waiter returned with the bill, Martin reached for it but paused.

"Do you want to move in together?" he blurted out.

She stared at him, incredulous. "Why would I want that?"

"It's just that … I understand how and why everything came up with Javier and wanting a child. A sense of family. And with him moving on, you've lost that."

"Thank you for the offer, but I'm fine."

She turned down Martin's offer of a drink on the way home. She felt the tug that always came when she was away from Dario for too long. Even if he'd already gone to bed and was sleeping, she wanted to be home with him.

In silence, she and Martin walked the four blocks back to her place. At her door, she bade him good night. Martin kissed her on the cheek as he always did, his hand falling to her waist.

"Good night," she told him.

His hand hadn't moved. A determined spark appeared in his eye and before she could react, he'd stepped closer, gripped her waist and kissed her on the lips. Firmly, possessively. She stepped back, breaking the seal of their lips. He released his grip and flushed a dull red. "Sorry," he mumbled, and ducked his head.

Dismay and a profound sense of disappointment replaced the comfortable feelings the evening with him had produced. So went the platonic feelings—at least for him. But when he looked up, contrition in his eyes, she couldn't help but feel a touch of pity. He'd been a steady friend, always kind and solicitous. She'd begrudge him this one sloppy gaffe. "Good night," she repeated more firmly.

"Good night. Until the next time."

Once inside, she leaned against the closed door and heaved a sigh of relief. "Hello?" she called out. "Anyone home?"

She heard a clank in the kitchen, followed by Javier's voice. "Be right out," he called. "Do you want a drink?"

"If you'll stay and have one with me."

"I can do that."

He returned with two glasses of red wine, and gladness filled her heart.

"How was he?" Katrina gestured upstairs to Dario's bedroom.

"Good." Javier took a sip of wine. "He wanted to argue with me about dinosaurs and extinction. He says they're not gone, they're just hiding. He didn't like my response. But I enjoyed watching him think about it. He gets that look on his face, that little brow furrowing."

"Exactly!" Katrina exclaimed, delighting in the way no detail about Dario was too small, too excessive, for Javier and her to discuss at length.

"Oh, I haven't told you the good news," he said, his face lighting up.

Hope sprang up instantly. "You're moving back in."

His shocked look was replaced by laughter. "No! Why would you think that?"

What had she been thinking? His mirth only made it worse. "I guess I was just hoping."

"No, not that. Never that. I wouldn't have moved in with Brent unless I thought it was something lasting." His expression softened. "Katja. You look so sad and lonely."

"I miss you."

"You need a romantic partner of your own."

"Does Martin count?" she joked.

"What do you mean?"

She told him about Martin's would-be proposal, expecting him to laugh and shake his head. Instead, he looked thoughtful.

"You should consider it. He fits all your immediate needs. You'd have the traditional family-security feeling you crave."

"He said the same thing. I'll give you the same answer. Which is, I don't think so."

"Give him a chance. Maybe you'll warm to the idea."

It disappointed her that Javier, who used to be able to read her so well and offer genuinely good advice, would propose something so unappealing.

"You said you had good news," she said stiffly.

"That's right! I have a new gig for us. A commercial photo shoot for an upscale jewelry line. Lucinda's given us the green light. We'll be well paid. Interested?"

She smiled. "Yes, I'm interested. Thank you."

"You're welcome." He looked at his watch. "It's getting late. I'm beat. Brent and I were up too late last night." He rose, polishing off the last of his wine. "See you tomorrow at the studios."

"Yes. Good night." She gave him a quick hug, resisting the urge to hang on tight and keep holding on.

"And do me a favor. Don't rule out Martin just yet."

She sighed and something well-behaved in her capitulated.

"All right. I won't."

Chapter 9

Kylie

In high school, just like middle school, girls always walked around in pairs or in little groups. It was their safety pod. But something was up with Kylie's own little group. Marisa was being downright unfriendly, and today, Lacey seemed particularly uncommunicative. When Kylie asked if she was okay, Lacey said she was fine, without looking at Kylie. "Just cramps. That time of the month," she mumbled.

There hadn't been room for Kylie at their lunch table, so she'd skipped lunch rather than sit alone, and met back up with her friends as they were leaving the cafeteria. The three of them walked without talking toward the girls' bathroom by the gym. Lacey went in and Kylie was about to follow until Marisa caught her arm. "Look," she said in a no-nonsense voice. "Just let her go in there without tagging along."

Tagging along? What was Marisa talking about?

Marisa sighed and glared at Kylie, gesturing for her to join her a few steps away. "You know, we were hoping you'd just get the hint. I feel bad for saying this, but, well, we need you to stop hanging around us. It looks bad. Like we're the same as you. And we're not. You're stressing Lacey out—can you not see that? Can you see anything besides yourself? You don't even try to fit in. And the thing is, we *want* to."

Girls were brushing past them, coming and going from the bathroom. Someone bumped Kylie's shoulder from behind, rattling her even more.

"Excuse me," Marisa said with finality. "I have to use the bathroom too."

"Maybe I do too." Kylie hated the way her voice quavered, like a little kid's.

"Yeah, well, can you try thinking of us for once? Give us the space we're asking for?"

She didn't wait for Kylie's reply. She turned and went into the bathroom.

Kylie swung around and marched blindly past the other girls, not caring that now she was the one bumping into people, eliciting a few indignant calls to watch it.

She hated Marisa right then, her big mouth and too-broad face and superior attitude. "I feel bad for saying this," she'd told Kylie. Bullshit. Marisa had always wanted their trio to be a duo. Now here she was, successfully poisoning Lacey with her thinking. For a moment, Kylie pondered running right back to them, asking Lacey, point blank, if she agreed with everything Marisa had said. But in the next moment, she knew, with a rush of despair, that to do that would make everything worse.

Her footsteps slowed. Dread filled her heart, still in free fall.

What did this mean for her? She'd be all alone, a girl without friends. In high school.

It felt like the end of the world.

Horribly, the three of them were all in the same history class, which came right after the lunch hour. It had seemed like the best thing imaginable, back in September, and now it was the worst thing imaginable. She wondered dully how much worse the day could get.

Mr. Lee, the teacher, waved a stack of graded assignments at them. "These are your responses to the prompt, "'How does my name reflect my history?'"

Which had been super easy for Kylie. She'd been named after Kyle Lee Manning. Her mom had told her the story, how, when she was pregnant, she and Kylie's dad had wanted to honor her mom's father, an admired and beloved physics professor, who'd died years earlier. When they found out it was a girl, her dad had instantly said, "Kyle Lee. Kylie. Kylie Manning Garvey," and he and Kylie's mom had looked at each other and right then, the baby in her stomach—meaning her, Kylie—leapt for the first time, as if to say, "yes!"

"But before I return these papers," Mr. Lee was saying, "I want to read a response that really stood out among the others."

She thought of hers. The intimacy of it. The love she'd felt for the dead grandfather she'd never known, her reverence for his talents and the pride she felt being named after him.

Please not mine. Please not mine.

"'Quantum Theory is a lofty topic to consider by any stretch of the imagination,'" Mr. Lee began to read. "'But when you throw the history of your name into the equation and it fits like a glove, you know your history is a rich one indeed.'"

There was her answer on how much worse the day could get.

Mr. Lee continued on and on as she sat there, frozen with mortification. It sounded just like classical music, with its clean form and elegant structure, which meant it was music to her ears and probably no one else's. She could almost hear Marisa whining, "why can't you write the way everyone our age does?"

And yet, this was her beloved relative, her never-known grandfather, that she'd written about. Her history and her name. This was nothing to be ashamed of. She was proud to be the daughter of Russell Garvey and the granddaughter of Kyle Manning. They were both geniuses. They'd both won scholarships to MIT, where they'd studied with the best of the best, and excelled. Her father was a Silicon Valley legend after his startup went big in 1992, and her mom's father, a distinguished university professor, had tutored her dad in physics and math when he was a teenager to help him achieve his potential.

The Quantum Theory discussion itself had taken place years ago. She'd been six and Jen seven, and their father was trying to explain it to them as they cuddled on either side of him on the sofa. "See, wave-particle duality is an example of what we call 'superposition,' a quantum object—quantum means teeny, teeny tiny—existing in multiple states at once," he told them. "An electron, for example, can be both 'here' and 'there' simultaneously. It's only once we do a theoretical experiment to find out where it is that it settles down into one or the other."

He proposed being in a pitch-black room and throwing soccer balls at a tennis ball in the center and trying to figure out, once you'd launched the soccer ball, where the tennis ball was.

"I would know where the tennis ball is," Jen told him eagerly.

Their father smiled. "Where would that be, exactly?"

"You'd hear a sound when the soccer ball hit it. That's where it is."

"But it moved," he said. "The soccer ball pushed it upon impact."

Jen thought about this, frowning in concentration.

"It would be impossible to know," Kylie said. "You could only make a good guess."

"Exactly!" Her father's eyes lit up as he pointed to Kylie, and she felt like she'd won the lottery. "It's all about probabilities. We can only say which state an object is most likely to be in once we look. These odds are encapsulated into a mathematical entity called the wave function. Making an observation is said to 'collapse' the wave function, destroying the superposition and forcing the object into just one of its many possible states."

This was trickier to understand. Jen looked even more baffled. Their mother, nearby, began to laugh. "Russell, they're little kids. You expect them to understand quantum physics?"

"These kids are your dad's progeny, April. Kyle Manning was a genius when it came to this stuff. They might be like him. Especially our Kylie here." He chuckled. "Did we give her the right name, or what?"

She couldn't have felt prouder. Of her grandfather, her own smart father, and for being privileged enough to carry her grandfather's name.

Kylie had shared this all in the assignment.

"'So it's with pride that I embrace the history that's inherent in my name,'" Mr. Lee read on. "'Kyle Lee Manning can live on because Kylie Manning Garvey, all waves and particles depending on how you observe her, will carry on his legacy.'"

He lowered the stack of papers and beamed at her.

The silence from the other students spoke volumes.

She was weird. Because she wrote weird stuff and liked weird music, and now they knew she had a guy's name for a first name and a last name for a middle name, and every class needs its sprinkling of weird kids that you could laugh at, or stay away from, and when you're a freshman in high school, you're desperate to not be that person.

Marisa seized the opportunity. "Kyle?" she asked in exaggerated confusion. "A *guy's* name?" She began to laugh and others joined her, until the room was buzzing with mirth.

It was the Schumann poem happening all over again. There was vindication in Marisa's eyes, too, that not only had the breakup been a good idea, it had happened just in time.

Lacey didn't laugh, but she didn't look up.

That was it. End of friendship.

"Stop it!" Kylie shouted, horrified that the words seemed to just burst out of her. "You should all be ashamed." She rose, shaking, face burning, muscles tense. An excited hum filled the room as everyone leaned in, wholly engaged for once, alert to real-life drama. Mr. Lee, trying to regain control, called out, "See here, this isn't the right way to critique another student's paper," but the whoosh of pounding blood surging past Kylie's ears blotted out everything. Without thinking, she grabbed her backpack and the loose items on her desk and stormed out, incapable of stopping to consider how very wrong this was.

What happened next? In the hallway, her steps slowed.

She didn't have a clue.

She realized that at this point, the best option was make her way to the administrative office and tell them she was afraid she was going to throw up. Maybe she *was* going to throw up. She ran to the girls' restroom for good measure and leaned against the cool tiles on the wall, panting like a trapped animal, until she was sure nothing was going to come up. Drawing a shaky breath, she left the bathroom and made her way to the administrative office.

There, the secretary, eyebrows arched in surprise, asked her why she was there. Instead of the "I felt sick" defense, though, she found herself telling the truth. "I couldn't stay. It was all too much. It's all too much." She could feel little prickles behind her eyes, and the itchy feeling in her nose, this cross between wanting to sneeze and to cry.

"Have a seat," the secretary told her, not unkindly, gesturing behind Kylie.

Very tired all of a sudden, she sank into one of the plastic chairs lining the wall. The room was silent except for the tick-tick of the clock and someone in another room in conversation. From her seat, she studied the carpet. Nearby was a brown splotch that Kylie was sure came from someone's spilled Coke. She knew because there'd been one like it at home, on the family-room carpet, for which she'd gotten blamed, even though it might have been Jen's spill.

"Kylie?" A big, imposing woman in a tailored navy-blue suit interrupted her reverie. "I'm Ms. Latimer, the vice principal. Let's talk in my office. Follow me."

Once in her office, Ms. Latimer didn't yell at her. Which was reassuring. At first. Then it became this tricky game, because she sensed the vice principal wanted to place her into some pre-designed box. Tricky child, pre-juvie troublemaker, artistic, autistic, problems at home, problems in the head. Genetic, environmental. She saw all this in Ms. Latimer's eyes. Not so wise and seeking as a counselor or psychologist, but more like checking questions off a list. "Are you having a good year, Kylie?" she asked. (Hardly.) "Are you friends with the same girls you were friends with in middle school?" (Bad day to be asking.) "Are you being bullied?" (No idea. Did being mocked, belittled, made to feel ashamed, constitute bullying?)

Kylie gave polite but vague answers to each one. Ms. Latimer didn't look satisfied.

"Why did you shout at your classmates?"

News traveled fast.

"Marisa, who *used* to be my friend, made fun of me and my grandfather's name," Kylie began. "I'm named after him. He's dead. I never got to meet him. He died when my mom was in her twenties. Writing about him, and my family, was personal. I didn't expect Mr. Lee to read it out loud.

"And the truth is," she continued heedlessly, "when I write, I want it to mean something. To be artful and thoughtful, and carry some insight. I feel changed inside when I write like that. It's painful, but I know I've done it right when it hurts. I know I've created something artful. Which is everything to me. And why it hurts so bad to get laughed at. I'm all raw, and they're just looking for someone or something to mock."

A part of her felt relief in saying how she truly felt. But when she looked up, she saw that the vice principal merely looked confused. "You're awfully young to be having such profound thoughts," she told Kylie.

What was she talking about? Kylie had had thoughts like these for years.

Ms. Latimer looked down at a file—apparently it was about Kylie, probably all those forms they made you fill out at the beginning of the year, or maybe the staff gathered to assess each new kid and jot down thoughts about whether they would be good students or bad, so that, at times like this, they could point to a sentence and say, "Aha, Mr. Lee had this weird student pegged."

Ms. Latimer studied the page. "Your father is Russell Garvey."

"Yes."

"Silicon Valley's Russell Garvey?"

"Yes."

"Ah. And I see your mother is April Manning Garvey. A top-level administrator with the West Coast Ballet Theatre."

"Yes."

"Busy parents," she murmured as she turned to the next page. "Accomplished. And Jennifer is your sister."

"Yes."

"She's doing fine here. Better than fine." A smile softened her expression. "A lovely girl."

Was she supposed to keep parroting "yes" to all of this? Yes, her family had distinguished accomplishments. Yes, the rest of them all stood out as winners. Yes, she was trying. No, she wasn't trying to be difficult or obstructionist. She was just being herself. Did everyone else in the world struggle like this? Did they just fake it, ignoring the urge to be original in order to appear the same as everyone else? There was room in the world, it seemed to her, for highly accomplished people, fit-in people, and dumber-than-average people. Where did that leave people like her?

A bell sounded.

"Are we finished?" Kylie asked, trying her best to sound polite. "I have one more class."

Ms. Latimer looked up and took off her reading classes. "Yes. Thank you for the clarity of your responses. You may go now."

Chapter 10

Katrina

"I've changed my mind," Edwin announced to Jimmy and Katrina, the moment he walked in—thirty minutes late and unapologetic—for their rehearsal. "This is no longer just a ballet about love. It's about sex, too. The animal drive of it. It's about passion. The messy kind. The chaos. The lunging and panting."

Katrina knew her face had gone red with embarrassment. She didn't dare glance at Jimmy to see how he was taking Edwin's announcement.

"The old steps are out. Watch as I show you the new opening passage," Edwin directed, and gestured to his assistant to keep notes. Curtis, from his seated spot in front of the room, took his own notes, but otherwise let Edwin run his show.

"It begins with you two passing each other, like strangers, but a moment later, you stop, turn, and run back to each other, catching hands. Then you drop them. Then you face front and for sixteen counts you stand still, side by side. Doing nothing, revealing nothing."

She swallowed her disappointment. She'd liked the smooth, lyrical nature of the original choreography. But he was within his rights to change the steps, as much or as often as he pleased. Now he was instructing Jimmy to support her by the waist as she made the leg motions of walking, only her feet weren't touching the floor. From there, an abrupt shift to an almost liquid draping over him, and Edwin had Jimmy take hold of her leg, the one closest to his face, and pull her through. They'd become more like snakes than people, coiling and uncoiling, sliding.

He told them to remain connected, yet try and separate, through yanks, kicks, half-turns and lunges, using each other as a counterweight to keep balance, which became a tug-of-war.

"Life, you see, is like that," Edwin said. "Sex is like that. Two sides, battling. Flowers ripped off, only the thorns remaining." His eyes flickered shut. "We are all thorns—they become the world beneath us. Like earthworms. Thorny earthworms. Chaos and a certain ugly beauty, the spew, the regurgitated sorrow of the earthworm experience." He opened his eyes and regarded them expectantly. "Yes? Do you see?"

It was so unfathomable and weird, Katrina wondered if he were on drugs and whether it was a poetic musing or genuine direction. ("More thorny for your earthworm! *Be* the earthworm!") She caught a glimpse of Curtis rolling his eyes before he resumed his normal unflappable expression.

"Now it needs to get more physical," Edwin said. "Jimmy, you slide your hands down her chest, slow, and both hands meet at the vee, where you clamp on. Really clamp on."

"What do you mean by the vee?" Jimmy asked faintly.

Katrina could feel her face burn. "He means my crotch. He wants you to grab my crotch."

"Oh." Jimmy visibly shrank.

He had them run the sixteen-count passage, culminating with the crotch grab. Jimmy looked mortified by the latter. While crotch-grabbing did occur in ballet sometimes, such as when a one-handed overhead lift and hold required it, that was different. The audience saw the lift and not the gesture. This was bold, overt, aggressive.

"Stop," Edwin snapped. "It's wrong. *You're* wrong." His phone trilled and he paused to glance at the number. He looked up at them. "I need to take this. Two-minute break."

She and Jimmy stood there as Edwin spoke rapidly into the phone and Curtis exchanged a few words with Edwin's private assistant.

"I surely don't feel right about this," Jimmy said. "Doing these things Mr. Hess is asking us to do. It feels disrespectful to you. I'm sorry as anything."

"Jimmy." Katrina waited until he met her eyes to speak again. "You can't be afraid to maul me. If it's what Edwin is demanding, you have to do it. I'm okay with that. In fact, I'll be angry if you're too tentative, because it'll leach the movements of their power. This isn't personal, and I know it."

His face was crimson. He looked miserable and helpless.

She took his hand, squeezed it for reassurance, and planted it firmly against her crotch. "This is not sexual. It's business. It's what you have to get comfortable with." She released his hand and it retracted swiftly like it had been spring-loaded. "I need your confidence so that I can trust you to lift me, grab me, throw me around, do what it takes. We need to trust each other."

He regarded her solemnly. "You're the greatest. I can't believe how lucky I am to be partnering you here. But I gotta be honest. I'm scared, Katrina. I don't want to let you or Anders down."

"You won't if you trust me. And trust that I'm not a fragile doll. If we're wholly aligned, on the same team, we'll get this down."

Edwin hung up from his phone call. "We'll try it with the music now." He gestured to his assistant, who inserted a CD and cranked up the sound. Music blared forth, a jittery, propulsive electronica.

She hated it.

The second half of the rehearsal was to be with the ensemble, the four male corps dancers he'd just selected. When the four dancers arrived,

Edwin surprised everyone by stating that they'd rehearse off-site, at Murphy's. Which was WCBT code for "let's go have a beer!" The corps guys seemed thrilled. Curtis politely waved off the invitation to join them. Katrina wanted to beg off as well. This was the last part of the day's last rehearsal, and she had to relieve Anna, her nanny, promptly at 6:20PM on Mondays, which meant leaving the studios right at six. It was already ten past five. But Edwin had that determined, manic smile on his face, so she stayed silent and dutifully joined them.

Murphy's was a WCBT institution since well before her arrival, a cool, gloomy dive located a block from the studios. The bar's creaky wooden floors had been replaced, and no more strewn peanut shells littered the floor beneath the once-wobbly Formica but now sleek, varnished wooden tables. Two big-screen televisions had replaced the juke box. There was still a pool table and a dart board in the back room and, like before, a half-dozen men hunched on stools around the bar, staring down at their drinks. Some things never changed.

A few of the tables in back had padded booth-style seating along the wall. Edwin ordered at the bar and proceeded to claim the biggest of the back tables. He sat and gestured for Katrina to take the spot beside him on the padded bench, like a king and his consort. The others settled themselves on chairs around the table as the server approached with their order, beers for them all and two shots of whiskey for Edwin. He tossed them both down in rapid succession before lifting his beer glass high in a toast.

"Are we going to talk out the choreography?" Katrina asked once they'd all taken a sip. "Or just discuss the ballet's intention?"

"None of the above." Edwin gave an expansive wave. "This was my point, right here. Being real with the dancers. Getting acclimated to each other's vibes. Odds and sods like that, you can't do in a studio."

So this wasn't to be a rehearsal in any way. Katrina's toes gripped her shoes' inner soles.

"What would you like to ask me?" Edwin addressed the group. "I know you must have questions. Ask away. Hollywood, what Kara Reed was really like to work with, in the movie."

"What was it like going from being a dancer to working in Hollywood?" Jimmy asked.

"Hollywood is a hornet's nest. A viper's nest. A very exciting and somewhat trashy place to spend a month. I'd hate to live there permanently."

"And Kara Reed?" one of the corps males asked.

"She's a bitch when she doesn't get her way. No more pretty face, that's for certain. And when she arrives in the morning, before going to Makeup, crikey, not pretty at all. Up close, you see she's older than you'd have thought. Another ten years and she won't be able to hide it, even with makeup."

"You used real dancers, right?" another asked.

"Had to. The actors couldn't dance. Then again, the dancers couldn't act. But that part wasn't my problem. I got paid either way, so I left it to the director to work it out."

It went on like this for fifteen minutes. From her spot, Katrina noticed a trio of females, in their early thirties, she guessed, who'd just arrived and were now sizing them up. Edwin noticed them as well. "Ah. Someone's about to get asked for an autograph. I can feel it. Do you see them, fishing around for paper and pen?" He squared his shoulders and sat taller.

Sure enough, they approached, excitement in their eyes. But they didn't go to Edwin. They went to Katrina. "Excuse me?" one of them said. "You're Katrina Devries, right?"

She nodded, avoiding Edwin's gaze.

"Can we have your autograph?"

She gave them a warm smile. "Yes, of course."

She could feel Edwin's resentment radiating from beside her as she chatted with them, asked their names, signed the scraps of paper they held out. She posed with them while they took selfies on their phones, then watched them skitter away, giggling among themselves.

"Stupid cows," Edwin murmured. "They're going to kick themselves when they realize who they *could* have gotten an autograph from. But that's the plight of a choreographer, even a celebrity one. People see your magic onstage but they don't see you. I won't complain. I was 'seen' plenty as a dancer with the Royal Ballet and, given the choice between the two, celebrity choreographer certainly lands easier on the mind. It pads the bank account much better, too. And the perks now, oh Lord. I am a spoiled man." He beamed at them all, before swiveling in the direction of the bar. "More drinks!" he shouted. "In fact, drinks for everyone here! Courtesy of Edwin Hess."

She heard a buzz of pleasure arise from the other patrons. The three women leaned in toward each other, murmuring. When they pulled back, they eyed Edwin with new appreciation.

The server eventually brought over a loaded tray, with second beers for everyone, even though Katrina had drunk less than half of her first one. She consulted her watch. "I can't linger much longer," she told Edwin. "My son's nanny has to leave promptly on Mondays."

He made a face. "You're being dull, dull. Come on, lighten up. Have some fun." Before she could answer, he'd turned to the others and commenced a new story about being on the movie set.

She regarded her two beers gloomily. Fun was getting home and spending time with her son. Fun was watching him in the bathtub, post-dinner, making hairdos with the shampoo suds, the way his body was as slippery as a dolphin's, and the way he'd crow with delight as he made up games and friends and adventures on the spot and told them to her in a conspiratorial voice that was pure music to her ears.

Edwin, having finished both his beers, reached for Katrina's second beer, which she'd nudged to the table's center for anyone to take. He was growing more animated, physically so. As he continued talking to the others, she was unnerved to feel his thigh press against hers. A moment later she realized, to her relief, that it was only his leather jacket sandwiched between them on the booth seat, a rather bulky article for San Francisco in warm, balmy October, but that was a Londoner for you.

Finally Edwin, tired of telling his own stories, turned to her. "My secretive muse, of whom I know so little still. Of course we all know you're Paris Opera Ballet-trained."

"I am." She smiled, affecting a warmth she didn't particularly feel.

"My former partner dances with the Paris Opera Ballet. Sophie Bocuse." He cocked his head at her expectantly, as if she might know the name.

Katrina shrugged apologetically. She'd maintained a relationship with only a few of her POBS classmates, mostly those who'd gone on to achieve principal ranking at other companies around the world. No matter; he talked on about Sophie.

"She and I were together for three years. She dances like an angel. She *is* an angel. Calm, soothing, beautiful, caring."

This, she had not expected. Some of the manic energy seemed to drain out of him as he spoke about her. His expression grew soft. "It was the best three years of my life. My choreography career was taking off and then I got the movie contract. But that meant I had to make a choice—Hollywood for a year, or pass up the opportunity and stay in Paris with her. She said no to a long-distance relationship, which was horribly selfish of her, in my mind. I came up with the perfect Plan B, procuring two free round-trip tickets for her to join me in Hollywood, spend a few weeks on the set. Not one trip, but two! I could have gotten her onto the film, even. I was sure she'd come around to the idea, because, what's not to love about it? Only she said no. She valued her career as a dancer—a mere *dancer*—over time with me on a film set."

He grabbed his beer and drank half of it down in two gulps. Afterward, he studied the beer glass. "Why couldn't she have waited for me?" he asked softly, almost to himself.

In spite of herself, Katrina felt sorry for him. Judging from the expression on his face, the genuine sorrow, she intuited the rest. Sophie had found someone else during his time in California. He'd gone on to celebrity and stardom, loved by many, except by the one love that had most mattered.

Or not. He must have caught her look of sympathy, because when he next glanced at her, his woeful look became a cool frown. "She and I are still friends, still talking. In truth, I think she's still got feelings for me, but I'm far too busy these days to cultivate *that* kind of relationship. She'll just have to stand in line." He chuckled over this, as if he'd just told a particularly good joke. "I got a text from her the other day, in fact." He picked up his phone and busily scrolled through his texts until he found the right one and showed it to Katrina, thrusting it under her nose. She glanced at it with some reluctance. Yes, it was a text from Sophie Bocuse, but she didn't particularly want to see what she'd written, nor what he'd written her. Too much information about someone she hadn't yet warmed to. He was her choreographer, not her friend.

"Hey Edwin, do you have any pics on your phone from the movie set?" Jimmy called out, for which she silently thanked him. Edwin's face bloomed into a happy smile.

"I do! Let me find you a good one."

She consulted her watch as Edwin showed the others his pics, and she wondered if she could leave politely. He passed his phone around and continued a stream of chatter, but a moment later his hand landed on her knee. It shocked her so much, her knee shot upward and smashed his hand beneath the too-low tabletop.

"Ow!" he cried, adopting a surprised, wounded look.

"I'm sorry," she stammered, embarrassed beyond measure. "Your hand—it startled me."

His gaze turned reproachful. "I was reaching for my jacket, that was all. Where did it go?"

It was now on the floor, they both saw, and this flustered her, too, because it had been this safe barrier between them and she was sure she'd felt it there when his hand landed on her knee. "I'm sorry if I made your jacket fall," she said, even as she was almost certain she hadn't.

"It's all right," he said, apparently pained, which made a part of her bristle with defensiveness. Why had she apologized? She wasn't the clumsy one who'd had two shots, two beers, and was pounding down a third. But it wasn't worth escalating the situation.

Why did you let him get away with that? a voice from a lifetime ago whispered. *He's not being kind to you. He's not being respectful. You say he's the boss and the celebrity. I say it doesn't matter who he is. Don't just sit there and take it.*

She ignored the misguided admonition—where had it come from, anyway? It was a childish, reactive response, like from her spoiled Katja days. Meanwhile, she had a solid reputation for getting along with all choreographers. That was worth a lot.

Her apologetic strategy paid off. In a matter of seconds, he became amused about the whole situation. "Look at you," he exclaimed, "your face is bright red. It's okay! My jacket will be fine." His hearty laughter caught the attention of the others at the table.

"My jacket slipped down and dear Katrina here took it to mean my hand was groping her," he told them.

"No, I didn't. I … I'm sorry."

He leaned down to pull the jacket from the floor and held it up like a prize. He was very deliberate about folding it and replacing it between them, making her feel, strangely, as though she'd been the one to make a pass, from which the coat now safeguarded him. "You probably need to leave now, don't you?" he told her, laughter still in his voice. "I think you've had enough to drink." He gave the others a theatrical *girls will be girls* eye-roll, which made her seethe. She'd never felt more uncomfortable and out of place as the lone female in a group of men. But at least Edwin had given her the opportunity she'd been seeking.

"Thank you, and yes, I do need to get going." She rose and sidled off the bench, stumbling a little in her haste, as if validating Edwin's comment that she'd had too much to drink. Everyone laughed. It helped, at least, to create the sense that she was an average person, after all. The the four corps guys smiled warmly at her. Jimmy reached over and gave her hand a goodbye squeeze.

She practically ran out of there, bursting out the door into the golden evening light. *I'm free, I'm free!* she wanted to cry as she began to walk briskly in the direction of her home, banning all thoughts of Edwin and his tricky nature from her mind. Relief filled her to finally be going home to her little boy.

You turned out so weak in the end, the voice, back again, admonished. *How could you?*

This sentiment infuriated her. *Because,* she wanted to tell the voice, *the stakes are too high.* You couldn't be at odds with your choreographer, a celebrity choreographer at that, not when he was setting something new and exciting on you. It was surely something wrong with Katrina, something about her, that was agitating him. In her student years at the POBS, the teachers were constantly finding fault with her, criticizing, shouting, even, in truth, hitting, although, with the changing times and political correctness, the harsh treatment became less physical, more psychological. "This is how you will learn best," were the consoling words from a kindly teacher. "Ballet is hard. Being a ballet professional is harder."

And it had ultimately worked for her, all of it.

I am not weak, she told the voice. *In the ballet world, I'm among the best of the best.*

And in life? the voice persisted.

Time to ignore the voice, she decided irritably, and strode faster toward home, to her son, the only thing outside her professional life that truly mattered.

Chapter 11

April

On Tuesday afternoon, April rehearsed her three casts for *Nutcracker*'s Arabian Dance, with Rebecca there to assist. "We'll start with our second-cast couple today," April announced, and Dena and Jimmy switched places with the first-cast couple in front.

Arabian Dance, with its slow, sultry music, acrobatic lifts and back arches, perfectly suited Dena and her recuperation, April decided. It was one sensuous, gorgeous movement into the next, and highlighted Dena's natural grace and long, leggy extensions.

Rebecca had danced this very role with Jimmy the year earlier. "I'm totally fine with just watching," she'd told April before rehearsal. "I'm so over being a dancer. By the end, I was in pain almost all the time." But, mid-dance, when April glanced at her out of the corner of her eye, she saw Rebecca impatiently swipe at a tear rolling down her face. Her heart contracted in sympathy. Watching others dance was a grueling task for any former dancer. True, there was less physical pain involved. But the emotional ache was huge.

April well remembered her own day of reckoning, the moment it hit home that her career as a performing dancer was about to end. She'd come back from maternity leave after baby Jen turned six months old, but in the studios, she was unable to regain her former energy, not to mention her body's leanness. There she was, with

Betty in Wardrobe, trying on her Odette/Odile costume for the season's *Swan Lake* production, mystified by how poorly the tutu bodice fit. Impossible to hook up around the waist. Breasts spilling out over the top. April, irrationally upset, cried to Betty that she *had* gotten rid of the baby weight already, so why was it coming back, now, when she needed her body to be rail-thin and high-functioning? Betty grew still as she studied April. "Oh, honey," she said, with both elation and sympathy in her voice, "you're pregnant again."

It felt like a death sentence at the time. She herself knew how much time off Anders would allow a mom dancer—there'd only been one, prior to her—and she'd already used it. Betty held her close as she sobbed, and assured her it would be all right, that the little one growing inside her was a gift, a treasure beyond any price.

Kylie had indeed been a treasure. Professionally, April had fared wonderfully in her shift of jobs, still an integral part of an organization that would have otherwise booted her out by now. Rebecca, too, would fare wonderfully. But right then, she knew better than to offer the younger woman cheap words of reassurance. When the dancers finished and Rebecca handed her the clipboard with notes, April met her eyes sympathetically.

Rebecca gave her a little nod of thanks.

April glanced through her notes but before she could share them with Dena and Jimmy, an assistant from the ballet school poked her head into the room. "April? I'm supposed to tell you that Jen is rehearsing as Clara today. As in, right now."

April's heart leapt. "Jen's actually dancing it?"

The assistant nodded.

"What a big deal for her!"

"They're in the big studio," the assistant added. "Ben's running the rehearsal and thought you might want to catch a peek."

April gazed hopefully at Rebecca.

Rebecca laughed, once again composed. "Go for it. I'll give Dena and Jimmy their notes and crack the whip."

April hesitated. "You're sure?"

"Absolutely."

"All right. I'll be back soon."

She hurried out of the room and down the hallway toward the sound of Tchaikovsky's battle-scene music, and a moment later, slipped into the room. The piano had been moved to the front corner, as the day's accompanist thundered through the score. This was the scene where oversized mice showed up to terrify and harass the young Clara, until the Nutcracker Prince arrived with his toy-soldier regiment to help her, and help battle the Mouse King. Oversized gift boxes were positioned on the studio floor where they'd be onstage, seven feet tall, with bows the size of kids, hilariously out of synch with reality. But that was the point. It had been Anders' way of "shrinking" Clara down to the size of mice, a blink-and-you-missed-it shift of scenery, wildly effective and a big crowd-pleaser.

Anders was standing in the front of the room, intent on watching the toy soldiers march down a ramp and toward center stage, as Jen, clad in a white nightgown, raced around the swarming mice. April joined him. He noticed her a moment later and smiled. "The proud mother, getting to watch her daughter?"

"I'm so glad I was told. Rebecca's covering the Arabian rehearsal for a few minutes."

Together they watched the action unfold. Jen was such a beautiful actress, with a gift for showing all sorts of emotion on her face without mugging it. That was one of the challenges of the role. Clara wasn't a dancing role so much as an acting role.

"Jennifer looks perfect in the role," Anders said. "She has that ideal look for the production, an adolescent girl on the cusp of something bigger." He smiled at her as he spoke. But it made April feel oddly uneasy. As she continued watching, she understood why.

Jen looked like an adolescent girl on the cusp of something *physically* bigger.

Budding breasts. Hips. Even her arms were starting to fill out.

It was the "something" no aspiring professional ballet dancer wanted. Ever.

Back at home, Jen was all smiles as the family ate dinner together, an increasingly rare setup in their busy lives. Even Schrodinger, the family cat, was present, hunkered by the table, purring.

"Tell me how the rehearsal went," Russell said to Jen. "I want to hear every detail."

"Okay, so there's always supposed to be two Claras and two understudies in each rehearsal," she explained. "But this was just one of those weird things, today. The first-cast Clara had to get her wrist x-rayed and she thought the other Clara could rehearse, no problem, only *she* had a dentist appointment that was running way late. Laura, the first-cast understudy, wasn't there yet, so it was just me. Anders showed up and said, 'no problem, let's see our young Miss Garvey dance it.' So he watched me dance it. Omigod, that made me so nervous! But he smiled at me afterwards and nodded. Mom was there, too, she saw it too." She turned to April. "Right, Mom? He seemed to like it, right?"

"He did," April assured her.

But there was some hesitation in her voice that Jen caught.

"What, Mom?"

"What do you mean?" April tried to play it innocent.

"Did he say something else?"

"He didn't, honey."

'I don't believe you."

"His exact words were, 'Jennifer looks perfect in the role.' That you had 'that ideal look for the production, an adolescent girl on the cusp of something bigger.'"

"Oh." Jen relaxed. "Okay. That's good. That's great."

"It is!" Russell exclaimed. "It's amazing!"

In the bedroom later that night, April wanted to discuss it further. "I have to be honest," she told Russell. "I'm a little concerned about her body type."

He was sitting in a tub chair reading the latest *Investor Business Daily* under the light of the floor lamp. He lowered the paper to regard her. "She's skinny as a beanpole! All three of you are."

"It's just that I worry."

"Of course you do. I worry about both our girls. Whether they're happy, whether they're thriving. Seems to me they both are."

"Really?" She eyed him skeptically. "You see Kylie as happy and thriving?"

He shrugged. "Okay, she's going through a bumpy stage. I had a lousy freshman year myself, so I get it. She'll be fine, though. I'm sure of it."

But Russell had been a math prodigy, his mind focused on that alone. Kylie was a different case entirely.

Russell seemed to recognize his Kylie defense had fallen short. "Okay, Kylie needs time, but surely there's not a thing about Jen you can find fault with," he said.

"Not in school. Not socially. But, well, I'm worried about whether Jen has what it takes to be a professional ballet dancer."

"Look. I know you think it's your job to manage your daughter's hypothetical future career, since it's so close to what you did. But, what if Jen doesn't *want* to have this be her whole life, her whole future? What if it's more fun to her than it is do-or-die?"

"Then the ballet school will kick her out." April moved through the room, releasing the curtains from their holders. When Russell didn't reply, she looked over at him. To her surprise, he looked grim, like she'd said something wrong. "What is it?" she asked.

"Just this. Don't ruin it for her. Don't steal her adolescence from her."

"What?" she protested, her mind spinning. "Ruining things? Stealing her adolescence? You make me sound like a villain, some crazed stage mom. I'm doing this for her. Supporting her."

"Are you sure?"

His words, his skepticism hurt. "I am simply trying to support Jen's aspirations," she said with great dignity, "in the way my parents seemed to balk at doing for me."

"They were trying to protect you. They loved you fiercely."

"They did. They just didn't want me to love ballet so much."

"I can appreciate that, now that I'm a parent. And I love that my daughter is having fun and enjoying life." He picked the newspaper back up, and like that, he'd switched his focus.

She suddenly felt tired about it all. "I'm going back downstairs," she said.

"Hmm. All right."

He hadn't looked up. He'd gone into his peaceful mind-bubble, where others' words didn't sink in. "I'm just going to go bifurcate a squirrel and plant tulips in the water heater," she said, testing her theory.

"Sure. All right."

She sighed, not sure whether to scream with frustration or laugh out loud.

Families. At least they kept your life interesting.

Chapter 12

Kylie

The shrill sound of the school bell announced the end of the last class for the day. Kylie stopped at her locker, then walked out into the golden sunlit October afternoon, where the leaves on the trees were rustling in the breeze and making a *shhhhh* sound. She made her way slowly; the bus wouldn't come for another ten minutes. But in the parking lot, to her surprise, was David. He was leaning against an old red sports car, his arms folded, a smile on his face as students paused to study the car. Well. The boys studied the car—it was a vintage Alfa Romeo—and the girls studied David. It wasn't just that he was good looking. It was the careless way he acted about it, the casual way he dressed, the way he let his blond hair stay loose and untamed. Like a gorgeous wild cat you might think twice about approaching. Unless the cat liked you.

If only you could freeze moments like this.

"Excuse me," she said airily as she brushed past Freeda and her group, who were gawking like the others. "He's here to see me, I think."

Which made them laugh in disbelief.

"You're about to be hilarious again, aren't you?" Freeda asked.

Something inside Kylie faltered. "No, I'm not," she retorted.

"Okay, so go greet him. We'll be watching."

"Fine." Kylie strode toward David's car, praying he was indeed there to see her and that this wasn't going to be some awful situation.

Then he saw her, and his smile came alive.

It would be okay.

She bounded over to him. "Hi! This is crazy."

"You asked, and I delivered. I had to see those mean girls for myself."

She laughed. "Some are right over there. They didn't believe I knew you."

"Well, they're about to feel very foolish." He widened his eyes theatrically and said, extra-loud, "It's so good to see you again!" Then he swept her up in a big bear hug.

It was only for a few seconds, and he'd only done it as a joke, but being encased in his arms was the most incredible feeling, and if she'd had a crush on him before, this was so much bigger.

This was love. Eternal love. She was sure of it. She had this sudden vision of years down the road, decades even, the two of them together, laughing as they told their kids, for the tenth time because the kids loved hearing the story, about how it was that moment, that golden afternoon, that they both realized they were meant for one another, and even though Kylie was so young and it meant having to go through all sorts of waiting and being patient, and some separation even, ultimately it was nothing.

He released her, opened the passenger door for her and she waved gaily to the now-dumbstruck girls standing there watching.

He started the car and she felt giddy enough to fly. "Home?" he asked as they waited in a line of cars for their turn to exit the parking lot.

"Do we have to? Can we do something fun first?"

David hesitated. "What do your parents allow?"

"Usually I go straight home and text my mom that I'm there. But last year, she started letting me do stuff with my friends, as long as I texted her beforehand, and then once I got home."

"What about this year?"

"No one's inviting me to do stuff." The giddy feeling evaporated.

"What happened to last year's friends?"

She considered not telling him what had happened. Her loner status—which was to say loser status—felt like leprosy. Once someone knew, that was it. They stayed away, except to make fun of her.

"Did they move, or go to a different high school?" David persisted.

She had to be honest. This was David, after all. "No. They're still there. It's just that … I was told I was ruining their reputation by trying to hang out with them. They asked me to stay away." Her voice had gone trembly, and she thought she might start crying, which would be so humiliating.

Silence greeted her pronouncement. She kept her eyes fixed on the carpeted floor mat, wondering if David was now trying to figure out how to politely get her out of the car. Horribly, the tears arose, unstoppable. She could feel them roll down her face and plop onto her backpack on her lap.

"That's despicable," David said in a low, furious voice.

She felt ten times better, even though the tears kept leaking out. "Yeah. But that's how high school works these days." She found a crumpled napkin in the front pocket of her backpack and used it to dab at her eyes.

"So, who were the girls you were talking to, when I saw you?"

"Those were some of the cool girls. Mean, still. But at least they make fun of everyone, not just me. And thanks." She offered him a wobbly smile. "I'll bet it shocked them, when you hugged me like I was some long-lost friend."

"What you missed was seeing their expressions. It was priceless.

Just like in the cartoons, when the jaw drops and stays open."

She began to laugh, just thinking about it. "That was the best thing that's ever happened to me, the whole year. Just seeing you there, waiting for me, was so great."

"I'm so glad I did it. Your mom thought it was a good idea, too."

This made her stop short. "You discussed this with my mom?"

"You came up in conversation, there at the studios. I told her I thought you were the greatest, and she agreed. I told her my idea—actually, your idea—to stop by the school if I was free, and she gave it a thumbs' up."

Elation battled with irritation. She didn't want her mom to have anything to do with the setup. She wanted David all for herself, with no parents or mom friends involved. It was a little like discovering her mom was in the back seat right then, listening in.

But he'd just said he thought she was the greatest. That he'd told her mom so.

That was something. A pretty amazing something. And the way he was smiling at her just then, like he didn't think it was a big deal, one way or another, that her mom was involved, made her relax. Besides, if her mom knew, it gave her freedom to do whatever.

"Let's go somewhere and get a hamburger," she proposed. "If my mom knows I'm with you, she won't mind."

"Text her, just to play it safe," David said. "But I love the idea. I haven't had lunch yet, and I'm starving."

"Me too!" She whipped out her phone and began busily texting. Her mom always kept her phone nearby after school, for things like this, and within seconds, had replied.

"Permission granted!" she exclaimed, holding up the phone for David to see. "She told me to have fun."

"Excellent. Let's go."

He asked for her recommendation on a great burger, and she said

Bill's Place, down Geary and over to Clement. It was way across town, which bought her extra time with him, but in that unfair way life could sometimes be, all the stoplights remained green as if just for them, and unfortunately they got there in record time. Once inside, they were greeted by the delicious smell of burgers sizzling on the grill behind the counter. Everything was white and chrome and cheery, with 1980s music blasting.

They claimed a booth that looked out the window onto the street, so they could people-watch. David made up stories about the people that passed by and she cracked up over his wild, inventive descriptions.

Over their burgers, they talked about music (her favorite composers were Tchaikovsky, Schumann and Saint-Saens, and his were Beethoven, Chopin and Liszt, but he loved all of hers too), meditation (while traveling in India two years earlier, he'd done a three-month yoga retreat and still meditated daily, something called *vipassana*), the way classical music felt like its own spiritual journey sometimes (definitely Debussy's "Prelude to the Afternoon of a Faun," they agreed). They talked about science, about high-energy physics, which he was surprised she knew about until she told him about Kyle Lee Manning. He told her that not only did he know about quantum theory, but he had a book in the back seat of his car that he'd bought *just last week*, called *The Tao of Physics*, and they marveled over what an amazing coincidence that was. He told her Kyle Lee Manning would have been so very proud of having such a cool, smart granddaughter, and it was such a nice thing to say, she almost cried.

They pulled out their iPhones and took selfies together, both of them being outrageous and laughing. She studied hers while he left to pay the bill, and saw the way her eyes were lit with something miraculous, something that made her instantly look more adult. More like someone who mattered.

Before going back home, they stopped at Sutro Tower because he said he hadn't been there for years and years. They stood up high on the observation deck, spellbound by the panorama of San Francisco, with its neat grid of streets, Market Street a long avenue that seemed to go on and on. Oakland, the Bay Bridge, South San Francisco, and in the other direction, the Golden Gate Bridge, the hills of Marin and beyond. Golden Gate was the name of the mouth of the bay, she informed him, and that was why it was called the Golden Gate Bridge, which also explained why it wasn't painted gold, but was instead orange. Or red. People argued over its exact color.

"How did I not know that?" David asked in wonder.

"I guess you've just hung out with the wrong people."

"I guess so." He gave a happy sigh as he looked all around. "What a great idea this was, Kylie. Thank you."

She was shivering from the brisk wind blowing from off the Pacific, and from something more, something that left her jittery in a wonderful, new way. "You're more than welcome. Look me up anytime. I'm full of surprises."

He chuckled. "I believe that about you. And you know what else?" He turned to look at her, serious now. "Don't ever change. You're perfect, just the way you are."

She tucked his words close to her heart as they headed back to the car, to Hayes Valley, to her home. She bade him goodbye, let herself into the house, texted her mom, and sank to the couch in a daze of happiness.

You're perfect, just the way you are.

/ Chapter 13

Katrina

Dario woke in the night, crying inconsolably. Through the darkened upstairs hallway, Katrina carried him back and forth, jiggling him, patting his back, but it changed nothing. His issue was inexplicable; he howled and cried, "My face, my face!" which didn't mean "my throat" or "my ear" or a headache or a neck ache, and before Katrina could figure out where he hurt exactly, he cried, "My nose is gone!" and kept repeating it, rejecting her assurances that it was still there.

Twenty minutes passed. She tried to set him back in his bed but his wailing increased and he climbed right back onto her, nimble as a monkey. Back to walking him. Twenty more minutes. She would not get to sleep again that night, she thought in despair. And there was no longer night in the world than one in which you were trying to soothe a crying child who resisted all your efforts. Finally she began to cry too, both of them wailing, which, ironically, was the thing that stopped him. "Mama?" he asked, in an alert voice. He patted her wet cheek, no further sign of whatever had been wrong with him—who knew what had been wrong? Gas? A bad dream? A molar coming in? An ear infection? A scratch or irritation inside his nose?

"It's time to sleep," she murmured.

"Okay," he said cheerfully.

She set him down on his bed and he fell instantly asleep. The sky was growing light as she made her way back to her own bed, wanting to weep at the injustice of a setup that allowed no backup support for these nighttime dramas.

Javier was curiously unsympathetic when she told him about it later that morning. They were in the big studio, stretching before company class. He looked skeptical as he hooked his left leg onto the barre. "What you're telling me is that he cried for the whole time you held him, but when you set him down, letting him solve it for himself, he went straight to sleep. Is that right?" He gazed at her, almost in disapproval, before he bent over to rest his torso on his extended leg.

She wanted to lash out and tell him he was twisting the facts around to support his own theory, but she was too tired to verbally spar. Javier, with his new bright-eyed, I-slept-well-and-something-more look, had clearly forgotten how hard parenting a small child could be. When Jimmy approached to wish her good morning, she welcomed the distraction. They chatted, commiserating over Edwin's latest choreographic change, which neither of them liked.

Ben entered the studio to teach class; it was almost time for it to begin.

Javier had been talking with Palmira in the same way she and Jimmy had been bantering, and when everyone took their places at the barre, Javier gestured for Palmira to stand behind him.

She and Palmira froze.

This was not how it was supposed to be.

Palmira looked both anxious and deferential. Today she was wearing a sleeveless, high-neck leotard with a design of red and white roses against a black background that made her look particularly youthful and pretty. Javier's glance flickered over the two of them. "It's good to shake things up from time to time, Katja," he said. "Keeps everything fresh."

She sensed Jimmy's bewilderment, and grabbed his arm before he could leave. "Please," she said in a choked voice. "Stand here." She took a step back and gestured to the now-vacant spot between her and Palmira. He took it, and she radioed gratitude with her eyes.

Grumbles arose behind her as the other dancers were forced to shift to accommodate the two new dancers. "Sorry," Katrina called over her shoulder. "Blame Javier."

Through pliés, an unfamiliar sense of isolation filled her, which she immediately pushed away. Javier wasn't her only friend among the dancers, she told herself sternly. Look at how she was starting to make friends with Jimmy, after all. And …

Well, no "and." No other good friends. She'd prioritized her relationship with Javier above all else. She caught a glimpse of David, today's accompanist, his easy smile, and right then she hated him for his effortless social skills.

She worked doggedly through barre, through adagio and petit allegro in center, forcing her tired body to deliver her trademark 110 percent. During grand allegro across the diagonal, she noticed the corps girls glancing in David's direction, how they seemed to be showing off for him, and the way he'd reward them with a smile. Which annoyed her as well. Today, everything annoyed her.

By the end of company class, she was sweaty, spent, and still grumpy. Limping from a pointe shoe that was overly broken in, too mushy in the toe, she opted to take the elevator and not the stairs. A mistake. She saw David inside the elevator only as she herself was stepping in.

"Look at this," he said as the doors closed, "we're finally alone."

"I don't know what you're talking about," she said stiffly.

"Oh, just that it seems like I encounter the other girls, but never you."

"Yes. You do encounter the other girls a lot, don't you?"

He chuckled, but didn't reply.

He was, as per normal, carrying a book. Today it was a weighty hardback, a biography of Winston Churchill. "You're a reader," she commented.

He looked down at the book, affecting great surprise. "Hey! How'd that get there?"

Before she could reply, he changed the subject. "So I've been wanting to pick your brain about what you think makes a successful accompanist. I'd love to take you out for a bite to eat sometime and chat."

"You can ask the others."

"Sure, but you're a senior principal and your opinion would be highly valuable to me."

"I'm a mom. That alone occupies my evenings."

"You found time to eat out, that one night I saw you. Was that your 'safe' boyfriend? The one who's just a cover so that no one knows you're harboring a secret crush on me?"

She cast him a chilly look.

"Sorry. Just a joke. Fine, so you don't have a secret crush on me. It would still be great if you and I could catch a bite of dinner some night and, you know, talk shop."

"I have no interest in going out with you." She spoke deliberately. "The accompanist's job is to play the music, unobtrusively, and to not harass the dancers."

So just leave me alone, she wanted to add, but she knew he'd gotten the point. Yet any sense of triumph she felt evaporated when he didn't reply. She knew, without looking, that the smile had left his face. She knew, as well, that she'd sounded like a bitch.

He became a different person when he wasn't smiling, she realized. More intimidating. She thought of the cross-legged meditator, still with focus, and realized how unknowable he could be. "You know," he said in a tone that echoed hers, "they told me you were aloof and kept to yourself. They said I shouldn't bother trying to make friends with you. And I told them, nonsense, everyone can use another friend. I suppose they were right, after all."

She didn't know what to say. As the elevator approached the lobby level, he stepped close to the door, his back to her, as if to block her presence from his mind. A ping sounded and the doors slid open. Waiting there were three corps girls—his harem, she thought viciously—who emitted pleased coos at the sight of him.

"You meant it!" David exclaimed, back to that easy, flirtatious tone. "You're really going to take me out to lunch!"

"We are!" they trilled in unison, and together, the four took off, laughing and chatting.

Katrina was slower to leave the elevator.

Fine. She was aloof. It meant she got to keep herself. Just as she preferred, anyway.

Alice had left her a message to call back about their next meetup, at Montserrat's performance in Menlo Park. Katrina rang Alice that evening. "The performance is still on, isn't it?" she asked anxiously. "I've got Javier coming over to watch Dario."

"Oh, sure, it's on," Alice said. "But her quintet had a last-minute casting change. Guess who will be stepping in?"

"I don't have a clue."

"David Lavigne! He's thrilled there will be a group of us he knows, in the audience. He's so cute—he's getting nervous, he told me. I said we'd be his cheering section."

Her heart sank. "Oh, my," was all she could manage.

"April will be driving you and Kylie there?" Alice asked.

"Yes, that's the plan."

"Great—I'll be on the Peninsula already, so I'll meet you ladies there. A night without our little boys—yippee!"

"Yes!" She hoped she sounded sufficiently enthusiastic. "Can't wait!"

The night of the performance, April picked her up, with Kylie shifting to the back seat so the two friends could chat. They talked about studio matters, about Hess and his eccentricities, the latest challenges he'd thrown at Katrina and Jimmy. "How are you doing, Kylie?" Katrina asked over her shoulder as April took the highway entrance and merged with traffic.

"Fine." Kylie sounded bored.

"How's school?"

"Fine."

Katrina kept trying. "Anything exciting to report?"

"No."

"Do you know what we're hearing tonight?"

"Sure." Kylie sat up eagerly, leaning forward. "It's that Dvorak quintet that Montserrat had David play a little bit of. Remember, that night he was there? I wonder if he's nervous? He seemed to play it really well that night."

"I imagine performing for four moms is quite different from performing as a substitute in a semi-professional quintet," April said. "I'd guess he's feeling nervous. But he strikes me as the type of person who's up for the challenge."

Forty minutes later they arrived at the venue, an enormous, airy church where, inside, they met Alice. Although they'd arrived early, it was already crowded. Montserrat was a celebrity in the classical music world, the big-ticket musician on the program. They bought their tickets and looked around.

"Montserrat told us to go toward the front and look for the reserved section," Alice said.

They spied Dena in the reserved section. When she saw them, she brightened and waved them over. "Neither Misha nor my mother-in-law could make it tonight," she told them as they approached. "So I am representing the family. I'm so glad to see you ladies. Familiar faces!"

They claimed the seats around her. A moment later Montserrat peered out from a side wing close to the temporary stage, and came out to greet them.

"Can we go say hi to David?" Dena asked her.

"Not a bad idea," Montserrat said. "I think he'd appreciate that."

"Oh, yes, Mom!" Kylie gave an excited bounce. "Please, can we?"

"I don't want to lose these great seats." April glanced at their spots.

"You three go ahead," Katrina said. "Alice and I will stay here and guard the seats."

April nodded. "Good plan. Thank you."

The church was set up arena style on three sides, and had a lovely high ceiling and stained glass windows. Four chairs, along with music stands, were situated on a platform stage in center front. Katrina met Alice's smile and relaxed. "It's good to see you," she said.

"You, too," Alice said. "I've been thinking of you and your domestic upheaval. How's Dario?"

She told Alice about the "my nose is gone!" wail, amusing now that it was in the past. Alice thought it was hilarious.

"Aside from losing his nose, how's Dario been doing with the transition?"

"Not too bad. He was over the moon to see Javier tonight. Just thrilled that Javier would be the one to kiss him goodnight. It kind of hurt my feelings."

Alice looked at her in sympathy. "I get it. It's tough to be the one who's always there, versus the flashy, less frequent one. When Niles travels, Granger acts inconsolable, even though it's rarely more than two nights. But tonight it's my turn." She gave a happy sigh. "I'm so glad to be out with my friends. I need this."

"I do too," Katrina admitted.

Alice caught sight of acquaintances and excused herself to go greet them. Katrina studied the program distractedly—there would be three groups performing, culminating with Montserrat's quintet—until Dena, April and Kylie returned. April and Dena paused in the aisle and it gave Katrina the chance to analyze Kylie, waiting behind them.

Kylie was changing. Seemingly overnight she'd gone from nondescript little girl, shorter than average, skinny in an awkward little-girl way, into something mysterious. She'd shot up three inches without gaining a pound and now you saw her lean, long lines. Leggy, like a dancer, and a distinct way of moving them, that, along with her skinny arms and expressive hands, seemed almost sexy, even though Kylie herself was too young and lacking in self-awareness to be doing it on purpose. Of April's two daughters, Jen was the outgoing, flirtatious one, and yet her personality was always so sweet and guileless. Kylie kept a lot of thoughts to herself. Katrina had a sneaking suspicion that Kylie was brighter than she, Jen and April combined. It didn't make for as comfortable a relationship.

The three of them returned to their seats. "David wants you to come say hi during the intermission," Kylie told Katrina.

"Really?" Katrina turned and eyed April uncertainly, but April only nodded. "How was he doing?"

"Poor thing, he really did look nervous," April said.

"Don't you think it would bother him if I went back there?"

"Nope."

Katrina hesitated. "I was rude to him, April," she said in a lower voice. "In the elevator earlier this week. Essentially I told him to back off with the chatty flirtation. He took offense—or as much as someone so easygoing can." Katrina recounted their exchange, with its chilly, awkward conclusion.

April nodded. "Clearly it was an effective method of communication for you both. He needed to learn that not everyone responds well to flirtation."

"Exactly!'

"Anyway, he knows you'll be honest with him, and that he can be honest with you. That's worth a lot. And he really did look like he needed the support."

"All right. During intermission."

Alice returned. The lights flickered a warning and the audience quieted down. A minute later the lights dimmed and the first group's four musicians strode out to the stage and took their seats, adjusting their chairs, the scores on their music stands. Then the four musicians met eyes, the first violinist gave a small nod, and they were off.

It was Schubert's "Death and the Maiden," his Quartet No. 14 in D minor. Kylie had given them a tutorial on the composition in the car. The second movement, she'd informed them, was based on an old French poem in which Death came to claim an adolescent girl, which sounded macabre to Katrina. But the music was sublime. The quartet, like all the groups that night, was composed of young musicians, conservatory graduates finding their way out in the bigger world.

The next group performed a Mozart quartet, polished but less thrilling than the Schubert, with Katrina silently fretting over what she was going to say to David. The music concluded to a burst of applause, and the lights brightened for intermission. People rose and stretched as a buzz of conversation filled the space. With some reluctance, she rose as well. Stagehands began to wheel the piano from its resting place in the corner to its new location right beside the platform stage.

'I'll just go say hi to David," Katrina said, half-wishing someone would offer to join her, but her friends only nodded. Alice and Dena began to chat and Kylie claimed April's attention as Katrina slowly made her way to the center aisle and off to the side door where the musicians were.

David, still in the musicians' changing room, seemed genuinely downcast. Beyond downcast. Panicked, as if he hadn't considered that this might be well above his abilities. And yet, wasn't he the type to embrace risk? She tentatively posed the question to him.

He didn't reply. Instead he studied his hands miserably. He was wearing a dark, surprisingly excellent suit, white shirt, his wavy gold locks tucked into a neat ponytail. It startled her that he didn't look like the young, irrepressible guy taking the new accompanist job. He looked like a man. An attractive man. Which was disconcerting.

"I know you're up to this," she tried again. "I'm sure you'll do great."

This time he met her eyes. "You think so?" he asked.

When she didn't respond immediately, a shadow seemed to fall over his eyes. "I'm a shallow, weak-willed, flirtatious guy. I know that's what you think I am. I flit here and there, and work hard at something until a shinier object catches my eye."

"That's not true!" she lied.

She'd never before considered him as a vulnerable individual. Then again, this was the major leagues. If he didn't have it in him to play at the professional, concert-hall level, he needed to discover that. Bravado and cockiness only got you so far, in the end.

She realized, in a flash, what she could give him. "Do this as well as I think you can, and it will be my honor to accept your invitation to go out and talk about your accompanist's job, and answer all your questions over dinner."

This time, she could see, the words got through.

"All right," he said quietly. "Thank you."

A knock sounded at the door. "Five minutes, Mr. Lavigne," a voice announced.

She rose. "I should go."

"Me too. I don't want Montserrat and the other musicians thinking I'm flaking on them."

He rose, tall and imposing, and Katrina realized he and Javier were the same height and build. It was the dress clothes, she decided. They made him seem bigger, more formidable. "*Merde*," she told him, the ballet world's good-luck wish. "Or, well, break a leg. Whatever one tells a musician before a performance."

He smiled. "Thank you."

Watching the quintet perform, Katrina couldn't decide who compelled her more. Her eyes went from David to Montserrat and back to David. She could tell he'd overcome his nerves and was now immersed in the music, in a place of perfect concentration. The quintet, following Montserrat's cues, flowed seamlessly through the first movement without mishap. David's piano opened the second movement. It was a pure, elegant sound. Kylie was sitting next to Katrina, and she could feel the younger girl's body tense and shiver, like she was in a meditative trance, at one with the music.

He fit in surprisingly well among the other musicians, she realized. His serious demeanor was not just professional but attractive. How to equate this David with the sloppy, grinning accompanist at the studios? It felt like a social experiment: put a young man in a suit, tame back his hair, place him in front of a discerning audience where there was no option to goof around, and watch to see whether he sank or swam.

David Lavigne swam.

When the quintet finished, she expelled the breath she hadn't realized she'd been holding. Over the roar of applause, she turned to Dena, whose eyes were bright with pride. "Did my brother-in-law hit the ball out of the park, or *what*?" Dena shouted over the applause.

"He did!" Katrina exclaimed, her mind still whirling. She turned the other way to exchange broad smiles with April, who gestured with her chin to Kylie.

Kylie looked like she was still in a trance. She stared straight ahead, clutching the program so tightly it was crumpled, and Katrina saw her furtively brush a tear from her eye. April's smile turned maternal. She reached over and stroked Kylie's shoulder, which made Kylie jump slightly and regard her mother in surprise.

"We go backstage?" April asked them over the ongoing applause. "Offer our congratulations?"

"Definitely," Alice said, and Katrina nodded.

She told herself it was the polite thing to do, after all, the professional dancers acknowledging and praising the artistry of the musicians.

It had nothing to do with wanting to see David, reach over and touch him, and marvel at the alchemy that had just occurred.

She just wanted to congratulate him.

Chapter 14

April

After the concert night, Kylie began acting strangely in a way April couldn't put a finger on. "How's school?" she asked late in the afternoon, the following week. Kylie was eating grapes at the table while April prepared dinner.

The light immediately faded from her daughter's eyes. "It's there."

"Can you tell me one thing about what made today interesting?"

"No," Kylie replied in a flat tone that told April they were done.

The experts said you were supposed to talk to your kids about school, engage with them, but April didn't know how to make it happen anymore. The adolescent Kylie was even more stubborn than her younger self; no longer could April or Russell easily strong-arm her into anything.

"Tell me what's new on your music playlist," she tried instead.

Kylie's expression brightened. "Oh, what they played at the concert that night. I went to the library the very next day and found two CDs of Dvorak's music. He wrote all sorts of chamber music I'd never heard. Like over a dozen quartets. There's one called 'The American' that's so good!

"He liked trains, did you know that?" she continued. "He lived in Iowa. That's where he got his ideas for the famous one, the *New*

World Symphony. You know that one, right?"

April studied her blankly. "No."

"Mom! Everyone should know that one."

"Maybe I've heard it but I just don't know it by name."

"I'm sure that's it. I'll play it on the living room stereo one night and have you listen to it."

"All right. That would be good."

Kylie dropped a grape, but aside from an offhanded "oops," continued eating the others, one by one, lost in a dreamy reverie.

The grape had rolled several inches away from the table. April frowned. "Excuse me, young lady? Kindly pick up that grape before someone steps on it."

Kylie snapped back to attention and giggled. She was barefoot, and April watched in amusement as her daughter's foot trawled the linoleum and tried to pick up the grape with her toes. Unless you were a primate, toes weren't like fingers, but Kylie's toes were different. It reminded April of the sensitive tip of an elephant's trunk, the way her toes curled around the grape, cradling it without squishing it. Kylie then lifted her foot so that it hovered over the table, where she released the grape.

"Kylie!" April cried, shocked.

Kylie looked abashed. "Sorry, Mom. I know, that was gross." She rose, retrieved the grape, and threw it in the trash.

But it hadn't been her bad manners that had shocked April. It was Kylie's dancer's feet. She'd had amazing feet when she was little, but so had Jen, and April had assumed it was a baby thing, to be able to point and flex and chew on your foot and wave it high in the air like a baton. But the older Jen now struggled with pointing her toe in the way every dancer craved, a high-arched extension that curved to the floor like an upside-down banana.

"Kylie. Point your toes," she instructed.

Kylie looked startled. "What, here?"

"Yes. Like you're at a barre and doing a tendu. Feet turned out, tendu heel forward."

Kylie did as she was told. April's heart leapt and sank at the same time.

She had it. Her non-dancing daughter had the foot type all ballet dancers coveted, with high arches, and toes that effortlessly pointed and curled downward. And she wasn't even trying. "Does it hurt?" April asked. "Is your foot cramping?"

Kylie looked mystified. "No. Why would it hurt? I'm only pointing my toes."

"Has Jen ever seen you do that?" she asked Kylie.

"Point my toes, you mean?"

April nodded.

"I guess so. Or, I don't know. It's not like she's watching and I do it on purpose. But what's the big deal, Mom?"

"You have nice feet, that's all. Dancers' feet. Jen physically struggles to point her toes like you're doing. Unfortunately, some things a person is just born with, and practicing, stretching, pushing the muscles, will only get you so far."

Kylie looked unimpressed. "So she has the looks, the charisma, the grace, the sociability, and I have the feet. Gee. And here I was feeling like a loser."

"Kylie! You're not a loser!"

The light behind Kylie's eyes had switched off, leaving her expression once again opaque, deadened.

"Right, Mom." Without another word, she turned and left the room.

April returned to her dinner prep, more puzzled than ever. Kylie's moods were all over the place these days. The higher-than-high of watching Montserrat and David perform. Her obsession with classical music. High school could be a time of experimentation, and she wondered if Kylie had tried something illicit, like marijuana or worse, but quickly dismissed the idea. Jen was so clean-cut, avoiding drugs, alcohol and unhealthy behavior, because she knew being a ballet dancer had to be her world, and her body had to be at its healthiest. Kylie always followed Jen's cues. Neither had started experimenting yet, April decided. This was something different.

And now she heard Kylie singing in the upstairs bathroom, her burble of laughter when the cat did something funny.

She was fine, April assured herself. She was a teenage girl, that was all.

The school counselor called April while she was at the studios, insistent that both she and Russell come in to talk. No, Kylie wasn't in trouble. It was just that she was, they decided, a Student of Concern, and they felt it needed to be discussed ASAP.

April called Russell, who groaned as she began to explain.

"I can't. Not today. I absolutely can't. I told you how crazy this week would be."

So April, cringing, had to apologize to a grim-faced Anders and thank God for Rebecca by her side, in the end. Rebecca told Anders coolly that she could cover, no problem, she knew the ballet being rehearsed inside and out, and there was no reason for him to go railing on April when she was doing the best she could. Anders narrowed his eyes at the both of them and tersely told April to go and get back as soon as she could.

Driving to the high school, April felt confident, even certain, that Kylie didn't have a "real" problem. It was just that she was sensitive and smart and was bumping around as she found her way. It had always been this way with her. Teachers expressing concern because she didn't fit into the mainstream. Those jagged cityscape drawings in charcoal-grey and magenta in the kindergarten classroom, when all the other little girls were drawing daisies and bungalows and pink things. First grade, more issues. Reading far above her school level. Writing that was called "inappropriate" simply because it surpassed the teacher's own literary preferences for the class. Russell scoffed at it all, including the suggestion that Kylie submit to a battery of psychological tests. "We just need to let her be a kid," he always insisted. "She's bright. She'll do fine."

At the high school, twenty minutes later, the team in the vice-principal's office invited April to take a seat. She felt immediately assaulted by the three women in their no-nonsense suits who scrutinized her even as they smiled politely.

"How are things at home?" the school psychologist asked.

"They're fine," April replied, although every time she got asked this, it made her feel like an inadequate mother, one who never delivered a traditional six o'clock dinner, with the entire family around the table at the same time, beaming at each other over their well-balanced meal. "What is this about?"

"I imagine Kylie told you about the way she behaved, well, erratically during the 'history of your name' presentation?" Karen Latimer regarded her expectantly.

What were they talking about? "I'm sorry, I guess not," April managed.

The other women exchanged glances and she felt like a criminal.

"Here's a recap." Karen Latimer cleared her throat and read the teacher's report from her laptop.

"Is Kylie in some sort of trouble for this? I can't believe she wouldn't tell us."

"No, not trouble. It's just that we're concerned about her."

"For getting angry when the students mocked her, and she reacted strongly?"

"No. Something more recent." Karen gestured to Kylie's literature teacher.

The teacher, a young woman, smiled tentatively at April. "This is an assignment Kylie turned in. She does like classical music, doesn't she? But I'm wondering if she's exploring it, perhaps, too deeply. In a dark way."

Already bristling with defensiveness, April took the pages the teacher handed her. She loved that Kylie loved classical music and its composers. No, it wasn't mainstream, but it was nothing to shrink in shame over. She read Kylie's assignment not in concern, but in increasing admiration.

The quartet's second movement was originally a song entitled "Death and the Maiden," which Schubert had composed seven years earlier, in 1817, based on the poem by Matthias Claudius. In it, Death comes to claim a frightened young woman, who sings:

> *Pass by, oh, pass by!*
> *Go, you savage skeleton!*
> *I am still young, go, dear!*
> *And do not touch me.*

And Death tries to soothe her:

> *Give me your hand, you fair and tender form.*
> *I am a friend and come not to punish.*
> *Be of good cheer! I am not savage.*
> *Gently in my arms shall you sleep.*

Even though Death is present, the music never turns ugly. That's the skillful part. I can hear the continued sweetness of the maiden's voice through the first violin. All that innocence and purity, up against Death. If I were watching this in a movie, around this time, I'd turn nervously away from the screen. But Schubert gives the story a twist. The maiden stops fighting. She gives in to Death's low, soothing voice. You can hear this in the music. The composition is in D minor, which is appropriately funereal and suits Death perfectly. But toward the end, when the maiden stops fighting Death and capitulates, the music switches from D minor to D major.

It changes everything. Just as, in life, looking death in the eye, with acceptance, with loss of fear, changes everything. There is even a certain grace, a nobility, in the closing phrases of the second movement, that seems so true to life — or death, in this case — that it gives me little prickles down my neck and makes me feel like I'm witnessing something transcendent.

April looked up. "That's Schubert's 'Death and the Maiden.'" She tried to sound confident and not defensive. "We attended a performance last week and heard it played live. I think this essay is beautifully written." Because, truly, it was artful and engaging, and all from a fourteen-year old. Was nobody noticing that?

"You're right, it is," the literature teacher admitted.

"Anyway," April said. "That's all this is about. It's Schubert and his music that she cares about. Nothing more."

Karen Latimer leaned in. "April. Are we sure about this?"

The "we" reference made April bristle with defensiveness.

The school psychologist, as if sensing her reaction, spoke up. "We care. Most parents are grateful that we point out things like this. As you yourself noted, kids don't always come home and share that they had a triggering incident—and mind you, we have a strict policy on aggressive behavior, which includes storming out of a classroom, but we opted for the benefit of the doubt there. We're not trying to wage a war, April. We simply want you to be aware of what we know."

It ended politely. April knew how to keep things from escalating in a potentially high-emotion situation. It was part of her job, after all. So she smiled at them, thanked them warmly, told them what they wanted to hear, that yes, she and Russell would keep an eye on Kylie at home, consider some psychotherapy (even as she knew Kylie would fiercely reject it and push back, like she'd done the other times it had been suggested). They all kept smiling at each other, which made April's face hurt, but she knew how to deliver a good performance.

Maybe she's a good mom after all! April could almost hear them think. *Maybe she does care for her kids and their welfare as much as she does that job of hers. And the husband! Where's the husband today? Priorities. Parents. They think they rule the world.*

It was approaching the end of the school day, so they allowed Kylie out early to go home with April. When Kylie appeared at the door, the administrators were warm and deferential toward her, which surprised April. The literature teacher gave Kylie a pat on the shoulder and said, "I hope you feel better." Which bothered April. Kylie wasn't sick, so why was the teacher treating her that way? But in her eyes—all their eyes—Kylie was now a Student of Concern.

She didn't know what to say to Kylie as they drove home. She didn't want to discuss the creepy implications of the "death" motif. And she knew better than to voice her frustration over how Kylie was compromising April's job, with all this eccentric behavior. One look at Kylie, the way she slouched, folding into herself in a way that made her seem all the more small and childlike, triggered April's maternal instincts. But she was still angry.

"Tell me about the fact that you had your own meeting with Ms. Latimer over a week ago." April kept her eyes on the road. "Wasn't that something worth bringing up? So I didn't have to find out here? Imagine if I'd been forewarned."

"I'm sorry, Mom. I was going to tell you." She sighed and looked out her window. "The teacher read my piece about my name-history to the class because he thought it was good, but the others laughed and I freaked. I walked out and went and talked to the vice principal about it. That was the end of it. I didn't think they'd call you in like this."

"They were worried about your essay. The one about the Schubert quartet."

"'Death and the Maiden?'" Kylie turned to her in interest. "Why? Did they like it? Or not get it?"

How did you explain this to your kid who was already acting a little unstable? April didn't want to go using "death" and "young girl" in the same sentence, the creepy way they alluded to it all. But she'd been the one to bring it up to Kylie.

"They thought it was … morbid. They'd rather you write about meadows and sunshine."

This made Kylie laugh, which made April feel better.

"Pink gazelles bounding through the air on the African savannah," Kylie added. "Not a predator in sight!" April laughed out loud, in equal parts amusement and relief.

They drove the rest of the way in a better mood. Once at the house, April looked at her watch. It was 2:30PM; she could still make the three o'clock rehearsal.

Kylie sensed her hesitation. "You can go, Mom. I'm good."

April studied Kylie's face for any sign of instability, trauma, depression. Nothing. "You're sure you're fine?" she asked.

"Absolutely."

"All right. I'll have my phone handy. Call if you need anything."

"I will. In fact, maybe I'll even stop by later. Say hi to Betty and the Wardrobe ladies."

"They'd love that. They adore you." April smiled at her.

"All right, I'll do that. I'll swing by the studios too, to wave hi to you."

"Excellent idea."

"It is." She gave a decisive nod. She looked so happy now, April's heart swelled.

This affection, this devotion, from her teen daughter.

And here she'd been worrying that Kylie was drifting away from them.

Chapter 15

Kylie

Kylie arrived at Katrina's house right on time to babysit Dario. But so far it had been ten minutes of hanging out in the living room, while Katrina was upstairs getting ready, with Dario refusing to leave his mother's side. Kylie was on the couch, reading the book she'd brought, when the phone rang.

"Could you get that?" Katrina called down to Kylie from her bedroom.

"Sure, no problem." She set down her book and went to answer the phone.

It was Javier. He sounded surprised to hear her voice.

"I'm watching Dario while Katrina goes out for a few hours," she explained.

"Ah. Put her on the line, would you?" He sounded pleasant enough, but there was this undercurrent of anger that Kylie couldn't help but pick up on.

"Sure!" she responded cheerily, pretending not to notice his irritation.

Katrina didn't look any happier when Kylie knocked on her door and told her who was on the phone. "Can you take a message?" she asked, regarding Kylie in the mirror reflection.

Kylie hesitated. "I can try. But something tells me he's going to insist. He's got that voice."

Katrina sighed and rose from her makeup table. "I understand. Make sure Dario doesn't get into my things here."

"Sure, no problem."

As Katrina descended to the main level, Kylie kept her eye on Dario from the hallway. He was on his belly in the middle of the bedroom floor, on a rug that doubled as a Hot Wheels racetrack. He made putt-putt noises as he drove one car after another down the track, only to crash them all at the end. Katrina's voice rose as she spoke with Javier. From Kylie's sentry spot in the hall, it was impossible not to hear her.

"No, no, Dario should stay home here. Kylie lives six blocks away, so she's a perfect sitter for a short outing."

A long pause ended in sputters of protest. "I'm *not* keeping him from you. If you want to spend the time with Dario, you can come right over and send Kylie home."

Another pause, and then, "Brent is better than *who*? Better with little boys than I am? Is that what you were about to say? You think a boy's mother's home isn't his safest zone? I beg to differ. A child's mother *is* his home. Period."

Kylie heard the plasticky clatter of a phone shoved back into its base. Next came the sound of the refrigerator being yanked open, the jars and bottles on the door tray inside sliding around and clanking. There was the distinct hiss of a soda can being opened. Dario, still engrossed with his Hot Wheels, hadn't even noticed his mother's departure, and didn't react when Katrina returned to the bedroom, Diet Coke in hand, once again composed. Kylie didn't mention the call and neither did Katrina.

"I'll just let you finish up here," Kylie said, feeling awkward and uncomfortable. Whether it was from witnessing Katrina's lapse of control or because Katrina, always so above it all, made her feel awkward for all the reasons she was Kylie and why the kids found her weird, wrong, not enough like Jen, whom everyone knew and liked.

Oh, to be Jen. To be not-Kylie. Sometimes the feeling welled up in her so much, she could hardly find room to draw a breath.

Katrina smiled at her. "Help yourself to a Cherry Coca-Cola. They're in the fridge. I bought them just for you."

"Thank you." Kylie smiled back at her, feeling a little better. She loved Cherry Cokes. Back downstairs, she got her soda and settled back on the couch with her book.

The doorbell sounded. "I'll get that," Kylie called out.

"Thank you," Katrina replied from upstairs.

She assumed Katrina was going out with her English boyfriend-but-not, but instead she opened the door to David. Pure, unexpected delight surged through her. She invited him in, drinking in the sight of him, overwhelmed by this new emotion filling her, all happiness and high flying.

"Be right down," Katrina called out.

David walked to the foot of the stairs and angled his head up. "Take your time. Kylie's here to entertain me." He grinned at her and she felt even more fluttery, her face heated like she had a fever.

What to say? How to make the time worthy? She could hear Dario fussing in Katrina's bedroom, an "I don't *want* her to be here. I want *you*. I want Daddy!" and right then Kylie decided she didn't much like Dario. But from now on, she'd take any job Katrina offered her, if it meant a chance to see David.

He took a seat in the armchair. "Tell me something interesting, Kylie."

She returned to her place on the couch, pondering the challenge. "Okay. We have a cat named Schrodinger."

Sure enough, he began to laugh. "Seriously? As in, the quantum theory 'is the cat dead or alive' thought experiment?"

She nodded.

"That's brilliant."

"There's a funny story attached. We got the cat less than a month after my dad told us the story about Schrodinger's cat. He brought it home in a box, the kind they give you at the SPCA for transport, and he set it down in the living room. We all stood there, but there was no sound, no movement from the box. Jen asked jokingly whether the cat was alive. My dad, thinking he was being so clever, said, 'I guess it depends on the observation.' I got the reference right away, the way quantum particles can be many states at once until the observation forces them into just one state, yadda, yadda, ya, but Jen had forgotten that conversation, and she looked just horrified. My mom told my dad it was a terrible thing to tell little girls, and he got flustered, saying it was a physics joke, and he was sure the kitty was fine. But now both our parents looked uneasy, which made Jen start to cry, saying, 'Our new cat is dead.'"

"How old were you girls?"

"Jen was seven, I was six."

He was grinning. "So what happened next?"

"There was this long terrible minute—probably only a few seconds actually, but you know how something awful seems to stretch out time—and finally I said something like, 'This is dumb; the cat's alive.' I marched over, opened the box and for one creepy second I hesitated, but then I plunged my hand in, pulled the kitty out and sure enough, he'd just been sleeping deeply. He was so cute, still just a baby. He let Jen cradle him like a baby until he woke up more and wanted to start exploring. I said, 'I guess we know his name,' and my dad started laughing. He had to explain the Schrodinger thing all over again to Jen. She wanted to call him 'Fluffy' because he really is pretty fluffy, but I stuck to my guns and eventually Fluffy went out the window. The name, I mean. Not the cat."

His laughter was rich and infectious. His eyes glowed with appreciation. It filled her with such pride, as if she'd just hit a home run with the bases loaded.

"All right, that qualifies as an interesting story. I knew you wouldn't let me down."

They heard Katrina hurrying down the stairs and a moment later, she entered the living room. "I'm sorry about the delay. Dario was being needy."

"No problem." David offered her a dazzling smile, which made Kylie's triumphant feeling fizzle out.

"We won't be out long," Katrina told her. "Just a casual bite to eat."

"She's allowing me to pick her brain on what constitutes a good accompanist," David explained to Kylie.

"That's cool," Kylie said as Dario entered the room and stopped short at the sight of David.

"Bye bye, sweetie," Katrina cooed. "Come give me a kiss."

He ran to her and she hugged him tight. "Now you be good for Kylie," she said.

"I don't wanna be good for Kylie!"

This made Katrina and David chuckle, but Kylie wasn't about to join in. Dario was becoming a brat, but all Katrina could see was how precious and adorable he was.

Once they left, Kylie and Dario eyed each other warily. She didn't feel like jumping through hoops to entertain him, so she went straight to the uncomplicated default.

"Should we watch one of your movies?" she asked him.

"Okay," he said.

"Which one do you want to watch?"

He chose a *Winnie the Pooh* video. Once he was engrossed, she left to use the bathroom, but instead of returning, she chose to explore the house. When she stepped into Katrina's bedroom, a curious feeling arose in her. Fascination. Envy. She wanted to be older, an adult who commanded respect. She wanted to dislike Katrina even as she desperately wanted to *be* her. To have so much talent that the waves parted for you as you made your way through the world.

Katrina's makeup table fascinated her. It was loaded with colorful tiles of eye shadow, rounds of blush. Bottles of foundation, a creamy pale color that matched Katrina's perfect skin. Powder puffs and various brushes. All of it, in such profusion. It made Kylie want to put on makeup, play dress-up. It made her yearn to be swept away, experience glamour and excitement. Katrina was a star and had star power, and even though Kylie had known Katrina all her life, there was still something untouchable and unknowable about her that was like a siren call. Even though she and David had looked all businesslike heading out to dinner, Kylie could tell that David was attracted to Katrina. She was famous and beautiful and elusive. Everyone who met her, who got this close to her, wanted more of her. It hardly seemed fair.

She heard Dario laugh and clap. She guiltily made her way out of Katrina's room and went back downstairs where she belonged.

David. *David.* A prolonged fantasy about him sprang up in her mind, unspooling before her like a film, one with a happy ending. When Dario asked for a snack, she and phantom David went in to the kitchen, where she poured some Pirate's Booty popcorn into a bowl. David got her a Cherry Coke and a beer for himself and the two of them, laughing and letting their hands brush against each other, returned to the living room. She set the popcorn down and both she and Dario took a handful. She conjured David's presence on the other side of Dario. She could almost feel him in the room, his warmth, the smell of him like when he hugged her that afternoon at the high school, the firmness of his arms around her, the way it had made her feel so shaky afterward, agog with the gift of his closeness.

Dario laughed again, engrossed in his movie as she and phantom David smiled at each other over Dario's head. *I love you,* she mouthed to him, and he smiled, a look of such warmth and affection that a shiver came over her. She snuggled closer to Dario, who didn't notice, and she watched the movie with unseeing eyes, basking in the presence of her fantasy lover. A little sigh slipped out, followed by one of those shaky intakes of breath that you get after a long cry. As if the world had magically realigned, and you now feel loved, secure and safe.

Utterly safe.

Chapter 16

Katrina

Katrina arrived early to stretch before company class, but also to plant a present for David. Over dinner the previous night, the subject of European chocolates had come up. David loved the ones that featured hazelnuts, chopped or whole, and hazelnut paste—called gianduja throughout Europe—and mourned their absence stateside. Why, they both wondered, weren't gianduja and hazelnut confections more popular in North America when they tasted so good? He told her he used to buy Baci Perugina chocolates by the handful, each one individually wrapped in blue and silver foil, like an exotic Hershey's Kiss, covered in dark chocolate and filled with a chocolate-hazelnut cream, minced hazelnut, and a whole nut in the center. She told him they were easy enough to find in San Francisco, but he'd been skeptical.

"Prove it," he'd said, so this morning, before class, she'd gone to Little Italy in North Beach, where she knew of a small coffee house that featured imported Italian goods. She found and bought a half-dozen of the Baci Perugina chocolates. Knowing David was the morning's accompanist for class, she'd set the chocolates in a row on the piano, before going to her normal spot to stretch.

The previous night's dinner, his "reward" for the impeccable performance, had been surprisingly effortless. There'd been no flirting, no strained conversation, no long-winded monologues on his part that left her mentally yawning. He'd pulled out a pad of paper and posed intelligent questions as they sipped wine and ate pizza. What tempo did she most prefer for tendus versus dégagés? And after the développé exercise, when the dancers were given an extra few minutes to do their own stretching? Did she prefer lush and lyrical there, or passionate and grand? During an adagio, was it acceptable to include a crescendo or did that distract the dancers? The grand allegro—should there be more or less bravura from the accompanist?

She'd answered each question and he'd written down the replies, sometimes telling her to slow down so he didn't miss anything. It was charming to watch his brow furrow with concentration as he pondered her words. "You're serious about this," she'd said at one point.

He'd offered a self-deprecating shrug. "I know I've given you reason to believe I take things too lightly, but I'll say this. When I'm serious about something, I become very, very serious."

Javier's arrival in the studio broke her reverie. He took his customary spot at the barre in front and greeted her like he always did, bending to kiss her forehead. She responded with a smile that was perhaps a little less warm these days. They'd kept the uncomfortable new setup of Palmira just behind Javier, and, thankfully, Jimmy stayed, too. No one else minded; everyone respected Javier and allowed him this. They allowed Javier to do most things. He could say as he pleased, rage as he pleased, bestow smiles or comments on the other dancers at whim. He was becoming more like Anders, utterly assured about his place in the WCBT and the world at large. She only hoped he didn't become like Edwin.

But Javier seemed grumpy this morning. "Who were you out with last night?" he asked. "A date?"

"No. Business."

"So, a business dinner."

"Yes."

"With whom?"

"David Lavigne." She winced as her stretch went too far for the throbbing sacroiliac joint, that spot between the glut and the bone that always flared up when she went too deep, too fast, into a stretch, and would linger through the season until she gave her body time off.

"*What?!*" Javier froze amid his own stretching to stare at her, and she realized belatedly that she should have given him a more ambiguous answer.

"We talked business. He sought my advice about being an effective accompanist and what he might do differently in order to improve."

"And that required a dinner together? Really?"

She frowned at him without replying. What business was it of his anyway?

"What about Martin?" Javier persisted. "You told Lucinda you'd set up something more regular with him."

"Why do you care?"

"Because Martin looks the part of someone who deserves to be seen with you. David Lavigne, are you kidding me? Maybe the corps girls can be dazzled by him, beg him for a date, but not a senior principal. Not my partner. Not my son's mother."

Just then, David came in and went to the piano. She paused, waiting to see his reaction to her gift.

Javier followed her gaze. They watched as David stood over the piano and a smile lit up his face. He looked up, caught Katrina's eye, and mouthed a *thank you*. He unwrapped a chocolate and held it aloft, head back, mouth open, before letting it drop in. As he chewed, he exaggerated an expression of drunken ecstasy, which made her laugh.

Javier, meanwhile, had remained frozen in his disapproving glare. She shot him an impatient look. "So he and I are sharing a joke together. I believe laughing constitutes 'lightening up,' which you regularly tell me to do."

"Just … don't be foolish."

She watched Jimmy and Palmira enter the studio together before she turned back to Javier. "Have I ever been foolish? Been imprudent or acted unwisely?"

"No," he admitted.

She stayed in the building for lunch, and, on impulse, went to the hidden spot where she'd sighted David before, in meditation. She smiled when she glimpsed someone there, only to discover, too late, that it was Edwin. He was looking at his phone with a murderous expression. She wondered who had aggravated him this time. He regularly took calls and read texts during rehearsals, and it was easy to tell which ones weren't to his liking. She wondered if exchanges with Sophie Bocuse had anything to do with the ensuing good moods. Then again, of late, there hadn't been so many good moods. Nor was this any exception. She'd never seen him look this angry before, and longed to sneak away before he could turn his anger on her.

Too late. Edwin looked up and saw her. He smiled, even as his eyes glittered with rage.

The warning kicked in, deep in her gut.

He is not a good person. He's a bad dude.

"Why, hello, Katrina," he said pleasantly.

"Hello, Edwin." She gestured to the phone. "Is everything all right?" She wanted to kick herself as soon as the words came out, but he only smiled.

"Of course. Why would you think otherwise?" He lifted the

phone in his hand. "I was just talking to an old friend. I'm angry for him. He's struggling with something." His mouth worked but no words came out, which was fine with her, because they would have undoubtedly been angry or caustic. "He certainly didn't deserve to have his call blocked," he bit out, as if to himself.

Before she could process this last comment, he switched tactics. "Talk to me, Katrina." He gave her a professional smile. "I don't know you well enough, and that's a problem. You keep throwing up barriers."

She did her best to sound casual even though his presence, not to mention his mercurial mood, made her uneasy. "It's just that I'm private. Sorry to disappoint you."

"Tell me about your days at the Paris Opera Ballet School. I need to see that younger, more vulnerable Katrina."

She didn't like the way his eyes seemed to glow when he said "vulnerable," as if he relished that in particular. "There's not much to tell. I joined the ballet school when I was eight. It was mid-year because a girl had left the program and, after auditioning, I was picked to replace her. I hadn't studied any ballet prior, so it was a challenge, but hard work and commitment paid off. Within two years, I was as competent as the others in my group."

"More than competent, I imagine," he replied. "Because you completed all six divisions of the program before you turned sixteen. You were never held back, were you? A star in the making."

Hardly, she thought wryly. She hadn't been one of the three dancers in her group picked to join the company, after all. "Anders thought so, fortunately. I owe much of my success to him."

"I'll bet the men really get hot over you. Such aloofness, when you want it. You and Sophie both. Is it something the Paris Opera school taught you? Or is it a natural thing?"

What did he want from her? How to shake off these questions, these subtle digs at her, without making him angry?

"Do you date?" he persisted. "What's the longest you've gone without a romantic encounter? Or, more simply put, had sex?"

She could feel her jaw drop over the rudeness of his question.

"When did you first kiss a boy?" he continued. "When did you first allow him to slip his hands down your pants? Did it excite you? What made you wet for the first time?"

She couldn't believe he was asking these terrible questions. She was certain he was doing it for entertainment. Her face, she knew, had flushed red. For a moment, she was speechless. Then rage billowed up. "I have no answers for you on such a disgusting topic. You have no right to grill me in this way."

"I have every right," he said, but in the blink of an eye, the deviousness disappeared and he began to laugh. The murderous expression disappeared, replaced by merriment. "I was teasing you! You're so serious! Frankly, I'm going to say it's a sign that you're undersexed. But that's your problem, not mine. What were you thinking? That I'm some sort of pervert? I'm an artist digging for material, that's all. And I'm trying to figure out how best to coax the best energy out of you. Look at you, all flushed and trembling. That's creative energy. That's untapped potential in your dancing. I'm going to create a masterpiece. Is it too much to ask that you emerge from your safety zone for a little while? Christ. Lighten up."

With that he brushed right past her, walking down the hall and into the stairwell, where his footsteps gradually receded. She stood there shaking, as despair coursed through her over the time she still needed to spend with him in order to learn his ballet.

What did I tell you? He's a bad dude. And you're giving him permission.

Martin called that evening just as she'd gotten Dario off to bed. She'd let Martin's last three calls go to voicemail, and she hadn't called him back. Normally a longer time would elapse between their dates and his phone calls, but apparently he'd taken the stolen kiss as the green light to escalate things. She wanted to tell him persistence here wouldn't intrigue her, it would turn her off. He deserved better, she thought guiltily. He was kind, so guileless, the complete opposite of Edwin Hess. So she took his call.

He seemed delighted to hear her voice, and she half-listened as he rambled on and on about what was new in his life. "But, alas," he said with new energy in his voice. "Methinks it is time for another dinner together. What say you, my fair and fine lady?"

She laughed even as she rolled her eyes.

"Next week?" he asked, his hope nakedly apparent.

"I'm just not sure what next week will look like."

"You still need to eat dinner."

She searched for an excuse. "It's Dario. The routine of dinner for him, here, is so important. As is the wind-down time."

"I eat late. You do too. We could wait till he's asleep. I know you have a trio of backup sitters for the evening."

"Not really."

"Of course you do. You told me so."

Caught. Damn.

"You're right. It's just that, well, this is a transition time. It was different when I knew Javier was home nightly, as well. And Dario knew it. Now, things are changed. His sleep is more fretful. He needs a week or two more of this new normal."

"I understand." He sounded disappointed. "But if not this or next week, the following, all right? I'll kidnap you, if need be." He laughed heartily at this, so she joined in, even as prickles of distaste raced down her spine.

"Maybe a daytime thing. Lunch. A weekend walk outdoors."

By the silence that greeted this, she could tell he was the one now rolling his eyes. Martin wasn't an outdoorsy type. And, the truth of the matter was, she didn't want to leave Dario alone on weekend days that she had free. She wanted a date that included her son, and that was never going to happen with Martin. Children made him nervous. He would have done it for her, to be with her, but it would have been a joyless experience for all of them.

"Call me in two weeks," she said. "We'll make a plan."

"All right."

She hung up and her shoulders drooped with relief. Two weeks was a long time away.

Thank goodness.

Chapter 17

April

Palmira fell out of a turn during her Don Q rehearsal with Javier. It was a tricky move, where the male spun the female while her right leg was out, à la seconde, and mid-turn she had to change her focus and angle her body down, like an arrow, into a deep partnered arabesque. Up to now, Palmira had aced it, along with the other challenging turns and partnered moves, leading April to admit that Javier's plan to switch partners and "share the wealth at the top" had been a good one. Palmira was definitely a major talent in the making.

A fall during rehearsal was no big deal. Except when you were under pressure to get up to speed, fast. And right then, April sensed she and Palmira shared the same thought.

Palmira might be out of her league here.

Javier hurried over to help her up, telling her congratulations, a fall meant taking a risk, and it was all good.

"Are you okay, sweetie?" April called out, going over to rub Palmira's delicate shoulders and give them a squeeze. "That looked like it hurt."

"I'm fine, I'm totally fine." She flashed April a smile but she could tell by the sudden brightness in Palmira's eyes that she was holding back her tears.

"That's a tricky turn," April said. "One of the trickiest. It's all about holding the core tight and not getting freaked out about your axis shifting. Well, and doing it impeccably three times in a row."

Fear flashed in Palmira's eyes.

"Do not fret this," April told her. "If need be, we'll take the whole rehearsal to do just this one move so that you've got it down pat."

Palmira looked relieved, but only for a moment. "It's just that there's no time to slow things down." She half-glanced at Javier and April knew he'd been coaching her, telling her, in a way he (alone) thought was productive, to get up to speed quicker.

"Sure there is," April said. "Rushing something creates its own problems."

Javier looked annoyed. Of course. His preference was to be running the entire pas de deux over and over by now, polishing it. With Katrina, that would have been the case.

Palmira might have been prodigiously talented, but she wasn't Katrina, and no amount of cajoling or bullying was going to change that. Javier, April decided, was going to have to learn—possibly the hard way—that he couldn't have everything he wanted.

That afternoon, April had a second, even more disturbed feeling when she peeked in on a Hess rehearsal. The rehearsal she'd been scheduled to run had been delayed for a Wardrobe fitting with the dancers, so she had a few minutes to kill. Edwin seemed to be having a good time, joking with the males as he demonstrated new steps. He directed Jimmy to "shove Katrina so hard she almost falls back." The first time Jimmy did it, Katrina was so unprepared for the force, she toppled right over like a bowling pin.

Edwin was highly entertained. "I wish I could use that. I so wish I could use that. But there's probably a slew of liability issues connected to keeping it in."

Jimmy looked miserable. He reached down for Katrina,

murmuring an apology as he pulled her to standing. April could tell the four male corps dancers were unsure whether or not to laugh along with Edwin.

Edwin saw her at the door and his expression cooled. "Can I help you, April?"

She assumed a bright, clueless smile and raised her voice higher when she spoke. Men with big egos seemed to find that less threatening. "Hi, no, I was just passing by." She peered around; neither Curtis nor Ben were there.

Edwin noticed the query in her gaze. "I told Curtis he needn't just stand around here, and that my own rehearsal assistant could pass on notes. He takes lots of notes." Edwin gestured to the slim, bored-looking young man standing nearby whom she'd seen daily but had never once heard speak. "Curtis has better things to do with his time."

"Well, that's very considerate of you, to think of Curtis's busy schedule, but, honest, this is how we like to run the business here. Always having a ballet master nearby, at your beck and call." April broadened her smile. He did not return it. Instead, childishly, he greeted her last comment with only a disapproving silence. She was determined to let him be next to speak. She'd done her apology; now she was going to stand there until he responded.

"I'm sure you have a rehearsal to go to," he said finally. "So I'll just let you be on your way."

"Thank you! And, tell you what. I'll send Rebecca over here to assist you."

"I. Do. Not. Need. Any. Assistance." He strode toward the door and April commanded herself to not shy away. He brought his face right up to hers, so close she could see the acne scars on his face, which made her realize how young he still was. There was even a pimple on his chin that had been topped with concealer.

"I don't like you," he said in a low, hostile voice. "I don't need you. I think you should keep to your own business and let me do my work. And I shouldn't think you'd want me to go complain to Anders. Ballet masters are expendable. There are three of you right here. A choreographer of my stature? I put this company on the world ballet map by accepting the commission."

A half-dozen heated retorts sprang to mind. They were already on the map. The company had been invited to perform in London eighteen months ago, and for this coming summer, Anders had accepted a prestigious invitation to perform for two weeks in Paris. But she kept the comments to herself.

"Thank you for your contribution to the company," she trilled instead. "I'm sure I speak on behalf of Anders and the entire artistic staff. Keep up the good work." She stood her ground, limbs shaking, but with the same bright smile pasted to her face.

He knew there was nothing further he could say. If April had no jurisdiction over him, he had none over her. Ultimately he gave her a curt nod and without another word, turned and headed back to the dancers. Jimmy flashed April an apologetic look. Katrina's glance was despairing, and it made April ache that this situation was to be Katrina's fate. And the gala—the night that proudly displayed the WCBT's best of the best—was fast approaching. Meanwhile, Edwin was still choreographing and re-choreographing, in what seemed to be an increasingly erratic, unpalatable style. It was profoundly disturbing, and yet there was nothing April could do or say. Anders, Javier, Ben and Curtis would perceive her as the bad guy for saying a word against Edwin.

Back in her own studio, the dancers still hadn't returned. Rebecca was there, however, and April found herself blurting out what had just happened.

Rebecca's eyes narrowed. "So it's true. You know, Leila would never trash another choreographer, out of professional courtesy, but she alluded to the fact that he thrived on being controversial. And not one but two of Sabine's dancers commented that he acted high on his own glory. Or high on something. Apparently he's got that reputation, too."

"That's gossip. That's not helpful here."

"I'm just telling you what I heard. And you're telling me what you saw. Edwin Hess strikes me as the epitome of a talented but mostly lucky self-absorbed male who's achieved so much in the ballet world because of his connections, gender and skin color. But, hey, did I mention Leila's latest award? Big recognition, not just in Belgium but throughout Europe. It'll win her more commissions, for sure."

"Good for her," April said. "I feel much better knowing there are determined, ambitious women like her, paving the way for females in the ballet world to find new success."

Rebecca regarded her in new appreciation. "I'm glad to hear you say that."

David, their accompanist for the rehearsal, poked his head in. "We're still waiting, I see."

"Come on in," April said. "They'll be here any minute."

Rebecca was still eyeing her intently. "The Leila thing. If the chance came up, would you back her? She needs an endorsement from the inside. We know from Ben that Anders prefers male choreographers and doesn't think it's a breakout time for female choreographers."

"I don't know how much power I have there," April said, and Rebecca's hopeful expression fell flat. "I'm sorry, Rebecca."

"With all due respect, you don't seem all that sorry. You don't want to rock the boat. I get it. But, I have to say, I'm sorry for that."

Dancers began coming into the room. Rebecca began to walk

away but stopped and turned to face April again. "You claim that you fight for your girls—the dancers—but, frankly, what I see is your being a pushover and pandering to anything Anders asks of you. You're letting the men run the show and giving them all the power."

April sighed to herself. Rebecca meant well. She remembered when she was Rebecca's age, how certain she felt about things, the way she believed enough positive attitude could affect change. "Anders is my boss. I'd like to keep my job and keep things smooth. I am not an activist; it's in my best interests here to stay apolitical. Does that seriously make me the bad guy?"

"You can't control chaos. You just think you're controlling it. Meanwhile, what is simmering beneath the surface is going to rear its head some day and you'll be unequipped to deal with it. Because it doesn't follow the tidy rules of the West Coast Ballet Theatre and the ballet world at large."

"Thank you for the life lesson. At forty-six, I'm sure I know less than you."

"I see things," Rebecca said. "I've stepped out of the bubble of oblivion."

"But look at you, here right now, and 'the enemy' is paying you, quite well. I should think you'd consider yourself to be lucky. You've escaped the clutches of being a corps dancer and are poised to move on to something better. But don't kid yourself. It's not going to happen without the support of 'those men.'"

Rebecca said nothing more, but her eyes flashed with spirit.

The dancers now filled the studio, chatting and in good moods.

"Rebecca. I appreciate all you've said," April told her. "Really, I do. But we have work to do right now. Can we agree to disagree, and move on?"

"All right," Rebecca said, and they both shifted their attention to the arriving dancers.

April knew she herself was on the right track. Her goals, while not lofty, were simple: keep moving, keep rehearsing, help keep everyone healthy and safe. What Rebecca couldn't understand was how compromise didn't mean capitulation.

Or did April have it all wrong? Was Rebecca proving to her that compromise was just that?

Chapter 18

Kylie

Her world came crashing down on Thursday afternoon at precisely four o'clock. She'd gone to the studios after school again, claiming she was searching for her mom, but was in truth hoping for a David sighting. She'd heard a pianist in a rehearsal room whose playing drew her in, Pied Piper-like, and she knew it had to be him, and, *ta da!* It was. She stood there, reveling in the sight of him, her body aflame with longing. He was leaning into his playing, like his heart was urging his body forward. He had those beautiful blond curls loose today that made him look even more like a angel. His shoulders were in a protective hunch over the keyboard, like the notes were so precious and fragile he had to protect them as they came out. He looked up with a gaze of perfect love and bliss, which Kylie took to be the emotions from playing the piece. She, too, felt that way inside just then.

The ballet master—ironically, her mom, after all—called out for him to stop, so he did, only the look of love didn't go away. It seemed almost sad now.

Kylie heard her mom pose a question. Javier replied. Then she felt a sickening thud when she heard Katrina, and as the three talked, David's longing look only grew stronger.

He thought no one could see him. If he'd had any idea Kylie

could, he'd have reverted in an instant to the lighthearted guy who could charm everyone. Everyone except Katrina.

He was in love with Katrina.

No. *No.*

Kylie stumbled back. She couldn't breathe. Was she having a heart attack? Could teenagers have heart attacks? Agony filled every nook and crevasse of her chest, pushing against her ribcage.

She had to get out of there. She whirled around abruptly, knocking over a pair of folding chairs propped against the wall behind her, which landed with a noisy clatter. Great. She was officially the clumsiest, most graceless creature alive. She wanted to disappear on the spot. Or die. Or both.

She lurched down the hallway, out the building, not even responding to the cheery "bye now!" of the security guard. She walked toward their house without registering anything except the roaring sense of pain and loss that David had succumbed to Katrina's allure, like everyone always did.

She had a babysitting job tonight. For Dario. It seemed like the cruelest, most ironic thing.

How was she going to babysit Dario tonight? How could she look Katrina in the eye ever again?

Back at the house, she texted her mom. "I don't think I can babysit Dario tonight."

A minute later, her mom responded. *Unless you have a good reason, yes, you will. Katrina is relying on you. Don't break promises and don't make promises you can't keep.*

Jen was at the Ballet School, being beautiful and promising. Her dad was still at the office, being heroic and all-knowing. Her mom was finishing up at the studios but texted an hour later to say she'd be home after Kylie left to go babysit. So Kylie had to walk over to Katrina's place at six o'clock, feeling almost physically ill over the prospect of seeing the beautiful, glowing Katrina, who didn't love David or even care that much about him, but it didn't matter because he was in love with her and would never have eyes for anyone else, especially not a nerdy freshman girl like her.

It was a small consolation that Anna, the nanny, answering the door instead of Katrina. Anna explained that Katrina planned to go to her evening event straight from the studios. "She says she'll be back around nine," Anna told her, "and you're to feed Dario and make sure he's in bed by eight o'clock."

Kylie managed a nod.

Anna hesitated. "Are you all right?"

"Sure. I guess I'm a little tired."

"Okay, have a nice evening."

Dario didn't seem happy to be with her. He wanted to see his mom. She told him too bad. She wasn't in the mood to deal with his whiny demands.

He wasn't in a good mood either. He didn't want her to read to him, and she didn't want to play Hot Wheels with him. They agreed on a movie again, even though she was aware Katrina didn't like Kylie sticking him in front of the television so much, but right then, exerting energy to nourish perfect little Dario's brain with kiddy flash cards or educational Lego structures was beyond her. She didn't want to interact with him. At all. She wanted to be alone to grieve. A sense of rage and despair came over her and she decided she officially hated Katrina. She hated her as much as everyone else admired and revered her. Something new took hold in her mind. She wanted to punish Katrina somehow. Or punish herself.

What to do with this feeling? It was eating her up.

She went into the kitchen to get a Cherry Coke from the fridge and, on impulse, opened the liquor cabinet. Inspiration seized her. In the movies, drinking always calmed you down when you were having a bad day. And her dad would come home sometimes and say, "Wow, what a day, I need a drink." She'd hear the *ssst* of a beer bottle being pried opened and a moment later, his satisfied, "Ahhh." There was brandy in the cabinet. Her mom liked a brandy when it was late and she was wired and needed to wind down to sleep.

It was a mostly full bottle, and she decided a little dribble wouldn't be missed. She pulled it down and poured herself a sip into a glass. It was bitter and harsh on her throat, which shocked her. Watching characters in movies sip it appreciatively made her think it would be like a combination of maple syrup and melted butter.

She went to the counter and grabbed the Cherry Coke she'd just opened. She drizzled it into the glass until the brandy tasted better. Not just better—the drink tasted great. She made another, adding more brandy this time. It was good, but maybe too much of the Coke. She found the perfect combination finally, and it turned out to have been a great idea, because now the room had begun to list from side to side, ever so slightly. At the same time, a warmth filled her inside and out and made her think that maybe life wasn't so bad after all. It was full of sadness and despair, yes, but the brandy was creating some disconnect, so that her life became like a movie she could sit back and watch. Poor, sad Kylie, kind of like a Cinderella, and everyone had gone to the ball, leaving her behind.

She liked the image so much, she began to waltz around the room, giggling to herself when she bumped into a chair. She paused to listen for Dario, and when she heard him laugh at something in the movie he was watching, she knew he was safe. She decided she liked the Cinderella feeling and when her drink was finished, she went to make another, because there was no way she could maintain this magical, life-doesn't-matter-so-much feeling without the brandy. No wonder people liked to drink brandy. It softened life's harsh edges. Which, she decided, was so profound, that she had to go write it down. A poem. She felt a poem coming on. Or, wait. She was *living* a poem.

"I'm hungry," Dario called out.

"Okay," Kylie said, in a better mood now. "In a little bit." She found some Pirate Booty popcorn in the pantry and brought it out to Dario. "Here. Eat this right now."

It was a big bag. He looked dubious. "Mommy says that's only for a special treat."

"I'm the boss and I say it's okay." She pulled the bag open, only she pulled too hard and popcorn flew out, making them both laugh. "Here you go," she said cheerily, handing him the bag. "Eat as much as you want. I'll be back."

Because she was liking this Kylie party she'd created, so she refreshed her drink and took it upstairs.

She went into Katrina's room. By now, the gentle listing had turned into sloshing waves, and she giggled every time she walked into something, or dropped a trinket of Katrina's she was holding up in the mirror. She sat at the little chair in front of Katrina's makeup table, feeling very posh and adult. She decided to put on makeup to look more glamorous. She dug a Q-tip into the makeup from those little artful squares of color, only one of them wasn't cooperating and she dug too hard and the square did a little half-flip and fell to the floor, face down, where it broke, because there was a hard clear plastic vinyl surface underneath the chair and over the carpet. The eyeshadow crumbled when she tried to pick it up and she realized that she might be drunk, because her fingers were as clumsy as anything.

"I'm hungry," she heard, and Dario appeared at the doorway, and Kylie realized it had been over an hour since she handed him the popcorn. He looked confused to see her there. "This is my mommy's room."

"I know it's your mommy's room," she said, suddenly really disliking Dario.

"You shouldn't be in here."

"I'm the one in charge, not you. And you're the one who needs to get out of here."

"It's my mommy's room," he repeated, stubbornly.

"Fine! And what do you want, anyway?"

"I'm hungry. You're s'posed to feed me."

Suddenly being drunk wasn't fun, it was annoying and complicated. She could feel her good spirits come crashing down around her. "Go make your own food," she told Dario. She'd meant it as a cutting remark, but his eyes lit up.

"Can I?"

"Yes," she said. "Go."

"A sandwich?"

"Yes. Go make yourself a sandwich."

He disappeared and a minute later she heard him downstairs, singing to himself in the kitchen. Kylie, meanwhile, doggedly smeared on the eyeshadow so she could look beautiful, the way her mom, who sometimes looked plain and washed out with no makeup, would come back into the room a half-hour later and look as beautiful as a model. But it wasn't working. Not the eyeshadow, not the mascara, which smudged her cheek and wouldn't come off, and not the blush that ended up on top of her cheekbones instead of beneath them and made her look like a clown.

She hated it, all of it. She hated herself. She hated life.

She thought of Schubert and that unforgettable quartet of his. How Death scared the maiden but instead of being scary, he tried to soothe her.

Give me your hand, you fair and tender form.

I am a friend and come not to punish.

She pondered that moment where the maiden stopped fighting so hard to stay alive. Was it a relief, maybe? Because, look at *her*.

Were her own shitty feelings, the dreary existence of high school and not fitting in, worth fighting so hard to stay alive for?

Be of good cheer! I am not savage.

Gently in my arms shall you sleep.

Downstairs there was a crash, followed by an "uh oh," and she knew that he'd just dropped the jelly jar. Now she would have to go downstairs and deal with the mess. In a sudden rage, she swept her arm over the makeup containers and they all went tumbling to the floor. "Oops," she announced grandly to the empty room, before rising unsteadily. She stopped in the bathroom to pee, then blearily regarded herself in the mirror. She looked beyond horrible. She felt the same. She opened the medicine cabinet to look for Rolaids or an antacid, which she didn't find, but there sat the pills she'd spotted while snooping last week. Wasn't Tylenol with codeine supposed to take away pain?

She took the prescription bottle downstairs, but stepped wrong and fell down the stairs in a horrible thumping and pinwheeling and loss of control that seemed to go on and on. Dario ran over to watch and when she finally landed on the ground floor, he laughed and clapped his hands. "That was funny! Do it again!"

"Shut up, you stupid little kid," she screamed, and began to cry, which made him cry.

"You're not s'posed to say shut up! You're not s'posed to say stupid. That's mean, and *you're* the stupid one."

"Leave me alone! I hurt myself!" She rose unsteadily and tested her legs one by one, and sure enough, the left ankle hurt horribly.

Good thing she had the Tylenol with codeine.

Without giving it another thought, she opened the bottle, shook out three, and popped them in her mouth, staggering and limping into the kitchen, where she sloshed brandy into the empty glass, along with more Cherry Coke, and washed down the pills.

"Will you make my sandwich now?" Dario pestered.

But the last gulps of her drink didn't sit so well. She sank to a seated position at the wall. "Give me a minute," she mumbled. "Wait till the medicine makes my pain go away."

"But I'm hungry!"

"There's candy in the cabinet."

"Really? I can eat?"

"Yes. And then leave me alone."

A mistake. I made a mistake.

That was what her brain was saying. She roused herself and realized that she'd fallen asleep. The house was silent. She tried to rise and winced. The Tylenol hadn't helped her ankle pain. And now her stomach and head were feeling much, much worse.

"Dario?" she called out. "Where are you?"

No answer.

A mistake. I made a big mistake

Chapter 19

April

April was attending a Nob Hill fundraising event when her phone chimed. She pulled the phone from her bag and smiled at the sight of Kylie's number. "Hi there," she sang into the phone, idly thinking that the puff-pastry crab appetizers had been worth trying to hunt down a few more.

"Mommy," Kylie cried in a high, unfamiliar voice, and all thoughts of appetizers disappeared. "Mommy, I don't feel good." Kylie gave a little moan that struck a chord of terror deep inside April.

"Sweetie? What's wrong? Are you at Katrina's?"

"Yes. I'm in trouble. I'm sick."

There was something unnerving about Kylie's voice that scared April all the more. "Is Dario all right?" she asked.

"I don't know. I don't know where he is."

"Oh, God," she half-whispered.

Kylie moaned again, followed by the ghastly sound of her retching and throwing up. April felt a dizzying sense that this was happening to someone else, and if she blinked a few times it would all go away.

"I'm leaving," she said. "I'll be right there."

She retrieved her jacket and raced out, flagging a taxi. With shaking hands and fear clawing at her heart, she called Russell, who was still engrossed in work at his office. She hardly registered his "I'm coming right home" over her frantic need to be at Katrina's house. When the taxi hit gridlocked traffic three blocks from her destination, she flung a twenty at the driver and told him she'd walk the rest of the way.

She ran.

An ambulance and a firetruck were parked in front of Katrina's building, and a crowd had gathered. The vivid flash of the emergency vehicles' rotating lights, triggering in the best of times, made her mind go blank with panic. She tried running faster on legs that now felt like wooden stumps, slow and ineffectual.

Katrina's front door was open. Neighbors and onlookers clustered on the sidewalk, chatting and speculating. Off to the side, she heard a boy wailing and saw it was Dario. A neighbor was holding him, trying to soothe him.

He was safe. Thank God.

She pushed her way through the throng and saw, to her horror, that Kylie was lying on the living room floor, apparently unconscious. An animal whimper slipped out of her. Someone from the fire department was blocking the entrance, but when April told him the girl lying on the floor was her daughter, he let her pass. In the living room, someone else warned her not to get into the EMT team's way as they hovered over Kylie. April stood as close as she could, unable to draw a full breath. The room reeked of alcohol and vomit, which made no sense.

Her ears registered a conversation among the onlookers outside. "Rob says the little boy came outside, and asked if we could make him a sandwich. I know, crazy or what? Good thing he left the door ajar. As soon as Rob saw the girl on the floor, he shouted for me to call 911."

"What the hell happened?" someone asked.

"Who knows?" the original speaker said. "She's a mess, though."

Even as she listened, April's gaze remained fixed on Kylie. When she finally stirred, April fell to her knees, thanking God and the angels and her mother and father in heaven for letting Kylie be alive. She began to sob, biting her clenched fist in an attempt to keep hysteria at bay.

"Pills," she heard one of the EMTs murmur. "Did you take pills?" she asked Kylie. When she didn't reply, they tried again.

"Her name is Kylie," April said, trying to steady her voice.

"Kylie. Did you take pills?"

"Yessss," she slurred.

"How many?"

"Dunno."

Another of the EMTs held up a small green prescription bottle. He shook it and it made a maraca-like sound, which meant Kylie hadn't taken them all. Thank God.

She heard panicked shouting from the distance and recognized it as Katrina. A moment later, Katrina's out-of-breath voice cried, "Where's Dario? Where's my baby?"

"He's right here," the woman who'd been talking earlier called out.

Dario's wails stopped abruptly, which April knew meant Katrina was now holding him. "Who are you," she heard Katrina demand. "Why were you holding my son? Where's his babysitter?"

The woman started repeating the story about seeing Dario outside, setting Katrina off.

"He was outside *on his own?*"

April rose shakily and stumbled outside to join her. Katrina, clutching Dario, looked more distraught than April had ever seen her. When she saw April, she looked shocked, then furious. "What are you doing here? You mean you came through here and left Dario alone with these people? The person he knows best, all these strangers, and you walked right past him? How could you?"

April stared at her in disbelief. "He's fine. Your neighbor was holding him."

"That's not my neighbor!"

The person, a portly middle-aged woman, looked flustered. "My husband Rob and I were just walking by. We saw the little boy alone, outside, and we knew something was wrong. We thought we could help."

With Dario in her arms, Katrina ran inside but stopped, aghast, to take in the chaos on her living room floor. "What happened?" She swung around to face April, who'd followed her back in. "She drank alcohol—I can smell it. And this disgusting vomit. How could she do this while Dario was under her watch? What has Kylie become?"

"Kylie has never touched alcohol before," April protested.

"The parents always think that." Katrina glared at her as she clutched Dario tighter, making him squall in protest.

"Ladies, we're going to have to ask you to move," one of the EMTs said to them, and April turned from Katrina to edge closer to her own child. Kylie was all that mattered. If she was fine, the rest could be managed.

With deft speed, they transported Kylie onto a stretcher and April followed them out. Allowed in the ambulance with them, she took Kylie's hand and held it tight. Kylie's eyes fluttered. "Mom," she murmured.

"I'm here, sweetie. You're going to be okay."

"I'm so sorry."

What happened? April wanted to cry. *This isn't you. Why did you do this?* But she knew better than to agitate her. And the truth was, she was almost afraid to know what drove Kylie to this. Her sweet little pixie had a deeper inner life now, one she didn't want her mother to see. The thought filled April with such fear, she wanted to wail.

Please let my little girl be safe. Please, God. Be merciful.

Russell met April at the emergency room and she fell into his embrace, unable to stop shaking. They sat and clutched hands as information was given to them in a slow drip. The emergency room doctor, a woman with curly black hair and a brisk demeanor, finally came out introduced herself as Dr. Gomez. She told them they were lucky and that, physically, Kylie no longer seemed to be in any danger. Groggy and nauseous, but able to answer a few questions. "We'd like to move her to the children's wing and have her observed overnight. Her body's been through a lot in the past few hours."

"So we come back tomorrow and bring her home?" Russell asked.

Dr. Gomez shook her head. "It's more complicated than that. She's fine but not. Taking pills and alcohol like this was a cry for help. Have you, as a family, discussed candidly her feelings of depression and anxiety?"

April had thought she'd gotten a grip on the situation, but the doctor's words swung the conversation so far from what she was expecting, she could only gape in shock.

"Whoa, just a minute here." Russell held up both hands. "Are you saying what I think you're saying?"

The doctor looked flustered. "This is better addressed with a qualified staff member present. Let me page her and have her meet us to talk in private. Follow me, please."

Russell clutched her hand tighter as they walked behind the doctor, and April knew he felt as rattled and stunned as she did.

In a small, boxy white room just big enough for four chairs, a social worker joined them.

"We'll need an official evaluation before confirmation," Dr.

Gomez said. "A child psychologist has been called in. But, pending authorization, it's our intention to hold Kylie on a 5150." She saw their blank looks. "That's a mandatory 72-hour hold for observation, when there's concern the person in question is at risk of hurting him or herself, or others."

"I can't believe I'm hearing this." Russell plowed his fingers through his hair. "Are you trying to tell me she did this on purpose? To … hurt herself?"

"Yes."

"That's absolutely impossible." Russell spoke in that bullish way of his that always silenced arguments at home.

But they weren't at home. "Mr. Garvey," the social worker said, "your daughter told Dr. Gomez she did it because she didn't want to be alive."

The ground seemed to disappear from beneath April and she felt herself falling, falling. She heard the social worker's next words through a fog. "We take these things very, very seriously, as we hope you would. If Kylie is placed on a 5150, which is what we anticipate, she'll be transported tomorrow to an adolescent inpatient behavioral health unit. It's most decidedly the safest place for her."

April sat there, stunned and mute, as Russell answered and asked a few more questions. Then the doctor and social worker excused themselves, leaving the two of them alone to process the news. After that, everything took on a dreamy unreality. Calls to Jen, to Russell's parents, to Montserrat. Feeling almost drugged from the shock and confusion. A nurse notified them that Kylie was being transferred to the children's wing, and that they could see her there once she was settled.

Atop April's messy cocktail of fear and pain was a bafflement as to what had happened. What terrible thing had made Kylie experiment with alcohol—and prescription drugs? What had turned her beloved child into a risk-taking stranger? Was it school? Trying to be "cool" so the other kids would respect her more? And during a babysitting job where she should have been the height of responsibility. April could hardly wrap her mind around it all.

What had happened?

But once Kylie was settled and more awake, an hour later, she refused to speak to them. April and Russell tried asking questions but her face remained a stony mask. They gave up and just sat there, waiting in silence for the child psychologist to arrive. When he did, she and Russell were unceremoniously booted out of the room, told to go take a walk and come back in thirty minutes.

Upon their return, they were given the verdict. Kylie was to be held for 72 hours; she would be transported the next morning to an inpatient adolescent behavioral health unit.

It was approaching midnight when she and Russell went home. They had another child, after all, and with the 5150 hold, Kylie would be under constant surveillance. At the very least, April knew she was safe.

At the house, Jen was on the couch, wide awake, and scared. Russell held her and rubbed her back as she cried and cried. "What's going to happen?" Jen asked afterward, dabbing at her face with a tissue.

"She'll be fine," Russell said. "They'll probably have her participate in some group therapy sessions, and talk privately to a therapist, the psychiatrist. Three days minimum, and we were told sometimes they want to keep the kids a week longer. For our part, we'll make sure she has all the support she needs."

He went into the kitchen to fetch them all cold drinks. Jen turned to April, seated beside her on the couch. "Why did she do this, Mom?"

"I was hoping you could tell me. Have you two talked lately? She used to come to you and tell you everything."

"No, she hasn't said anything." Jen gave a delicate sniffle. "She's been so moody lately. I know school's harder for her this year. I'm not sure I can relate. School works for me. I don't get why she *resists* everything. Even her friends don't want to hang around with her anymore. Freshmen eat lunch at a different time, but I've heard she eats alone."

She regarded the bunched tissue in her hand. "I thought it was something she'd get used to and start enjoying. I didn't know she hated everything that much. And now that I think of it, there's a guy. She told me he was just a friend, but I can tell she's got a massive crush on him. Except he's way too old for her."

April felt queasy. "Who's the guy?"

"I can't remember his name. She showed me a picture of the two of them, though. They'd gone out on a date, she told me. I think she was exaggerating. I think it was just grabbing a hamburger together after school one day."

A bad feeling came over April. From her bag she pulled Kylie's phone, which she'd been handed at the hospital for safeguarding. "Do you know her phone's password?"

Jen nodded.

"Can you find me the picture she showed you?"

"I can try."

April passed her the phone. Jen unlocked it with the password and began to scroll through Kylie's photos. "Here you go." She handed the phone back to April.

Oh, good Lord. It was David with Kylie. The afternoon outing that she herself had sanctioned, even encouraged. David was holding up his Coke, with that irresistible smile of his, and Kylie looked happy enough to float away.

How had she not seen that coming? She'd seen the adoration in Kylie's eyes the night they watched him and Montserrat perform, but she'd assumed Kylie was too young to fall in love.

Everything else slotted into place, as well. Kylie, not coming into the studio that afternoon to say hi, even though that had been her plan. Later, her text, begging off the babysitting job. Something that day had been her breaking point—April knew that now. But she'd texted Kylie to say no, that an obligation was an obligation. At the time, she'd felt so noble, thinking she was teaching her daughter responsibility. Instead, she might have inadvertently caused her daughter untold pain.

It was like the time she was showing a five-year-old Kylie how dangerous a sharp knife could be. She'd delivered a lofty speech before handing Kylie the knife to cut into a nectarine so she could see for herself. "You need to press the sharp side harder into the nectarine," April had insisted when nothing was happening, except for a little dent in the nectarine. So Kylie sawed harder. Nothing. Until she dropped the nectarine and knife with a cry and April saw she'd positioned the knife in Kylie's hand with the sharp side facing her palm. Blood poured from Kylie's little hand, making her wail. April had felt beyond terrible.

Much like she felt now.

No, this was much worse.

How did you forgive yourself for allowing your child to get so badly hurt?

Jen was angry with April the next day for saying she needed to go to school. "My sister is in the hospital!" she announced dramatically. "I need to be by her side!"

April waved her theatrics away with the spatula she was using to make eggs she knew no one would eat. "You'll do better in your normal routine. It'll distract you." Meanwhile, nothing could distract April, not even sleep. Through the night, she'd jolted awake hourly to process this new, terrifying reality, her daughter lying in a hospital bed after nearly killing herself. And it was unconscionable, unbearable, to consider what they were saying, that she'd done it on purpose. But in front of Jen, April needed to sound calm and pragmatic. "We need to find out what facility they're going to move her to. After they've placed her, we can talk about how visiting will go."

After Jen went off to school, April and Russell headed out too. At the hospital, Kylie was sleeping deeply, which, they were told, was good. They'd found her a bed at an adolescent behavior health unit—apparently the spaces were in high demand, and you went where they found one, even if it was 50 to 100 miles away. Fortunately for them, Kylie's destination was 20 miles south of San Francisco, on the Peninsula, a straight shot down Hwy 101. They transported her via ambulance as April and Russell followed behind, to a smaller hospital and a locked facility where, on the third floor, visitors had to be buzzed in not once but twice.

Inside the main living area, April caught a glimpse of a handful of young teens, boys and girls alike, some off in the corner reading, others congregating in the center. The staff member who looked through April's bag, as well as the bag she brought for Kylie, told her no shoelaces, no pens. "You can't imagine what these kids will try," he said, matter-of-factly. "Some of them are so determined to succeed." It made April queasy to realize he was referring to suicide. It seemed impossible to imagine that the four girls on the couch, singing a little ditty together and laughing, were at such high risk. But they were. Otherwise, they wouldn't be here.

Kylie disappeared for an intake appointment, which was just as well, because she was still refusing to speak to Russell or April. They left and returned, then left and returned.

Over the next two days, April didn't even think of work. Nor did Russell even consider trying to run or attend his usual meetings. They visited a continued uncommunicative Kylie during the hours allowed, and on off hours, Russell and April ran errands together, took walks together, and returned to the house to be there for Jen. On Sunday, Jen had no Nutcracker rehearsals, so she joined them for the day. It felt weirdly idyllic, a bubble of calm amid a sea of upheaval.

A very temporary bubble, as it turned out. On Monday, Russell came to the breakfast table wearing sweats, hair still tousled. "I just talked to work. Ron told me to take all the time I needed. I think I'll make it a few more days."

April gazed at him and bit her lip, knowing the decisions and responsibilities of her own job needed to be addressed. Anders had been tolerant of her absence, but had told her he still expected her attendance at a meeting taking place that day. "I'm sure Megann in HR would tell me to take as much time as I need," she told Russell, then hesitated.

"—But Anders won't," Russell finished.

April studied the swirls of steam rising from her cup of coffee. "You and I both know family comes first. The question I'm asking myself now, is, can I do both?"

Russell reached over and gave her hand a squeeze. "Do what you have to do."

She decided she had to at least try.

April pushed through the meeting and the reception that followed, mimicking the language and behavior of a normal person. She didn't bring up the issue—few of the guests present knew her personally—

and no one, including Anders and Gil, brought it up. Even in skirting around the issue, however, she found interacting with everyone to be pure torture. It took so much effort simply to appear relaxed. She moved slowly, carefully, feeling as though she were made of glass, and if someone pushed her, she wouldn't explode or fire back, she'd just silently shatter.

She survived the meeting. Feeling more confident, she made her way to the studios for the afternoon *Nutcracker* rehearsal. To her dismay, she saw she'd been scheduled to run a rehearsal with Javier and Katrina, for their Snow King and Queen pas de deux. She hadn't exchanged any words with Katrina directly, but she'd had Russell call her on the second day, offer a craven apology, ask how she was doing, offer another apology, and tell her their family cared. Javier, bless his heart, had called April, to let her know Dario was fine.

"He hadn't even processed the danger of what he'd been doing," he told her. "He'd opened the door to go outside and find someone to make him a sandwich." Javier chuckled to himself. "When I got there, the night it happened, all Dario wanted to talk about was how he'd had to wait a long time to have a sandwich, and that the front door was very big and heavy. That was it. He's been told that he shouldn't open it again and I'm confident he'll comply. I think the sirens right outside the house unnerved him."

The closer April drew to the studio, the more her footsteps slowed. Seeing Katrina inside, she felt so dizzy she had to pause with her hand on the wall to steady herself before she could enter. Everyone was there: the accompanist, the second and third-cast couples, Rebecca with a pen and pad of paper. April drew a steadying breath and entered, greeting everyone crisply, without meeting anyone's eye. "Glad everyone's here on time, let's get started right up. Katrina and Javier, let's take it from the second entrance."

But being crisp couldn't cover up a bad rehearsal. And it was a bad one, full of clumsy starts and stops. Katrina stumbled out of one of her pirouettes and could only produce anemic leaps. Finally she came to a dead stop just before a partnered leap. "I can't," she said, as if it had been fifteen hours of rehearsing and not fifteen minutes.

Javier's expression darkened. April suggested the others take a five-minute a break, and once everyone had left, Javier lit into Katrina. April had the sense they'd been arguing before the rehearsal, and were picking it up right where they'd stopped.

"You're being weak and that's not acceptable," he told her.

"I'm struggling!"

"It's the way you coddle Dario like he's a baby. He's looking for more freedom. More exploration."

"I'm his mother!"

"I'm his father! By the time I was five, I was allowed to come and go as I pleased. In Havana! That's two years away. You are not preparing him to be a young man. You want him to be a baby forever."

She'd never seen Javier this angry toward Katrina without stepping in to defend her. But when April reached out to touch her arm, Katrina reacted as though she'd been scalded.

"Don't you touch me!" Her eyes were wild with hostility. "I don't trust you anymore! You should have known your daughter was unstable."

It was the most hurtful thing Katrina could have said.

The two of them regarded each other as if they were strangers. And in some ways they were. April didn't know this hateful Katrina.

Apparently she didn't even know herself. She'd never failed this deeply before, not in her work, not with her family. But clearly there was a first time for everything. "I'm done here," she heard herself say in a raw, ragged voice. She let the clipboard fall from her hands with a clatter. There was a ringing in her ears as she turned away from the two of them and walked out.

Rebecca was in the hallway, right outside the door. Apparently she hadn't taken a break like April had told her to do. Instead, she'd been eavesdropping. But April couldn't yell at her, not when she could hardly speak.

Rebecca took one look at her. "Go," she said. "I'll cover."

"Thanks," was all April could manage. She let her feet guide her, through the hallway, down the stairs to the lobby, and out into the cool, bracing air. Mind blank, she walked and walked, from Van Ness to Market, and a long, straight slog down Market Street, mostly because it didn't require a decision. When she reached the Financial District, she saw thirty minutes had passed, so she turned around and walked back.

Gradually her wits returned. It was unthinkable for a ballet master to walk out of a rehearsal. It was unspeakable that she'd stayed off property for that entire hour. She was screwing up, badly.

She walked back into the main building and went straight to HR, where she told Megann in a shaky voice that she needed to leave.

She wasn't ready yet, after all.

Chapter 20

Katrina

The photo shoot could hardly have been worse timing, but she and Javier were being well paid for the day, so her feelings did not factor into the equation. At the photographer's SOMA loft, she donned her first costume in a makeshift changing stall. Across the wide room, an enormous three-sided white panel had been set up, as had tripod lights in various spots, their cables taped to the floor.

She'd slept poorly every night since the drama, waking hourly, convinced Dario was in danger. She'd go into his room to check, but each time, he was fine. Early this morning, she couldn't get back to sleep after the 1:00AM visit. Knowing she needed her sleep to look good for the photo shoot, she took a sleeping pill, which, back in bed, she immediately regretted. She visualized still being deep in sleep when Dario woke, free to wander, free to open that front door again. She flung the sheets back and went down to the living room, making a bed from the padded armchair and ottoman nearest to the door, never pausing to consider that the door's security chain already kept it from being accidentally opened. When she woke before him at seven o'clock, with a crick in her neck and groggy from the pill, she realized how complicated she'd made her life.

High windows spilled late-morning light into the loft, but in the working corner, the lighting remained artificial and meticulously adjusted. She took the vacant spot near Javier at the makeup table, as the makeup artist expertly worked over his face. Javier was still acting testy and judgmental toward her. She knew better than to share the sleeping-pill-and-Dario incident.

There were a dozen people assembled, including a hair stylist, makeup artist, costume assistant, photographer's assistant, lighting director, art director, and two men in suits standing apart from the others. The clients, likely. Nearby stood a rolling rack with costumes and a table with a laptop for the photographer to consult with the art director and his assistant. Fans whirred to circulate the air. Even though it was early still, it was on track to become one of those hot October days that even twenty years of living in the Bay Area hadn't prepared her for. Warm Octobers and chilly, foggy summers. Welcome to San Francisco.

The hair stylist labored to create a curly, tangled look for Katrina's long blonde hair as the lighting person discussed positioning with the photographer, how to best rearrange lights for each segment of the shoot. Out came the jewelry, oversized gold and glittery pieces that felt heavy against her chest. The clients were owners of a luxury jewelry chain with a big advertising budget. They were after a subtle approach, the glamorous dancers rendering the adornments almost secondary. Magazine readers would catch the elegance, beauty, luxury represented, and, although they couldn't become ballet dancers, they could buy the jewelry—if they could afford the five-figure price tag.

"Javier and Katrina, are we ready?" the art director asked.

They both nodded and made their way to the white-paneled area.

Photo shoots were a study in "hurry up and wait." You warmed up but then were asked to keep still, hold a pose, or wait ages for the next cue as the photographer mulled over every minute detail. If it made a muscle cramp and ache, that was your burden to bear in silence. You stood there after the pose, rubbing the aching body part and waiting, as the shots were studied and discussed. Then it started all over again.

Her body hated photo shoots.

They commenced with simple poses, to acclimate their bodies to the work, and the photographer's eye to their bodies in space. Tendus. Cambrés with a luxurious back arch. Développés.

"Let's take that first pose we discussed," the photographer called out. "Smile and move toward it, through it, as slowly as possible."

Attitude devant. Leg développé out and step into arabesque. Javier took her hands and they bent, twisted, pretzeled into a more contemporary pose.

"Yes! Hold that. Hold that, please!"

Click, click, click.

Her face hurt from trying to affect the joyous, carefree look the photographer wanted.

Click, click. Murmurs.

"All right, release," the photographer finally said.

The art director, photographer and crew hovered around the laptop to compare the last ten shots and talk among themselves, which gave her and Javier the opportunity to speak, whether or not that was a good idea.

They were still feuding over her reaction to the terrible night. "I still can't believe you skipped work that next day in order to stay locked inside the house with him." Javier reached for a hand towel on the makeup artist's table to dab at the sweat around his eyes. "That was so wrong."

"It was just for that first day! I felt too distraught to even consider company class and rehearsal." Angrily she gave her costume, riding up, a yank down. "Have I ever done that before? No, never! I can't believe you're so unsympathetic over what happened! He was alone and unsupervised, and *he opened the front door.* Can I ever turn my back on him again?"

"You're a professional ballet dancer. You know, as well as I, that you've just got to take that scared, shaken, 'this could happen again' feeling and ignore it. Those performances where you've fallen, or that performance where the backdrop came crashing down—did we stop the performance? No! We kept dancing. Does the risk remain, that a backdrop might crash? That a massive power failure could destroy the entire night's performance? That a bad landing on a jump can mean the end of our careers? Imagine if you were as protective about performing as you were about parenting. I'll say this—you would not be a principal dancer."

"Looking good," the photographer called out. "Now let's see you in the *Romeo and Juliet* costumes for this next shoot."

The costume assistant approached to help with the quick change. Katrina felt so angry with Javier's lack of sympathy, it was all she could do to breathe in and out, affect a neutral expression, as the assistant unzipped her from behind, then held out the new costume as she stripped in the changing stall. Right then, she was glad, defiantly glad, that she wouldn't be dancing a pas de deux with Javier in the gala.

"How about that overhead lift we talked about last week?" the art director asked, once they were dressed and ready.

Overhead lifts were good. She didn't have to meet Javier's eye and she could look upward and create the illusion of even more space between them.

"Excellent," the art director said after twenty minutes of poses. "I think that last one, in particular," he added to the photographer. They turned to look at the two men in suits, arms folded, who nodded.

The crew once again congregated by the laptop to look at the newest round of photos.

"I would like to take Dario for a night," Javier said. "I think you need it."

His words terrified her. "That would be cruel beyond words right now."

"No, quite the opposite. I am his father, and I have as much right to my son as you do. He couldn't be safer than when he's with me."

His expression softened. "*Chica*," he said in a gentler voice. "Dario will be fine. He will always be safe when his father is around. He loves his bedroom at our place. I don't mean to be cruel and act as though I don't feel the trauma. I do. That's why I would like a night with him."

"Come back to the house to sleep, then."

He shook his head. "That's not the right way forward."

A more reasonable part of her understood that for her to deny Javier this would be unfair. They'd agreed to share responsibility for Dario, not heaping the burden on one parent or another. He, too, needed nights with his son. And maybe he was right. She needed a night of sleep free of fear and the hourly compulsion to check on a sleeping child who, ironically, had slept through the night for the past three nights, a new record for him.

"Great," the art director called out. "On to the close-ups."

Which ended their conversation. Which was fine with her.

The photo shoot lasted until five o'clock. Since it was a relatively early end to their workday, Javier came back to the house with her. Anna, opening the door for them, greeted him. "I miss seeing you!" she exclaimed.

"I miss you too!" Javier gave her a warm hug. "All of you!"

"Papi, Papi, Papi!" Dario screamed from the other room. Katrina heard the thud of his footsteps and a few moments later he burst into the living room, hurling himself into Javier's arms. Seeing their delight in each other's company sent a different kind of pain through her.

He had a point. She had no right to keep father from son. "You can take him tonight, if you want," she said, forcing the words out.

Javier looked thrilled. "Really? I can bring the little man home with me?"

"Yes. If Dario would like that."

Of course Dario loved the idea. Which hurt even more.

"Call one of the other moms," he urged once he'd set down Dario, who tore off to fetch all his favorite things for the sleepover. "Alice, or Montserrat. You have the night free now, after all. Go out to dinner and have a glass of wine. Relax. You need it. You deserve it."

Neither of them mentioned April, even though Katrina knew the rawness she was feeling was parallel to April's own. They'd never been so close in experience and so far apart as friends. She couldn't believe how destabilized it made her feel.

"They're moms. They won't be free."

"Call Martin, then. He'd love that."

"Thank you," she snapped, "I can plan my own evening."

In the end, she called Alice first. But Alice was in her own misery, it turned out, with Niles away and Granger battling the flu. She told Katrina that Montserrat was traveling, as well. Katrina felt disappointed enough to cry.

"Let's try for next week, or the next," Alice said. "It's too important, with all that's going on. We need to connect with each other, bond closer, not drift apart."

Katrina heard Granger wailing in the background. "I'm thinking you have to go."

"I do." Alice sounded tearful. "I hope you'll have a better night than I will."

Doubtful, she thought, after the call. She sat alone in the darkening living room without turning on any lights, because that would have required energy and motivation. Huddled there, she felt her aloneness like a fever. She replayed the bad night over and over, her terror and trauma over seeing her front door open with strangers entering, not knowing where Dario was, the ambulance, the heart-stopping fear. The way Javier's predominant mood since then had been not sympathy but anger.

The home phone rang. To her surprise, it was David.

"I don't want to bother you, or push a closeness you don't feel," he said, "but I'm calling just to say hey, are you okay? I heard at the studios about all that's been going on."

"I'm not sure," Katrina admitted, and any residual antipathy toward him evaporated. When you felt fragile and broken and life handed you one person with a sympathetic voice, offering to help, you'd be a fool to not accept.

"Okay, so here's what I wanted to say." David cleared his throat nervously. "I know I don't have kids and I can't know what it feels like to be a parent in crisis. But I will tell you my own very scary experience. Once, I took my sister's five-year-old son to the circus, plying him with ice cream and hot dogs and sodas, thinking I was the coolest uncle in the world. Then I lost him. In a packed 30,000-seat arena. I went through thirty minutes of living hell until we were reunited, and those were the scariest thirty minutes of my life, which is saying a lot. I still have dreams about it."

"Is this a real story?" Katrina asked suspiciously.

"Of course it is! Do you think I'd make up a story so personally humiliating just to grab your attention?"

This made Katrina laugh. A sudden desire seized her, to invite him over, so they could continue the easy conversation over a glass of wine. But before she could act on the admittedly risky impulse, her phone clicked to announce a new caller.

"I should take this incoming call," she said. "I can't see who the caller is but it might be Javier with Dario."

"Very important to take it. Good to talk to you. Call me anytime."

To her intense disappointment, it was Martin. Why, oh why, hadn't she gotten up to check the caller ID box?

"Curiously, I just received a message from Javier," he said.

"What?" she exclaimed. "Why?"

He didn't answer the question. "You are alone tonight! This is the happiest coincidence imaginable. I'm free, and lonely to go out. Join me. I absolutely insist."

She wanted to throttle Javier. He must have called or texted Martin, in some misguided attempt to find her company that he (and, admittedly, Lucinda) deemed "proper" for her. Regret filled her, that she hadn't invited David over, which would have been the perfect bucket of water over Martin's fiery ardor. She was a poor liar; he knew, by her silence, that she had no plans. She sighed in defeat.

"Fine. You can take me out. Give me an hour." She heard his pleased murmur—clearly he'd expected a rejection—and without waiting for a more coherent reply, she hung up. She half hoped he'd get the hint and decide she was too rude and too uninterested in him to pursue. Dully she showered and readied herself. Her doorbell rang an hour later, on the dot.

She opened the door. He stood there, flushed and smiling, in a rumpled business suit. He smelled like cigarettes and booze.

"I've been in meetings all day that culminated in happy hour," he explained as he lumbered in, uncharacteristically loud and clumsy. "And now, it seems happy hour has come to me! Which is to say, being with you. I recognize that I came to you and you haven't come to me, so that statement is not quite accurate. But here we are! I'm so happy!"

He was drunk. More drunk than she'd ever seen him.

"Are you all right?" she asked cautiously.

"I'm wonderful!"

"Shall we go out, then?"

"Or we can stay right here and have our own little party." He swayed and leered at her.

Not a chance.

"I don't think you need a party, Martin," she said in a frostier voice. "I think you need a cup of coffee."

"Party pooper!" He gave a clownish wave of his hand that accidentally smacked his own face. He hardly seemed to notice.

"I'm going to go make us some coffee," she said, walking into the kitchen. She didn't trust this Martin. He looked unhinged, capable of anything. Had this, too, been Javier's prompting?

Don't take no for an answer. Be determined about what you want. Go for it!

"No coffee. Let's dance!" He swayed headlong into the kitchen and took her arm, clumsily waltzing her around. She spun away in annoyance, but he was persistent. Even as she gripped the refrigerator handle to anchor herself, he grabbed her by the waist, pressed into her and began to plant feverish kisses on her neck.

"Stop this, Martin!" She wrenched herself free and strode into the living room. He followed close behind. As they approached the sofa, he tackled her, landing both of them lengthwise on the cushions. He was heavy, and she couldn't breathe. His own breath, meanwhile, washed all over her, the cloying sweet fumes of metabolizing alcohol.

"Let me up," she demanded. "Get off me or I'll scream."

"Then I'll cover your mouth. With mine!"

She managed to roll over, all prepared to scream when he planted his mouth on hers, his thick tongue filling her mouth, making her want to gag.

With all her strength, she pushed him off her and he rolled like a log onto the floor. She sprang up, tore to the bathroom and locked the door so he couldn't get in. Her heart banged so loudly against her chest, she couldn't hear his response, or whether he'd gotten up and was approaching.

She stood there in the dark, her breath slowly returning to normal, and realized he hadn't made a noise. She waited there another two minutes, rigid with mistrust.

No sound.

Finally she crept out, cagey as a feral cat. "Martin?" she called out.

No answer.

She made her way silently into the living room. He was still on the floor, lying face down, unmoving.

Dear God. She'd killed him.

She approached and cautiously poked at him, terrified he would come to life and grab her, and equally terrified he was dead.

A second poke, and suddenly a noisy snore arose.

He was asleep. He'd passed out.

She perched herself out of reach on an armchair and waited, frozen with indecision. Ten minutes passed. He didn't stir and she didn't try to rouse him. After another ten minutes, however, she realized she might be stuck with him all night. She wanted him out of her house. He would not sleep here, she decided. Nor would she sleep until he was gone. But how to get rid of him?

David. He was the one who could help her here. Not Javier, who'd played a big part in this disaster, so glib in his assurance that this was what she needed.

She called David, praying it wasn't too late. It wasn't; he answered on the second ring. "This is insane," she began. "But, can you come over? I have a problem."

"Uh oh. Rodents?"

Which made her laugh hysterically. Eventually she calmed down enough to explain.

Just as she'd hoped, David seemed unfazed. "I can be there in less than fifteen minutes. Will he still be there? More importantly, will you still not want him there?"

"Probably yes, and definitely yes."

"I'll be right over."

He showed up ten minutes later. She was so happy to see him, she had to resist the impulse to fling her arms around his neck. He followed her into the living room and together they assessed the sleeping figure on her floor.

"He's bulky," she said.

"No problem," David said. "I've encountered worse." He squatted alongside Martin, giving Katrina a wicked grin before assuming a high, cheery voice. "Let's go, Martin. The party is moving back to your place! Katrina needs her beauty sleep."

He somehow managed to rouse Martin, who was groggy and unable to walk on his own. It took the two of them to get him outside, down the steps and into David's car, where he promptly fell asleep again. David walked with her back into the living room, where she wrote down Martin's address for him.

"You should sleep better now." He offered her a reassuring smile as he pocketed the note.

She looked at him in abject gratitude.

He was standing there, close enough to touch, and instead of the usual distance she kept between herself and most men in her personal life, an irrational desire came over her, to put her hand on his chest, even slide her arms around his waist and press her body into his. It was just a flash, one more unexpected aspect of the night's surreal nature. A rogue blip, and it was gone, even as something deep within her pelvis continued to quiver, making her knees feel curiously weak.

"Thank you for all your help." To her relief, her voice sounded normal. "Seriously, I can't thank you enough. I owe you."

"You don't owe me anything. I'm glad I could help."

"Not half as glad as I am. I wouldn't have slept a wink, knowing he was in the house."

"Speaking of which, I'd better get to him." He glanced out the window. "The last thing we need is for him to wake and come lumbering back in here, like Frankenstein."

"That's a scary image," she said.

"Agreed." They smiled at each other.

"Okay. Good night," he said.

"Good night. Thank you."

Chapter 21

Kylie

She refused to speak in the various group programs the first few days. Even here, it seemed, she was an outsider. The other kids were older. No one else was a freshman. Some of them drove. A few of them had already paired up and acted like a couple. It was against the rules but they did it anyway and every time Kylie caught them nuzzling each other, it felt like a knife in her heart.

From the outside the building had looked like a hotel, with its circular front drive and big white columns flanking the front doors, but inside it was office-building bland meets hospital. The food served three times a day was generic and awful. If you were depressed enough to get sent here in the first place, how could they think you'd ever consider eating such food?

Everything was awful. Cold linoleum floor. Creaky beds. No privacy. Nothing comforting. One flat pillow and scratchy blanket. No private bathroom. All horrid. Like a prison.

She shared a room—just two beds, two nightstands, two lamps—with a girl who never spoke. Two days later she was gone. A day after that, a new girl appeared in her room. She wanted to talk and Kylie didn't.

"You can't leave until you open up, Kylie," the counselors told her.

"I don't want to talk. There's nothing to 'discover.' Life sucks, period. I hate high school and I hate being a teenager. Is there anything I can say to change that?"

"No," her assigned counselor admitted.

Her parents and sometimes Jen came during evening visiting hours, and her dad dropped by during the lunchtime hour. The team had told her parents they wanted Kylie to stay for seven to ten days to participate in their specialized therapy, that it would greatly help her. They were wrong. Leafing irritably through the binder she'd been given, Kylie couldn't bear how simplistic it all was.

Thoughts are things that most of us don't think about, and when we feel bad we don't realize it's because of the thought.

Or: *sometimes we wonder why we're feeling blue, but we should know that it's normal to feel blue sometimes.*

Seriously? she wanted to ask. *People are this oblivious?*

She didn't belong here. This place was just making her more depressed.

"I need to go home," she told them. "I'm feeling worse with each day here."

"You need to open up and talk first, Kylie," they kept saying.

On the fifth day, over lunchtime visiting hours, the best and the worst thing happened. David showed up. He'd brought a big pizza. "Do you want this?" he asked. "Your call. The pizza, or me, or neither, or both. Because I want to talk, but maybe you don't want to see me. Or maybe it will just make you feel worse."

She wasn't sure. Wild elation battled with unspeakable sorrow. She loved him so much it hurt. And all he could offer her was pizza. Worse, she saw pity in his eyes. He probably knew she was in love with him, and she definitely knew he was in love with Katrina.

But she was starving, having ignored the crappy lunch on offer.

And a David who wasn't her beloved was still better than a world without him.

"Stay," she told him. "I'll take both."

"I'm glad."

As they munched their way through a slice each, the other kids noticed him. The girls looked both impressed and sympathetic. They'd likely taken one look at Kylie's sad face and guessed what was going on. The guys came up and asked if they could have a slice of the pizza, and David said sure, go ahead, and they grinned and joked with David while munching on their slice. Even here, David could make friends effortlessly.

He seemed nervous around her, too jokey. She was a great detector of bullshit and saw clearly that he was faking his joviality. It dawned on her that he might be here out of a sense of obligation.

"Did my mom tell you to come visit me?" she challenged.

Her question surprised him. "No! I made that decision on my own." He hesitated. "But I did call and ask her opinion on visiting you before I came."

It was like the time he'd shown up at the high school, and she learned he'd discussed it with her mom. It ruined the good feeling. It made her hate her mom just then.

She'd blown it. Everything. It had seemed like such a great idea that night, an "I'll show them" gesture, fueled by the brandy, and she couldn't believe how horribly it had backfired. Things were way, way worse now. And to see David regarding her with a wariness behind his smile—this was the worst.

He was trying, at least. "Tell me something interesting," he proposed in that newly fake way.

She wasn't about to take fake bait. "I guess I'm drawing a blank today."

"Wrong place to go pick up new, funny jokes, huh?" A

mischievous glimmer appeared in his eyes, but faded when she didn't even crack a smile.

In truth, some of the kids could be wildly funny and make everyone (else) laugh. It wasn't a funeral home, in the end. Emotions, high and low, swirled around the rooms all the time. But in response to David's comment, she merely shrugged.

He looked around the big room with its bookshelves, its musical instruments in the corner—two guitars and a ukulele—its armchairs, couches and bean bags. "How long do they plan to keep you here?"

"Up to ten days. They want me to participate more first."

"Well, once you've set your mind to it, I'm sure you'll do great here," he said, which was so false and un-David-like, she emitted a little gasp and dropped her second pizza slice.

"What do you want me to say?" he protested. "You're not answering my questions anyway. I feel like we're good enough friends that I can be honest with you here."

"Then be honest! Don't give me some disingenuous shit about 'You're going to do great.' I can get that from the counselors. You? I thought you'd really have something special to say. But you don't. In the end, you're just like all the others."

The disappointment of it all was like a boulder crashing on top of her, like in the old Road Runner cartoons, where the coyote stands there dumb and oblivious one second, and is crushed the next.

David rose, his expression cold.

This was it. She was losing him now, too.

She would lose him forever if he walked out that door. Panic swept over her at the thought. She quickly reconfigured her strategy. "Fine, I'll answer. In fact, I'll ask *you* a question. An important one." She felt a dizzying sense of relief when he sat back down.

"Ask away," he said, but he looked wary.

"What would you do in my situation? If everything they plan to 'teach' in the group therapy is so simplistic, you just want to retch, but instead you have to participate?"

The wariness disappeared. He smiled at her. "All right. Here's how you should play it. Act like you're an anthropologist, not there to learn so much as observe how the others are learning. Or imagine yourself deaf, and you can only rely on body language and reading lips."

He tossed out further ideas, none of which she retained, because she was so shaken with relief that she'd managed to save the train that was their friendship from derailing. She gave small nods from time to time as he spoke, something about finding genuine people in her life, and taking her pain and using it to make art, or something like that. The words went in one ear and out the next, as she fixed her gaze on the returning warmth in his eyes.

He left ten minutes later, and even though she couldn't remember his advice, beyond acting like an anthropologist, the memory of his presence was like a trail of bread crumbs. Showing her how to get back to where she'd been, where they'd been. How to readjust to a greyer reality while maybe, just maybe, keeping his friendship.

It was up to her, she realized.

To get out of here was up to her.

That afternoon she agreed to participate in group. If she didn't, they would let her rot here, eating their terrible food and sleeping on their terrible bed.

First in group came "check in" time. Participation was not optional. She listened to the four people before her, dreading her turn more and more.

Silence. Then ten pairs of eyes fixated on her. "Kylie?" the therapist called out.

She studied the floor. "I'm Kylie. I live in San Francisco and I'm a freshman. I don't do sports and I don't play a musical instrument. I don't have a big hobby. Well. Music. But not … the right kind for someone my age." This was excruciating. She wanted to stop, but judging by the therapist's silence, she knew, miserably, that she had to say more.

The silence built and so did the tension inside her, until all at once, like verbal vomit, everything spewed out.

"I'm weird. I don't fit in. Nobody understands. I just want to fit in and I can't. The rest of my family is beautiful or brilliant or accomplished, or actually they're all three at once, and then there's funny little me. I don't look the right size, and I say the wrong words—I guess it's some great sin to have a polysyllabic vocabulary when you're a kid—and I'm just … desperate." Tears spilled out faster than she could blink them away. Someone reached for the Kleenex box in the center and thrust it at her. She pulled out tissues, one, two, three of them, and bunched them in her hand. "I feel all this stuff inside, what's beautiful, what's magical, what makes my heart pound, and somehow it's seen as all wrong, all weird."

Nobody said anything and for that she was grateful, because if the facilitator had asked, in that sanctimonious tone, what "weird" meant to her, or how all this made her feel, Kylie would have snarled and bared her teeth like an animal, and maybe done more, except that would likely keep her stuck in this prison-like place even longer and she had no intention of giving them any opportunity to keep her here longer.

And David. Beautiful, adored, unreachable David. The thought of him made her double over with pain, folding her arms around herself. "They think fourteen is too young to find true love and it's not, and it hurts, and I want to die because there's not a chance with him and me."

Silence greeted her words. It almost didn't matter to her what the others thought, or what their expressions were. She hadn't planned to say any of this.

She lifted her eyes. Time to face the firing squad.

Everyone was studying their hands like they didn't know what to say.

Finally a girl spoke. "You just told my story."

"Mine too," another said.

The relief of having unburdened it all was staggering. So was the relief of these two girls meeting Kylie's eyes, their own filling with tears. One of them had shorn hair and glasses, and the other was a beautiful but aggressively unfriendly girl who now looked at Kylie with pure gratitude, as if she'd been drowning and Kylie had just thrown her a life raft.

"Me too," a third girl said, but then Kylie realized it was a guy dressed like a girl, with a bow in their hair. The agony in their eyes when they met hers made her heart contract and feel like they were each seeing each other, deep inside. She began to sniffle again, but the other two girls were crying audibly, so she took a final tissue for herself before passing the box along to the other side of the circle. No one spoke anymore but instead sniffled and motioned for the Kleenex box, and it almost became one of those kids' party games, like Hot Potato, with that ticking thing you'd toss from person to person and whoever was holding it when it went off was the loser and oh, how Kylie had hated the stress of that game.

You'd think the Kleenex box was down to its last tissues, by the way they were all clamoring for one, now laughing about it, and it was exactly like Hot Potato, only the Kleenex box never went off. It just kept dispensing tissue after tissue. Kylie glanced at the facilitator, expecting to see annoyance that they were wasting Kleenex just for fun, but the woman had the same carefully neutral expression she'd had the whole session. Except that, as Kylie watched, the corners of her mouth turned up, just a bit, and she gave a little nod, and looked down at her clipboard, making a check or a dash or a three-word comment that Kylie could only guess at.

Kylie Garvey. Interesting.

Chapter 22

Katrina

There was something increasingly unhinged about Edwin's rehearsals of late. He continued to change the choreography in spite of the ever-closer approach of the gala, which left Katrina lying awake at night, rigid with anxiety. With each day, the fear of failure grew in her. She went to Anders' office late one afternoon to voice her concern, but Anders brushed aside her words. Javier was there, too, listening in. Anders told her he had confidence in her abilities to roll with the punches, as well as any changes, and Javier nodded his agreement.

She tried to tell them this wasn't about her, that it was about Edwin. Neither wanted to hear this. "Do your job," Anders said with a smile, except there was an edge in his voice, too.

She looked from one set face to the other.

There was no room for dissent here.

"All right," she said dully, mechanically—because what else *could* she tell her boss?—and took her leave.

And sure enough, the next day, Edwin walked into rehearsal (thirty minutes late, again) and announced, "I hate it all. We're starting from scratch again. It's not about love, or even passion. It's about war. Aggression and war."

The choreography he proposed surpassed all the others in its awfulness. Edwin had decided that no, Jimmy hadn't been killed after all, that he'd returned, and now despised his beloved for her own survival. He was to walk with a limp, but with his dignity fully intact. Katrina, meanwhile, was to throw herself at her former beloved, who rejected her because the bad guy had had his way with her, and now she was sullied and broken. Even the two males who, in the last version had lent her their support, were now to turn their backs to her. Literally. She was to fling herself onto their backs, one after the other, and slither down as they began to walk. Once on the ground, she was to cling to one ankle, yanked along for four counts before the male stopped, legs out, arms folded, a soldier's repose.

They ran it. It was uncomfortable on so many levels. Her elbows and knees stung. Her pride stung. She felt sick with shame, as if she herself had done the shameful thing (because apparently being raped meant you were shameful). Once they finished, she wanted nothing more than to run out of the studio and take a long hot shower.

He had them run it again. It made her feel worse. Degraded. Violated.

You've sold yourself, the little girl inside her cried.

Shut the fuck up, she thought viciously, and now she turned against the voice, suffocating it and its unwelcome advice, squeezing her fists as if she were squeezing the life from the little girl who didn't understand how things were in the real world.

"Brilliant," Edwin breathed from his place in front. "Just brilliant."

Finally she'd pleased him, but at what price? As her rage-fueled thoughts subsided, the darkest of despairs took their place. What was she going to do? She couldn't take Edwin's mercurial nature much longer, his irrational anger against tiny issues that shouldn't have mattered. And the way all the males in the cast were trying to ignore his increasingly loud outbursts. They still admired and sought to please him. Only Jimmy reached out to her, trying to shield her from some of Edwin's wrath—which never worked because Edwin told him to stop and Edwin was the boss, so all Jimmy could do in the end was squeeze her hand, hug her during breaks and murmur that she was a champion.

Which left one person who'd be both sympathetic and proactive about Katrina's plight. But her easy connection with April had been destroyed. She herself had killed it, just like she'd killed her inner Katja.

She had to try.

She sent April a text, asking her if they could meet at their old spot, a window alcove on the top floor at the end of a little-used hallway. A lifetime ago, their first year with the WCBT, April had found Katrina huddled and crying there one day, so overwhelmed and scared of failing. It became their special nook, the perfect spot for a private chat, to hash out Katrina's worries and challenges together.

Can meet you there ten minutes before afternoon rehearsals start, April texted back.

Thank you, Katrina replied. *See you then.*

Right on time, April was there. It was like old times, and yet nothing like old times. All that had happened between them recently hung heavily in the air. Katrina thought of her "You should have known your daughter was unstable!" outburst and felt a desperate wish to delete it all.

She had to address that first. It was too big to ignore.

"How is Kylie doing?" she asked.

"Russell's bringing her home today," April replied. "She's very happy about that. But we'll all have to be super vigilant for a while."

She saw the shadows under April's eyes, the new gauntness in her face. "I'm so sorry," Katrina began. "For my harsh words at a bad time. That was so wrong of me."

"Thank you." April sounded all business. "But I don't imagine you arranged for this meeting in order to say just that. What is it? What's the problem?"

April's cool, assessing manner helped Katrina focus on the problem at hand.

"I'm scared about Edwin and his ballet." Katrina clenched and unclenched the sweater knotted around her waist. "I'm genuinely afraid it's going to go bad."

"He's made it clear that I'm not welcome in the studio when he's working with you. I'm sorry, but I can't step out of my jurisdiction here. Curtis is the ballet master in charge."

"Here's the thing," Katrina said. "Edwin has become good friends with Curtis. In some ways, it's almost like he did it to have a cover, so he can dismiss Curtis with a friendly wave and tell him he's not needed. Curtis doesn't want to be annoying, so he leaves."

April's cool expression softened into sorrow. "That would be awful. Curtis is a good guy. You'd think the most senior ballet master would have seen all the tricks."

"I don't know what to do. Anders and Javier told me to just do my job. Meaning, to shut up and take it."

"Talk to Curtis. That's all I can offer you. I can't put my own job on the line here."

The decisiveness in April's tone, the lack of warmth and love, was like a blow to Katrina.

April turned to leave.

"April." The word came out as a gasp. Katrina lunged forward and clutched April's hand. "Help me. Please. Curtis won't get it. I'm scared and I don't have anyone else to turn to."

April looked down at their connected hands and emitted a little sigh. Katrina couldn't tell if it was one of defeat or sympathy.

"I can't make any promises." She gave Katrina's hand a squeeze.

"But I'll try." When Katrina released her grip, April turned and walked away without a backward glance.

The following afternoon, rehearsal with Edwin was, if possible, even worse, with him flinging new choreography at them and angry when they didn't instantly intuit his intention.

"I don't want you to be strong," he shouted at Katrina, banging the floor with the folding chair for emphasis. "You are weak and rely on them and none of these five men are your ally."

Jimmy and the four ensemble males remained silent, gazes downward.

A thought sprang up, vivid and subversive, swallowing her whole. *I don't think I can do this ballet.*

This was the end. She felt it in her bones. She'd reached the breaking point.

Even the spirited little girl was gone. Katrina had killed her.

The loss of little Katja felt so enormous right then, as if she'd actually killed something, like a beloved longtime pet, and she hadn't known how big a part it had played in her life, her happiness and well-being, until it was gone.

Oh, the sorrow. The loss. The irretrievable loss.

And right then, to her relief—a relief so great that she wanted to weep—April appeared at the doorway. Katrina saw her expression turn stony, her hands balled into fists as Edwin demonstrated what he wanted more of (which was violence toward her) and had Katrina and the males try again.

She did the best her deadened mind would allow. The chassé passage, the piqué arabesque, trying to lean on one male after the next, only to be rebuffed. Next, a pas de chat that crashed to the ground. Her as a broken human, trying to recover, only to be figuratively stomped on by the males and their entre-chat quatre jumps.

Thirty-two counts in, Edwin screamed "NO!" and lifted the folding chair overhead. He turned to face the group and at the last moment, as if catching sight of April, he hurled the chair not at them, but just off to the side.

The moment seemed to freeze time. Katrina took in the rage of his wild, bloodshot, dilated eyes, amid the understanding that he'd wanted to physically hurt her. She'd never felt so afraid of a choreographer before.

April's angry voice broke the spell. "I'm sorry, Edwin, but this is absolutely unacceptable."

He swung to face her. "You keep out of this," he screamed. "I'm the choreographer."

April rose to her tallest height and walked right up to him, nose to nose. "And I am the ballet master and these are my dancers and I saw the way you almost threw that chair at them, and that is inexcusable."

"You … you—" he began, sputtering, but April was louder, and angrier.

"You're a mean-spirited, small-minded person. And the way you're treating the cast's lone female is despicable. Don't say it's your muse. You're a misogynist through and through, and this ballet"— she stabbed a finger in the direction of the dancers, still cowed and shaken—"is cheap, obvious, artless, over-the-top propaganda about how women are weak and men rule the world."

He stared at her, eyes bulging. "You two," he bellowed, gesturing first to April and then Katrina, "do not belong here if you can't comply with my vision."

"No. It's you who do not belong here," April shouted back. "We have standards of what is acceptable, and you have exceeded them."

"That you should speak to me in this way? With my credits in theater and film? Commissions lined up as far as the eye can see, and

I deigned to take this on, out of the kindness of my heart. If this is the thanks I get from this company, I want nothing of it."

"Then go! Leave! Allow me to escort you out. Let's find Anders together, shall we?"

"I'm leaving," he shouted. "Don't think I'll come back, either."

"Good. We don't need your darkness in our midst."

"You'll regret this!"

"I promise you I will not."

He snapped for his assistant to *hurry, hurry, goddammit,* and the two made a noisy, clumsy exit, the assistant dropping things while Edwin shouted. Katrina's limbs shook so badly, she sank to the ground, drew her knees up and roped her arms around them like a child.

It had never ended so poorly before, not in twenty-one years as a professional. What was going to happen next? Were they out of the gala for good? Would she and April be out of a job?

It didn't matter, in the end. All that mattered was the deep, pervading comfort filling her from the inside, as she watched Edwin Hess storm out of the room and out of her life.

Chapter 23

April

The gathering in Anders' office was toxic beyond measure. All the males—which was to say all the others in the room—were furious with April. Anders was angry with her for several reasons, not least of which were dashed hopes for an exciting commission to promote. Gil from development was livid for the same reason. He stood there, arms folded, glowering at her. April met his gaze, lifted her chin and slowly, deliberately folded her arms in the same way.

Ben, at least, looked more troubled than angry. With reason: he wanted to stay in Rebecca's good graces, and Rebecca hated Edwin as much as April did.

"What do we even know about the reason Edwin had this commission time open?" April asked the others. "Did anyone ever follow up?"

"What are you insinuating?" Gil asked.

"I'm saying that maybe this isn't a lone incident."

Gil paled. "You are *so* out of line in saying that."

"Excuse me? I am a ballet master and you were not there to observe what I did. He's been acting increasingly unstable. I'm hard pressed to believe a month in San Francisco caused it."

"Curtis?" Gil's gaze swung his way. "Did you see this behavior? *Did* you?"

"Not so much," Curtis said. "But … I could have missed it." He looked shamefaced, which told April he knew he'd been shirking his job and placing too much trust in Edwin.

Before Gil could respond, Lucinda called. Anders put her on speaker for all to hear.

"What the *hell* is going on? I want answers! I want them immediately. Someone better get over to my office *now*."

"You'll have them," Anders snapped. "We're talking here first."

After disconnecting, he glared at April. "You be the one to tell her. Go." He made shooing motions with his hands, as if she were a cockroach that had ambled into a sitting room during a tea party.

"I'll be glad to do that." She stalked out.

The discussion with Lucinda went smoother. Lucinda agreed that if Katrina had perceived herself in harm's way, that was all that mattered. Their conversation was downright soothing, after the firing squad in Anders' office.

"There's something I can't put a finger to," April said. "It was beyond his being an artist with a big ego. There was something not right about the way he was acting, even thinking. If only you or Anders could have seen it, you'd have no concerns that I'd done the right thing."

"Something not right, like what?"

"Unhinged. Like he was on amphetamines or something. Or maybe not drugs, but some huge issue he's hiding, that's affecting his behavior. And, if we're seeing it, maybe it's a personal problem that's shown up elsewhere, too."

Lucinda mulled over April's words. "If there is a problem, it's flying under the radar. He's booked well into the next two years with commissions."

"The English Ballet Theatre," April pressed. "They're saying nothing is amiss?"

"Their official word is that he's artist-in-residence there, and that they're proud of the exciting new works he's brought the EBT." She chewed her pen thoughtfully, then set it down. "Enough said. What's done is done. What I need to know is how we plan to spin this?"

April exhaled, sounding tired and defeated even to her own ears. "I need to talk to Anders more. We'll have better answers for you tomorrow."

"All right. Keep me in the loop." She paused. "How are things, otherwise? At home? Kylie, I mean."

This surprised April. Then again, she'd been surprised a lot lately. Those she was sure would have reached out, hadn't. Others, whom she'd perceived as brusque or unsympathetic to domestic affairs, did.

"Thanks for asking." She offered Lucinda a wan smile. "We're making our way through things."

Lucinda's piercing gaze hadn't dropped. That was another thing. People had been averting April's eyes since learning about Kylie's hospitalization, on which she hadn't elaborated. She'd never before fully appreciated the strength, the power of conviction Lucinda's eyes projected. She sensed very little shocked Lucinda or made her feel insecure. Right then, April needed someone like her.

Lucinda waited another moment before speaking. "I was hospitalized when I was fifteen. And again the following year. First anorexia, then suicidal thoughts. It was discreetly referred to, back then, as 'anxious feelings,' when it had to be discussed. Which was, basically, never. You'd be amazed how these things got covered up, back then. Not even my grandparents were told. You'd have thought I'd committed a crime and done time in juvenile hall."

She eyed April steadily. "These aren't those kinds of times anymore."

April drew an unsteady breath. "Kylie was held on a 5150 as a suicide risk. She tried to hurt herself at Katrina's house while babysitting." She had to force the words out. Her only comfort was that saying it didn't make her burst into tears anymore.

"Has she stabilized?"

"We think so. We hope so. Only time will tell."

Lucinda nodded thoughtfully. "You probably can't imagine right now that she won't always seem so fragile. I know I didn't believe, back then, that my situation, my thoughts, could ever change. But, of course they changed. *I* changed. We're wired for survival, in the end. And teens are wired for high drama, continual instability and irrational thinking. As a family, you just ride the storm until it all settles down."

Lucinda's comforting words played over in April's head as she returned to Anders' office, only to discover the meeting had broken up. His personal assistant, just departing, informed her that he was still on property. April thanked her and sank into a chair, where she texted him. They had unfinished business, after all.

He didn't reply.

She called and left a voice message. She re-sent the text with an "urgent" in caps added.

He didn't reply.

Anger stirred in her. They'd known each other for almost twenty-five years, sharing highs and lows, achievements and near disasters. She deserved better than this. She rose from the chair and went down two levels to the administrators' break room. Pulling a Coke Zero from the refrigerator, she felt the anger in her increase to a slow boil.

She sent him another text. *We need to talk.*

He replied, finally. *No time.*

Soda in hand, she headed back upstairs, where she spied him striding to his office. He didn't see her; she'd used the stairwell and was behind him. She re-texted her entreaty and heard the little ping as his phone received the text. She saw him look at it and shake his head. Unaware that April was watching, he texted back, not even noticing the muffled ping of her own phone receiving the text. She read it.

Am in a meeting. No time for you.

She responded, fingers moving busily. *I know you're not in a meeting. Turn around.*

He turned around. Under any other circumstance, it would have been hilarious. But he didn't laugh, or even smile. Neither did April. When he turned and strode into his office, she followed him in and claimed the seat he wasn't inviting her to take.

"We aren't done talking about the problem Hess was causing," she said.

"Frankly, I don't see this current problem as one originating with Edwin."

She tried to keep her patience. "Trouble was brewing. Really dangerous, wait-till-the-dancers'-union-hears-about-this kind of trouble."

"There is always drama brewing in a company at any given moment. You chose to turn personal bias into very harmful action."

There went the patience.

"Stop this!" April shot to her feet, slapping her hands down on his desk. He recoiled in surprise. "Shame on you for trying to keep Edwin Hess happy at the cost of your dancers' well-being!"

"I am doing no such thing!" He echoed her furious tone.

"By not doing anything, you are."

"Has it escaped your notice that we have a gala in three weeks? A Hess commission was our goddamned meal ticket. And now we've spent all that money and we chased away the golden goose."

A solution came to April. A perfect one. "Sabine can help you here, and you know it."

"What the hell are you talking about?"

"You rejected Sabine's endorsement, her offer to have Leila Bertrand set a short ballet on the dancers. She gave Leila high marks and you ignored the offer. And now it's a chance, a way for the company to stand out. Discovering a major new talent. So don't tell me you have no options. Not to mention at a tenth of the price."

"Her price is low for a reason. Her work is unknown in North America."

"All the more reason we'll benefit when she delivers a winning commission."

"That would be 'if,' and not 'when.'"

"She's got Sabine's endorsement—what higher praise can you want?"

"Sabine is my ex-wife. That should make it clear that we don't see eye to eye."

"You and I both know there's more that binds you to Sabine than separates you."

"We need a solution ASAP. Action tomorrow. Brussels is too far away."

"Leila is in New York."

"How do you know so much about Leila and her whereabouts?"

April hesitated. "Because, well, Rebecca keeps me in the loop about her."

Enraged, he threw his arms up theatrically. His office chair squeaked in protest as the motion sent him backward. "Again, trouble with Rebecca Lindgren at the center. Will she never keep herself in line and simply, quietly, effectively do her damned job? What is it about some of you, being this thorn in my side?"

"What you mean to say is, why won't we female subordinates quietly behave and do our jobs demurely and without a ruffle of any feathers?"

"Oh, stop. You make it sound worse than it is."

"No, *you* make it sound worse than it is. I think we're going to find at some point that Edwin is in hot water somewhere, and that's why he was free. And that we will appreciate that we cut ties with him. We will appreciate that we've brought in a seasoned female choreographer to replace him. Mark my word. We will be remembered for all this, and in a good way."

He eyed her irritably. "You're pinning your hopes on some fantastical scenario. Stop spinning it like it's all good, and that I should go thanking you and Rebecca."

"You forgot Sabine."

He flung his arms up again, his eyes following as if in a *why me, God?* plea.

This time, April couldn't help but laugh. She knew capitulation when she saw it. "Shall we fly her out? Leila, I mean."

His lips were pinched together so tightly, they'd turned white.

She tried to soften her tone. "Note that I am respectfully asking your permission."

"No you aren't. You're stating what you plan to do, with a little 'shall we?' in there to make it sound like it's a consensus."

"There's no harm in flying her out and you know it. You've done the same with lesser choreographers."

He studied her for a long moment, his expression stormy. April summoned her inner-Lucinda and calmly stared him down. Finally he gave a sigh of defeat.

"I'll call her. If, and only if, she can fly out and start tomorrow, I'll let her give it a try."

Chapter 24

Katrina

Katrina's phone rang early on Friday morning, but she was already awake, queasy with anticipation over her fate in the aftermath of The Great Edwin Hess Departure.

It was April. "It's a done deal," she told Katrina. "We've got Leila Bertrand flying in as we speak. Rebecca will pick her up at the airport, get her to the studios for a lunch meeting with Anders and myself. There'll be a 2:00PM audition for new ensemble dancers, and you should plan to be there with Jimmy, at the main studio, an hour later."

"Wow. Okay." She felt dizzy with the speed of the change. "That's great."

"It is. No word from Hess, or lawyers or spokespersons. Nothing on social media, even. I thought he'd shout it out to the world, this 'terrible injustice.'" Her last words dripped with sarcasm. "How are you doing today?"

"Tired. Relieved. Worried but hopeful. You?"

"Energized. Of course I'm in the doghouse with pretty much all the males, but that's their problem, not mine. Oh, and guess what? When Leila and Anders and I talked last night to confirm things, she told him she's planning on the Ravel Violin Sonata for the music." She paused expectantly.

"Which means?" Katrina asked, mystified.

"Know of any concert soloists whose rarified skills might be used for this? A hint—there are only two musicians, a pianist and a violinist. Leila's already got a world-class pianist picked out."

"Wait. Montserrat?!"

"Precisely. Anders is speaking to her. He told me to stay out of the negotiations. He's furious with me."

"We haven't lost our jobs?"

"Oh, no. Definitely not." April sounded confident, but the hesitation between the two sentences made Katrina's blood run cold.

Oh, God. What had they done?

Then again, had there been a choice?

"What if Leila can't produce a winner?" Katrina quavered.

"Then we're screwed. At least I am."

"No. If you go down, we both go down."

"Don't say that."

"I'm serious. You saved me."

"You're sweet," April said. "But no one needs to go down here. I've only talked with Leila by phone, but she sounds smart, calm and focused. Everything Edwin Hess wasn't. It'll work. We'll make it work."

From behind, as Katrina entered the studio that afternoon, Leila Bertrand looked like any other dancer-turned-choreographer in her late 40's, casually dressed in black leggings and a tee shirt. She was talking to April and Rebecca. But when she swung around to face Katrina, there was an instant familiarity to her dark eyes and lashes, her broad, agreeable smile.

She was a dead ringer for Nabila, right down to the same dusting of light freckles across the bridge of her nose. For a psychedelic moment, Katrina felt as if she'd stepped back in time.

Cairo.

April made the introductions. Katrina and Leila shook hands. Leila paused afterward, as if sensing Katrina's confusion.

"Are you Egyptian?" Katrina blurted out. Only not in English, and, perhaps more surprisingly, not in French, which she knew they both spoke fluently. She'd spoken in Arabic.

Leila looked astonished. "How could you …? Wait. Did you just speak in Arabic?"

Katrina felt dizzy. "Did I? I'm no longer sure."

"You did," Leila said, and switched to Arabic. "You spoke Arabic in the dialect of Egypt. How is this possible?"

April and Rebecca gaped at them in shock.

"I lived there," Katrina replied in Arabic. "In Cairo. It was another life. A—how do you say?" She shut her eyes and the language's music flowed right back into her mind. "A dream. That is how it felt. That is how this feels now. It is so long ago, speaking Arabic." She opened her eyes and switched to English. "I don't know where that came from." Her voice sounded like someone else's echoing around in her head.

"You called it correctly," Leila said. "My mother is Egyptian and my father is Belgian. I was born in Alexandria and lived there as a kid. But we moved to Brussels when I was seven, so my childhood memories are dim."

"I lived there when I was eight," Katrina said. "My memories are dim, as well."

Except they weren't. That dream, from weeks ago, spilling out the memories again. Katrina stood there, disoriented, as Leila excused herself to address the group of dancers who'd been auditioning for a place in the ballet's ensemble. She thanked everyone before dismissing the ones who hadn't been chosen. Eight of them left glumly as the four remaining dancers, including Rebecca's sister,

Dena, gleefully high-fived each other over their 11th hour fortune.

Leila turned back around. "April, your violinist confirmed with Anders and she's a go. She and I will meet tomorrow afternoon, go over things, and she'll join us for rehearsals next week."

"Excellent." April smiled.

Jimmy burst into the studio. "Am I on time? I really wanted to be here early but I got stuck in the last rehearsal. But here I am! Hello, ma'am, I'm Jimmy," he called out to Leila. He strode right up to her and vigorously shook her hand. "Welcome to America!"

"She's been in New York the past month, cowboy," Rebecca teased.

Jimmy grinned over at Rebecca but didn't stop pumping Leila's hand. "Then welcome to the West Coast Ballet Theatre, ma'am! We're glad you're here."

It was, in the end, surprisingly uncomplicated to learn much of a two-movement ballet in the course of three hours. All you needed was a confident, seasoned choreographer—one without an oversized ego—two lead dancers who'd been through everything and could now handle anything, and a motivated ensemble of four dancers, all happy to have been given this opportunity. Leila presented, and they implemented.

Her choreography was contemporary and original, but still grounded in the classical ballet idiom. Everything was clean and concise. There was a story, a flirtatious interlude. The entire second movement was witty and elegant, with a pleasing yet edgy dissonance in the music.

The rehearsal time flew. Jimmy lifted, responded, supported, smiling and eager for each new step. Dena and the other three ensemble dancers bounded through each new move.

Only one snag arose for Katrina, during a section that felt tense and stilted, but which Leila told Katrina they could work on the next day. "Maybe meet forty-five minutes before the others?" Leila asked, and she agreed.

"I'm pleased," Leila said to all of them at the end of the rehearsal. "Let's put in a solid three hours tomorrow—sorry to hold you for so long on a Saturday, but it can't be helped—and I've a hunch we'll be in great shape."

On Saturday morning, Leila and Katrina got right down to business, just the two of them, working in starts and stops. "There," Leila said, after about twenty minutes. "That movement, right there. You're too controlled. It's energetic and tense, but the wrong kind of tension."

The *you're too controlled* assessment filled Katrina with unease, reminiscent as it was of Edwin and the way he'd bait her. Even the mere thought of him seemed to re-introduce his bad energy into the room.

Leila peered closer at her. "Everything okay?"

"Definitely," Katrina said.

"Because I feel like you threw up a huge defensive wall just now, and I don't want to pry, but if there's any way to clear the air, I'd feel better."

Leila stood there, open and expectant, waiting for an answer. Katrina picked through the debris of her memory and plucked out enough details to keep the explanation bearable. "Edwin accused me of being aloof, and that it was a problem for him. And then he started prying, using inappropriate language and graphic suggestions. He did it to provoke a reaction, he told me. Break through my controlled persona so I could 'access my creativity.' It's hard to explain, in retrospect, how threatening it felt."

She shook her head, as if that could shake the memory of him out of her mind.

"I get it," Leila said. "He's not a nice human being. I hate saying that about a fellow choreographer, but that's becoming his reputation."

"He was nice to the guys in our cast, and the males in charge. All the males, in fact. They still think he's the greatest. Anders refused to believe there was a real problem brewing."

"That kind of gender favoritism—and harassment—is his reputation, too." Leila hesitated. "I'm going tell you something that's public knowledge, so it's not like I'm perpetuating false gossip. There's a female Paris Opera Ballet dancer who's filed multiple complaints, and finally received a protective order against him. He's prohibited from contacting her or physically approaching her. Except he contacts her anyway. It's a mess."

Katrina knew who the dancer was, instantly. "Sophie Bocuse?"

Leila's eyes widened. "Wait. You knew, then?"

"No." She felt sick. "But he talked about her, to me. It always seemed like a kind of trigger. Always, after talking about her, or maybe even talking *to* her, he'd show up at rehearsal in a dark mood and say he was making changes. Every time, the new steps, or their intent, would be darker, more violent. Not toward the five male dancers. Toward me."

Something akin to panic enclosed her like a vise grip. She hadn't intended to ever share anything about how low and sleazy and personal Edwin had gotten, the way it had felt like the psychological equivalent of sexual assault.

She fell silent and fixed her gaze on the floor.

"Keep talking," Leila said.

She shook her head. She was afraid saying anything more would make her puke.

"Katrina. Talk to me."

She looked up reluctantly.

Leila's eyes were filled with concern. "You might be thinking if you can avoid that thing that's making you feel this way, you'll be safer and your dancing will be more secure. But my perspective is that if you keep avoiding it, that won't breed security. Instead, it's the opposite. It has power. He left behind a dark power that you're still under the influence of."

She had a point. Katrina wondered if Leila had been a therapist in a past life.

"Please," Leila said more softly.

"All right."

Leila gestured to the folding chairs nearby, and they sat.

Katrina looked down, wanting to be anywhere but there. "It's like he decided to stage an assault on me—with words. It was the way he'd say things, like, 'I'll bet the men really get hot over you.'" She shut her eyes, as if somehow that could make her invisible. "And worse, like, 'when did you first allow a male to slip his hands down your pants?' I think he wanted to arouse me, not sexually but fearfully. It's like it aroused him to see fear in me."

Leila sucked in a deep breath. "That despicable man."

Now that she'd opened up, it all came rushing out. "He made a pass at me at Murphy's, this bar we'd all gone to instead of rehearsing. When I reacted, he turned it all around, insinuating that *I'd* been the one to do something inappropriate. When he got darker—and now that I know about Sophie Bocuse, I realize how much a part that played—the way he took it out on me was just terrible. And effective."

On and on she continued, with words that came from her gut, from that scared little inner-Katja she'd killed, who all along had been trying to tell her what had turned out to be the truth.

She started crying in a raw, wracked way, wrapping her arms around herself. "He killed something in me. No, worse. He pushed me until I was the one to kill it. I killed the little girl inside me. The fiercer Katrina, who knew what was best for me. I choked the life out of her."

Leila handed her Kleenexes, which Katrina used to dab at her eyes, but the tears wouldn't stop coming. Leila remained silent now, calm, like they had all the time in the world.

Neither of them spoke. Finally the tears, the agonized sorrow, began to recede. Even the thought of Edwin wasn't so devastating, now that she'd blurted out every bad thing to Leila.

Leila reached over and pulled from her bag an unopened bottle of mineral water. Katrina accepted it with gratitude and glugged half of it down in one breath. Afterward she regarded the bottle, feeling spent but somehow lighter. "I would have never said all of that to anyone else."

"Thank you." Leila smiled. "I know what it must have cost you. Am I a bully for forcing it out of you?"

Katrina considered this. "No. Hess was a bully. You're just … horribly pushy."

They both laughed.

"One last thing and then we can drop all of this," Leila said. "I want you to know. The little girl isn't dead. She's just waiting till she feels safe to come out again."

Voices in the hallway signaled the early arrival of other dancers. Katrina dabbed hastily at her face.

Leila handed her a fresh Kleenex. "I realize you probably don't trust me anymore, but do you want to grab dinner together some night? Just easy chatting, like our Cairo memories."

Two dancers came through the doorway, engrossed in their own conversation.

"That would be nice," Katrina admitted. "In fact, Javier, my son's father, has got Dario today and tonight, so I'm free."

"Perfect. I'm free tonight too. I've been told there's a good little Egyptian restaurant here, nothing fancy, but I think that would be perfect."

"Do they have … koshari?"

Leila, hearing the hope in her voice, smiled. "I'm certain they do.

Could you imagine any restaurant in Egypt without koshari?"

Katrina laughed in delight. "No."

The restaurant was a gem. Katrina couldn't believe it had been there, in her city, all this time, without her knowing it. The place itself was humble, with Formica tables and bright overhead lights and poster art featuring Cairo on the walls, but the food was authentic and the conversation flowed easily.

Leila shared her own memories, mostly from visits back there. Katrina talked about the glorious days of exploring the city with her father, followed by her girlish obsession with belly dancing. "I fell wildly in love with it, and that was that. I was such a pampered child, and so willful. Only now, as a parent, do I realize how hard it must have been for my mother. I could talk my father into anything. I'd make up my mind to do some outrageous thing, and then I'd relentlessly push to make it happen."

She told Leila about the turbulent year when Grandmother swept her off to Paris and she started at the Paris Opera Ballet School as one of its youngest students. How, against the odds, she not only survived, she thrived. How, within the year, her grandmother had replaced her parents as the most influential adult in her life. Years later, Katrina shared, there'd been the huge disappointment of not being offered a contract with the company upon completion of training. They'd allowed her to repeat her final year, given her still-young age, but mere weeks later, she'd been snapped up by Anders and the WCBT, and had never looked back.

They talked about European dancers they both knew. Many were still dancing, but some had become directors of their own companies, others choreographers. When conversation shifted to Javier, who was world-renowned and considered to be one of the top North American male dancers, Katrina found herself opening up about his less charming side. His disapproval of late. His attempt to hook her up with Martin the night of the photo shoot, and afterward, the way he'd waved off her angry words, telling her she needed to get out more. Not to mention his sullenness over the Hess debacle, no discussion beyond a cursory "are you all right?" and a formal, pained, "I'm sorry it didn't work out." Even there, his regret seemed to be more about his own personal loss of face than her trauma.

Katrina hesitated. "I'm sorry, I don't know why I'm attacking Javier. He's a model father to Dario—I have no complaints there. The negative stuff just popped up out of nowhere."

"Ballet dancers are trained from their earliest days to be compliant, agreeable, to not have—or at least not express—strong opinions. Particularly the females. But just now, when you were recounting your days in Cairo, you became a different person. Physically, even. Your shoulders relaxed. Your jaw. Your eyes sparkled. It was beautiful to see."

"I was remembering my days of being a stubborn, willful girl."

"I'm curious. What would happen if you allowed that stubborn, willful self to come through now, and stay?"

Katrina laughed. "It would be chaos."

"What if, from that chaos, a new, empowered you emerged?"

She was about to tell Leila she was being ridiculous, stopped herself.

What *if?*

Why should Javier be the only one to transform into a newly empowered person?

Leila was watching her closely. "There's something incredibly powerful in just considering the concept. Don't overthink it. Take that, and tuck it away to consider later." She leaned in, eyes flashing.

"Something's waking up in you, Katrina. I'm certain. And it's a very good thing."

Chapter 25

Kylie

It was a creepy feeling going into school on Monday, after more than a week away. Kylie began the day in the counselor's office, but even there, and in administration, things had changed. There were no questions because they already knew everything; they *needed* to know everything, her parents had told her. They were to be her soft landing place now. Any time she felt overwhelmed by re-entry, she was free to leave class and walk over to the counselor's office. All her teachers knew she'd been hospitalized. Her literature teacher asked to speak to her after class. "I understand things are hard, and take your time getting in last week's assignments, as well as this week's," she said gently. "The whole semester. Just let me know."

She pointedly ignored Lacey and Marisa. The pain of not just being rejected but being mocked by girls you'd thought were your forever friends was an ache that might never subside.

Lacey did try. There was genuine distress on her face when she approached Kylie—making sure it was a time where the hallway was empty, Kylie noted scornfully—and asked if she was okay, since she'd been absent from school the entire previous week.

"I was in the hospital," Kylie tossed out recklessly.

"The *hospital?* Kylie! What's wrong?"

"Obviously nothing that couldn't be fixed."

Lacey flinched at the chilly tone. Kylie might have cared in the past if she'd hurt her former best friend's feelings, but Lacey had made her choice and she'd made hers.

"But … are you okay?" Lacey persisted.

Kylie had been sifting through her locker, but hearing the concern in Lacey's voice, she swung around to face her ex-friend. "I am so much better than I was a month ago," she said in a cold, clear voice. "Back when I was deluded about who my friends were. So. Thank you for helping me achieve clarity there."

The big words, the way she spoke like something out of a textbook—she didn't give a shit anymore. She was weird and different and she would try to stop hating that about herself. She was going to make friends who lifted her up and didn't tear her down. That was what the therapists in group had counseled the teens to do. In the end Kylie had bonded with her fellow patients, and they were now friends online, where they'd chat and post funny, uplifting stuff or darkly humorous cartoons that only they seemed to find hilarious. It was nice.

Lacey gazed at Kylie, her pretty blue eyes stricken. "All of this has been hard for me, too," she said in a low voice. "It's not easy for anyone, you know. Sometimes I wish we were back in eighth grade."

A flash of hope that they could go back to how things had been passed through Kylie, but was gone an instant later, replaced by the understanding that the friendship was over, period, and that time didn't move backward. Lacey and eighth grade were her past. This, now, however crappy it felt, was how it was. This alone would lead her into the future.

"Well, too bad, and I'm sure you'd do fine." Kylie hesitated. Being cruel and uncaring didn't feel as great as she'd expected. Not toward Lacey, at least. "Anyway, thanks," she added grudgingly. "For asking how I'm doing. And the answer is, I'll be fine."

Lacey just stood there, saying nothing.

A lump rose in Kylie's throat—why did Lacey have to be like this *now*, when she, Kylie, didn't need it anymore? Abruptly she swung back toward her locker so Lacey wouldn't catch the tears creeping into her eyes. She clattered about in the locker, pointlessly rearranging items, focusing on the noise, the cold metal against her hand, keeping busy until she knew she was once again alone.

After school, she took the bus to the studios and made her way to Wardrobe. She wasn't allowed to be at home alone for the next four weeks, because she was still considered "at risk of self-harm" even though she knew she'd never try anything so stupid again. It made her feel physically ill, just to think about how sick she'd been that night, so sick she'd been terrified that she might really die. They'd told her later, in the hospital, that the amount she'd ingested into her little body could indeed have killed her, a thought so appalling and oversized and unfathomable, she'd burst into tears and had spent the next few hours sobbing uncontrollably, unable to shake the horror of it.

Her father had readjusted his work schedule to come home at lunch on Wednesdays and Fridays, working the rest of the day from his home office. She was cool with that. She was cool with the temporary return on Tuesdays and Thursdays of Amelie, a college-aged student who'd come over when Kylie was in middle school. But neither her dad nor Amelie were available on Monday afternoons. Her mom had wanted Kylie to come inside the studios and hang out there with her. Kylie's response had been a resounding *no, absolutely not.* To see David in this humbled, reduced state? To encounter Katrina and feel mortified over the damage she'd caused that night? No way.

The solution: Kylie could go to Wardrobe, in a different building, circumventing the studios entirely. It was familiar, homey, and Betty was eager to have her there, according to her mom.

Except that Betty didn't look eager and smiling when Kylie entered the department that Monday. The bright lights and clattering sewing machines, the smell of fabric being ironed, were all familiar and reassuring, but Betty's expression when she saw Kylie was not. "I want to talk to you in private," she said in a low, angry voice.

Kylie shrank. What had she done? She nodded and followed meekly behind Betty to her office, a small room with a desk, chairs, a tailor's dummy, and side tables stacked high with fabric bolts. Betty gestured for Kylie to sit. "I want to hear it from you," Betty said. "What you did that landed you in a hospital, and why."

She'd never made Betty this angry before, even the time she'd had chocolate on her fingertips from a Hershey's bar and was reaching toward one of the costumes. Unnerved, Kylie drew a breath and launched into her non-David version, how she felt alone, sad, unappreciated, unliked, all grey inside, hating herself so fiercely that the urge to hurt herself had overpowered her. The last bit surprised her; it was more than she'd told her parents. Right then, though, she feared Betty, feared being caught out for not telling the truth. "And there was a guy," she found herself adding.

Betty sat and expelled a slow, knowing breath. "Teens and hormones," she said, as if to herself. "So you poisoned yourself so bad, you had to be rushed to the emergency room."

It sounded so awful, the way Betty put it. Reluctantly, Kylie nodded.

Betty's cheeks reddened with outrage. "How could you do this?" she demanded. "Do you have any idea how precious you are to us? You're like this little miracle we've watched grow up. To think you were stupid enough to almost ruin your entire life, by poisoning yourself." She was shaking now, eyes bright with tears.

Kylie felt six inches tall. "I'm sorry."

Betty continued on. "When I think of how we could have lost you, I … Well, I'm just sick, thinking of it. Your poor mama. Do you have *any idea* how traumatic it is for a parent to be at risk of losing a child? Do you?"

This was worse than being yelled at by her parents. "No," Kylie whispered.

"I love you and your sister. I'd fight like a bear to protect you both. But I love your mama too, and she needs protecting just as much. You did a terrible thing to her."

Kylie nodded miserably, even though she'd never thought of it that way before.

"Now I want you to promise me, right now, that you'll never *ever* do such a stupid, risky thing again," Betty commanded. "Tell me. Right now."

"I won't ever do such a stupid thing again. I promise."

Betty rose. "Good. Now give me a hug."

Kylie stood and Betty's arms enfolded her. Betty had always been the best hugger, with a firm grip but soft and cushiony in all the right places. Kylie's muscles untensed. Betty was strong and powerful— and pretty scary right then.

She would never let Kylie fall.

Chapter 26

April

In April's dream, she and Leila were in the studio, and Leila was trying to downplay her panic, even as they both knew they were in deep trouble. Suddenly, Edwin was there, saying in a smooth voice, "I've got this covered." And poof, Leila was gone and the dancers were smiling, happy at his return. Then he turned to April and said, "Oh, I've got you covered, too." The way his eyes glittered said it all.

You're screwed. You went against me and now you'll pay.

Her eyes flew open as she jerked awake with a gasp. Adrenaline and anxiety coursed through her system.

Nothing was safe. Nothing was secure. Kylie was proof of that. The gala changes were proof of that.

It was 3:30AM. Russell was sleeping peacefully by her side. Fifteen wide-eyed minutes later, she knew she wouldn't be able to get back to sleep, so she quietly eased herself out of bed, put on a robe and went downstairs. In the quiet of the kitchen, with only Schrodinger for company, she made herself a tea, then sat and sternly reminded herself that anxiety was simply fear over what you couldn't control. It was irrational and insubstantial.

And it was doing a number on her.

Leila's ballet was coming along surprisingly well. So why, then, the repeating dream, still clawing at her insides? It alternated with the other nightmare of Kylie, with that deadened look, saying, "I don't want to be alive anymore."

She'd failed Kylie. She'd nearly failed Katrina. It chilled her, the fact that she almost hadn't gone over to the studio that fateful day. Thinking, *let Katrina solve this herself.* But then she'd gone, and the violence in the studio, with Edwin at its center, had stunned her. The crazed glow in Edwin's eyes told her he'd gone over the edge. This wasn't just rage or an abuse of power—it was more. He'd stepped inside his fantasy world. He wholly believed his own narrative, that he was a god and could do anything he felt like, and no one would stop him.

He could still come back, exact his revenge. He could threaten litigation unless they fired April. He could smear Katrina's reputation via social media and cause irreparable harm, to her and the WCBT's good reputation.

She was not an insecure person, nor was she easily swayed by her emotions. Then again, up until recently, her daughter had never expressed suicidal ideations, nor attempted to harm herself. Up until recently, she'd never seen a choreographer go rogue and use his ballet to attack an unsuspecting female. Why had he harbored so much vitriol against Katrina? Katrina was the most accommodating, compliant person April knew. She literally never complained on the job.

Something was not right with Edwin Hess. And she had no proof, no power, to challenge that, or him. Nothing was going to change that.

In that way, he'd won.

In spite of her truncated night's sleep and the anxiety that churned in her gut, the day's rehearsals went smoothly. In Leila's ballet, the chemistry between the dancers was excellent. Leila had an even-keeled nature that made everyone enjoy working with her. Including Anders. April could tell he also enjoyed having Montserrat in the studios as part of the team.

He showed up frequently at Leila's rehearsals. Today he and April stood side by side as they watched. They didn't speak, but she took that as a good thing, because Anders mostly spoke when he didn't like what he saw or how the ballet was going. No comment meant no issues. Out of the corner of her eye, she saw him smile and nod to himself.

"It's going well, I think," she said to him when Leila stopped the music to discuss a passage with the ensemble dancers.

He shrugged. "It's early. We thought the Hess commission was going well, until it wasn't."

Maybe you *did,* April thought darkly, but kept the comment to herself.

"How are the Don Q rehearsals going?" he asked her.

She smiled brightly. "The pas de deux is … still a work in progress."

He frowned. "What does that mean? Will it be ready or not?"

How to answer? If she told the truth, it would be a poor reflection on her, as the ballet master in charge. If she blustered her way through with false confidence, she'd end up in a different kind of hot water. "I think you should come to a rehearsal and judge for yourself," she told him.

His frown deepened. "When's their next rehearsal?"

"This afternoon at four o'clock."

"Fine. I'll stop by."

When Anders showed up an hour into rehearsal, April proposed having Javier and Palmira run the entire pas de deux straight through. Anders motioned impatiently with his hand, so she cued the accompanist.

She and Anders watched in silence from the front as the two dancers made their way through the first movement. Palmira hadn't fallen out of any of her turns since the day that she'd taken a tumble, but a shadow had remained, a creasing of her brow, even a look of fear. Today, her unsupported balances in back arabesque wobbled, and in the partnered pirouettes, she reduced the triple revolutions to doubles. It was clear she wanted to play it safe.

It was a bad idea to merely "play it safe" when Anders was watching.

April's stomach clenched. Her gut sense was that Palmira simply could not match Javier's power. Few could, even among the seasoned dancers. Javier was doing his best to make her appear strong, but his stellar technique, his space-devouring leaps and jumps, only served to highlight the disparity.

They completed the adagio. Palmira smiled brightly, but her chin trembled. Javier's performing smile soured the instant the music stopped. Nothing had gone amiss, April told herself. But "not bad" wasn't enough. Not for a gala.

"Onto the solo variations?" she asked Anders, her voice high with tension.

Anders shook his head.

April called for Palmira and Javier to take a three-minute break, and once they left the studio, Anders turned to her. "What happened? Three weeks ago, they danced it far better."

"A lot has been placed on Palmira's shoulders right now," she said. "We both know it's not uncommon for a new member to start off strong and then struggle. They're used to the student's pace, one ballet to polish per season. Right now she's rehearsing four ballets in addition to this, and understudying two more roles. She's wearing pointe shoes seven hours a day. It's a dramatic adjustment for any new company member."

"We don't have time for excuses. This was supposed to be your job, to refine the rough spots. Not to drag it all down. It looks terrible."

"I'm sorry," she said miserably. "You're right."

He muttered a few angry words in Danish under his breath and shook his head. "It's as though you're trying, this season, to be a liability."

April sucked in a deep breath. "Is this about the time I took off for Kylie?"

"Of course not. What sort of unfeeling bastard do you take me for?"

She chose not to answer that one. "Is this still about Hess, then?"

His lips pinched together. "You might have cost the company dearly."

So she hadn't been forgiven. "You keep saying that. You keep acting as though he was producing a miracle of a ballet. He wasn't. Stop kidding yourself about that. In the meantime, Leila's ballet is already shaping up to be something solid, not to mention fresh and original."

"The full piece is still an unknown," he said. "No matter how cleverly you try and spin it, we are taking a big risk."

"Fine. If Leila's ballet proves to be a liability—which I'm certain it won't—you will have my resignation."

His expression didn't change. They'd been at this contentious, saber-rattling place before. He'd threatened to fire her more than once. Over twenty years of working together closely tended to include a few bumps, after all. "If it fails," he said, "I will accept that resignation."

This had not happened before. This was more than saber rattling. April stared at his calm, unchanged expression, and something in her snapped.

"Why wait?" The words tumbled right out. She was so tired all of a sudden. Tired of all the work she'd put in, day in, day out. She wasn't looking for praise or flowers, but was it too much to ask that she got a little appreciation for the juggling act that was her life? "You can have my resignation now. At season's end, I'll leave."

Before he could reply, Ben appeared at the doorway. "Anders, glad I found you. I think your phone's off. Lucinda wants to know if you're free for twenty minutes before she leaves."

"I'm available right now. We're done here."

She wanted to scream, or punch something. Instead she dug her fingernails into her palms and called out for Javier and Palmira, hovering by the doorway too, to come back in. She told them she wanted to see their solo variations. They both brightened. They had their solos down pat. April didn't even need to run them. But what she needed was something stabilizing, something that would allow her thoughts to run wild as she watched the dancers.

Because she might have just resigned. And Anders didn't care.

At six o'clock, she went home. Russell appeared to be on a conference call in his office. Jen and Kylie were in their respective rooms. In the kitchen, she clanked pans and bowls as she stormily started dinner prep. Russell came in five minutes later and asked her absently how her day had been, April's cue to reply "oh, fine," so that he could stay in his bubble of concentration.

"Well, I don't know if I'll be employed beyond May," she said grimly, plunging the knife into a chicken breast.

He looked up, startled. "What does that mean?"

"It means just what I said. I'm considering resigning." Setting down the knife, she stomped over to the refrigerator and tried to yank the bag of spring greens from the produce bin, only it kept getting stuck on something, so she had to yank harder, until it broke free, with a tear, sending spring greens flying everywhere.

Russell approached and gently took the bag from her. Ignoring the greens, he shut the refrigerator and led her to sit at the table. "Elaborate, please," he said. "Ignore the food."

She explained.

And of course that morphed into her feelings about the Hess issue. On and on, April raged. Russell, to his credit, listened to it all. When she was done, he took her hand.

"Let it go, sweetheart. Answers don't always come just because we want them to. Or, who knows? An answer might drop down to earth some day and vindicate you. Regardless, I'd bet money Anders won't let you leave."

"It's not his choice."

"Okay. *You* won't let you leave. That group is your second family. You'd sooner walk out on me than quit the Ballet Theatre because of a spat with your boss. Because, don't hit me here, but if you take away the drama and the wounded feelings, that seems to be at the core. He's angry at what you chose to do, and it seems you're angry that he overlooks your considerable efforts."

He stopped short. "Well, maybe I do the same. Overlook your efforts, I mean."

"I guess I'll go pack up, then."

She'd meant it as a joke, but the bitterness that had crept into her voice killed any humor that might have arisen. He looked at her with the kind of puppy-eyed expression he'd used back when they were newly in love, giddy and optimistic, and life seemed effortless.

"I think it's time for me to show my appreciation for all that you do here, by taking over dinner," he told her. He went to the counter, poured a glass of wine and set it in front of her. "Shoo. Go away. In fact, go talk to Jen. She's excited about something in school. It's charming."

"All right. I'll do that. You really have dinner covered?"

"I do."

"Thank you."

She took a sip of the wine, then went upstairs to Jen's room and knocked. Jen called out for her to come in.

Her daughter's room was decorated in all pinks, neat and organized, with dance posters adorning the walls. April joined her on her bed as Jen chatted, all animated. Today it wasn't about ballet classes or Nut rehearsals but instead about school. There'd been much more enthusiasm about school this year compared to past years.

"We're working on an oceanography unit at school that's so much fun! I didn't think I'd like marine biology so much, but I do. As an extra-credit part of our project, we can opt to go on an afternoon field trip to Monterey and Pacific Grove, visit the tidepools. Afterwards, we get to be part of an event at the Monterey Bay Aquarium, with food and everything! All I need is your signature on the permission form and a check for forty dollars. You won't have to drive or anything."

"I can get you those things. But this is going to clash with your ballet class and rehearsals."

"It's a one-time event. That's what I promised them at the ballet school, too." She smiled. "I love doing these events. They make me feel more connected. There's always something fun going on in a high school."

She smiled at Jen's enthusiasm. "Enjoy it while you can. You're approaching the last two levels at the ballet school, which, as you know, mean ballet classes earlier in the day and a switching of high schools to accommodate that."

The enthusiasm faded from Jen's face. "I forgot about that. They can't make exceptions?"

"They can't," April said gently. It was one of the unfortunate aspects of dance training in the U.S. Independent study through an alternative high school was how most pre-professional level dancers earned their high school diplomas while completing their dance training. She herself, training in New York, had been thrilled for the opportunity not to attend traditional high school, keeping most of her focus on dance.

"Those last two years, the training gets much harder, doesn't it?" Jen asked.

"It does," April admitted. "The stakes are so much higher."

Jen fell silent, now wholly downcast. April thought of Russell's words from weeks earlier, his *don't steal her adolescence from her,* and she recognized an opportunity that would disappear in seconds. Then again, she argued to herself, *not* addressing it now wasn't the end of the world. She could save it all for another day, for a calmer period in their lives.

But this was her daughter, pondering her future. Considering the adult life *she* wanted, not the one April wanted for her.

"You know," April began, and faltered. There would be no going back, after all, once she voiced this thought.

It had to be said. For Jen's sake.

"So," she began again. "Next year, you could very possibly repeat the level of training you're at right now. Not move up to the level that requires a change of schools."

Jen looked up in surprise. April tried to keep her expression neutral, even as inside she was crying, *no, no! It's a terrible idea. It's the beginning of the end. You'll never make it all the way if you're prioritizing a high-school social life over your ballet training.*

"I can do that?" Hope bloomed in Jen's eyes, dashing the last of April's own hopes.

Her dance daughter wanted to abdicate. There it was. Time now for April to ignore the pain in her heart—she'd wanted it a lot more than she'd realized—and truly support her daughter. "I think it could be arranged," she told Jen, congratulating herself on her calm, reasonable tone. "Most students hate being told they need to repeat a level. The girls in your group would be glad, frankly, to have you out of the competition for Level Seven."

"Oh, I would *love* to do Level Six again!" Jen bounced on her bed in excitement. "I love ballet, but I like this high school stuff too. And Dad says he's game to take me on college campus tours starting next year. See what's out there and such."

She'd made her choice already, April realized. An immersive high-school experience, a rich social life, in anticipation of a four-year college, possibly far from home.

She was the mom; it was her job to make this easier for Jen, no matter her own hurt or disappointment. "That's a sound idea. And what you might want to do is research which colleges and universities have good dance departments. So that you can … have dance on the side. Maybe as part of a degree, or maybe just for fun." She had to force the last words out.

"That was my thought exactly!" Jen hesitated and her enthusiasm dimmed. "Would that be all right with you?"

There was only one right answer here.

"Of course it's okay! I want you to be happy. I want you to follow your dreams and do what feels right to you, not me."

"This is so great! My friends are starting to plan what colleges they want to visit next year, too. I need to tell them ASAP that I'm in. They'll be stoked." She picked up her phone and started texting.

April rose. "I'll let you get back to what you were doing."

"Okay." She didn't even look up. "Thanks, Mom."

April made her way slowly down the stairs and into the kitchen. She felt punched in the gut, ironically by her own hand. Russell, who'd just put a pan into the oven, smiled at her. "All good?"

"Can you just hold me for a few minutes? And don't tell me not to cry."

The gentle, loving look on his face made the tears well up faster. He held out his arms—he was still wearing oven mitts, the sight of which made April laugh even as she cried.

He wrapped his arms around her. "Everything okay?" he murmured.

"Yes. It'll all be fine."

It would be. She understood that now.

Maybe just not right away.

Chapter 27

Katrina

Friday afternoon's rehearsal with Leila hit an impasse during the pas de deux with Jimmy. Something essential seemed missing from the equation which Katrina sensed was her fault, a hunch that proved correct when Leila dismissed the others, in order to brainstorm with Katrina alone. Even April was excused. Only David, as the accompanist, remained.

Leila caught her worried expression. "It's just about getting the appropriate amount of sass for the second movement," she assured Katrina. "Nothing to fret about. We just need to dig."

"Sure." Katrina tried to mirror Leila's confident smile. "All right."

"Because it's saucy, sexy, yet very classical and somehow aloof. It has to be all of that at once, or the intention will get lost. Do you remember how Montserrat played her violin in that section? Sassy, flirtatious, but when it repeats, its intensity is even deeper, maybe even haughty."

A Cairo memory came to Katrina's mind, unvisited for decades. "Nabila's sister, Yasmine—remember my telling you about her?"

Leila nodded.

"She danced like what you just described. You'd think belly dancing was all about sensuality and seduction, but it was what she held back on that made it so powerful. She was so regal and aloof, it made something in you almost craven with longing."

Leila looked delighted. "That's it. That's it precisely. Keep in mind what you just said while you run it through again. I'll dance Jimmy's part. Seduce me. But, at the same time, show restraint. You are unattainable, except when you yourself decide otherwise." She cued David to recommence the music.

Katrina was glad no one else was in the room besides him as she "seduced" Leila, through a series of tango-like movements. Even then, she could hear David's laughter from across the room. "You there, accompanist," she called out. "Shut up."

Which made them all laugh and it became nothing short of hilarious. Katrina turned her head coyly away from Leila, playing hard-to-get, only to run her hand sexily down Leila's arm. She then used her pointe shoe to draw a line up Leila's leg, an improvisation that was so original and funny, Leila cried out, "That is *so* staying!"

After running it twice more, complete with an even more obvious pointe-shoe caress, Leila declared it perfect and called it a day.

"What's Jimmy going to say about the leg caress?" Katrina asked.

"Let's not tell him." Leila grinned. "His reaction will be classic, and that will work perfectly, too. In fact, do this. Let your foot travel even higher, like it's headed for his groin, and I'll bet you anything he slaps it down." They both broke into peals of laughter at the thought of Jimmy's farm-boy eyes widening with shock at the unexpected stimulation.

"Great work." Leila nodded in satisfaction. "No Saturday rehearsal after all. We're in good shape now. But I do have an assignment for you, in its place."

Katrina looked up from her spot on the floor, where she was easing off her pointe shoes. "What is it?"

"Tomorrow, do something different from your usual routine."

"My friend Martin keeps begging me for a daytime date," she

mused. Something to make up for his terrible gaffe that night, he'd told her over the phone the day he called to beg her forgiveness. She hadn't had the heart to tell him nothing would ever make up for his behavior.

Leila sensed her dilemma. "Did I mention it was to be fun, as well as different?"

"Like letting the accompanist take you and your son to the zoo?" David's voice came from the other side of the room, but in a flash he was right there with them.

Katrina rose, flustered, as Leila sized him up in interest. "Yes." She turned back to Katrina. "That would qualify as fun and different."

Had Leila observed Katrina's growing attraction to David? Even now, his nearby presence was making her face, her whole body, grow warm. And yet, trying something fun and different in choreography was very different from doing it in her personal life.

"Katrina," Leila said. "It starts with saying 'maybe yes' to new things. New prospects."

David tactfully excused himself to go get a drink of water. Leila's firm gaze didn't waver.

"Do it. Just play. Have fun. What he's proposing is the perfect opportunity. He seems to be a nice guy who will respect whichever way you choose to steer the day."

Katrina looked into those uncannily familiar brown eyes and it was as if she were eight again, considering the hand Nabila had offered.

"All right, I'll do it," she heard herself say, and instantly worried that it had been a mistake. But Leila was smiling at her in the same warm, approving way Nabila used to.

"Good. Have fun. That's all you need to do."

Dario connected with David from the moment he showed up at the house Saturday morning. David was carrying a big plastic tub full of

Hot Wheels cars that, he informed them, were from his own childhood. He set it down with a thud. "We can share them now," he told Dario as he dropped to all fours beside him. Dario's eyes rounded with delight. Speechless, he stared at the cars, then David, then the cars again, before thrusting his hands into the tub and pulling out handfuls of the cars, quickly, as if afraid David would change his mind.

"I'll just go finish getting ready," she said, but neither of them looked up.

"Sure," David said. "Take your time. We're good here."

She busied herself upstairs, humming a little tune. She was absurdly excited about the date, lighthearted about the prospect of a day of entertainment that didn't require her choosing between Dario and an engaging adult. She picked out an outfit with extra care and roped her hair into a high ponytail. She heard David and Dario talking about the cars and she smiled. David knew much more about each little Hot Wheel car than Javier did. Javier wasn't into cars.

Grabbing a light jacket, she hurried down the stairs, feeling like Princess April from *The Sleeping Beauty* skipping down the palace staircase at her 16th birthday party. "Ready to go!" she announced.

David looked up from the cars, his eyes softening in admiration. "Look at you. You're so pretty. You're the prettiest mom I've ever seen, bar none."

He turned to Dario. "Is she not the prettiest mom you've ever seen? Do you realize how lucky you are?"

Dario looked bewildered. "She's my mommy, is all."

David and Katrina looked at each other and laughed.

Giddy enough to laugh: that described her mood perfectly. Laughing on the drive to the zoo, at David's stories about being a kid, how he'd once dropped a big bag of Hot Wheels in a grocery store, setting them off in every direction and causing chaos. Laughing when Dario informed them that he could drive David's car, because he could drive a Hot Wheels and they were the same thing.

At the zoo, she gasped with laughter over the antics of the monkeys. She chuckled over the ungainly nature of running giraffes, and found the stiffly formal penguins hilarious. In the aviary, the screaming chatter of so many birds made her laugh hysterically, even as Dario shrank from the noise, lifting his arms up for David to hold him. She laughed so hard she had to wipe the tears from her eyes.

Outside the aviary, David, bemused, asked her if she always laughed this much at the zoo, which, of course, made her laugh more.

"I guess I'm just very happy today, right now."

His smile grew warmer. "I'm glad. I'm so happy you're happy."

Impulsively, she took his hand. "Dario's getting ahead of us. Come on!"

It took only a few steps to reach Dario, but they continued holding hands. It felt so easy, and yet, so shocking. Like a kiss, it wasn't something one could undo. It was there, this vibrant thing between the two of them. It sped things up. And later, in the reptile room, when Dario was given permission in the presentation to run up with the other kids and stroke the reptile the handler was presenting, David said, "There goes our Dario," it felt precisely like that. As if, at that moment, Dario *was* theirs.

It took her back, to a dreamier, more nostalgic time, when she'd been so sure that parenting would be just like this. Fun, carefree times, the three of them so happy and relaxed. The indestructible sense of family she and Javier would cultivate. And while she hadn't been wrong about the latter, the former had proven elusive. She and Javier weren't, by nature, fun and carefree. Case in point: the lone time they'd all gone to the zoo, Javier had been distracted, almost artificial, as if they were actors playing a role. Sure enough, people had recognized them, asked for an autograph, and from that moment on, he'd been more concerned about how they were presenting themselves, rather than whether they were enjoying themselves.

Javier would have never leapt at the chance to buy them all hot dogs, like David had. Dario's eyes had lit up like he'd been offered a grand gift and the three of them had plopped down on the grass, munched down hot dogs and potato chips, laughing at the flecks of mustard on Dario's chin and the tip of Katrina's nose. Javier eating hot dogs in public with his family, easy with laughter? Never. Letting the day be about enjoying the air, the sights, each other? Never.

This was what she'd always yearned for. This, here, now.

The thought passed through her in a flash, a clear insight free from any need for further interpretation. She drew in a slower breath and exhaled in wonder. She saw David glance at her. When she turned to face him, the witty thing he was about to say died on his lips. He sat there, silent, expectant.

How could she possibly explain? The feeling had gone beyond words.

Instead of speaking, she leaned over and kissed him. She felt his lips part beneath hers in shock and allowed her lips to do the same, knowing then that this was no "thank you for the day" peck, like she'd offer Martin sometimes. This was an invitation. One that woke something inside her that had been curled up and sleeping for the longest time. She pulled back and they regarded each other, both of them speechless.

"Mama! David! Lookie! C'mere!"

Dario's cry broke the trance. David, chuckling, rose. "I'll do the honors."

"Thank you." She hoped she sounded calmer than she felt just then, amid this sense of astonishment at the leap she'd just taken. "I'm glad one of us likes snakes."

"I love 'em. So, apparently, does your son." He sauntered over to

Dario, who excitedly grabbed his hand and led him closer to the snake. She watched the two of them and felt her heart contract, a feeling both joyous and painful, and decided she'd never quite loved the world as much as she did right then.

Two hours later, as the sun began its golden descent, they made their way back toward the car. Dario, all resistant about being placed in the stroller, now sagged against her chest, asleep. "What are your evening plans?" Katrina asked David, and immediately regretted it when his expression lit up.

"I'm crossing my fingers that maybe I've got a hot date."

Disappointment landed in her stomach with a giant thud. Of course. What had she been thinking? He was popular with all the girls at the WCBT. She'd gotten lulled into the image of the David he'd been with her and Dario today.

"I've got a hot date with my son," she offered, trying to keep her voice light. "Who needs a nap, dinner and a bath. That's my night."

"You need dinner."

"Doesn't matter." She shrugged, and he glanced at her curiously.

"Dario looks heavy. Let me put him in the stroller."

"He'll wake up."

"I'll bet he doesn't. Give him to me."

She deposited Dario into his arms and watched, skeptical, as he inserted Dario into the stroller. Dario gave a sigh but, as predicted, didn't wake up. "You're good," she observed.

"Beginner's luck."

They resumed walking. Her arms felt lighter but her heart stayed heavy.

"Back to the subject of dinner," he said. "What do you mean, it doesn't matter?"

"When it's only me, I just grab something small."

"So … you're not going to let me make you dinner?" A hurt note had crept into his voice.

Her turn to regard him curiously. "What do you mean? You just said you had a hot date."

He laughed. "Katrina, I'm hoping I've got a date. With *you*. To make you dinner."

"Seriously?" she stammered.

"Dead serious. Spaghetti Bolognese and red wine. *Italians* have praised my Bolognese sauce. It would be a terrible mistake for you to pass it up."

Relief welled up, spreading through her like melted butter. "Oh. *Oh*! How would I have guessed that? I thought you meant someone else."

"Absolutely not. So, is that a yes or a no?"

"Yes. Yes!"

"Good."

Not only was his spaghetti Bolognese as good as he'd bragged—even impossible-to-please Dario clamored for seconds—but after dinner, he shooed her and Dario out of the kitchen and told them to enjoy their own evening routine while he cleaned. And not just a slapdash effort either. When she came back downstairs forty-five minutes later, once Dario had been tucked into bed, she heard the soft whirr of the dishwasher running and smelled the pleasing lemony odor of counters sprayed clean and wiped down. The coffee maker gurgled. "I took the liberty of making some coffee," David told her, sleeves rolled up from cleaning, a damp red kitchen towel slung over one shoulder. "Does that work for you? It's decaf."

She looked at him, the sparkling counters, the washed pots and pans on the drying rack, and began to laugh. "No one has ever cleaned my kitchen so well, much less made me coffee without being asked. I'm in heaven. And yes, coffee most decidedly works. It smells delicious."

"Good. Go relax in the living room. I'll bring the coffees in once they're ready."

He brought a tray into the living room five minutes later, with steaming mugs alongside spoons, sugar, and a plate of dark chocolate squares with sea salt and almond (her favorite – how could he have known?). She decided happily that this was like spending the night in an all-inclusive B&B, except without the burden of leaving home. They nibbled, sipped, and reclined on the couch, chatting easily about movies, literature, the books he liked to read.

She mentioned the thick Winston Churchill hardback she'd seen tucked under his arm that day in the elevator. He nodded.

"My reading preferences have evolved pretty dramatically in the past year. Before it used to be paperback thrillers, or bestseller nonfiction, the kind with lots of hype and promises. Or scandals. Frivolous stuff, most of it. Now it's the opposite. I love reading biographies of historical figures, analyzing their greatness and what made them such powerful human beings. That and Eastern philosophy. Buddhism. A writer called Pema Chödrön. Her every written word speaks to me."

"Why the change?"

"Oh, I had a real before-and-after experience last spring. I'm sure you've got something similar. You know, where your life changes overnight, and there's no going back?" He eyed her expectantly.

She thought instantly of Dario. "Having a baby. I can hardly remember that other, pre-child self, so preoccupied with *me.*"

"My sister would probably concur." He glanced over at her empty coffee cup. "Refill? There's more in the kitchen, keeping warm."

"Sure, thanks." She watched him disappear into the kitchen and return with the coffee, filling their cups before setting the now-empty pot nearby.

"All right, I told you my before-and-after experience," she said once he took his seat back beside her. "I'm curious to know what yours is."

He was slow to respond. He took a sip of his coffee, then another, before speaking.

"So, last spring, I kind of almost died."

He was not smiling; he was not joking.

He nodded at her shocked expression. "I was in a motorcycle accident in Barbados, while visiting a friend. Sponging off that friend, to be honest. Living a hedonistic, irresponsible life. Truthfully, I had been for years. One minute I was speeding down the road, giddy and uncaring, and then, *bam.* I suppose. I remember nothing. Apparently another vehicle ran a red light and plowed into my motorcycle. My friend called my brother from the hospital two hours later. She told him he should be on the next flight to Barbados, if he wanted any chance to say goodbye. I'd sustained a ruptured spleen, fractured femur and internal bleeding. The doctors weren't expecting me to even make it through the night."

He fell silent. She herself felt too stunned to speak. This vibrant person, with his oversized personality and charm and good looks, on the cusp of life and death. The thought of David dying felt like a reverberating blow to her gut.

"I knew none of this at the time, of course." He lifted his coffee mug and examined it. "I woke a day later in a hospital, my brother there in the room. When I mumbled his name and he saw I was conscious, he started crying. My big brother, weeping. God." He set the coffee mug down abruptly and expelled a heavy breath. "What I put my poor brother through. My mom and sister, too. I'd been acting out since our father's death, years earlier. Being irresponsible, almost manic, as a way of running from that pain. Squandering the opportunity for a career as a concert pianist in order to goof around.

"Later that first day, I had this spiritual reckoning, for lack of a better phrase. I saw my entire life, this vast panorama of selfish choices I'd made, this pursuit of things that felt good, exciting, only now I saw the colossal emptiness of it all. The way I'd so deeply hurt the ones who loved me most. My dad—what would he have thought of what I'd become? That was it. That afternoon was the catalyst. From that moment on, I've been a different me."

Silence hung over his last words. She felt transformed by all he'd shared. It was his serious side she'd always gravitated to, and she'd wanted to get to the core of what made him tick. But now that they were here, his vulnerability laid out for her to kick around, she felt terrible. Who had she been to judge him, anyway?

"David. I'm so sorry." Her words broke the silence.

He eyed her quizzically. "For what?"

"For everything. For not knowing. For assuming you hadn't experienced pain."

"Thanks." He gave a little self-deprecating shrug. "I'm good at hiding what's not pretty about myself. Easier just to be a charming flirt and let people think that's me."

There was more she needed to say. "I stand humbled. And surprised. And … pleased."

"Pleased?" This last thing caught his attention and made a hint of laughter return to his voice. "Now that's something I'm curious to hear more about."

"All right." She chuckled. "Allow me to explain. I like seeing that other side of you. Seeing a flirtatious, good-looking guy get quiet and act serious is an incredible turn-on."

He looked stunned. His mouth opened and closed without any words coming out.

"Staying silent in lieu of tossing out something flirtatious or clever also qualifies."

He began to laugh. "Anything else? Because I'm mentally taking notes here."

"Sure. Doing the dishes, wiping down the counters, even washing the pans. That was a very sexy thing to do."

God, she was flirting.

It went beyond that.

She wanted him. Plain and simple. It was like watching Yasmine dance and feeling this yearning come over her, saturating her, inside and out.

The ball was in her court. His eyes—they were so beautiful, ocean-colored and lit from within, and slavishly compliant—told her she could torment him, tease him, and he'd take it.

"May I tell you something now?" he asked.

"I think you've earned the right."

"I absolutely loved watching yesterday in rehearsal when you 'seduced' Leila with your movements. Your expression, your whole body energy, transformed you into a different person. I could almost see you as the young girl you must have once been."

"Hmm. Tell me what you think I was like, back then."

"Let's see. Long, flowing blonde hair. Stubborn, willful. Quick to laugh. Mischievous. Demanding. The apple of your parents' eyes."

She narrowed her eyes. "Did Leila give you those details?"

"Nope. I'm just good at guessing. Was I right?"

"Spot on."

"I deserve a reward for getting it so right, don't you think?"

She laughed. "It depends. What kind of reward are you asking for?"

"How about another viewing of that cat-like move Leila set on you yesterday."

"You mean the belly-dancer like move?"

"Yes. I think we're talking about the same thing. Show me. Please?"

As she studied him, a reckless giddiness seized her. Greedy, life-seizing, demanding little Katja had returned, then. "All right, I'll humor you. You did clean my kitchen, after all."

She rose and stepped to the nearest open space. Humming the music, she tossed out a pirouette, the lunge that followed, and segued into the move that Leila had created, a swirl of the hips followed by an exaggerated undulation of her spine.

"That's it. You're like a cat. Your moves are so feline."

She emitted a low chuckle. Dropping down to all fours, she began to make her way to him, a movement both feline and dominant. Not a housecat. A tiger. One who'd spied delectable prey. The helpless, entranced expression on his face delighted her. She felt as powerful and confident as Javier.

She came up to the spot on the couch where he was sitting. She rested her hands on his knees before sliding them up his thighs and down to the cushion, planting them on either side of his hips. She did one more spine undulation until her chest rested against his. "Meow," she breathed into his ear, and, hardly believing her own daring, kissed his neck, letting her tongue work a soft trail down, until his hands cupped her face and with a neat shifting of bodies, he was lengthwise against her on the couch, kissing her deeply, passionately.

You didn't realize how desperately lonely you'd been until someone was touching you, someone desirable with strong hands, and not ballet-dancer partner hands, but hands that have yearned to touch you, as well.

Pressing her pelvis into his, she hooked a leg up and around one of his, essentially locking him into place. She tugged at his shirt and slipped her hands beneath. She felt his hands on the back of her neck, her shoulders, before they slid down and up her own blouse. His hand glided under the skimpy bra she wore more for decorum than need; she was as flat-chested as an adolescent. But that didn't mean her nipple was any less sensitive to the soft flicker from his thumb, eliciting a soft moan from her even as they kissed.

His phone dinged to signal a text.

He ignored it. They both did.

But it dinged again to let them know the unread text was still there.

They ignored it.

Until thirty seconds later, another ding announced a new text.

This time he pulled back, with a groan. "I should check that. I don't want it to be something horrible that later I'll regret not having addressed."

Katrina scrambled awkwardly to a more dignified sitting position. All she could think was that it was one of the pretty corps girls, wanting his attention.

He read the text and smiled. "How cute is this?" he said to himself as he scrolled to a second text, obviously a picture.

"'Schrodinger is now defying gravity,'" he read out loud.

He showed her the image on his phone. To her confusion, she recognized the Garveys' enormous tabby cat.

"Wait … who just texted you that?"

"Kylie. I told her to text me any time."

This baffled her even more. "That's nice of you," she began. "Is this … a recent thing?"

"Just trying to help her through this strange time in her life," he said, and his expression softened, almost like what Javier's did when he was talking about Dario. Except something more. Like the time Javier had let Dario take a tumble and he'd felt terrible about it.

"Poor Kylie," she said, trying to employ the same warm, concerned tone. "Hopefully soon she'll be done with all that weird instability."

She thought she was being relatable, that they were on the same page. But when David looked up from his phone, he suddenly appeared less friendly.

"Have you ever tried talking to Kylie? Beyond, 'will you babysit Dario?'"

Wrong question to ask her. "For the record, she's never babysitting Dario again," she said, unable to keep the frostiness from her voice.

"Gee. That'll make her feel much better."

She drew in a deep breath, staggered by how they'd gone from kissing to this veiled hostility in the course of a minute. "You called me that one night, if you remember, to say you understood what it felt like to have a little boy get lost. But I don't think you understand, after all, what it feels like to be a parent who afterward keeps having the 'what if?' replay over and over in their mind, haunting them nonstop."

He didn't reply immediately, but the anger left his eyes. She'd risen to her feet, but he came back now, sat, and gently tugged her down to sitting as well.

"I'm sorry I forgot about the Dario connection, the trauma it brought you," he said. "Forgive me. I was thinking about Kylie's burden and not yours."

They sat there in silence. When he took her hand, laid it on his thigh and covered it with the warmth of his other hand, she felt a flutter deep in the belly again. It shocked her that she could be thinking about sex, how she'd happily throw the conversation out the door and start making out with him again.

"Kylie's such a great kid," he was saying. "I feel like I owe her something. I let her down."

An uneasy prickle traveled up her spine. She thought of Kylie's tears the night of David's performance, her look of stunned adoration. Katrina had assumed it was the music that had made such an impression. But what if it had been David himself? A crush like no other.

Another memory arose. The crash of folding chairs right outside the hallway when she and Javier had been rehearsing a *Nutcracker* pas de deux with April. David had peered out into the hallway and reported seeing Kylie, only Kylie never reappeared, even though April, too, had been expecting to see her.

What if Kylie, so observant and eerily intuitive, had discerned David's interest in Katrina?

It would have been so upsetting.

It might have made her want to hurt herself.

Oh, dear Lord. That would mean she, too, had played a big part in Kylie's pain. And all she'd done since that terrible night was point fingers and accuse.

She forced the words out with difficulty. "You said you feel like you owe her something. It's because she has a crush on you, isn't it? A big one."

He sank his face into his hands. "I think you're right."

She felt sick. She couldn't speak.

"I'm fourteen years older than her," David protested. "She's a high-school freshman and I'm a college graduate. What was she thinking?"

"Teen girls fall in love—there's little thinking or analysis involved. It's all flying high with no protection, no guard rails." A wave of sadness washed over her. "Poor Kylie. I feel terrible."

"I made sure to set the matter straight," David said. "I told her I hoped we could still be friends. And that, as a friend, she should feel free to text me anytime."

"I feel somehow responsible. Like I owe her something too."

He shook his head. "I was the one who let her read too much into a friendship. My fault entirely. But if I can be a text buddy to her as a consolation, it makes me feel a little better."

"Just maybe … don't text her to say where you are right now."

An hour later, she lay in bed alone, too agitated to sleep. Partly because her sensual side had been awakened and she was regretting not inviting David to come upstairs and into her bed. But then again, the Kylie situation had killed the mood for them both. Now, she found herself mulling over how difficult it was to be a teen girl grappling with a first crush, discovering just how hard you could fall. Poor Kylie.

And now, knowing all she did, how to proceed?

How on earth to make amends?

Chapter 28

April

Bumps kept appearing in Leila's ballet, newly christened *Sonata for Six,* on day ten of rehearsing. This worried April, because in six days they'd start full dress rehearsals, where each gala piece was expected to be perfected and polished to a sheen for the Friday performance.

"No problem," Leila called out when the ensemble males missed their musical cue to lift Katrina off Jimmy's back. "We'll tackle that spot tomorrow. Let's just keep moving."

The unison in the ensemble section was off today, as well. April exchanged worried looks with Rebecca, taking April's notes, but Leila seemed unfazed. "You're good, just keep going," Leila called out.

But when Dena nearly collided with Jimmy as they passed each other in piqué turns, Leila let out a tired exhale. April's insides clenched at the sound.

Leila waved for the musicians to stop. "You're tired," she told the dancers. "Let's stop and talk through what's going on."

As the dancers plopped down on the floor with weary sighs, April considered her own unease. What would legitimate failure look like for Leila's ballet? She told herself they were far from that place. And yet, something could show great potential and still hold dangerous risk.

Leila looked around at the dancers. "I'm thrilled at the way you've got the steps and basic intention down. What's not working today is relatively minor. But something's up, and, if left unaddressed, it risks leaving those sections earthbound. And we need it to fly. In fact, the whole movement requires this sense of flight."

"It's that ensemble section, toward the end," Dena said. "I feel like we're somehow clashing, except, at the same time, we're wary of each other."

"Good point," Leila said. "Keep talking."

"Maybe it's an issue of trust?"

"I agree," Katrina said. "It made me nervous, when the two guys weren't there right when they needed to be."

"We didn't want to get in yours or Jimmy's way, beforehand," one of them said, and the other nodded. "It's tricky timing."

"And I want to keep it tricky," Leila said. "Tricky equals clever, and the audience loves that. But in regards to spacing. It's almost like we need …" She rubbed her chin reflectively.

"Aha." Her eyes brightened. "I've got it." She strode over to her oversized bag and rummaged around. "Here you go," she said a moment later, holding up a fistful of what appeared to be bandannas. "We'll do that thirty-two count ensemble passage with these on."

Jimmy stared at the red bandanna she handed him. "You want us to dance blindfolded?"

"I do."

The dancers stared at her in horror. April could only laugh. She heard Rebecca and the musicians chuckling too.

"Trust me here," Leila said. "You don't have to dance full out. Just mark the trickier steps and the lifts. It's your bodies moving through space I want you to focus on."

Unsurprisingly, the dancers were slower and clumsier when blindfolded, with plenty of laughter and bumping into each other. But there was also a sense of gentleness as they moved, a kinetic awareness of everyone else's presence. They weren't just looking out for themselves anymore.

The moment Leila told everyone they could remove their blindfolds, they ripped them off and began chattering about how hilarious and chaotic it had been. Katrina and one of the males were laughing over how she'd groped him, thinking he was Jimmy, and meanwhile Jimmy had gone after Dena and not Katrina.

"There," Leila said. "That's a new perspective for you."

Rebecca gestured pointedly to the clock on the wall and Leila looked at her own watch in surprise. "Darn it, we're out of time. All right, hear me out. This was a bad rehearsal, but in a good way. Nothing goes unequivocally smoothly, and we've been coasting along for day after day. This was our hurdle day. Tomorrow, hopefully you'll remember the feeling of wearing the blindfold and having to rely on instinct, on trust. That's the connection every last one of you needs to have. You are six individuals, but at the same time, you are one unit. You have to be."

"Got it." Jimmy rolled his bandanna into a tight ball and tossed it like a jump shot into Leila's bag, thirty feet away, prompting whistles of appreciation.

Leila excused everyone and the two corps males bounded right out. The other dancers dropped to the floor, chatting as they removed their shoes and dug through their bags for dry clothes. A text ping diverted April's attention. It was from Russell.

Made way too much cornbread. Which goes with the way too much chili. Feel free to invite any and all over for dinner.

She laughed and repeated the message to everyone. "Anyone interested in a hot, free meal, four blocks away?" All hands shot in the air, even Katrina's. "Javier's got Dario tonight," she announced. "My turn to play."

"Must call Alice," Montserrat said from the musician's corner, whipping out her phone.

Jimmy rose. "April, I sure hope you don't mind, but I think we've got a party in the making."

April grinned. "What're we waiting for? Let's go. Party time!"

Minutes later, they all trooped over together and noisily spilled into the Garvey house. In no time, it was like the old days, when impromptu WCBT parties would double in size in less than an hour. Alice arrived. Ben arrived, lugging a half-case of wine. "Just to play it safe," he told April. "I remember our parties here from the past." Rebecca sidled up to him cozily and claimed two of the bottles, which together they opened and began to serve.

Russell produced his double-sized serving of chili—made on purpose because he liked to freeze the second half for a later meal—and his double-sized serving of cornbread, made accidentally because he'd been distracted and had forgotten to halve the industrial-sized recipe. "Come and help yourself, gang," he called out, and the kitchen became a loud, cheerful madhouse.

April moved to the far corner of the kitchen, where she could survey the activity from a distance. Montserrat joined her. "Now all you need is Anders here," she said.

April's lip curled. "I don't think so."

Montserrat looked at her curiously. "What's up between you two? I mean, you told me he was peeved that you drove out Hess, but clearly he's happy about the shape of Leila's ballet now, right?"

"Right."

"So it's something more. What aren't you telling me?"

April offered only a noncommittal shrug.

"I can appreciate that you might not want others in the company to hear you gripe," Montserrat said, "but something's up that's impacting you. I'm your friend. Take advantage of my outsider-ness and tell me."

She met Montserrat's expectant gaze. "Fine. He and I bickered last week, the same issue, that I might have caused irreparable harm, yadda, yadda, ya, and I told him that if Leila's ballet tanked, I'd offer my resignation. And he told me that if the ballet tanked, he'd take that resignation. To which I replied something along the lines of 'why wait, you can have my resignation now.' And I told him that at season's end, I'd leave."

Montserrat looked horrified. "What was his reply?"

"No reply. Ben called for him and they left the studio together."

She felt sick about it all over again.

"Oh, poor you," Montserrat said softly. "You've been having a bad month."

"Yeah, that's safe to say."

"It's just theatrics," Montserrat assured her. "He would *not* let you leave. You're too valuable."

"That's what Russell keeps insisting. But what you and Russell don't see is how, this time, it feels different," April insisted.

"It's a tense time and emotions are sky-high. My God, you've been put through the wringer. It's absolutely the wrong time for you to even consider making a big decision."

"What's done is done. Neither of us can un-say our words."

"Hey, April," Jimmy called out from across the kitchen as he held up an empty bowl. "Any chance there's more cheddar?"

"There is," she called back. "I'm on it." She left Montserrat to hunt down the cheese, secretly relieved to have ended the excruciating discussion about Anders.

She grated more cheese and chopped more onion. The kitchen gradually quieted as everyone took their bowls and plates into the living room, where the animated conversation and laughter continued.

Montserrat had slipped away but now returned to the kitchen, sliding her phone into her back pocket. "Well, that's done," she murmured to herself.

"What's done?" April asked.

Montserrat looked abashed, but only for a moment. "Okay, well, Anders is coming over."

April stared at her in disbelief. "Why?" she cried.

"Because I think this is what you two need. A more relaxed environment, away from the studios. And besides, stop thinking you're all alone. I'm here. Anders likes me. He desperately wants to play the Ravel sonata with me—he tells me so every time I see him at the studios. It's the perfect chance. And please tell me your piano is tuned."

"It is."

"Good. So. Just let me handle him, okay?"

"Fine," April snapped. "You answer the door, play host to him."

"I will. I promise."

April poured herself more wine and went upstairs to sit and cool down. Right then she felt as rebellious as a teen, upstairs sulking in her room, unwilling to admit that Montserrat might have come up with a good solution.

She heard Anders arrive and sneered into her wine. She stayed there through noisy greetings and laughter, the announcement that he and Montserrat would play the Ravel sonata, and the subsiding of conversation. Finally she heard the two of them start to play, and the anger wafted away. Montserrat's violin playing always did that to her.

April left the room and crept down the stairs. She saw that Kylie and Jen had joined the group. Russell was visible from the hallway, smiling as he watched Montserrat and Anders play.

Montserrat had been right. Watching Anders play the piano made a person instantly like him more. He was a stunning pianist, classically trained, and he loved playing. His expression changed when he played classical music, as did his body language. He softened. It allowed the music to flow through him, and cast his listeners in a spell. Every last person in the living room looked entranced.

Leila was sitting beside Anders on the bench, turning pages for him, a smile on her face as he and Montserrat played all three movements straight through. Leila's ballet used only the first two movements and a short coda to finish. The third movement was rapid-fire and electrifying, and hearing the sonata in its entirety made it all the more exhilarating. The moment the music ended, everyone began cheering and clapping.

"This is such a marvel, this sonata," Anders said.

"It is!" Leila exclaimed.

"Why aren't we using it all?" Anders asked her. "That whole third movement. It has such potential."

"I agree," Leila said. "I actually choreographed to it because I couldn't bear not to."

Anders cocked his head. "Tell me more."

She talked it out. Russell and Ben cleared the coffee table from the center and moved a few chairs so she could demonstrate. For Katrina, a quick solo. She'd be joined by another female, then joined by Jimmy. The three would have an exchange, through the incredibly fast music—the movement was called *Perpetuum Mobile* for a reason. "They run off, replaced by the ensemble, which mirrors what they did," Leila explained. "Then it cuts back to the three dancers, and finally everyone together."

"How long does it run with all three movements?" Anders asked.

"Seventeen and a half minutes," Leila said, "but there are repeating passages that could be cut. I've clocked the truncated version at fifteen minutes."

"That's a full ballet," Ben commented.

"Agreed," Leila admitted. "I knew it would be too long for a gala."

Anders looked thoughtful, as if he were genuinely considering it. Ben, meanwhile, was trying to radio his discomfort. "A full ballet in a gala," he told Anders, "would be highly irregular."

"True," Anders said. "People would talk about it after the performance, wouldn't they?"

Ben's jaw sagged. He started to say more, but Rebecca placed a warning hand on his thigh. April kept quiet, hardly daring to believe that Anders might highlight Leila's ballet in this way.

Alice broke the trance. "What the hell, Anders," she said, in a way only she could, because she didn't work for Anders or the WCBT anymore. "It's your company, your gala. Do what you want. Put it all in. Make a statement. This bold new commission that eclipses what you'd planned. All in a good way."

"For what it's worth," Leila said, "we could compress it all. Keep the dancers mostly onstage and the three movements could become one long one. The dancers could lounge by the musicians' corner when they're not 'onstage,' and that could add to the whimsy."

Anders pondered this and consulted Ben. "The timing of the program is already tight. Where can we shave a few minutes?"

"Nowhere," Ben retorted. "Not unless you pull something else."

"Something that's not up to speed yet," April interjected, which was probably unwise on her part, since she and Anders were at odds and, unlike Alice, she didn't have any kind of safe distance.

Anders knew, of course, which "something" she was talking about. He studied her, and she could almost see his thoughts circling.

"In a year, Palmira will ace the Don Q pas de deux," she said in a lower voice meant for just him. "She'll be a prize. Not rushing it this year will pay off for you."

He drew in a slow breath and expelled it.

"I want to see this third movement used." He turned to Ben. "Don Q is on hold."

Alice gave a loud whoop and Rebecca hugged Leila. Katrina, Jimmy and Dena stared at each other in shock.

"Anders, are you sure?" Ben asked. He didn't sound happy. "I'm feeling a bit uncomfortable with this impulse decision."

Anders shrugged. "That's your problem, not mine."

"What's Javier going to say?"

"Let's find out."

Anders picked up his phone and called Javier. He got straight to the point.

"The Don Q is out. A good idea, but it's not its time. Next year's gala, maybe."

April watched as Anders listened to Javier sputter his outrage. Anders' expression didn't change, except when Javier proposed something and Anders chuckled. "I'll ask her," he said. He pulled the phone from his ear and addressed Katrina. "He wants to know if you'd consider going back to the original setup."

She looked incredulous. "The one where he and I dance the Don Q pas de deux?"

Anders nodded.

"Not a chance! I *like* the new setup. This one right here."

Javier continued raging, how he hated that decisions were being made at a group gathering—and why hadn't he been invited? And suddenly *Katrina* was the one calling the shots, whispering into Anders' ear? "Put me on speaker phone," they heard him demand, which Anders, with a grin, had already done. He set the phone on the coffee table, where it seemed to vibrate with Javier's wrath.

"What do I get now?" Javier demanded. "This is absolute insanity."

"Don't get your knickers in a twist," Anders said mildly. "A solo. The Don Q men's solo variation?"

"It's too short!"

"The *Le Corsaire* variation," April proposed. "It's longer."

"That's dramatic and the crowd would love it," Anders agreed.

"But it's still too short!" Javier's broadcast voice shook with wrath.

"The solo from last year's world premiere?" Ben suggested. "That's longer."

"It's not dramatic enough for me!" Javier exclaimed. "Do you know what the audiences are expecting from someone of my stature? Big music, big, dramatic leaps and turns."

"Which brings us back to *Le Corsaire*," Anders said. "Think about it. You can tell me tomorrow which of the options you prefer. Come to my office before class."

He disconnected over Javier's continued protests, as April sat there, stunned by the speed in which fortunes had switched. Leila's ballet had just increased in size by a third, making it, for all intents and purposes, the gala's headliner. This was the biggest chance imaginable for Leila, but everything had to proceed just right. There would be no margin for error.

Leila's eyes met hers and April saw in them the same wild elation and gut-churning insecurity she was feeling.

Win big or lose big. Those were the only two options here.

Chapter 29

April

It was the conversation April dreaded having with Kylie. *Why did you do it?*

And the awkward, horrible, *do you still want to hurt yourself?*

She'd rehearsed and gauged the best time, but had continued to put it off. It was too terrifying, too overwhelming. What if it triggered Kylie and sent them all back to that place?

But then Katrina had said her bit, just before leaving the previous night's chili party. Speaking in private, she'd offered April a tearful *I am so, so sorry at any part I played in causing both Kylie and you pain.* The hug between them afterward had felt so comforting, so instantly settling, it gave April the courage to seek a similar closure with Kylie.

So here she was now, in the kitchen with Kylie, late the following afternoon. She drew a deep breath and blurted out both questions. Then she waited, heart hammering, for Kylie's reply.

Kylie's expression didn't change as she considered the questions. "I guess I did it because everything had just gotten so bad," she said finally. "I dunno, I just sort of crashed. I wasn't thinking straight that night. And, no, I don't want to hurt myself like that ever again. Yuck." She grimaced. "But it doesn't mean I feel all sunshiny and happy to be alive."

"What would make you feel happy to be alive?" She sounded like a therapist, and, indeed, had been coached by a therapist and told specifically how to ask these seemingly unaskable questions. Kylie didn't seem annoyed by how clumsy and stupid April sounded. Maybe she, too, had been coached by her therapist on how to respond to a well-meaning parent's awkward fumbling.

"I don't know," Kylie replied. "A place in life where I fit in. Where everything didn't hurt so much. Where people liked me, approved of me. And where the guy I was into was into me."

This was more than Kylie had ever confided to her. April was afraid to mention David's name for fear of breaking the spell. But it, too, needed to be voiced. She gestured to the kitchen table and they both sat, side by side, not looking at each other.

"Kylie," she began, "I see things at the studio, and I have this feeling that, well, David and Katrina are starting to explore a … closer, more personal relationship."

Kylie rolled her eyes and April felt like a fool.

"I'm not blind, Mom. I've been watching what's been going on. David's still my friend. I'd be a jerk if I didn't at least try to support him getting the thing he wanted most."

"I'm glad to hear that."

There was more. April hated herself for pushing it, but now was the time. "Katrina is someone who's been important in my life, *our* life, for so long, I'd like to keep that relationship going. But not if it hurts you. You and your feelings come first here. If it's too painful, I'll step away. She knows she'll always have the support of the other moms in our group."

Kylie didn't respond at first. She just looked at April with those big blue-green eyes that dominated her face. It was a jolt, seeing how Kylie had changed, just in these past few weeks, from a girl to a young woman. One showing early signs of an uncommon beauty. No, not Jen's beauty. Something more singular.

"I'm fine with Katrina, Mom. I know I still owe her an apology for shirking my responsibility that night. I messed up her makeup, too, and I know I need to replace it. How should I go about doing that?"

Fourteen years old, and already sounding so mature, so calmly resigned to the world's unfairness. April wanted to reach over, gather Kylie in her arms and hold her close, make all her daughter's pain go away. But she couldn't do that, any more than she could solve Katrina's problems.

"I think a nice gesture would be to get Katrina a gift card for Sephora or Nordstrom. Say, for fifty dollars. I'll cover half, in fact. But, in return, I'd like you to find the time to come to the studios and give it to her in person. It can be during a rehearsal I'm running. And know this—Katrina feels contrite in the same way. She understands now that she played a part in hurting you."

Kylie shook her head. "She doesn't owe me an apology for anything."

"It's what she's feeling inside. She's known you since you were a baby. All of us moms—we feel the responsibility for the well-being of all you kids, not just our own."

"Well, that's nice of her. And I think the gift-card idea is a good one."

"Great." April hesitated. "There's one last thing I need to say."

"Yeah?" Kylie looked up, alerted by April's change of tone.

"That terrible afternoon. You texted and told me you didn't think you could babysit that night. And I insisted. I think I lectured you. I'm sorry, honey. I'm so sorry."

The memory of her glib "you *will* go" demand made a sob arise in April's throat, and that was it—the dam burst, pent up for too long. She buried her face in her hands, appalled by the noisy sobs that kept coming, yet helpless to stop them.

"Oh, Mommy," she heard Kylie say softly. She stood behind April and draped her arms over her mother's shoulders, her body like a warm blanket. April reached up a hand and clutched at Kylie's arm.

How strong she'd become, this curious, wayward daughter of hers. How like her father, in her ability to provide comfort at the important times.

"I love you," April managed.

"I love you, too, Mom. Don't apologize for telling me I had to go. You're teaching me responsibility."

For a moment, neither of them spoke, but April could feel her own heaviness lessen as Kylie withdrew her arms and returned to her chair.

"Montserrat asked me if I could watch Emma on a weekday afternoon once a week, starting next month," Kylie said. "She'd be there, upstairs in her rehearsal studio, working. I told her okay if you thought it was okay. I like Emma. I like girls. She's both serious and cute. And very smart."

"Yes. I think that would be a great fit. 'Serious, cute and smart.' That could describe you at that age, too. You'll have to call her Little Kylie. I'll bet she'd like that."

She chuckled. "Montserrat said the same thing."

"She did? Well, there you have it. Great minds—"

"—think alike," Kylie and April said at the same time, and they both laughed.

April rose. "Okay, enough of this being weepy and emotional. I've got a dinner to make."

"Want help?"

"I do." She glanced over at Kylie in surprise. This was new.

This was good.

As they worked together, Kylie scrubbing red potatoes as April prepped a pork roast for the oven, a peaceful silence descended over them. Which wasn't to say April felt peaceful inside. The familiar worries resumed their hum inside her brain. Frets about the various rehearsals and demands from Anders. Concerns about Leila's fledgling ballet, and the deep shit she'd be in if it didn't bloom into something amazing. Then she stopped to consider that life couldn't have offered her a bigger gift than the one she had right here, standing beside her, absently humming a tune. This daughter of hers who had not been lost, after all, no matter how perilous it had seemed that night, that week, and who, miraculously, was finding her own way through healing.

The miracle won.

Chapter 30

Katrina

The ladies' room on the WCBT's executive level had a spacious lounge area, with full-length mirror, coffee table and a pair of comfortable armchairs. What it also had was privacy. With ten minutes before her next rehearsal, Katrina entered and happily sank into one of the armchairs to mentally replay her just-concluded encounter with David. Since that first night's kiss, they'd strived to interact professionally around each other in the studios, but ten minutes earlier, when they'd crossed paths in the empty back stairwell, they'd immediately lunged at each other in an uninhibited tango of grabbing, kissing and laughing, that thrilled her to the core and filled her with an overflowing sense of physical well-being.

She relaxed deeper into the armchair to further consider the pleasure of the encounter. How silken and warm the skin on his backside had felt, how arousing when his lips traveled up and down her neck, his pelvis pressing into hers, igniting something frenzied in her.

Her thoughts were interrupted by the sound of a stifled sob. She craned her neck and saw, in the mirror's reflection, a pair of feet beneath a closed stall door. The pink satin footwear gave it away: a dancer. She recognized the brightly flowered dance bag on the floor, as well.

It was Palmira. She was crying. And probably praying Katrina would just go away.

It would have been Katrina's instinct to do just that, a few weeks prior. A younger dancer's drama wasn't her problem. Now, with her continued guilt in the aftermath of the Kylie crisis, she'd found herself wanting to reach out and help. It was an April kind of thing to do.

Another sob arose from within the stall. That solved it, Katrina decided. She simply couldn't ignore a young dancer in that kind of pain.

She approached the stall. "Palmira? It's Katrina. Come out here. Let's talk."

"Please go away," Palmira said in a shaky voice.

"You'll feel better if you talk about it."

"No I won't. Please just go."

"I'm not going to do that. I'm just going to wait till you're ready to come out."

Palmira gave a sigh, a mix of despair and exasperation. "Fine," she said, and a moment later, the stall door opened.

She looked so young, her eyes red, her makeup smudged, that it made Katrina's maternal heart lurch. After Palmira washed her hands and dabbed at her face, Katrina gestured to the armchairs.

They took a seat in silence, as Katrina debated over what April might say. "It'll be okay," she told Palmira, cringing at the ineptitude of her words. "No matter how jagged and painful it might feel right now."

"Thanks, but it's not going to be okay." Palmira said. "It'll be anything but okay."

"Tell me what's up."

"I'm out of the gala, just like that, and I have family members coming to the performance. Six of them. They've already bought their plane tickets, their gala tickets. It was a big investment on their part, and my moment to show them all that their sacrifices for me had been worth it. And now? I won't even be on the stage."

Her eyes filled with tears again. "And then there's this—I let Javier down. I'm the reason Don Q got pulled. He's angry with me, and so am I." She covered her face with her hands and her body shook with sobs.

Javier and his moods again, Katrina thought wryly. Since losing Don Q for the gala, they'd barely spoken, his eyes channeling fury toward her, as if it had somehow been her fault. She could handle his moods. What was unfair was his foisting them onto a young dancer intimidated by his magnificence, one who'd been doing the best she could. "Javier is a spoiled man-child who's used to having everything his way," Katrina burst out. "He should be understanding, not angry toward you. I mean, is Anders acting angry toward you?"

"No," Palmira admitted. "He was blunt about it when he told us, but not in a mean way."

"There you go. Anders is business. Javier lets his emotions get in the way."

Palmira said nothing in reply, but she seemed calmer, patting away the last of the tears and drawing in deeper breaths.

They sat there, mulling over the situation, when an idea sprang up. Leila had yet to finish choreographing the new section of her ballet; she planned to do it in today's rehearsal, based on the dancers' input.

Palmira could fit into it like the last puzzle piece.

Katrina leapt to her feet. "I've got a fabulous idea, one you and your family would love. Come with me right now."

Palmira was slower to rise. "But what? Why?"

"No time to explain." She grabbed her dance bag from the floor and motioned for Palmira to grab hers. "Let's go."

Minutes later, she and Palmira arrived at the studio. Leila, Montserrat and April were already there, chatting by the musicians' corner. Palmira hung back at the door, but Katrina took her hand and tugged her in.

"I've got this amazing idea," Katrina called out to Leila. "I really like it, and I'm hoping you'll feel the same."

Leila smiled at her. "Tell me. I like the fire in your eyes. In fact, I'm tempted to say 'yes' based on that alone."

The others laughed as Katrina gazed fixedly at Leila. "Palmira should be our third female in the new section. Remember when you explained it to Anders in April's living room, you described it as a sort of demi-soloist role? Palmira's perfect for it."

Palmira emitted a little gasp. Leila paused to consider this before turning to April. "You've seen her dance and I haven't," she said in a quiet voice meant for April alone, but of course they were all listening. "Would she be a good fit?"

April glanced at Katrina before responding, and her expression grew soft, like that of a proud mother watching her child ace something on the first try. She turned back to Leila. "Yes. I think Katrina's suggestion is perfect."

Rebecca and Dena came into the studio and stopped short at the sight of them. Palmira had started sniffling again, wiping her eyes, as April slung an arm over her shoulder, giving her a warm squeeze.

"What's up?" Dena asked. "Don't tell me something bad has happened."

"Something good," Leila said. "Meet our seventh cast member."

Amid the exclamations and congratulations that followed, Rebecca paused. "But we just told Marketing that your ballet is called *Sonata for Six*. As in, six cast members, right?"

"I guess we're changing the name," Leila said, laughter in her voice.

"What if the playbills have already gone to print?" Rebecca persisted. "I know the promotional material already has."

"They'll just have to cross out the six and add a seven," April joked.

"Wait!" Leila clutched at April's arm. "Let's do that anyway!"

Rebecca wrinkled her nose. "You mean like this?"

She walked over to the dry-erase board by the door and wrote it out: *Sonata for ~~Six~~ Seven*

Now they were all whooping with laughter, over its wit, its irony for this eleventh-hour ballet with its eleventh-hour section added and now, an eleventh-hour cast member.

"It's a keeper!" Leila cried, and everyone agreed.

It all worked. Leila tweaked the already-completed sections, and the ensemble adapted to the changes. Palmira and Dena connected instantly, each working to help make the other even stronger. The new choreography included a section where the two of them danced together, holding hands like young girls, supporting each other through leaps and aerial cartwheels. Seeing the joy in both their eyes as they waltzed and cavorted made Katrina feel absurdly happy.

She had the power to help younger females, she realized. Not just here but throughout the company. And beyond.

As in, Kylie.

Leila and Katrina had planned one last koshari dinner together, on a night when Javier had Dario. As they dug into their meals, Katrina brought up Kylie.

"I liked meeting her at April's chili party," Leila mused. "What a cutie. So smart."

"Very smart," Katrina agreed. "In truth, she intimidates me. I'm closer with Jen, April's other daughter, because we speak the same language—ballet. But I can't take that avenue with Kylie."

There was more, of course. She hesitated, then blurted out the rest. "I don't know if you've noticed, but David and I have gotten involved."

Leila hooted with laughter and Katrina felt her ears burn. Leila, noting her discomfort, patted Katrina's hand. "Yes. I noticed. We all have. I think it's wonderful."

"What you might not know is that Kylie was harboring a massive crush on David."

Leila grew serious. "Oh, no. And does that mean it played a part in her emotional breakdown?"

"That's my hunch. But it's not something I feel like I can share with anyone besides you. So it goes nowhere beyond this table, please."

"Absolutely."

"Anyway. In regards to my own David development, I feel so happy and carefree, it almost seems unfair. Like, maybe I don't deserve this happiness right now."

Leila shook her head. "Don't go there. You're an adult woman who's earned this chance to have a lot of fun. You and David are fantastic together. You're drawing out his more serious side and he's making you more playful. It's so much fun to see. Kylie's plight here is heartbreaking, agreed, but it's something every teen has to go through." She tore off a piece of pita bread and chewed reflectively. "But, that said, you can help her in a unique way."

"How?"

"Befriend her publicly. You're a celebrity, and teens groove on being connected to fame. Even a casual friendship with Kylie, going out for ice cream cones, or popping into one of those pricey boutiques on Hayes Street, would pay off for her in dividends."

Katrina was hesitant. "I hear what you're saying. But I'm socially awkward. An introvert. Kylie would see through it instantly."

Out of nowhere arose the memory of the Cairo dream from weeks earlier. She told Leila about it, the way she and Kylie, both just girls, were fighting over a bowl of koshari. Dreams always seemed so absurd when you recounted them later, and by the end, she was laughing, shaking her head over it.

But Leila wasn't laughing. Instead, she looked keen, alert.

"I have it. I know how you can bridge that gap with Kylie."

"How?" Katrina leaned in, intrigued.

Leila shook her head. "I have to create it first."

"Give me a hint!"

"Hmm." Leila looked mischievous. So like Nabila. "I'll say this. The answer is all around you." She gestured to the restaurant's walls, with its posters and Egyptian memorabilia.

"What does that mean?!"

"Something for you to think about. I'll say no more."

Chapter 31

Katrina

A flawless performance of Leila's ballet would have been nice on gala night, but that wasn't what they got. And yet, somehow, that made it all the more electric.

Amid the minimalist set design—blue gel lights against a textured backdrop, with tall Grecian columns in each corner—the group of them waltzed, scampered, twisted, jumped and flowed. A jeweled bodice affixed to chiffon skirts for the women, in colors that matched the men's slacks and tops, had been created in record time, although a bodice malfunction forced Dena to dart backstage eight counts early, where a Wardrobe member hastily restitched the open seam just in time for her to step out right at her next timed cue.

Other little gaffes appeared, here and there, reminiscent of the time they'd groped around blindfolded, keenly aware of the others in a kinetic, protective way. When, at one point, Katrina slipped out of Jimmy's grasp because his hand was so sweaty, the two ensemble males, eyes round with horror, reached out simultaneously to catch her from falling and flung her right back into Jimmy's arms. The audience laughed, clearly assuming it was all part of the whimsical touch.

From that moment on, it all became pure, riotous fun. Katrina relished the second movement's duet with Jimmy, the problem spot solved in the intimate Friday rehearsal with just Leila, her and David. When Katrina's pointe shoe slid up Jimmy's leg, Montserrat's violin sounded positively flirtatious. The audience loved it. Jimmy hammed up the look of shocked reproof as he slapped her meandering foot down, and the audience burst into laughter, right where Leila had hoped they would.

The third movement, frenzied and distilled, flew. As an ensemble, all seven of them executed the last sixteen counts in perfect unison, right down to the moment they leapt in the air and the lights went out just as the music ended, all of them still airborne. They landed in the darkness, laughing in sheer exhilaration, as they scrambled to clear the stage for a return of the stage lights, and curtain call. First the ensemble dancers. Then Jimmy and Katrina.

The cries of approval intensified as she sank in her curtsy. A second curtsy, deeper and more reflective, expressed what she couldn't put into words. Gratitude. Relief. The rightness of the risks taken so that she could be here right now, instead of being caught in the grips of Edwin's darkness.

Thanks to April and Leila.

She'd never felt so humbled and elated at the same time.

For the first time since forever, Katrina had a date at the gala after-party, with someone she was deeply attracted to, a relationship so full of promise, it thrilled her even as it unnerved her. Before fun, though, came work: company-mandated socializing at the party with donors, guests, anyone wishing to engage with the company stars. Javier was by her side, as per normal, but keeping a chilly emotional distance. He'd gotten a roaring standing ovation for his solo performance, but he was still miffed, she could tell.

David was nearby, engaged in conversation with Brent. Seeing her date, a sweet fluttering feeling shot through her, tinted with worry.

Two days earlier they'd been alone in the hallway, holding hands, but at the sound of approaching dancers, she'd abruptly yanked her hand away. He'd called her on it later, asking if her intention was to keep their relationship a "forever" secret in public. "If it's a 'not just yet' thing," he'd said, "I'm totally on board with that. The gala, and all. But if we're going to continue operating in the shadows because you don't plan to ever take a relationship with me seriously, that's different."

She'd protested that yes, she was taking it seriously, and how could he think otherwise?

"I guess it's because I see how comfortable all you dancers are with illusion, keeping a façade. And of course you have to be, to perform so convincingly. But I wonder if all of you notice how it seeps into your personal lives. And not necessarily for the better."

He'd immediately apologized, saying it had come out all wrong, and for her to just ignore his words, but the matter had weighed on her since.

Now she studied him from several feet away. Both David and Brent were extraordinarily good-looking men, well dressed in their fine wool suits, much the same height, separated only by their ages. Even then, it was tricky. Brent, in his mid-forties, still looked youthful, and David, not yet thirty, had cut his hair short, which instantly transformed him from easygoing Gen Xer to ageless urban hottie. He now looked like Brad Pitt.

She'd always had a thing for Brad Pitt.

She herself had dressed more daringly than usual, in a shimmery red satin evening gown with a halter neck and bare back. It was a dress intended to make a statement, to seduce—one person in particular. Javier looked startled when he first noticed the backside exposure.

"Is that appropriate?" he asked in disapproval.

"I should think so."

"For one of the corps girls, maybe. But for a 37-year old? The mother of a child? I should think not."

She would not take his bait, she vowed. She would not let him bring her down tonight.

Guests approached to congratulate them on their performances and to chat. Several inquired about Dario.

"Your son's asleep at home, I imagine," a portly, silver-haired woman said to them.

Javier replied first. "Same as always, with his favorite sitter. He knows the drill now."

"You three make *such* a lovely family."

Javier's arm tightened around Katrina's waist. "Thank you. Is it wrong of me to think the same? My family—such a treasure. I feel like the most fortunate man in the world!"

Why was he acting as if nothing had changed? she wondered irritably.

Because he wanted it both ways, she realized: his real life and the one he displayed to the public. David's words came rushing back to her.

He'd been absolutely right. She and Javier were no different, in the end. Both of them had profited well from the illusion of a domestic partnership. *This* was why Javier didn't like her budding relationship with David, and why he kept pushing Martin at her. David was real. He had no interest in illusion. Martin would have been happy to play the Javier game.

As Javier continued offering the patron more of his favorite Dario-and-his-parents stories—growing increasingly stale—Katrina fantasized about going "real" with the conversation.

Being a single mom sure is a challenge! But Javier's twice-a-week dad duty gives me time off and I'm learning to embrace it. Like this Saturday night, where I plan to get naked and seduce a younger man that I'm wildly attracted to, and boy, can you believe I've gone a full decade since having that feeling? I'll tell you what, this weekend my plan is to make up for lost time.

She snickered to herself, which made Javier, in the middle of his story, cast her a sideways glance. As soon as the woman moved on, he turned to her in a huff. "I was trying to share a tender moment! It's like you weren't even paying attention. That was rude. And to have you *laugh* about it?"

"I wasn't laughing about the story. I was just thinking of something funny."

"Well, stop it. We're here to promote the company and our place at the top of the company roster. We're expected to behave in an exemplary fashion."

"What, and tell Dario stories that are past their best-by date?"

His expression darkened. "What's gotten into you lately? It's like you're set on destroying tradition, decorum, off on some selfish tirade of late."

The thought was so lopsided and wrong, she didn't know whether to argue the point that he was merely projecting, or to sneer in his face.

She was suddenly so tired of him.

"See you later. I'm done here."

She swung around, sensing Javier's shock. It wasn't part of their routine. She, meanwhile, walked right over to David and Brent, who welcomed her with smiles, making her feel better immediately. The heaviness returned the moment Javier joined them, silent and sullen, in a way that had even Brent shooting him concerned looks. She ignored him and focused on the anecdote David was sharing, which was hilarious, tender, and self-effacing. Anders joined their group, greeting Brent and David, content to listen as David finished his story with a quirky conclusion that left them all chuckling.

Anders turned to Javier and Katrina. "A few minutes of your time, you two?" Anders gestured to a private alcove. She and Javier nodded, and the three of them made their way through the friendly, boisterous crowd.

Once in the alcove, Katrina noticed that Anders looked particularly happy. "I just had a nice conversation with Mr. and Mrs. Kaplan. They thought you and *Sonata for Seven* were stunning," he told Katrina. "Helen Kaplan gushed that you revealed a brand-new you tonight. They'd like to see the ballet included in next year's repertory season. They're willing to be lead sponsors for it."

The Kaplans and their foundation were one of the WCBT's top donors. Their word was gold; if they said they wanted to see *Sonata for Seven* and financially support it, Anders could bank on it.

Which explained the gleam in Anders' smile.

"Did Mrs. Kaplan mention liking anything else in particular?" Javier asked.

"As in, your *Le Corsaire* solo?"

"Precisely." Javier looked both eager and expectant.

"In truth, she just wanted to talk about *Sonata for Seven*. She did ask about you, though. Wondered why you and Katrina weren't dancing together. I explained how you felt it would profit you both to mix things up, perform with some of the up-and-coming talent."

"But I didn't!" Javier protested. "You didn't let me!"

"A mere delay. Next year, perhaps." A frown replaced Anders' smile. "Now let's talk about this sulky mood of yours. When the world doesn't go your way, my friend, you need to smile and take it. Like you and I told Katrina to do, just a few short weeks back."

Javier scowled. "Excuse me, but it seems to me you're taking her side on everything all of a sudden."

"Nonsense. There are no 'sides'. There is simply the company, moving forward. Finishing an important performance and moving on to the next one."

Katrina glanced over at David and saw, to her alarm, that he and Brent were now surrounded by a trio of corps girls, utterly lovely in their long, shimmery gowns, so dewy and fresh in their youth. The old sense of despair flashed through her; he couldn't possibly find her more desirable than these girls. She watched them flirt with him and, to her dismay, one of them tugged at his arm, gesturing toward the dance floor. David, however, only shook his head, smiled and gestured to Brent, as if their conversation were too compelling for him to leave. The girls put on mock-pouts and good-natured shrugs before leaving to find someone else to dance with.

The muscles she hadn't realized she'd clenched began to relax.

Javier had noticed the exchange.

"He's your date tonight, isn't he?" he asked, spitting out the question like it was bitter.

"Yes. And?"

Anders crossed his arms and watched the two of them in amusement.

"He's eye candy. I saw him just now, flirting with the girls. What kind of date is that?"

"One who politely declines the offer to join them on the dance floor in order to remain in conversation with—oh, look, it's *your* date. Which you're allowed to have, and yet, I'm not?"

"David Lavigne is a boy. A junior accompanist." Javier turned to Anders. "She's gotten romantically involved with him. Were you aware?"

He made it sound like she'd committed a felony.

"She is your star female principal," Javier continued. "Doesn't she deserve to be seen with someone of the highest caliber, the highest standards?"

"Like … you?" Anders inquired dryly.

"Exactly!" Javier exclaimed, unaware it had been a joke.

One thing Javier hadn't noticed around the studios: Anders liked David. Each admired the other's skills on the piano and they frequently conversed about the challenges and nuances of various piano compositions.

"A mere piano player." Javier wrinkled his nose, digging himself into a deeper hole. Katrina, meanwhile, knew when to keep her mouth shut.

"Do you know how good a pianist David Lavigne is?" Anders asked Javier, in a tone that was both pleasant and withering. "I'd like to think I'm a very competent pianist, but he's leagues above me. Not just me, but all our accompanists. His talent, his musical instincts are huge. A competition gold medal is all that stands between him and an illustrious career as a concert soloist. He might still get there. In the meantime, I deem it our privilege to have him on staff. You should reconsider your attitude."

Anders looked over their shoulder and nodded to someone. "Excuse me. It appears I'm needed elsewhere. Now please go back out and be the golden couple our patrons love." He offered them a smile that mirrored his confidence that they'd be obedient and comply without question.

Except that, maybe, she was done with blind compliance. She tested out the idea on inner Katja, who sputtered with laughter.

Oh, my. Yes.

"Thanks, I think I'll take a pass," she announced airily. "I'm spending the rest of the evening with my date. Holding his hand. Maybe even holding his ass. Because I can."

They stared at her, dumbstruck, which amused her. Had she ever so effectively silenced the two of them before?

"You know, I'm all about sustaining an illusion onstage," she continued. "And look at how diligently I've sustained our 'family of three' image, that so appeals to our public. But things have changed, haven't they?"

Javier found his voice. "What hasn't changed is that you and I are supposed to be side-by-side at this event, spending time with our patrons."

"I have no problem spending time with our patrons, nor being by your side. But I'm going to ask my date to be on my other side. Which isn't so far-fetched, is it?" She turned to Anders. "See how David and Brent have hit it off beautifully—how convenient is that? We can be a happy, chatty group of four. None of us pretending something's not there, or pretending that something *is* there." She turned back to Javier. "And for the record, why are you talking to the patrons as if the three of us still live together as a family? We don't. Why aren't you proud of your emancipation? This big change in your life you were so eager about making. And I'm asking myself now why I should have to hide my own new relationship. Why I can't publicly display affection toward him—how stupid is that?"

Javier sputtered to find the right retort as Anders regarded her warily. "What happened to our sweet, compliant Katja?"

"Oh, Anders." She had to laugh. "Katja was never compliant. Not the real Katja. She was just sleeping."

She tossed back the last gulp of her champagne before handing the glass to a passing server. "I'm going to rejoin Brent and David. That's where the fun is. Feel free to join me, Javier." Without waiting for a response, she walked away.

David looked up, as if sensing her new intention. He set down his own glass on a nearby cocktail table and watched her approach. She marveled over the truth of the cliché of feeling like the only ones in the room. She saw in his eyes a reflection of her own wonder and delight.

She was his grand prize.

Had she ever felt so cherished before, by someone she herself was so attracted to?

Time to claim her own grand prize.

She strode right up to him and did the thing she'd wanted to do in the studios, the hallways, every time she saw him. She pressed her body right into his, arms around his neck, pelvis against pelvis, lips millimeters from his face.

She sensed his surprise, but he adapted quickly. Soon, his hands were sliding up and down over her bare back. "This is an incredible dress," he murmured into her ear, and she laughed.

"If you want to come home with me," she whispered back, "I've also got a negligée, same color, same material. Well, maybe less material. Okay, a lot less."

His chuckle vibrated through her chest. "I'd love to see that."

"I've also got a spare men's robe, a spare toothbrush. Should you opt to stay the night."

"Good to know. I make really good pancakes, by the way. If the offer to stay should extend into the morning."

"That is highly possible. Dario's crazy about pancakes."

"I'm so glad. About both things." He gave her a soft squeeze that made her breathless with happiness.

She heard Javier's petulant voice and Brent's soothing reply. She sensed that people around them were watching. She even heard murmurs, a distinct "would you look at *that?*" followed by the click of someone snapping a picture. She lifted her gaze, met David's eyes, and kissed him, a slow, luscious, anything-but-chaste kiss.

"Excuse me." Javier's voice broke through. "This is embarrassing. Katja, stop it!"

Laughing, they pulled apart. Katrina took David's hand and held on tight, through the next hour, as the four of them circulated, smiling, chatting, greeting patrons and donors. No one commented that she was holding one man's hand and Javier was holding another man's hand, but she saw their eyes take it all in with great interest.

"I guess it's a new stage in their lives," she heard someone say. And, to her amusement, a hushed "wow, he's a hottie. Lucky her."

Lucky me. Lucky, lucky me.

Chapter 32

Kylie

Saturday afternoon, the day after the gala, several members of the company gravitated to the Garvey house, looking for a place to celebrate. More joined them, as well as outside friends like Alice and Montserrat, and by nightfall, it had officially become another party. This time the group included Javier and his partner Brent, both of whom were keeping an eye on Dario. Good thing, because Kylie would have said "not a chance" to a request that she watch Dario while the adults had fun.

The gala had been well received. Print newspaper reviews and printouts of online reviews were accruing on the kitchen table, and every now and then there was a cry of pleasure when a new online review was published, which her dad printed out and added to the pile. Anders was almost unrecognizable, all chatty and amiable, roping his arm around her mom's shoulders, giving her a kiss on the cheek and telling her how much he loved her.

The *New York Times* had been very approving of Leila's ballet. Her dad, smiling, had handed Kylie the article. "Read the second half," he said.

Her eyes raced to the spot.

Particularly memorable was Leila Bertrand's smart, sassy, world premiere of Sonata for ~~Six~~ Seven, *which closed the program. Lead dancers Katrina Devries and James Reinhardt burst forth with an uncanny energy and appealing synergy that held strong through the three movements. Bertrand, in her first North American commission, judiciously utilized a backup ensemble of five dancers in a brisk, propulsive ballet that explored personal relationships between couples and beyond. A tender pas de deux between Devries and Reinhardt utilized stillness as effectively as the tumultuous partnered movements that followed. All the dancers dazzled in a final ensemble flurry of dancing laced with witty touches. Set to Ravel's Violin Sonata, performed by Queen Elisabeth Competition laureates Montserrat Benes Fortray (violin, 1998) and Fedir Melnyk (piano, 2002), featuring Carolyn Wright's costumes and Lee Kassav's scenic design,* Sonata for ~~Six~~ Seven *flies, leaving one clamoring for more, more. Kudos to savvy, risk-taking programming decisions by artistic director Anders Gunst, which should pay off in dividends for seasons to come.*

Her dad opened bottle after bottle of champagne, as more people kept showing up to join the celebration. But what Kylie hadn't counted on was that David would show up with Katrina.

The first thing she noticed: he'd cut his hair. She hated it. It made him look so much older. He'd done it for Katrina, she was certain. The second thing she'd noticed: they'd become physically as well as romantically involved. She saw the way they stood so close, touching each other's backsides. It hurt. Beyond hurt. She went to the top floor, into the tiny bathroom, locked the door, and cried for five minutes straight.

Finally she wiped off her face and went to her dad's study, which had a little fridge. She pulled out a Coke and drank it so fast, it burned going down and sent pinpricks through the inside of her nose. She sneezed, and a second later, up came a big, satisfying burp, which made her feel better. Thus reinforced, she went downstairs and joined the others.

She found David and Katrina in the living room and walked toward them, her footsteps slowing as she drew closer. From across the room, she caught the look of alarm in her mother's eyes. Fear, even. It made her own heart thump double time. For an instant she thought of bolting, unseen, to safety, but something stern inside her told her there was no way around this. Otherwise, it would just be the elephant in the room, forever.

Katrina's face lit up when she saw Kylie, which confused but pleased her. It made up for the fact that David only slowly, reluctantly looked from Katrina (the prize) to Kylie (the liability). Katrina beckoned her closer and then reached over to grab a gift bag from a nearby end table. The bag was colorful and festive, with tissue blooming out like a giant flower, and apparently it was for Kylie.

"It's from Leila," Katrina explained.

"Wait. Leila, like the choreographer?" she asked, and instantly regretted how stupid she sounded.

But Katrina only nodded, a sense of excitement brightening her gaze.

"Wow," Kylie said. "That was nice of her. But … why?"

"I don't know," Katrina admitted. "But it seemed very important to her. She handed it to me at our farewell lunch today, and told me I was to be there, next to you, when you opened it."

Kylie had liked Leila. At the last Garvey party, they'd talked about classical music, and Leila had told Kylie about a CD she loved that blended Mozart and North African music. She'd promised to try and get Kylie a copy. Probably, Kylie decided, that was what this was all about.

"Let's sit at the table," Katrina proposed as she passed the bag to Kylie. "I think there's multiple things in the bag." She turned to David and handed him her empty glass. "Fetch me a refill, *mon amour?*"

"Nothing would make me happier," he replied in a silken bedroom voice.

It felt like swallowing knives, being around their intimacy. Kylie wanted to retreat inside herself and shut down, except that now David turned to smile at her, too. "And Kylie? My favorite young friend in the world?"

Their eyes met, hers with difficulty, his laden with something like entreaty, which was a million times better than the unease he'd displayed when visiting her at the behavioral health unit. *Can we still be friends?* his eyes seemed to be asking.

She considered this and gave him a grudging nod. "All right. I'll take a Cherry Coke." She hesitated. "Thank you."

She and Katrina situated themselves at the corner of the dining room table. As Katrina watched, Kylie pulled out what was, sure enough, the CD. "She found a copy after all!" she exclaimed. In spite of herself, she grinned. "She wasn't sure how widely distributed it was. She got her own copy in Paris." She fingered the CD's outer case. It looked Egyptian, a dusty gold with writing on it like it was an ancient map, with a superimposed giant eye. "That must be the title in Egyptian," she said, handing the CD to Katrina.

"I think you're right." Katrina gently traced the cover with her finger. "The eye artwork, too, is very Egyptian. It's gorgeous. The whole cover is." She looked up. "What else is in the bag? It felt heavy."

Kylie plunged her hand back into the bag and pulled out more items wrapped in tissue. Store-bought cookies, the packaging, curiously, written in Arabic. A packet of dates. A tiny flask of an essential-oil blend, that smelled heavenly, like cardamom, roses, and something rich, earthy and spicy. "Frankincense, I'll bet," Katrina said after taking a sniff.

It seemed everything shared a North African theme. Kylie's excitement built. Katrina, beside her, seemed just as excited. With each item Kylie pulled out and unwrapped, Katrina would laugh, a girlish peal that made her seem so much younger. A small, colorful, fabric coin purse with a thin shoulder strap. A little carved cat figurine, long and lean, looking very regal. A silver ring that had a flat surface on top, Arabic script, and some sort of bird. "This is *so* Egyptian." Katrina gestured to the design of the ring. "See the way the coils branch out, like vines or snakes? That's how Egyptian women love their jewelry. You don't see this kind of specific detail here very often. Not like in Cairo." Her voice grew soft. "This is the kind of thing Nabila, my nanny, would wear. Sometimes five rings at once. All the women did that."

"An Egyptian nanny?"

"She was hired help, not really a nanny. But she was my closest friend and, yes, she was Egyptian. Like Zahra, our housekeeper."

"Were there a lot of Egyptians in Paris, or something?"

"This wasn't Paris. My parents and I lived in Egypt."

Kylie gaped at her in surprise. She'd been so sure she knew everything about Katrina already. "You lived in *Egypt*?"

"I did. When I was eight, we moved to Cairo."

She struggled to take this all in. Katrina was so Parisian, even though Kylie knew she was half-Dutch and Dutch-born. But this news scrambled everything in her mind.

"Is that it?" Katrina gestured to the bag.

"No, there's more." Kylie drew out a bulky object and unwrapped it. It was a bigger figurine, glossy ebony, a warrior with a dog's face, sporting a gold wrap around his waist and one around his neck, like a collar.

"Ooh, that's Anubis, the Egyptian god of mummification," Katrina said. "He was also the protector of the dead and a guide for the souls in the afterlife."

"Is he a dog or a man?"

"He had the body of a man and the head of a jackal." She chuckled and shook her head. "I haven't thought of Anubis since I lived in Cairo. Nabila was the one to tell me all about the Egyptian gods. What a strange feeling to think about it now."

The two of them regarded the treasures in silence.

"Why did Leila give me all this?" Kylie asked finally. "And why did she give it to you to give to me?"

Katrina smiled wistfully. "I have a feeling she wanted me to tell you about Cairo. Tell my stories."

Kylie peered into the bag. "Oh, there's something more. It's much lighter." She pulled out the package and unwrapped it. There lay a long gossamer scarf, translucent blue, almost weightless against Kylie's fingers. She held it up and gazed at it in wonder. It was like something out of *The Arabian Nights*.

Katrina laughed out loud. "Oh, that was definitely her plan. She is so clever."

"Why? What's this?"

"All right, the secret's out. I learned to belly dance before I ever had a ballet lesson. I took it quite seriously. My first costume consisted of scarves like that, tucked into my shorts."

"A belly dancer?! You're kidding."

"I'm not."

She stared at Katrina in delight. Never in a million years would she have guessed Katrina would have such an interesting story to tell.

David returned with the drinks. "Sorry, I got derailed by

conversation," he explained, but Katrina's news was much more compelling and for once, the attention didn't realign to focus on him. Katrina, too, kept her gaze on Kylie, mirth in her eyes.

"I'll tell you about it later," she said.

"Promise?" Kylie asked.

"Promise."

There was an envelope in the bottom of the bag. Kylie opened it to reveal a handmade gift certificate that said "Good for one free serving of koshari"—whatever koshari was—and stated, in legalese, that Katrina would serve as Leila's proxy in making it happen.

Katrina burst into laughter when she read it. "Perfect. How clever of Leila. We'll do a koshari date and that'll be when I tell you the rest."

"Is koshari good?" Kylie asked eagerly.

"It is. It's Egyptian comfort food. Warm and savory and tasty. Leila and I found a restaurant on Geary with true Egyptian food."

"Do I get to go too?" David asked, and Katrina looked surprised.

"Of course not. It's supposed to be just Kylie and me. I think Leila wanted it that way." Katrina looked at Kylie and they both nodded.

"All right," David said. "But Kylie, she's not allowed to join us when you and I go out on our next burger date. I say that's fair. Agreed?"

"Agreed," Katrina and Kylie said at the same time, and they all laughed.

Anders called out to Katrina from across the room, gesturing for her and David to join him.

"I think we're being summoned," Katrina said. She looked down at Leila's gifts and smiled. "Enjoy. Thank you for letting me share that with you. That was amazing."

"You're welcome."

Kylie hardly noticed the other revelers, so engrossed was she in her new treasures. These adorable gifts. That was how life went, she decided wryly. Katrina had David, and Kylie had these new acquisitions and new insight on Katrina. You lost something big, you gained something small, and little by little, the small became bigger and the loss became less painful. She gently fingered the smooth ebony surface of the cat figurine and felt something tight inside her soften.

She couldn't wait to check out the CD.

Mondays were always hard days. They scared her, because important stuff happened over the weekend when you had an active social life. Which of course she didn't, aside from online chatting with her new friends from the adolescent behavioral health unit, which was nice, but didn't help her know what was going on in the world of her classmates.

As it turned out, the important news was gleefully broadcast through the school before the end of first hour. A Saturday night party had been busted and a bunch of freshman had gotten into big trouble, including Freeda and her friends. Everyone was mad at someone, it seemed, including Lacey and Marisa. Kylie didn't bother to seek out the details. She was content to take a back seat to it all and just observe the others' dramas. It made the day seem more tolerable, and when loneliness swept over her during the lunch hour, she thought of Leila's bag of gifts and the intriguing invitation for koshari with Katrina.

An interesting history class made the afternoon go faster and the final bell signaling the end of the school day was, in and of itself, a celebration. A day successfully navigated, a Monday she wouldn't have to face again. She was walking toward the parking lot and the bus stop, when, to her surprise, Freeda appeared by her side.

"So," Freeda began without preamble, "my mom went to the ballet gala on Friday."

Kylie sensed an attack. "Did she like it?"

"Yeah, but she'd heard about the big-name choreographer, the one who did the work on that dance movie, whose ballet was supposed to be part of the program. She'd been looking forward to that. She wants to know what went wrong. I told her I'd ask you."

Freeda studied her expectantly. Kylie was grateful her own mom had told her the stories. She shared the details now, one satisfying tidbit after another, gratified by Freeda's shocked reaction. "He'd become so hateful toward Katrina, it was totally harassment. My mom caught him in the act. He was screaming, and actually threw a chair at Katrina. It almost hit her and the other dancers. My mom witnessed it all."

"Whoa," Freeda said in a hushed voice. "Wait till I tell my mom."

"Something's really wrong with Edwin Hess, my mom says. She thinks the English Ballet Theatre is trying to protect him by saying nothing. But my mom thinks it's just a matter of time, one outrageous situation too many. She's the one who made Leila Bertrand happen, by the way. She went to Anders and talked him into it. Actually, I think there was a lot of shouting involved. But last Saturday night, they were buddies again. Everyone was in a great mood at our house."

"Everyone, like Anders and your family?"

"More. A couple dozen Ballet Theatre members and administrators all came over. It was a big party, which is funny, because we didn't have company parties for a long time, and now we've had two in two weeks."

"Damn. Those must be so cool. Are you, like, nervous around so many stars?"

"Hardly," she scoffed. "I've known most of them since I was little. They're like uncles and aunts." By now they'd reached the parking lot. Kylie found herself looking around for David, as if wishing hard enough could alter the facts of reality.

Freeda noticed. "Is your guy friend going to meet you again?"

"Not this week. He's got loads of accompanist hours at the studios. Maybe next week, we agreed."

"So, he really is your good friend? You weren't just trying to put us on?"

"Of course he is. What were you thinking?" She allowed disdain to creep into her voice—who gave a toss that others saw Freeda as someone important?

Freeda didn't seem offended by Kylie's tone, but she didn't look fully convinced either. "If he's such a close friend, tell me something I wouldn't otherwise know."

"Fine." Kylie paused, then thought, *why not?* "Can you keep a secret?"

Of course Freeda couldn't keep a secret. But it didn't matter anyway; it was no longer a secret. She decided irritably that if Katrina and David were going to show up together at the Garvey house, publicly displaying their simmering chemistry and sexual hunger, she saw no need to pretend like she hadn't seen it.

Freeda's eyes widened. "Sure!"

Kylie leaned in closer. "David and Katrina Devries have become a couple."

Freeda's hand flew to her mouth. "No way!"

"I'm serious."

"Oh. My. God. Lucky her. Lucky him!"

"I know, right?" She tried to sound unconcerned.

Freeda stopped, squinted and groaned out loud. "My older brother's here." She gestured to a red Lexus nearby where the driver was peering intently at his phone. "I'm grounded for two weeks and my mom doesn't trust me to come straight home. This is bullshit."

"Yeah, well, what can you do?"

She realized she sounded bored, which Lacey and Marisa would have deemed the biggest social gaffe imaginable because one didn't talk that way to a queen bee. But Lacey and Marisa could jump off a bridge for all she cared. "Maybe I'll go drop by the studios and spy on the lovers. Or just to crack a joke with David."

"Damn, you're lucky," Freeda breathed.

She met Freeda's envious gaze. "You should come to the studios with me."

Now pure longing filled Freeda's eyes. Then she frowned. "Um, didn't I just tell you I was grounded?"

"What if my mom called your mom to invite you?" Kylie hesitated, on purpose. "Nah, never mind. My mom is way too busy there. Like, nonstop. Anders needs her to stay on top of so many things."

Freeda looked stricken. "No, wait. Please? That would be *so* much better than going straight home. That would be amazing. Let me ask her tonight, okay? Because, if you *could* get your mom's permission, it would be totally legit. And besides, she'd be dying to know what it was like inside the studios. She'd want me to go so I could tell her."

"Hmm." Kylie pretended to think about it. "Well, if you want, ask your mom. Just let me know. Like I said, I'm free to go there whenever, so it's all cool with me." She glanced at the bus, and gestured apologetically. "Gotta catch that bus."

"Sure, of course. Talk to you tomorrow!"

Kylie walked briskly toward the bus, and it was only when she was in line with the others, waiting to get on, that she realized how normal the exchange had been.

Maybe she'd survive this year after all.

Chapter 33

April

"I have a gift for you," Russell announced when April came down to the kitchen one morning, two weeks after the gala. He beckoned her closer and pointed to his laptop screen.

It was the "Entertainment & Arts" section of the BBC News website. Halfway down the page, a photo and name sprang out at her.

Edwin Hess.

Russell smiled at her agape expression, and clicked on the link. She leaned in, her eyes racing through the text.

British newspaper *The Daily Chronicle* has reported that the English Ballet Theatre suspended one of its star choreographers, Edwin Hess, in early September, amid allegations of sexual harassment and sexual assault. Three females have come forward, including a former partner of three years. Hess has denied all charges.

Hess, 30, is Artist in Residence at the English Ballet Theatre, and has fast become one of the world's most admired young choreographers. The English Ballet Theatre had been expected to present his acclaimed 2010 production of *Wax Works* in May.

A spokesperson for the EBT said in a statement released this afternoon that the production was now on hold, as were plans for further engagements with Hess, pending the results of the investigation currently underway.

Further allegations of harassment, by two female EBT corps de ballet dancers, have arisen. Coupled with reports of violence amid recurring substance-abuse episodes, Hess has been banned from the premises until further notice.

In a press statement today, an American Ballet Theatre spokesperson said that the company's own decision to pull a recent Hess commission from their repertory season was made "out of respect for the ongoing inquiry in London, the dance community at large, patrons of American Ballet Theatre and artists of the company." Other professional dance companies around the world are expected to follow suit.

Well. She drew in her breath and gazed at Russell, speechless.

"Merry early Christmas," he said.

Elation welled up inside her, making her want to dance around the kitchen. But when she spoke, it was in a calm, unflappable voice.

"Is it wrong, do you suppose, that I feel glad about this?"

"Nope."

"Even that I feel like dancing and singing?"

"Nope. The guy was a jerk to you. And it's sounding like he was more than a jerk to more than one woman."

"I'm exonerated."

"You are. Allow me to be the first to congratulate you."

Laughing, April launched herself into his arms the way she used to, straddling him and roping her arms around his neck to hug him fiercely.

"What's going on?" Jen, behind them, sounded sleepy and cross. "Yuck, you look like you're making out."

Sheepish, April disentangled herself from Russell, who maintained his broad grin.

"We are celebrating a moral victory, Jennifer. You should be happy."

"What is it? What happened?"

April angled the laptop Jen's way, who leaned closer. Kylie appeared, and read the article over Jen's shoulder.

"This was the choreographer who was being such a psycho?" Kylie asked.

April nodded, trying unsuccessfully to look solemn and regretful.

"Whoa." Kylie brightened. "I can't wait to tell Freeda about this."

"This calls for a celebration," Russell said. "How about my broiler cinnamon toast?"

"White bread, too much butter and too much sugar?" April couldn't keep from wincing.

"Yes, yes!" Kylie exclaimed, and even Jen nodded eagerly.

"Guess I'm outnumbered," April said. "Russell, the oven is all yours. I'll take a piece, too."

Sharing the news and its implications with Jen and Kylie turned into a lively conversation as they munched through slices of Russell's cinnamon toast. But school still mattered, so eventually April sent both girls to get ready. She heard Kylie's laughter upstairs over the intermittent thundering of a racing cat. "You're playing with Schrodinger, aren't you?" she called up the stairs. "Stop goofing around and get ready for school. I want to get to the studios early, and my plans do not include driving you."

Kylie laughed again. "Okay, Sergeant Mom, got it!"

Normalcy. Or at least closer to it.

She would never again take it for granted.

It wasn't yet nine o'clock when she arrived at the studios. She'd printed out a copy of the article, and planned to find the right time to show it to the others. Right then, she enjoyed the secret warmth it gave her. In the staff room, April poured herself a cup of coffee and ambled through the quiet hallway. She heard piano music and followed it to its source in the big studio.

David was playing something by Chopin, deliciously melodic and romantic. Anders stood next to him, arms folded, head cocked to one side, listening. When he held up a finger, David stopped and looked up at him.

"That middle part should have more oomph, right there, concurrent with the soft arpeggiated notes."

"Show me." David slid to one end of the bench, and Anders sat down.

April surveyed the mostly empty room and saw Katrina, on the floor in sweats, warming up as she sipped a hot drink. She looked relaxed and happy.

"I'm thinking this," Anders said. He spread his elbows, fingers lightly skimming the keys as a warm up, before he began to play. On the bench, side by side, he and David concentrated, both intent on the music being made.

Katrina, from her spot, caught sight of April and smiled. She smiled back. Her news was going to make Katrina's day. But right then, Katrina radiated a perfect contentment. She didn't need anything more than what she had at the moment.

David took his turn playing the passage.

"That was better," Anders said.

"It needs work. Hours and hours. I wish I had day-and-night access to this piano."

"Hmm." Anders rose and rubbed his chin. "Katrina?" he called out.

"Yes?" she called back.

"How trustworthy is this young man?"

"I'd give him pretty high marks."

"Would you entrust him with a key to your home?"

"I would." She hesitated. "I have, actually."

"Ah." Anders pondered this before turning back to David.

"There's a Steinway at my big, empty, silent home. Find my personal assistant and have her make you a key. I'm gone most days and most evenings. Do anything to my home, cause any damage, and I'll tear you from ear to ear. Lose the house key, the same. Share this privilege with anyone—besides the two women in this room—the same."

"Of course." David responded pleasantly.

Katrina smiled at them both, as much at peace as April had ever seen her.

So much to feel optimistic about.

THE END

Author's Note

This note of thanks is first and foremost to you, dear reader, and all of you who've sought out each ensuing book in the series. I took a big risk, back in 2014, after my agent's efforts to find a traditional publisher for my novels fell flat, three books in five [very insecure and uncomfortable] years. Finally I pulled myself from the game and went with my gut instinct, daring to believe there was an audience for my novels, in a time when there were few ballet-centric novels for adults, certainly not ones with a women's fiction slant. And so Classical Girl Press was born. You took your own risk, dear reader, and bought my books, left thoughtful reviews on Amazon, like "Well, I jumped on this third book in the series with high expectations, and it did not disappoint" and "There are only a few books that I keep and read more than once and this book has joined that short list." Thank you so very much, all of you. Your kind words and interest kept me going, and trusting, this fictional world of the West Coast Ballet Theatre. This book concludes the series; my heart is full.

Thank you, friends and family, fellow writers, early readers, endorsers through the journey, including Kathleen Hermes, Donna Zimmerman, Tara Staley, Kelly Mustian, Lauren Rico, Grier Cooper, Kristina Riggle, Carolyn Burns Bass, Annette Hadley, John Dalton, Karen Dionne and the gang at Backspace, Adrienne Sharp, Zippora Karz, MarySue Hermes, Lauren Jonas, Kathryn Craft, Tasha

Alexander, Sari Wilson, Leigh Purtill, Anne Clermont, Marika Brussel, and editors Sandra Kring, Lauren Baratz-Logsted and Guy Crucianelli. To my own beloved KVDT dance tribe, including Jerri Clark, Ken Stewart, Alberta Wright and artistic director Kristin Benjamin. For gorgeous cover art, all four times, I'm indebted to James T. Egan of Bookfly Design, and to Jason Anderson at Polgarus Studios, for impeccable formatting. To the dancers of the San Francisco Ballet, whose performances it has been a privilege to watch and write about, both as a creative writer and a dance reviewer. While my own characters are fictionalized and none specifically resemble those I watch onstage, I've gained so much through observing these supremely talented and devoted professionals.

Finally, love and thanks to my husband Peter and son Jonathan, for celebrating every milestone with me, and tolerating my bouts of both artistic fervor and writerly angst through my years of writing the Ballet Theatre Chronicles series. I love you two so much.

About the Author

Terez Mertes Rose is a writer and former ballet dancer whose work has appeared in the *Crab Orchard Review*, *Women Who Eat* (Seal Press), *A Woman's Europe* (Travelers' Tales), the *Philadelphia Inquirer* and the *San Jose Mercury News*. She is the author of the Ballet Theatre Chronicles *(Off Balance, Outside the Limelight, Ballet Orphans)* and *A Dancer's Guide to Africa* (2018). She reviews dance performances for Bachtrack.com and blogs about ballet and classical music at The Classical Girl (www.theclassicalgirl.com). She makes her home in the Santa Cruz Mountains with her husband and son. You can visit her at www.terezrose.com.

More Books by Terez Mertes Rose

Off Balance
Outside the Limelight
A Dancer's Guide to Africa
Ballet Orphans

Off Balance, Book 1 of the Ballet Theatre Chronicles
https://www.amazon.com/dp/B00WB224IQ/

Alice thinks she's accepted the loss of her ballet career, injury having forced her to trade in pointe shoes onstage for spreadsheets upstairs. That is, until the day Alice's boss asks her to befriend Lana, a pretty new company member he's got his eye on. Lana represents all Alice has lost, not just as a ballet dancer, but as a motherless daughter. It's pain she's kept hidden, even from herself, as every good ballet dancer knows to do.

Lana, lonely and unmoored, desperately needs some help, and her mother, back home, vows eternal support. But when Lana begins to profit from Alice's advice and help, her mother's constant attention curdles into something more sinister.

Together, both women must embark on a journey of painful rediscoveries, not just about career opportunities won and lost, but the mothers they thought they knew.

OFF BALANCE takes the reader beyond the glitter of the stage to expose the sweat and struggle, amid the mandate to sustain the illusion at all cost.

Outside the Limelight, **Book 2 of the Ballet Theatre Chronicles**
https://www.amazon.com/dp/B01M0NIIX0/

Named a Best Book of 2017 by **Kirkus Reviews**
"A lovely and engaging tale of sibling rivalry in the high-stakes dance world." (Starred review)

Ballet star Dena Lindgren's dream career is knocked off its axis when a puzzling onstage fall results in a crushing diagnosis: a brain tumor. Looming surgery and its long recovery period prompt the company's artistic director, Anders Gunst, to shift his attention to an overshadowed company dancer: Dena's older sister, Rebecca, with whom Anders once shared a special relationship.

Under the heady glow of Anders' attention, Rebecca thrives, even as her recuperating sister, hobbled and unnoticed, languishes on the sidelines of a world that demands beauty and perfection. Rebecca ultimately faces a painful choice: play by the artistic director's rules and profit, or take shocking action to help her sister.

Exposing the glamorous onstage world of professional ballet, as well as its shadowed wings and dark underbelly, OUTSIDE THE LIMELIGHT examines loyalty, beauty, artistic passion, and asks what might be worth losing in order to help the ones you love.

A Dancer's Guide to Africa
https://www.amazon.com/dp/B07FYGND7F

Fiona Garvey, ballet dancer and new college graduate, is desperate to escape her sister's betrayal and a failed relationship. Vowing to restart as far from home as possible, she accepts a two-year teaching position with the Peace Corps in Africa. It's a role she's sure she can perform. But in no time, Fiona realizes she's traded her problems in Omaha for bigger ones in Gabon, a country as beautiful as it is filled with contradictions.

Emotionally derailed by Christophe, a charismatic and privileged Gabonese man who can teach her to let go of her inhibitions but can't commit to anything more, threatened by an overly familiar student with a menacing fixation on her, and drawn into the compelling but potentially dangerous local dance ceremonies, Fiona finds herself at increasing risk. And when matters come to a shocking head, she must reach inside herself, find her dancer's power, and fight back.

Blending humor and pathos, A DANCER'S GUIDE TO AFRICA takes the reader along on a suspense-laden, sensual journey through Africa's complex beauty, mystery and mysticism.

Ballet Orphans, **Book 3 of the Ballet Theatre Chronicles**
https://www.amazon.com/dp/B08KSL1JZZ

It's 1990, and New York soloist April Manning is trying to rebalance her world in the aftermath of her parents' deaths. An offer to join the struggling West Coast Ballet Theatre as a principal dancer seems like the perfect opportunity for a fresh start—a new life in San Francisco, an exciting step up in her career, and the hope of a redefined sense of family.

But the other dancers are wary, clannish and tight-lipped, particularly about an incident that hastened the departure of their beloved artistic director, leading to the arrival of his replacement, the young, inexperienced Anders Gunst. And no one wants to talk about Jana, a former company member who defiantly walked out rather than work under Anders. It is Jana herself who offers April hints about the incident, and even friendship, where she reveals a loneliness and hunger to belong that newly orphaned April well understands. But there is something troubling about Jana, and what April doesn't know could prove deadly.

A prequel to the Ballet Theatre Chronicles, BALLET ORPHANS explores the work and sacrifices required to arrive at the highest tiers of the professional ballet world, coupled with the primal, universal desire to belong, to love and be loved, and the lengths we'll go to protect those we call family.

9 7 9 8 9 8 8 5 2 1 2 1 1